Christobel Kent

The Viper

CORVUS

Published in trade paperback in Great Britain in 2020 by Corvus,
an imprint of Atlantic Books Ltd.

This paperback edition published in 2021.

10 9 8 7 6 5 4 3 2 1

A CIP catalogue record for this book is available from the British Library.

Paperback ISBN: 978 0 85789 336 9
E-book ISBN: 978 0 85789 335 2

To Europe, that made me welcome

The day was cold, early

HE WENT IN THROUGH the side gate, more out of long-ago habit than any fear that he would be detained for trespassing after all this time. It had once been painted but now the metal had reverted almost to nature, greenish, mottled and flaking, camouflaged against the late-summer hillside. But it didn't creak for once; carefully, he latched it behind him with a gloved hand. The sky curving over them was pale, streaked with morning pink. Autumn in the air.

'*Via,*' he said, hoarse, throwing his hands out, and Gelsomina ran ahead, panting, nose down, ears flopping in the leaves that carpeted the hill that climbed behind the house. He didn't believe there were truffles here, but she'd always been a stupid dog. The thought made him laugh, the old joke. *And the hound.*

He hurried past the house, averting his eyes, the flaking wall at his shoulder, the sweeping roof-high marks left on the stucco from years, decades earlier, the lines traced, curving and intersecting, by a long-gone hand. He experienced an uneasy shifting of relief when he started the climb and left it behind, although it had been empty for years. There had been rumours perhaps ten years back that more foreigners wanted the place – they'd make something out of it for other foreigners and the odd rich Florentine, a yoga retreat or a health farm – but if the plans had ever been real, they'd fallen through. Even if you didn't know anything about it, the first sight of it would be enough to send you back to your hire car and down the neglected road to your luxury hotel room: La Vipera – The Viper, named for the snakes that rustled in the dry leaves all around it – sat in a damp wooded cleft with its face turned into the hillside, and after a week of September rains it was dank and slimy.

He didn't know why anyone would come up here these days. He shifted, uneasy still. He wouldn't be here himself, but money was money.

Truffles were fussy, temperamental organisms, and there was no mystery about their disappearance, fewer each year and then none at all. The clue was in the roar of traffic down there in the valley, winding out across the widening plain from the great red low-lying city; it was in the poisoned air. They had signs now, on certain days, illuminated signs at the entrance to Florence forbidding traffic.

But the fewer truffles there were, the higher the price.

Up the hill ahead of him, under the trees, Gelsomina moved between the mossy stones, her rear end wagging with excitement.

He paused and turned as the dog raised her head and ran on after the scent; he looked back down the hill.

A mist had drifted in after him. It hung in the dark canopy of the forest and most of the house sat invisible below it now. Only a corner of the red roof jutted out, half caved-in where a storm had knocked a chimney down four, five years earlier. The whole place should have gone then, by rights, but it seemed to hold on, through the rains, a heavy snowfall, blistering summers; doggedly, maliciously it endured. He turned back uphill and whistled for the dog.

Silence. He walked on, until the roof of a tiny shepherd's hut appeared. Although the mist had crept higher, it clung, leaving a sheen on the summer-darkened leaves. He could have done this with his eyes closed, never mind the fog; he knew each stone. '*Mina!*' he bellowed, angry, waiting for the rustle of the returning bitch, his hand out to administer a clout to her stupid old head. When still he heard nothing, he stopped and raised his head, sniffing the air.

His heart rate didn't rise, there wasn't much would cause that at his age, but he felt an adjustment all the same, a shift in chemical composition as his body turned itself, like a sunflower to the sun, towards the threat. He walked on, steadily uphill. She was gone – he knew that before he pushed aside the door that hung from one hinge and saw her lying there on the dirt floor with her teeth bared – but because he had long since consigned emotion to the category of wasted energy, he just stood there in the doorway and waited for what would come next.

It wasn't, in the end, what he expected. The last thing he experienced, as he stepped into the hut for a closer look at what sat in the shadows, was surprise, which some would have considered more than he deserved.

Chapter One

La Vipera.

'YOU DO REMEMBER IT, RIGHT?'

Closing his eyes now and feeling the last warmth of the sun falling through his own kitchen window, it was the smell that Sandro Cellini remembered, incense rising in the rooms where the shutters had been closed against the low evening light. He remembered brushing against something that tinkled as he came inside. Dust motes hanging in the light that slanted through the shutters, and a chill inside the house's thick walls. He remembered the exact proportions of the big kitchen and the odd sadness he had felt on entering it. A room like his grandparents' kitchen, a marble slab for working pasta and a huge smoke-blackened chimney breast, only the sight of this one would have made his grandmother weep, the marble loaded with the detritus of a disordered household, beer bottles and spilled food and half a motorcycle engine dismantled in black grease.

And he remembered the drawings that covered every inch of the kitchen's crumbling plaster walls and scrawled and looped

5

outside too, on the wall facing into the hillside. Some passing artist, one of them had said. One of the women had told him that and, as he remembered, a face swam into view, small square chin, defiant.

Five women, one man: he could visualise them, in a kind of arrow formation, and there she was, *her*, their leader, at the arrow's head, tall, the long hair, the long slender fingers, the pale eyes. Her lover, the Italian guy, at her left hand, the small one, with her defiant look, at her right.

'I remember it,' said Sandro, opening his eyes to see his own kitchen, in the present day, and Pietro still in front of him, the mild, cheerful, inquiring face of his ex-partner in the Polizia dello Stato – after the thirty seconds' reverie that had taken Sandro back nearly forty years – older now than when he'd closed them. 'I don't remember the names. Well – except hers. Nielsson.'

'And the place?' said Pietro. 'Sant'Anna?'

Sandro shifted in his chair, uneasy. 'A miserable little place, really, it was then. A handful of little smallholdings, a bar, the big house up on the hill. A hundred inhabitants?'

'Not even that,' said Pietro.

Sandro sighed. 'It was a long time ago,' he said. 'And the investigation was –' He hesitated. 'Something and nothing.'

Sandro had been a rookie back in 1976, when the call had come in. Anonymous: informing on a handful of hippies, some wealthy, some not, some Italian, some not, living in a decaying farmhouse on the edge of the village of Sant'Anna, itself just over the southern hills that ringed Florence. Forty years ago. The caller – almost certainly a resentful local, a slighted tradesman, a farmer used to using the neglected land, it was common enough even now – had accused them of various kinds of immorality, including prostituting minors. Sandro, wet behind the ears, had gone along, his supervising officer that old thug Baratti, long since retired, probably dead. There had been no minors on the premises and no evidence of prostitution. They had been up there three times and found nothing to prosecute, closed the case. Long ago and far away.

Except. Except. Except now an old countrywoman had stumbled across two bodies in a hut, a hundred metres from the place. La Vipera: The Viper, although no poisonous snakes were in the frame for this one. Unless vipers had learned to stab people to death.

'I couldn't believe it,' said Pietro. 'I mean, it was luck enough that the record of the investigation hadn't been lost. But when I saw your name on it!' He was gleeful, delighted. 'We need you, Sandro. And the boss has agreed to it. You're on the team. A consultant.'

Luisa set down the coffee-pot gently and stepped back. It wasn't like her to stay so silent.

'It's very kind of you,' said Sandro, his fingers uncharacteristically nervous on the tabletop, 'but really, I –'

'Kind?' exploded Pietro. 'Didn't you hear what I said? We *need* you.' And he shoved the tablet towards him across the table.

On the table in front of him in his own kitchen, Pietro's tablet, its screen split between two windows, showed Sandro the first page of a police report on one side and a couple of columns of *La Nazione*, complete with photograph, on the other. Sandro made himself focus on the facts.

The bodies of a man and woman were found yesterday in an outbuilding of the estate of La Vipera, in the riserva statale of Vallombrosa in the province of Florence. The man is believed to be Giancarlo Loutti, 76, butcher, who was last seen on Friday last. The remains of the female have proved more difficult to identify owing to advanced decomposition, but the police laboratory is 'making progress'. La Vipera attained notoriety in the mid-1970s when it was acquired by Danish heiress Johanna Nielsson and a communal-living experiment was established there (by Ms Nielsson and her lover Marcantonio Gorgone) on the principles of free love and socialism. Ms Nielsson has not been located for comment, although it is believed the property is still legally in her possession. Gorgone's whereabouts are not known.

There was a photograph of a hillside where the remains of a rooftop were just visible through trees still in full leaf.

'They haven't got much,' said Sandro, staring at the picture, remembering the haze inside that house, the tinkling, and faces, now, faces after all this time. Johanna Nielsson. She had had a long, pale face, grey eyes, unblinking.

'*La Nazione?*' said Pietro. 'The reporters lasted two days in Sant'Anna before they gave up.' He sighed. 'I could have told them they wouldn't get anything out of the locals – they wouldn't talk to us either.' Gently he prodded the iPad back towards Sandro. 'I think we should probably be glad they aren't going to town on it – yet. Do you want journalists tramping all over that hillside?'

'Who found them, did you say?' said Sandro, and he felt it begin to stir, the old investigative instinct.

'A lady called Maria Clara Martinelli,' he said, swiping the screen left.

Three headshots appeared and instinctively Sandro reached up over his shoulder, and there was Luisa behind him, one hand meeting his, the other coming to rest gently on his shoulder.

Maria Clara Martinelli was named on the left: Sandro didn't believe he had ever seen her before. The shot looked like it had been taken in the door to the local bar, where she was standing to attention for the camera. A square un-made-up mannish face that was at odds with a monumental bosom and a too-tight skirt suit, a hank of thick straight hair falling to either side, she was grinning broadly at the photographer. He almost found himself smiling back, like a fool.

'A *contadina*,' said Pietro. 'Widow woman. She has a smallholding just over the ridge and she was looking for a sow that had got loose. Found the beast in this little lean-to just above La Vipera. Attracted by the smell, probably.' Pietro stood up abruptly. 'She claimed to be able to identify the female victim. Though there was considerable decomposition.'

Under Sandro's eye Pietro took a step or two to the window, still open to the street this damp, warm afternoon. Florence might be a big city but there were farmhouses still under the flyovers and ring roads, and they both had enough experience of the countryside to know pigs would eat anything.

At the table, Sandro moved his finger across the hard, bright screen. The photograph in the centre of the spread was of another woman, but she might have been a different species, she was so far distant from Maria Clara Martinelli. An old photograph, forty years and more. The way she dressed, the way she stood, the way she wore her hair, all said it. An A-line mini-dress, high at the neck, a hand on her hip, one long slim leg straight and the other extended in front of her in a dancer's position. Her dark blonde hair was long and unbrushed and parted at the centre, and although she was standing in the rubble of an untidy country farmyard, her feet were bare. She stared out from the frame of her hair, hostile and beautiful. Johanna Nielsson.

There was a sigh behind Sandro and Luisa was gone, clattering at the stove, unscrewing the coffee-pot. For a fleeting moment, he thought of Luisa back then, wondered how much *she* remembered of a case that had come up when they had been barely an item still.

From the window Pietro said, without turning round, 'I don't think there's a man on the team capable of solving anything more complicated than a domestic murder, Sandro.' He cleared his throat. 'We need you. No one can get people to talk like you – and you know these people.'

'I *did* know them,' said Sandro, but he was lost, and he knew it.

All very nice. But now he had to actually walk into the police station and get started. He sighed. 'I'm in,' he said.

But, beginning to walk back towards him from the window, Pietro started talking like he hadn't heard, or like he'd taken Sandro's agreement for granted all along. 'They think there's a good chance it could be her,' he said. 'The dead female. They think it could be Nielsson.'

Chapter Two

JUST ENOUGH HAD CHANGED at the police headquarters for Sandro to feel comprehensively disoriented. It was rather like dreaming about his childhood home, which he did regularly still, those dreams where nostalgia turns you feeble and longing and then you trip over a strange dog and start awake.

He remembered the operations room with its view of the back wall of an old cinema, although the graffiti had changed. The long whiteboard tacked with crime scene shots: Sandro averted his eyes. Two long tables, three computer screens, behind each of them a lad: they all scrambled to their feet when Pietro – Commissario Pietro – walked in. He proceeded to introduce them to Sandro while they waited for the new superintendent, who was in a meeting. They consisted of a stocky ginger boy called Parini, another called Panayotis – of Greek origin, very dark – and a whippet of a kid called Ceri, just graduated to agent, with fancy sideburns and whose knee jiggled constantly when he returned to his seat.

Sandro's eye was drawn back to the pictures, gliding over

them just slowly enough to register that seven were of the crime scene, two mortuary shots.

Then the door opened and the lads were all on their feet again because the super walked in.

A recent appointment, a replacement, Pietro had told Sandro, for that arsehole Scacchi who had accepted Sandro's resignation from the force with total indifference all those years back. A real new broom, Pietro had said, with a sidelong look whose significance became clear only as the door opened. Manzoni was a woman: a tall, dry, pale woman with a level gaze.

'Superintendente,' Pietro began, 'this is –'

She put out her hand to shake Sandro's, saying drily, 'Your reputation precedes you, Mr Cellini.'

'Oh, dear,' he said, and was rewarded with the briefest ghost of a smile, then that was it.

He didn't look at Pietro: the bastard. Had he thought Sandro would say no if he'd known the new boss was female? He'd have been wrong. But she was speaking.

'For your benefit, Mr Cellini,' she said. 'That's why we're here.' Sandro inclined his head and she went on. 'The victims died approximately a month apart. The female victim, whom tentative identification by the woman who discovered her suggests may be Johanna Nielsson –'

Sandro raised a finger. 'Hold on,' he said. 'If I may. Tentative identification?' Manzoni's head was on one side, waiting. 'We're talking about a body unprotected for a month at least, during the summer. A woman who hadn't been seen in the area for forty years. What was it that suggested her identity to this – this Martinelli?'

'The woman's body had a tattoo,' said Manzoni, brusque, and then he did remember. A tiny curled figure, like a snail, as Johanna Nielsson held out her hand to shake his.

'I see,' he said. 'Yes.' Had Sandro ever seen a tattoo on a woman before, at the age of twenty-three back in the seventies? He had not. He had seen them on men, and many since, on the living and on the dead of both sexes: they were useful for identification. He'd marvelled at them on the beach that summer; he'd said to Luisa, these children, inking their flesh with strange and marvellous designs, they never think they'll get old and the flesh will sag. They think they'll live forever. But back then – the snail on the inside of Johanna Nielsson's wrist was the first one he'd seen on a young woman.

Yes. He remembered Nielsson's tattoo.

'So Martinelli had dealings with her forty years ago.' Sandro searched his memory for the stocky woman with her iron-grey fringe, trying to imagine her younger. Something flickered, but he couldn't pin it down.

'It would appear so.' Manzoni still spoke easily but Sandro detected the faintest trace of impatience. 'She wasn't forthcoming in the initial statement, only said that she had worked in the village bar back then and served Nielsson on occasion. That tattoos weren't common in those days.' She smiled. 'Does that answer your question?'

Sandro nodded. 'Please,' he said. 'Go on.'

'Preliminary findings suggest cause of death in the female to be knife wounds to the lower body, most significantly the severing of the femoral artery, although there were more than twenty other wounds. Bound ante mortem to a chair with some kind of plastic ties still *in situ* – and, yes, we're working on a source for those, possibly agricultural – stab wounds to the abdomen with a sharp short-bladed knife and had been dead just over a month when the bodies were found. The male – a local butcher, Giancarlo Lotti, and his dog, a truffle hound known as Gelsomina – had been dead only between two and three days. No one had reported him missing.'

The photographs were just far enough from where Sandro sat to be out of focus. He kept it that way.

'This is to be *your* investigation,' said Manzoni, looking from one of them to the next, resting a beat on each, perhaps a beat and a half on Sandro, finishing on Pietro. 'As you know, there is a major administrative and disciplinary recalibration under way here' – hirings and firings, thought Sandro, still relaxed because it wasn't anything to do with him any more – 'which will require my attention, although homicide, and violence in general, against both men and women, is never,' the superintendent paused, '*never* going to come second to bureaucracy on my watch.'

There was a general murmuring of sheepish agreement, but she was still talking. 'There's been preliminary door to door in the village: Commissario Cavallaro and the agents have already covered some significant ground –' A minute hesitation in which Sandro understood that no one had told them a blind thing and most of the doors had been kept firmly closed. 'And they will bring you up to date on their findings so far.' And then she paused. 'Before I leave you, these are our questions.' She held up a finger. 'First, if this *is* Johanna Nielsson, what was she doing back here after what appears to be a significant absence? Second, is there a link between these two victims, and if so, what is that link? Your own historic connection with this case, Mr Cellini,' nodding, 'will be invaluable in answering these questions. The killing may have nothing to do with the commune or it may have everything to do with it, but I want anyone connected with La Vipera back then who's still alive to be traced and interviewed, and I want you to do it.'

Sandro nodded, his heart slowing, slowing. He focused on his clasped fingers in his lap and she went on.

'And lastly, if, as we must assume, these killings are connected, why was there a month between them?'

There was a pause, and heads turned to Sandro, who said, 'But he didn't kill her,' pausing a beat, 'and then come back a month later, wracked with remorse, to plead with her corpse for forgiveness then kill himself out of unassuaged guilt.' They all stared at him.

Manzoni was examining him, head tilted. 'Because?' she said.

'Because you wouldn't have needed to involve me if it was that easy, would you?' said Sandro, and he got to his feet.

He took a step, then another, past her, towards the photographs on the whiteboard.

*

The long blue bus pulled up in the tiny triangular piazza of Sant'Anna in Chianti and Luisa, who had been standing impatiently in the aisle for several minutes, climbed off, nodding to the bus driver behind his mirrored sunglasses so he'd think she was just another old lady with a shopping bag.

There was an app, these days, that told you everything – timetables, bus stops, walking distances – and Luisa had that app, extolled its virtues to Sandro, chided him for being a fuddy-duddy when he expressed scepticism, but under most circumstances she too would still rather ask a human being. Today, though, she didn't want anyone knowing her destination – or asking questions. Like, what do you think you're doing?

Sandro didn't know she was coming here, to Sant'Anna. Sandro had gone in to the police station.

Luisa had seen that piece in the paper before Pietro had come in with it, and said nothing. She was fairly sure Sandro had no clue that she remembered that case, that time long ago – and that woman, that woman Johanna Nielsson – rather well. And what Luisa was doing here, in answer to the question, was she was curious. There'd been a time she'd wanted Johanna Nielsson dead herself because the foreign woman had taken Sandro as her lover.

Turning in the little square to decide her next move, the image of Giuli was there behind her eyes, glaring in her face. *Never!* The girl idolised Sandro. Giuli jutting out her chin and saying, *But how do you know?*

You just know.

She didn't know how casual or fleeting or forgettable it had been on the woman's part – Luisa had only had one lover; maybe you forgot easily if you'd had a hundred – because it had never, ever been acknowledged between them, but Luisa knew. And she knew Sandro hadn't forgotten Johanna Nielsson.

Pietro snaps his fingers and Sandro jumps. Was that it? Or

was it *her*? The tall, fair foreign woman. Even dead, she could draw Sandro in, even after all this time.

Luisa had said none of it. Partly out of pragmatism because it had been a slow year in the private detection business and Luisa had stopped work herself after a lifetime at Frollini, the haberdasher turned ladieswear turned 'multibrand boutique' whose relentless march had left her behind at last, weary. Partly because it was not, in the end, her decision to make. And partly, mostly, because she didn't quite trust herself on this particular subject, this particular case.

You didn't forget, did you? You never forgot a woman who could take your man with a single look from those pale eyes: Johanna Nielsson.

So she had let him pace up and down in the kitchen without saying anything, she had asked him what he wanted for dinner, she had kissed him on the cheek when he left, smiled when he looked back anxiously at the bend in the stairs. And when he'd gone, Luisa, with time on her hands these days, had got her handbag and looked at the app and bought a bus ticket.

Luisa could have stayed on at Frollini; offers had been made, kindly, by the owner, part-time or working in the huge outlet in the countryside five miles or so from where she stood, but even leaving out the little matter of breast cancer – six years down the line and off their books if not in the clear in her own head – Luisa was running out of the patience required to be a thoughtful, discriminating vendeuse, and they both knew it.

Luisa stood a moment in the dim little piazza, feeling a warm gust as a solitary truck trundled by: was it gossip she was after? Early afternoon and there was no one to be seen, life not quite back to normal after a long hot summer and a week of storms – but it was more than that. The bus driver had nodded when she had asked him if it was the right stop for her destination, nodded again, and she could see his eyebrows lifting behind the mirrored lenses at the mention of the name. La Vipera.

Forty years ago Luisa and Sandro had been out walking along the river to Settignano, the day after he'd been out to La Vipera. The night before he hadn't called, which even at that early stage in their relationship had been unusual. He had called her at work the following lunchtime to ask if she would like to go for a walk. 'Not the movies,' he'd said, 'not tonight.'

She remembered it all, as if she'd known from the beginning there was something about this place, these people, that was going to stir up the mud, the riverbed of their lives. She even remembered his face, gazing across the Arno at something she couldn't discern. 'They were – educated people,' he had told her, disbelieving. 'And not all foreigners, either. *She* was –' and she'd known then, with the pause. 'But the place – the kitchen was such a – such a mess. The disorder.'

They both came from quite ordinary backgrounds, she and Sandro, with mothers who scrubbed their kitchen floors twice daily. This door to La Vipera's kitchen opened on another world whose boundary they couldn't discern. 'She's from one of those northern countries, Denmark,' he'd told her, frowning. 'Maybe it's different there.'

'Maybe,' Luisa had said drily.

Their relationship up until that point had been circumspect. Introduced by her friend Livia, at some parade or other, whispering in her ear, *He's a police cadet*, as he marched beside them, head up.

It was what she loved about him, his seriousness – even at twenty-three, the frown that would come over him when something he didn't understand cropped up, as he tried to work it out. Sandro had never been one to jump to conclusions: his livelier, louder colleagues laughed at him for it. Changing their tune to grudging respect as he turned out so often to be right.

He had looked at her, in the warm evening by the river, holding her hand tight still. 'You don't understand,' he said slowly.

She'd stayed silent, bridling, until she could trust herself to say, 'Maybe not.'

He told Luisa her name only later, Johanna Nielsson, casually. The case had taken up three weeks of investigation and she knew La Vipera had been on the radar for a time after, but Sandro hadn't really talked about her again. Luisa knew, though, that he thought about her. The foreign woman glittered in his imagination, like the fireflies in the trees around the city on warm dark evenings.

Luisa took a deep breath and walked into the bar. Eleven o'clock in the morning. A handful of men were standing at the far end, drinking white wine: they didn't seem to notice her. However discreet a presence Sandro could make himself, a woman in late middle age carrying a shopping bag was invisible. She asked for a coffee in her meekest voice, selected a pastry from the cabinet and turned to find a seat. She saw that one of the men was, in fact, a woman, stocky, dressed in jeans and workman's jacket, but with an unmistakable bosom.

They muttered, with occasional outbursts of laughter. The barman was summoned for a refill and discreetly she moved her chair. The mannish woman was in conversation principally with a lean iron-haired man. Then things sobered: they were talking about someone called Gelsomina – there appeared to have been three bodies found, not two. The woman was quite exercised about this death and Luisa couldn't work it out, why Sandro hadn't been told, why it hadn't been in the papers, until she realised Gelsomina was a dog. 'I can see about the other two but why punish the dog?'

Discreetly, Luisa shifted so she could get a better look at the speaker. With a shock of recognition she realised Sandro had shown her the picture of a younger version, uncomfortably skirted at a wedding or something like it, of the stocky woman. She was Maria Clara Martinelli, who'd found the bodies. As Luisa watched, the tall silver-haired man clapped her on the shoulder, heartily, country people together, with no pretensions, no nice manners. But he didn't have quite the right look for a farmer: lean and pale, with high cheekbones. More of a monk.

Luisa took a bite of her pastry and found it so disappointing she almost tutted out loud. Thick and greasy, it stuck stubbornly to the roof of her mouth; she took another bite to be polite and pushed it away. The coffee was good.

Did country people rank the death of a dog higher than those of two human beings? Not unless they had a fairly low opinion of the human beings in question. Luisa remembered reading that Martinelli was a widow: she looked as though she worked hard, which was the widow's lot. Another man, a barfly with a red face and bloodshot eyes, was gesturing for a third round of drinks. Martinelli was shaking her head.

The bodies. A butcher and a Danish heiress, a stolid working man and a wild child from the seventies. She would have been twenty-eight when she set up at La Vipera with her lover, a good-looking heroin addict from the wealthy industrial north, Marcantonio Gorgone. Did Sandro know how much Luisa knew about the case? What an interest she had taken behind his back, all those years ago? Luisa had only met Nielsson but once, and Sandro had known nothing of that meeting. Only once, but once had been enough.

If Luisa closed her eyes she would be able to see Johanna Nielsson as she had been, her tall body made out of straight lines and angles, long, slender thighs, pale straight hair, a level grey gaze. Wearing a long dress of pleats and folds, embroidered at the neck, something from a distant continent, India or South America. Flat-chested as a boy. Luisa put a hand to her remaining breast reflexively, to feel its weight, but stopped herself for fear they would see the movement from where they stood at the bar and wonder *what on earth*. Luisa had always been small, round hipped, narrow shouldered, but she had been proud of her bosom back then, getting to her feet, standing up straight when she had seen Johanna Nielsson approaching, though still a head shorter.

She'd come with a few of her gang. From where Luisa had sat, in the early evening that long-ago summer, on the ledge running along the back of the Loggia dei Lanzi, half-hidden by Perseus holding up the Medusa's head, she had watched them approach, Nielsson spearheading. A small blonde, a dark Italian-looking girl, the man, Gorgone. They stopped at the foot of the few steps up to the loggia and standing, moving forward, she had heard them speak. Nielsson had touched each of them lightly on the shoulder, like a blessing, and off they went, trooping away down the great flank of the Palazzo Vecchio.

And now, in the dim little café with the taste of the bun's cheap shortening in her mouth, Luisa wondered if any of Nielsson's ménage might still be around. They might be living in those woods or gone underground, changed beyond recognition in the intervening years, greying or sober or simply silent. The idea was fanciful: the locals wouldn't have assimilated them and no one could live on chestnuts and roadkill for forty years.

Maria Clara Martinelli was making her move. Luisa waited two minutes, then followed.

Chapter Three

SKIRTING THE BIG OLD WALL of the city under the speckled trunks of plane trees, Giulietta Sarto – Giuli to everyone but the authorities – could smell the autumn. Exhaust fumes and woodsmoke and the drift of leaves damp in the gutters – and another year gone. Another winter waiting. Giuli most decidedly did not like getting old.

Ten in the morning – well, she would be at work for 10.04; Sandro wouldn't be bothered anyhow but Sandro wasn't there this morning to *be* bothered – and Giuli was already tired. For a month now, maybe more, she had been starting awake at five, five thirty, the metallic taste of fear in her mouth and thumping panic in her chest, while beside her on the pillow Enzo still slept peaceably, the sleep of the just. By lunchtime she would be yawning.

Was forty-five old? Not to some, not to most, she was prepared to concede that. But Giuli, anorexic at fourteen, drug addicted by fifteen, on the streets for the twenty years following, had never expected to have to worry about old age. Her own mother had died at forty-two, looking seventy. Giuli paused, stooped to examine her reflection in the wing mirror of a parked car. Grimaced at her pallor, frowned at the bags under her eyes. Was there something different, something new? She'd never been vain, was more one to avoid her own face in the mirror once the obligatory eyeliner had been applied, but she thought she looked puffy and ill.

She straightened and plodded on, shouldering her bag with a hand to her nose: the diesel fumes this morning felt like they were choking her, turning her stomach.

Some people – Sandro and she – were born old, born sceptical about the future, born looking for what would go wrong, not looking forward. Giuli had thought that would protect her, perhaps. She'd never had any expectations – there always seemed more urgent things to worry about than a thickening waistline or aches and pains or losing her marbles.

Once or twice in the last few weeks she had tried to start the conversation with Enzo and changed her mind. They had barely been married a year, after all – there was no need to start talking about her little worries. Will you still love me if I turn into a nonna-type, round as a barrel and only interested in what's for dinner and putting my feet up in front of the TV? He'd married whippety, nervy, spiky-purple-haired Giuli. She needed to get her roots done, but she was too tired.

Sometimes it pissed her off deeply to be female. Every five minutes a different set of hoops to jump through. Periods. Boobs – or not, in her case. Motherhood – or not, in her case. Then suddenly you get a hair sprouting on your chin and you feel the urge to rant ten times a day and it's all over, boom, menopause.

Now you're an old lady, next stop oblivion. Giuli stopped at the lights, cars roaring past, other people going somewhere while she, she was only –

Hungry.

Giuli diverted. She crossed the road, turned into the Piazza Tasso and there it was again, the comforting whiff of buns – she could almost see them, a tray of pastries smelling of vanilla and butter, a golden crust of sugar on top. Her stomach growled: perhaps that was her problem. She was only hungry.

Sandro's office – *Sandro Cellini, Private Investigator*, he'd grumbled over the cost of the brass plaque but six years on he was still in business – was in sight, but she turned the other way into the bar, Le Tramway, following her nose. A plate, a napkin, a *briosc alla crema*, make that two. Giuli munched, contented, leaning against the bar, catching sight of herself in the pink-tinged mirroring behind the array of bottles. She had cheeks, pouchy little hamster cheeks – maybe that was what was different. She chewed, swallowed, set the bun down a second, discontented, then picked it up again, but it wasn't the same.

What woke Giulietta Sarto up in the morning was fear of death. Which was also new. When she woke she knew she would die, for certain: it wasn't that alone, exactly, that was new – she'd lived most of her youth not expecting to wake up at all. Now she felt it, in her body, in her ageing, dying, changing cells, in the difference, the new taste in her mouth. The most significant difference was that these days she passionately, fervently, with every one of those mutating cells, did not want to die.

Something wrong with her kidneys? That puffed you up, she'd seen it. Addicts often ended with the organs packing up, one after the other.

Giuli paid and left, her stomach full and churning. Across the piazza was the scruffy exterior of her old place of work, even if part-time: the women's centre, with the usual crew of restless, reluctant dads and chain-smoking women patrolling the pavement outside it. If she had still been there, she could have wandered down one of the corridors and collared a trauma doctor or gynae, a rehab worker, an addiction counsellor, even the STD crew at a pinch – more or less anyone would do given the range of Giuli's misdemeanours. She could casually mention – asking for a friend – her history, her symptoms: the palpitations, breathlessness, nausea, panic, tiredness, mood swings. Extreme bloody tiredness.

But Giuli didn't work there any more. And she was too tired to lift up the phone and ask for an appointment.

She could hear it ringing upstairs from the pavement, her key in the door. She couldn't have hurried if her life depended on it but as luck – or not – would have it, the phone was still ringing when she let herself in to the first-floor office.

'Hello?'

At first she thought they'd hung up, and all she could hear was background noise or the sound of her own blood rushing, but then it took shape, it became the sound of someone sobbing quietly.

'Hello?' And at last it came.

A tiny voice, tiny. 'Help me,' it said. 'Please help me.' And the line went dead.

*

Sandro didn't look at the photographs. Not yet. He stood in front of the names.

They must have got them from the old case files. Names, dates and places of birth. That had been Sandro's job, getting their documents from them, out of hippy backpacks and greasy bright-coloured Indian trousers, writing it all down, and there they were after all these years. They milled around him, ghostly, drifting from La Vipera's kitchen into the old hallway, the man with his curls and his faraway look, the small blonde watching him from the doorway, their voices calling up the stairs.

> *Johanna Nielsson, b. 1949 Copenhagen*
> *Marcantonio Gorgone, b. 1951 Reggio-Emilia*
> *Martine Kaufmann, b. 1956 Regensburg*
> *Lucia Grenzi, b. 1955 Trentino*
> *Helen Mason, b. 1947 Montreal*
> *Chantal Buisson, b. 1939 Toulouse*

Behind him now Manzoni was saying something about identification and dental records, but it was as if she was a long way off or he was underwater. He took a step to one side and he was in front of the crime scene pictures.

A dirt floor, sticks and leaves, a humped shape that could be a pile of old clothes against a chair but for the hair. Coarse greying hair, scurf on the collar of a padded greenish jacket of the sort countrymen and hunters wore. Then the dog, half under its owner, a black and white spaniel of some kind – although Sandro knew nothing about dogs – its head tipped back at an odd angle, neck broken. Teeth bared. On the soil floor of the hut under the man's outstretched hand – blunt-nailed, black hairs across his knuckles – was a knife, a hunting knife, the blade approximately six inches long and black with blood.

'He might have killed her,' Sandro said without turning round, 'but as suicide methods go, stabbing yourself in the chest is fairly unusual.' From behind him a murmur of agreement. 'And a countryman doesn't kill his dog like that. He'd have shot it and shot himself after. You wouldn't care, you see, about the noise.'

Belatedly Manzoni's words caught up with him. Dental records: yes. For identifying her. Something about her having kept a low profile, out of touch with her family, a loner, a drifter. Johanna Nielsson, whose light eyes had rested on him in the green haze of an upper room in La Vipera forty years ago, of course she had drifted. That was what she'd been all about, no strings, no ties – he'd heard her say those words, explaining to the dimwitted policemen what their commune was for. And now without his volition his eyes drifted, finally, to rest on her. There, with the dead man's head almost in her lap, she sat.

What was left of her sat. On a wooden chair in the corner of the hut, her head tipping forward: she had been pinioned at the arms with plastic ties, faded blue, holding the body in position. The long hair. Long hair, the hair of a witch or a wise woman, long and dirty white, fell across her body: some of it had begun to shed, a hank halfway down her sleeve. It obscured some of her face but not enough: he could see the gleam of her teeth exposed by the puffing of the lips, white against dark stretched skin. Small and white and even.

That mouth, her head thrown back and laughing at him by the long windows of La Vipera.

In Sandro's head began a kind of incantation, a child squeezing its eyes shut and chanting *the stages of decomposition are* ... Are significantly dependent on temperature. It had not been an unusually hot summer but the temperature had remained above thirty-five for the whole of August and into September. He and Luisa had quarrelled over whether to go to the sea or the hills; they had sat holding hands in the brightly lit restaurant of a seaside hotel; they had made it up in the humid sea air, paddling at twilight. And all the time this had been happening. The processes of decomposition.

In a corner of the hut what was left of Johanna Nielsson sat. The body was dressed in a long high-necked loose dress, antique in style, printed cotton that draped itself over the bloated limbs. A dark stain spread at its centre and there were brownish areas where decomposition had stuck to it, but the design was quite clearly discernible, tiny flowers, the kind of dress they used to laugh at, when fashionable forty years ago, a night gown for an old lady.

Sandro's hand was at his mouth, the edge of his index finger pressing up against the nostrils as if to block the smell that was not in the room with them so much as buzzing in his ears, glittering behind his eyes.

'You're still not sure – of her identity?' Sandro said, his voice coming out rough.

'We've tracked down a relative in Denmark,' said Manzoni, behind him. 'They hadn't seen her in years but provided a DNA sample. So we soon will be.'

But Sandro knew. It was her. He turned.

'So who do we have?' he said.

Chapter Four

I T APPEARED THAT Maria Clara Martinelli lived at the top of the village, in a small untidy farmstead under sparse trees – an ancient tractor with weeds growing through it, a mildewed car and the smell of pigs.

Martinelli and the lean man had come out of the bar and, after a nod, gone their separate ways.

It had been a long walk uphill, and Luisa had had to leave plenty of space between herself and Martinelli, walking ahead – with an awkward rolling gait, but fast – in her man's jacket and cap, allowing the other woman to disappear at regular intervals above her then hurrying in a panic to catch up, trying to muffle the sound of her footsteps on the verge. The village houses fell away abruptly and then it was all woodland. The leaves weren't yet turning but a cool, damp smell drifted out, the mushroomy scent of wet leaves and trickling streams after the previous week's rains.

A pair of crumbling stone pillars flanking an ornate rusted gate came into view at one point, but Martinelli kept going up the road with her strange rolling walk. Luisa had turned to look at the gateway: an overgrown drive seemed to peter out beyond it, leading nowhere. Up ahead Martinelli had not broken stride.

Luisa stood on the verge and wondered. Tried to visualise it: the discovery of the bodies somewhere above her. She had understood from what she had overheard in the bar that Martinelli and the lean, tall man with his hooded eyes had no doubt at all about the identities of the corpses she had found and harboured not an ounce of sorrow or pity for either death.

And she wondered where Nielsson had been all these years.

She had thought of her now and again, of course she had. This woman she'd met once, at twilight among the statues under the Loggia dei Lanzi, forty years ago. Luisa had heard about the disintegration of La Vipera two years after the investigation from Enrico Frollini, her erstwhile employer, or rather overheard. Gone: she remembered it as if it had been yesterday. She's gone.

Enrico – Mr Frollini to her back then, an inveterate gossip and social climber still – had been at the front desk, beside the silver-keyed cash till they would shortly trade in for an ugly modern one, leaning confidentially on his elbows. Christmas 1978. He had been talking to the Princess Salieri, chatelaine of the big villa above Sant'Anna, whose lands adjoined La Vipera and who had been waging her silent one-sided war on Nielsson since the Danish woman had, shortly after her arrival, without warning or consultation, paid for a wall to be built along their boundary – or at least that was why she said she hated the woman. The truth, Luisa suspected, had been more complicated.

The princess, being like most of the nobility tight-fisted – or frugal, as they would prefer it – had bought nothing in the shop since 1974, but Frollini had generally been relaxed about that if she brought news instead. She ignored Luisa, largely, but was aware of her enough to turn her back and whisper now and again.

'Gone, packed up overnight, men came in a pantechnicon with foreign writing on it – God knows, those languages, they're barbaric, I don't know where it was from – and good riddance.' Stiff and angry.

'*Addirittura!*' Never! Frollini whispered avid encouragement, and Luisa could see Salieri now, sighing, setting her big old ugly Gucci portmanteau down on the counter. The princess would then have been something like forty-five. Luisa remembered Salieri searching in the bag, as big as a tool bag, for the Russian cigarettes she smoked, with gold tips, lighting up in the shop, as would have been quite normal in those days.

She had had a husband, with an aristocratic speech impediment, who occasionally accompanied her to the shop, murmuring unintelligibly in the background as he caressed the gentlemen's tweeds, but on this occasion he must have stayed behind, sighing at the windows of their handsome hill-top villa.

That was where he had stood when Luisa had been summoned to the wedding of their daughter at the villa the year before, to assist in the dressing of half a dozen bridesmaids. The estate had been the size of a small hamlet, with its topiary and olive press and faded state rooms, and you could see a corner of La Vipera's roof from those windows. Luisa knew that because when the bridesmaids had departed in their cloud of perfume and a chorus of high-pitched complaints she had gone to look. The red tiles of the roof and the line of the newly built wall were also visible here and there as a thinning of the trees, the occasional ugly clearing.

And now, walking at a discreet distance behind Maria Clara Martinelli under low skies, Luisa glimpsed the Salieri place on the top of the far hillside, its imposing crenellated façade unchanged by forty years – or four hundred for that matter. She didn't even know if the old woman, the princess, was still alive and kicking: she must be eighty-five if she was a day.

Benedetta came in once or twice in the years after her marriage, always silent in her mother's wake, submitting to garments being thrust at her, trying on without emerging from her cubicle. Not for a long time, but then some women stopped buying clothes once they hit the middle years.

The softly murmuring Prince Salieri – he'd been much older – had died perhaps thirty years ago, not so long after the disbanding of the community at La Vipera and hastily, with a curious lack of fanfare, no displays of grief, public or private, but then it had probably been one of those marriages. The rich, as Luisa had often commented, aren't like the rest of us. Up ahead, Martinelli turned off the road and let herself into a low cottage under the trees, on one side the vegetable patch and agricultural flotsam of a smallholding.

La Vipera was around the next bend, perhaps half a mile on: Martinelli its neighbour on this side, the Salieri estate's boundary curving around most of the rest. Luisa turned her head to look. The raw gashes in the forest made by the wall that Luisa had seen from the Salieri windows all that time ago had long since healed over. The wall was invisible from where she stood now: it might still be there, or it might be fallen.

The countryside and its inhabitants had only ever to be patient and wait for the status quo to return. They generally didn't go in for attention-grabbing killings to speed things up.

From below in the village Luisa heard the buzz of a *motorino* winding up the hill towards her.

She should leave.

The knowledge came to her urgently. But it was already too late: Martinelli's door banged abruptly open and the woman was striding down, heading right for her. The whine of the *motorino* was louder now. Luisa turned to look behind her but it was not yet visible, then she looked back at Maria Clara Martinelli. There was no mistaking the anger in her face.

*

'So,' said Pietro, reaching for a plastic tray. He set it down on the shelf next to Sandro's and they shuffled forwards. 'What do you think?'

They had convened to the cafeteria for lunch. Same old conveyor belt, side by side, same dull clatter, same glare of overhead lighting, same row of lunch ladies in their hairnets and white aprons.

'She seems all right,' he said, 'Manzoni,' and sighed, looking at a plate of tagliatelle with ragu before helping himself to one of the prepared salads covered in cling film. Luisa had him on a diet. Beside him, Pietro thoughtlessly accepted the pasta. They sat.

So who have we got?

When he had turned back to Manzoni she had been smiling, broadly. 'A man after my own heart,' she said. She wanted a list of suspects. 'Based on whatever you want. Means, motive, opportunity and your own intuition: you don't have to have all of them at once. Come on, lads. You know how it's done.'

Shaking salt over his tagliatelle, Pietro shrugged. 'She's all right,' he said. 'And like she said, she's leaving us to it, which is the main thing.'

'Nice lads, too,' said Sandro eyeing his salad.

Pietro nodded, his mouth already full.

They'd been respectful. When the door had closed behind Manzoni, Pietro had taken the floor, the three young officers relaxed now but quiet. Seeing his old friend's authority, how he had moved on since the old days, Sandro had wondered all over again what he needed an old lag like him for.

'Cellini is here because he was in on the original investigation into La Vipera,' Pietro had said, pacing, his eye on all of them. 'I want you to liaise with both of us equally. He may be retired –' the briefest pause here while Pietro wrestled (Sandro knew him so well) with the evasion, as they both knew Sandro had more or less been fired '– and he's not going to be in the office much. But you should consider him to have the same authority in the investigation as I do.'

Sandro, who had not blushed in twenty years, had felt a certain warmth at his collar and cleared his throat while Pietro went on. 'I'd like you to bring him up to date on the work you've done so far.'

Panayotis, the Greek, kicked off. Stolid, thorough, only a hint of an accent so he was probably born here, thought Sandro. 'Forensics went over Lotti's house with a fine toothcomb,' he said. 'Clean and cold as a morgue.' He grunted. 'Or a butcher's shop. They say he had been dead more than two days, less than a week, but there was the rain –' He broke off and Sandro nodded.

Two days back. Routine these days, the storms that brought summer to an end: they seemed to be more violent than they'd ever been in Sandro's childhood and this one had knocked tiles off the roof next to theirs and turned the river yellow. Any evidence on that hillside would have ended up in the Arno by now, tangled in one of the great bird's nests of debris that the flooding river brought up against the bridges.

Panayotis sighed. 'Anyway, they came up with nothing, is the upshot. Rain is a bastard.'

Then it was Parini's turn, the cheery ginger kid. 'We did the house-to-house –' There was a collective sigh, and he grimaced. 'But no one says anything. Not seen anything, not done anything, didn't know anything. Don't remember anything, not in the bar, not in the market square. The barman expressed sympathy for the dog and said Lotti liked it more than any human being but that wasn't saying much – and then he shut up. Some of them just look at you through the window and shrug.'

Ceri had been in charge of compiling the list of those who'd lived at La Vipera. 'So far I have one dead,' he said, frowning, 'Chantal Buisson. She died of breast cancer ten years ago in France. One living in a religious community in Canada – Helen Mason? The phone just rings and rings and there's no email address, but I'll keep trying.' Bouncing on the balls of his feet. 'I may have a lead on Gorgone.' And abruptly he'd sat down again, and after that they'd dispersed for lunch.

'They don't eat in the canteen,' Pietro had said as they followed the younger men down the corridor. 'It's all energy drinks and gym sessions for their generation. So we can relax.'

Now they paused before the drinks cabinet: no more wine, though, it seemed, not even the quarter bottles that used to be de rigueur. There was a row of low-alcohol beers and soft drinks in cans. Sandro poured each of them a glass of tap water from a jug and pushed the trays onwards.

'You went on the house-to-house too,' he said. 'Who did you talk to?'

'I went up to the Salieri place on the hill,' said Pietro. 'The old lady was there but she's not dealing from a full deck these days. I gathered from the housekeeper she spends most of her time in bed.'

He hesitated and Sandro jumped in, remembering something dimly involving Luisa, a wedding. 'Any kids? The old lady – didn't she have a daughter?'

Pietro took a forkful of pasta, nodding. 'The old lady's son lives at home but had been away with his sister at some spa or something. Sister lives in town. He turned up as I was leaving, Luca Bartolini. Very civil, very forthcoming. Was in Greece in the early part of August, then at this spa at the time we assume Lotti to have been killed. Gave me the hotel names, the dates, all that.'

They looked down at their food.

'What do you think about the murder–suicide idea?' said Sandro, reaching for the bottle of oil. 'It would make life a lot easier, wouldn't it? Although we'd need to know why he killed her in the first place.'

Pietro gave him a quick look. 'I think you're right: he might have killed her but I don't think he killed himself. I don't get the sense that he was a man given to introspection or remorse – he was a butcher. But if he *was* going to commit a murder and then find himself overcome by his finer feelings, I don't believe it would be weeks later. Also, in addition to the knife wounds, he had a contusion to one temple and nothing on the floor of the hut to indicate that he struck his head when he fell. And he was fond of the dog.'

'So,' said Sandro, 'just coincidence?' Chewing the leaves without enthusiasm. 'I don't remember a butcher's in the village back then,' he said. 'I only remember the bar.' He hadn't remembered even that until that very moment. A little place on a square. A lean blue-jawed barman, a stocky barmaid. He realised that could have been Martinelli, the woman who found the bodies, an old woman now.

'No reason why you should,' said Pietro equably, forking pasta into his mouth. 'It probably didn't even have a sign back then.' He sighed. 'Lotti was retired and a widower. No children. No connection with Johanna Nielsson that anyone will admit to, although he did live in the village when she and her entourage were at La Vipera. He was twenty-five or twenty-six and still living at home at that time. He married in his mid-thirties, after the death of his parents. Wife died of cancer after fifteen years.'

'And these days?'

'He lived alone with his dog,' said Pietro. 'No history of – trouble of any sort on file. Along with a lot of other men all over Tuscany, he was interviewed over the Monster killings because he was in the right place at the right time for one of them, not the others. Although Martinelli recognised him, we did also track down a cousin for the formal identification. Quite easily, as a matter of fact, she lives in San Frediano.'

'All right,' said Sandro, chewing, already thinking ahead. 'So first off, we go to Sant'Anna and talk to a few people, right?' The village bar: he bet those young agents had gone about it all wrong. Maybe the barman would still be there.

'Well, not quite,' said Pietro carefully. Sandro waited and his partner went on. 'We've done the preliminaries there, haven't we? You don't want to give the lads the impression you don't trust them to do a thorough job. And the residents of Sant'Anna aren't going anywhere – they can wait a day.'

'Wait for what?'

'You heard Manzoni,' he said, sighing. 'She wants you to focus on La Vipera. Those guys. And you know what Ceri said about a lead on Gorgone? Well, it turns out he lives in Modena, of all places.'

'*Modena?*' He couldn't imagine it. Modena was a place of sober business and good food and sensible behaviour. Wasn't it? More Ferraris than hippies. The last time Sandro had seen Gorgone, his hair had hung to his nipples – which had been visible because his shirt had been unbuttoned to the waist – and he had played with the ends of it as he talked to Sandro, like a child, his eyes unfocused.

Pietro smiled wanly, putting down his fork. 'And he runs a chain of gyms, if you can believe that. Wellness centres, all that business. Rather top-end.'

Sandro stared. 'You're sure it's the same guy?'

Pietro held up his phone with a picture on it from a professional social media site and Sandro took it, peering.

The hair was short and grey, the eyes behind heavy-rimmed expensive glasses. In the photograph, at least, which looked like it had been taken professionally, he looked in unfairly good nick for a man two years older than Sandro. Three years younger than Johanna Nielsson.

'He's roughly the right age, I suppose,' said Sandro grudgingly. 'Is he a suspect?' Nielsson and a butcher called Lotti, lying on a dirt floor in that filthy embrace, and for a second all he could perceive as a motive was jealousy and Gorgone still her lover.

Pietro shrugged, just barely. 'You tell me,' he said.

'So we'll –' Sandro paused, hearing the lift in his voice, raising his head to look at his old partner with an unexpected bubble of exhilaration rising somewhere inside him. He checked himself, looking back down at the page open on Pietro's phone again, the smooth-skinned silver-haired businessman, the cold eyes behind the glasses. The man's company had an address in the Piazza Duomo, the historic centre of the city.

'So we'll go up there and interview him,' he said, handing the phone back.

Pietro smiled. '*You* will,' he said, fork in his hand.

*

Giuli tried Sandro first but the call went straight to answerphone. She hesitated – but what message could she leave that wouldn't make her sound hysterical or a fool – and hung up. A little girl phoned to ask for help. For a mad moment Giuli wondered if she had even imagined it. It was irrational: she'd retrieved the number and called it back and it had rung and rung. But the small frightened voice was so like the voice she had heard inside her own head for so many years. *Please help me.* The little girl had called Sandro: how had she got his number? She'd probably found it in the *Pagine Gialle*, the yellow pages, under private detectives: it was even online, these days, and so were five-year-olds. Acting out some story?

But there was no need to leave a message. Sandro's phone would tell him the office had called. Was it worth getting Sandro to trace the number, get an address?

Luisa had been oddly cagey about why he was going back into the police station after all this time. Giuli had never really thought what he did to get himself kicked off the force – giving information to a bereaved father about the man they suspected of his daughter's murder – had been wrong in the first place, but then she had been in a position to know for sure the suspect was guilty.

Sandro's pride and his scruples in the years since, his pain at being excluded from a club he despised, she had sort of understood – but Giuli was a pragmatist. If you had spent time on the streets as a junkie, if you had done terrible things, only some of which you were ashamed of, you had to be very careful around guilt and responsibility. You could die of guilt quite easily, and Giuli didn't want to die. Not any more.

Sitting back at the desk in the warm September light, Giuli let it bathe her. Closed her eyes, feeling the fatigue like a weight. She'd try calling the number again first. Give it an hour. The girl's voice was in her head, a bat squeak from far off, floating as though in space, a tiny astronaut untethered. Giuli's eyes sprang open.

She picked up the phone again but on the table beside her the mobile rang. Enzo, bang on cue. She hesitated – this was work time – and then picked up anyway.

'Sweetheart,' she said.

'Just checking on you,' said Enzo, her husband of thirteen months.

Giuli sighed. 'I'm fine. Just a bit tired.'

A silence. 'Maybe you're not sleeping, maybe it's the mattress. Maybe it's the job – Giuli, couldn't you take a break from it?'

She thought again of the tiny voice: there was no denying, it would keep her awake tonight unless she solved the mystery.

Children called the police, didn't they, all the time, to tell them their brother had stolen their sweets or whatever? She relaxed fractionally.

'There's work in the shop, behind the counter, you know that.'

'Darling, I –' She couldn't tell him. She loved him to pieces, her daft, shy, fond husband, but there was no way, no bloody way, their marriage would survive working side by side, day in, day out, in his father's hardware store on the edge of town, where the day's excitement would peak with a pensioner's purchase of some duck tape and a Stanley knife.

'I love my job,' she finished lamely. 'I probably need supplements or something.'

Enzo leapt in. 'Yes!' he said. 'I've booked you in for blood tests. Tomorrow evening.'

Terrific. 'You're so – that's so – thoughtful,' she said, trying to sound bright. 'Um – where?'

'The big lab on the Via Verdi,' said Enzo promptly, and she could tell he was relieved she hadn't gone off on one. 'Six tomorrow evening.'

'Thank you, sweetheart,' she said, dutiful. 'Home at seven, okay?'

'I'll do dinner,' he said and rang off, cheerful.

Giuli sighed and immediately googled the number of the lab on the Via Verdi. He'd never know she hadn't gone; she could tell him everything was fine. It wasn't that she was scared – she'd reschedule, of course she would – just now wasn't the right time.

She'd know if she was ill. She didn't need doctors, tests, all that.

Her hand hovered over the phone, but the tiny voice intruded. *Help me.*

Of course, Sandro would be at the police station – he could be in a meeting with some bigwig, and there she was, butting in. She felt a sweat come over her, engulfing her, and with it the desire to burst into tears. Her, Giuli, crying. Giuli who never cried, not ever, except she had, hadn't she? On her wedding day. It was all a huge mistake. Marriage was for kids, for the young, it wasn't for her, marriage and hot sweats, all in the space of a year. What a fool. What a fool you've been, Giulietta Sarto.

When you don't know, ask. When you need help, ask. How many times had Sandro said that to her? But Sandro was in an office with hot sweats of his own to deal with, and this wasn't his sort of problem: this was one involving women and emotion and children and blood tests and feeling completely and utterly out of control. *Help me.*

She dialled.

Chapter Five

I N LUISA'S HANDBAG HER PHONE, on cue, began to
buzz angrily, and the sound of the *motorino* was louder – it
was just around the bend below them. It appeared just as Maria
Clara Martinelli, breathing heavily, arrived in front of Luisa
on the verge, so close that she could smell sour breath. Luisa
looked from her to the rider. It was the man she'd seen with
Martinelli in the bar, ridiculously lanky on the tiny machine,
and he brought it to a halt behind her, trapping her.

Luisa, her heart beating so fast it hurt, scrabbled for her
phone in an attempt to pretend all of this was normal, they were
ordinary folk, this was a chance encounter on a country road.
She tried to force an apologetic smile as she retrieved the phone,
but her face was stiff. Martinelli glared back at her, mulish, the
shadow of a moustache on her upper lip making her look like a
tough. The man pulled off his motorcycle helmet with an easy
motion and stood there watching.

'Giuli,' said Luisa into the phone, but Giuli was already off
and talking in a rush, which wasn't like her. Something about

a child calling the office, something about being tired, not sleeping. 'Giuli? Slow down.' The man rubbed a hand through grey hair flattened by the helmet and began to walk over, slowly. They were an odd pair. He looked almost aristocratic, with his long fingers and deep-set eyes. Martinelli glared: she must have seen Luisa, must have called him. 'Look, is it – can it wait, Giuli? It's just that I'm in the middle of something.' A silence on the line. Giuli in a huff – the last thing she needed. 'Giuli.'

'It can wait.' The line was dead. Slowly Luisa put the phone away, wishing there'd been a way of letting Giuli know where she was without provoking a torrent of questions. The tall man came to a halt in front of them, the helmet under his arm, and the country road suddenly seemed very empty, very remote. It was cold in the shadow of the forest.

'What do you think you're up to, following me?' burst out Martinelli. The man set a long-fingered hand on her arm, and in that second Luisa detected something between them, a small spark of connection, and she subsided. A couple? Not these two, surely? But something.

The man frowned at Luisa. 'Excuse us,' he said. 'We're a bit jumpy at the moment. Not used to – tourists, you see.'

He didn't mean holidaymakers: there wasn't anywhere in Tuscany unused to tourists, not even a corner as unprepossessing as this one. He was talking about murder tourism. They must, Luisa reflected, have had plenty of that back in the day, when the Monster patrolled these hills.

'I'm –' *sorry* was what Luisa wanted to say, but that would have been an admission of guilt '– out for a walk,' she finished lamely. She'd come thinking she'd be invisible: so much for that theory. Under other circumstances she might have found it a cheering thought, that sixty years of good grooming and care over her appearance made a difference, but it was only inconvenient.

Martinelli scoffed. 'In those shoes?' They all looked at Luisa's feet. She had chosen her oldest, lowest pumps, but Martinelli had a point. They were calfskin, the heel was two inches and they were cut low over the instep.

'She doesn't look like a journalist, either,' said the man, sounding almost amused, as if Luisa wasn't there.

'I'm Luisa Cellini,' said Luisa, drawing herself up a little. They turned to look at her and she had to decide. She'd never been any good at lying. Sandro always said she shouldn't take up a life of crime. 'I used to – know the woman who died.'

Martinelli's eyes narrowed, but she didn't say anything. Luisa went on bravely. 'You're Maria Clara Martinelli? You found her.'

'I don't know how you'd know that,' said Martinelli, but before Luisa had to answer the man spoke.

'Maria Clara,' he said gently, 'I should think most of Florence knows.' He turned to Luisa. 'I'm Luca Bartolini,' he said, offering his hand. 'I'm a neighbour of Signora Martinelli.' A smile. 'We country people have to stick together.'

As if. If Luisa was identifiable by her shoes, Bartolini's elegant manicured nails gave the lie to any pretence that he was a man of the soil. She shook his hand briefly, registering that he would be about her own age. 'You were a friend of Johanna Nielsson's?' he said, watching her. His eyes were deep-set, hooded.

'I met her,' said Luisa warily. He'd said he was a neighbour of Martinelli's: she must in that case have walked past his house on the way up. The stone archway.

The Salieri house.

She went on. 'We had a – connection, forty years ago.' The woman's dead, she told herself. Be civil. 'You only had to meet her once and you couldn't forget her, I think,' she said. Which was true.

There was a grunt from Maria Clara Martinelli, staring down at her feet.

'You're sure it was her?' Luisa said quickly.

Martinelli lifted her head, slowly, and looked at her. 'I'm sure,' she said, brusque but not hostile now, and sighed. 'At first, well, I had no idea what I was looking at.' She put her hand up to her neck in a vulnerable, anxious gesture. 'Just a bundle of clothes and him on the ground. I knew the dog straight away. And it was her property – they were on her property, you see.' And for a second the square weathered face, the blunt fringe, had a childlike quality, and Luisa felt a pang of pity – and guilt.

Luisa suddenly shivered. 'I'm sorry,' she said, and she felt it. 'I can see how it looked. I'm not a gawker, I'm not a journalist, I just needed to – I remember those days. How it was. The Monster, all that.' And then the words escaped her. 'My husband doesn't know I'm here.' *Damn*, she thought, *damn, damn*. They didn't need to know, for heaven's sake. The shadow of something passed over Martinelli's face, of understanding, then curiosity. Wondering, thought Luisa, if Nielsson stole my man back then. Not wondering if her husband was Sandro Cellini, investigating officer – so let them think that, a useful smokescreen. Not wondering if both, in fact, might be true.

'I mean,' said Luisa quickly, 'he'd think what you think, that it's ghoulish.'

'You knew her when she lived here, then,' said Martinelli. Her voice was deep, like a man's, and rough.

'I met her in the city,' said Luisa. 'I never came out here. I worked in a shop in the city.' All true.

Martinelli nodded. 'They did spend time in the city. Art, they were always on about art.' Seeming mollified. Seeming to have had enough, dismissing her to turn back to her smallholding, the abandoned vehicles under the trees, the tilting stone house with dark windows.

The man, Bartolini, spoke. Luisa had the feeling he'd waited until the woman was out of earshot. 'I expect you'd like to see the place?' he said. 'La Vipera? I mean, that's why you came, isn't it? To –' he smiled gently, not with any malice that she could see '– pay your respects?' And he inclined his head respectfully. 'I could take you.'

'Well, I –' She hesitated. She would have liked to talk to Maria Clara Martinelli, but the woman was already ambling across the road, starting up the uneven ground as Luisa watched. She turned back to see Bartolini examining her with a frown – and then his face cleared.

He smiled. He had a nice smile; it reached his eyes. 'I'm not expecting you to get on the back of the *motorino*, Signora Cellini,' he said, his mouth turning down now in mock seriousness, pocketing the key, gesturing up the hill. 'We can walk. It's not far.'

*

No time like the present.

Sandro was on the three o'clock train, the fast train – the sleek Frecciarossa to Bologna, where he would change for Modena –

and experiencing the unfamiliar sensation of being on expenses. They'd put him in business class: leather seats, free coffee and newspapers, a tiny plastic packet of crackers. He eyed his fellow passengers, trying to settle down in the presence of businessmen – and women. One opposite him, with long glossy hair, was on her laptop, busily tapping, occasionally avoiding his eyes over the raised screen. Clearly, these days, in order to look like a businessperson you had to abjure all friendliness. He wished he was in steerage.

Good preparation, Sandro told himself. He needed to be relaxed when he walked into Gorgone's office.

The uniformed steward had given Sandro what he was sure was a sceptical look as he declined the aperitivo with reluctance and took the tiny watery coffee instead, and the biscuits. And opened them straight away, stuffing his hand inside. Catching a glance, a head turning here and there at the noisy crackle of the packet, he'd looked around then and saw that, while some of his travelling companions had accepted a newspaper, they had all declined refreshments.

He ate the crackers and wondered about following the steward down the aisle and asking for another, just on principle. Who was he trying to kid? Principles weren't involved here. He was still hungry. Modena was the gourmet capital of Italy and therefore of the universe. How was he going to survive an hour there – he was booked on the six o'clock train home – on rocket salad and water?

Pietro had offered him a squad car and a driver and Sandro, with sinking heart, had been about to accept when Pietro had followed it up with, 'Of course, you can't be uniformed, you understand that?'

Of course, yes, Sandro understood that. But still, the thought of sitting in the back seat with some rookie driver as though he was a hundred years old, as though, more to the point, he, Sandro, was the criminal, that ageing fraudster of his nightmares, that got him stuttering. Mercifully, Pietro had understood straight away: twenty years as partners did that for you.

'There's always the train,' he'd said, seamless as you like, as though he'd only just thought of it. 'Much faster, these days.' Diplomatically. 'Half the time, in fact.'

They had worked out a cover story, too, and Pietro had already cleared it with Gorgone. Sandro had been brought out of (*recent! You don't want him thinking I'm ninety!*) retirement because of his earlier involvement with Nielsson and La Vipera.

'You come,' said Sandro, blunt. 'Why don't you?' Pietro had smiled at that, mischievous, thank God, and not pitying, and said, 'Sandro, you're my secret weapon. *Our* secret weapon. I want to lull him into a false sense of security.'

'You do suspect him, then.'

Pietro had shrugged at that. 'When I called to arrange the interview Gorgone informed me rather quickly that he was out of town on business for two weeks either side of her estimated date of death,' he said. 'And do you think Nielsson was killed by someone who didn't know her? The woman was found in a place she hadn't lived in for years: we can't rule out the possibility – probability – that she was brought there, before or after death. Her killer took care over the presentation of the body, so perhaps returned to it at regular intervals.' A pause. 'Which may be how he – or she – happened to be there when Lotti turned up, unfortunately for him.'

Coincidence then? Sandro didn't believe it.

As it turned out, he would barely have had time to eat a second packet of crackers because the journey – a headlong dark rush through tunnels – took only thirty-five minutes. His phone blipped as they emerged briefly to a flash of bright sunshine and a glimpse of soft green slopes: missed call, from the office. It must have come while they were underground. He tried to call back immediately but the darkness swallowed them again, the signal disappeared and he put the phone back in his pocket.

At Bologna he switched to a *regionale*, moving more slowly. He hadn't been up here in years and even then had only been on his way somewhere else. The flat plains stretched into misty distance – in winter it would all be blanketed by the sudden thick fogs for which the region was famous, rising off the great winding Po river. Blinded, traffic would slow on the huge motorways that met here, would turn muffled and mysterious, but now it could not seem more gentle and open a landscape.

So Marcantonio Gorgone had come home, here, to possibly the quietest, safest, least dramatic city there was. Good for him.

He wondered if Gorgone would remember him. He looked out through the train window across the flat pale landscape; a figure appeared, tiny in black silhouette, walking a dog along a dusty path between fields. The two figures in easy companionship, the dog waiting for the man then running on.

Lotti's dog had been a truffle hound. It had been killed, they assumed, because it would alert someone to Lotti's death very quickly if allowed to run off in distress, but there could be other reasons. Malice? The dog was killed before Lotti – its body beneath his. Someone had expected him to appear after it? Certainly. Who could kill a dog ruthlessly? Most country people. And again the image of a figure waiting patiently in the dark came into his mind. Not coincidence, as Manzoni had proposed, but design.

Houses began to appear, closing off the wide vista, the man with his dog disappeared and then they were rattling slowly into Modena station. Sandro consulted his phone for a route into the town and began to walk.

'You can play it how you like, Alessandro,' Pietro had said, his smile widening. 'You can play it friendly, or grumpy, or bumbling, or nostalgic. God knows, you can play senile if you feel it'll get you somewhere.' And he winked.

But now, Sandro had to remind himself, he'd been working alone for six years, and he could manage this little fishing expedition in his sleep.

Standing at the centre of the big cobbled Piazza Duomo, he took a moment, overcome by how unfamiliar he was with his own country, how foreign it looked. He paused by the creamy-pink bulk of the cathedral, a thousand years old, two grinning lions guarding the entrance. Its pillared bell-tower leaned gently away from the duomo in the soft afternoon light, at its base a roll-call of partisans fallen in the Second World War.

Sandro had been born not long after the end of that war, as Marcantonio Gorgone must have been, a child in a poor country, a landscape trampled and wrecked by three armies. Florence had been still half-ruined when he started school and yet it had grown over, been rebuilt with all the grumbling, painstaking slowness in which his countrymen were expert, the status quo restored, but nothing was quite the same. We don't want things to change, thought Sandro, and yet they do. Or is it that we think we are changing all the time, we think we have grown up, but we find ourselves creeping back to old habits, old places?

Gorgone's offices were in a soft red-brick arcaded façade in the sixteenth-century style where a row of highly polished bell-pushes sat beside a vast wooden door. An accountancy firm, an architect, a psychotherapist. Upmarket was right.

He got out his phone to turn it to silent and saw the little icon with its red alert and remembered the missed call. The mobile was very useful, of course, but Sandro wasn't sure at his age if what he wanted was any more red alerts in his life.

Just a missed call.

There was no time to call Giuli back right now. His appointment with Gorgone was four o'clock and it was two minutes to. If it had been urgent she'd have tried again.

He pressed the bell-push that said Studio Fitness Gorgone. The door buzzed back and he was admitted. A dim vaulted entrance hall smelling faintly of something like expensive church incense, a wide stone staircase. A young woman behind a desk, with shiny centre-parted dark hair and severe black-framed glasses that did not disguise her perfect good looks, smiled at him, rising to her feet. Behind her were blown-up photographs of what looked to Sandro like shining torture chambers but were in fact gym interiors. A lot of fitness equipment. Rows of cycling machines and treadmills and a blonde with very white teeth laughing in a Jacuzzi.

And then there he was, after all these years, a glint of gold in his mouth, tucking his tie into a pair of very narrow, very well-cut trousers with an air of self-satisfaction, then holding out the hand to Sandro. His smooth, tanned face quite blank, no sign of recognition at all. None.

Chapter Six

BUSINESS WAS OBVIOUSLY GOOD for Marcantonio Gorgone, to judge by the old-school elegance of his offices, the cut of his suit and the deference of the assistant (that didn't come cheap) as she brought them in coffees on a tiny silver tray.

The dark-haired beauty let the door close behind her, and Sandro felt Gorgone's eyes settle on him, thoughtfully.

'Mr Gorgone,' he said, hesitating under his look, and it came to Sandro in that pause that the man had been born into money, hadn't he? You didn't get access to this kind of prime office space without connections – and something came to him dimly from the past, that small German blonde standing in a doorway at La Vipera, forty years ago, looking sidelong at Gorgone and muttering something about pigs that Sandro had at first assumed to be a reference to him as a police officer. Pigs – of course. Emilia Romagna was the home of the prestige pig: culatello, salame, prosciutto, zampone. The Gorgone money came from pigs. The Po's wide plains harboured hectares upon hectares of pig barns, their pungent fragrance drifting through the orchards and villas.

Odd how much of La Vipera was still there in his head, just waiting to be stirred into life. It was what happened five minutes ago he forgot, a missed call. He remembered that blonde, the way she stood, hands in her pockets, watching. Michelle? Martine.

He straightened in his chair – old leather, polished to a high shine – at the thought. 'Mr Gorgone,' he said again. His instinct was to begin by getting more details on the alibi, as Pietro had instructed him in no uncertain terms. 'I'd like to –'

'I *do* know you,' said Gorgone, delighted as a child suddenly, interrupting him, leaning forward in his excitement so Sandro got a whiff of foul breath under peppermint. Getting to his feet. 'You were the little cop who – you –'

Sandro wondered exactly how many and what drugs Gorgone had taken back then. He had the air of a man with a good few synapses blown, and his delight at remembering Sandro had something of the simpleton about it. *Little cop*.

'And now you're into – wellness,' said Sandro drily, balancing a smile on his face.

The man sat back, pleased. 'It's excellent business,' he said.

And you don't have to have many brain cells to pound a treadmill, thought Sandro, surrendering to peevishness. 'I'm sure,' he said. Gorgone went on looking pleased with himself for a good thirty seconds before he remembered why Sandro was there and hurriedly assumed the appearance of sorrowful sobriety.

'Of course,' he said earnestly, 'since those days we have very much all gone our separate ways. I can tell you straight away

I haven't seen Johanna in ten, no, probably twenty years.' The smile crafty. 'Hadn't.'

'Is it ten or is it twenty?' said Sandro, feeling weary already.

Gorgone spread his hands in a rueful gesture. 'I'm rather poor at dates,' he said, then, grasping at some dim concept, 'in this business it's all about the future, you see.' Sandro smiled a little – a very little – and said nothing. Gorgone went on hopefully. 'It was before the millennium, I know that,' he said.

Sandro sighed. 'So you have no idea of where she'd been living, any of that?'

'Oh, I didn't say that,' said Gorgone, with a professional frown. Sandro resisted the urge to lean across his desk and yank on his silk tie.

Gorgone inspected his manicured hands before going on. 'She went back to Germany when we left La Vipera. I lived in Berlin with her for a couple of years and then ...' he affected a blasé air, 'we grew apart.'

She kicked him out, thought Sandro, she got bored, and he was aware of something, that fierce little stab he'd felt all those years ago. What had she been doing with a fool like Gorgone? She had been so much more than him, he'd seen that, back then, more in a bad way – but more.

'After that, I bumped into her once in Los Angeles, I think late nineties, and,' Gorgone shrugged, 'that was it.'

Los Angeles, thought Sandro, who'd never been to America. Los Angeles seemed to him a place for people like this. La Vipera had been called a community but it came to him now that it had never been a community. A group of twenty-somethings each with their own agenda wasn't a community.

'She didn't marry?' he asked. 'Have a family, children, all that?'

Gorgone shook his head. 'I don't believe so.' He opened his mouth then closed it again.

'How do you know,' said Sandro, curious, 'if you lost touch?'

'A friend caught up with her – this summer, as a matter of fact.' Gorgone waved a hand vaguely. 'Up in Liguria somewhere. Near the Cinque Terre, travelling, you know. On the road.' He caught Sandro's interrogative glance and for once was ahead of him. 'Who was the friend? Martine Kaufmann. She was – one of us. Living at La Vipera back then.' He flushed.

Martine. The watchful blonde standing in the doorway. And quite suddenly Sandro remembered her turning away as Johanna Nielsson had touched him lightly on the hand and asked him if he wanted to check the upper floors, in the second he hesitated before following her up the stairs.

'Can we get hold of Miss Kaufmann?' said Sandro, clearing his throat.

'Oh yes,' said Gorgone. 'I'm sure. She's lived in Florence for the last ten years or so – she paints, teaches, I don't know. I bumped into her months ago, on the platform at Bologna – everyone ends up passing through Bologna, don't you find? Our paths do cross now and again, although we – we're very much on separate tracks these days. She's – I believe she's into good works, all that.' A slight grimace of embarrassment.

Sandro watched Gorgone, saying nothing. His colour still high as though emotions were beginning to kick in, as though the implications of all this were finally beginning to dawn on him, the businessman pulled open a drawer in his desk and began to rummage agitatedly. He brought out a brochure and handed it to Sandro. A cursory glance revealed some garish oils in a vaulted space and the indistinct figure of a fair-haired woman half-hidden behind a canvas. 'Martine gave me this,' he said. 'It's her business. I mean, if you want to contact her.'

Sandro stashed it in his pocket. 'Are you in touch with anyone else from that time?'

Gorgone shook his head. 'I think quite possibly only Martine and I are still alive,' he said, offhand. 'A few went abroad. There was a girl I can't quite – her name escapes me. I'll, I'll put some thought into it. Italian, I think she's running a ski school in the Dolomites, or was. If I remember ...' Earnest, willing.

'Thank you,' said Sandro, and leaning forward he said, lowering his voice in an attempt to engage with whatever vulnerability was making Gorgone nervous, 'my condolences. Really. I know back then we didn't – it wasn't the best footing for – you must realise now,' looking around the handsome four-hundred-year-old space, 'that perhaps rural Tuscany wasn't quite ready for experiments in communal living.'

Gorgone stared at him blankly. 'Well, no,' he said, impatient. 'It's how the world was then. We were young, there was a bit of experimentation. I mean, good heavens, look at the world these days and how people carry on.' Pompous. He might still fit into his 30-inch trousers, thought Sandro, but Gorgone was most definitely middle-aged these days. 'My goodness, it was all very innocent by comparison.' His eyes went vague again, his mouth clamped shut, deciding, Sandro guessed, against cataloguing drugs consumed or sexual variations experimented with.

'We don't think,' Sandro said carefully, 'that Ms Nielsson was killed down there, in the grounds of La Vipera, a place she hadn't lived for forty years, by chance or coincidence. How did you get on with the locals? The woman who found the bodies is called Maria Clara Martinelli – do you remember her? Worked in the bar?' Gorgone shrugged and he went on. 'Was there anyone with – I don't know, a grudge against you?' He paused. 'Did you have any idea, for example, who contacted us with those ... allegations, all that time ago?'

'Unfounded allegations,' said Gorgone sullenly, then leaned abruptly forwards. 'None of them could stand us, bloody Tuscan peasants. I can't remember individuals. They simply disliked us because we were – different.' He looked down his nose at Sandro, who just nodded and smiled.

'What about a man called Lotti?' he said carefully. The name of the second victim had not appeared in the preliminary newspaper reports and Gorgone looked blank. 'The other body,' he said and Gorgone paled. He went on. 'A butcher from the village, sixty-something, would have been in his twenties back then.'

Gorgone shook his head. 'I'm a lifelong vegetarian,' he said. A vegetarian whose money comes from pig-farming, thought Sandro. 'At La Vipera we practised veganism for the most part – Johanna was ahead of her time in that. We had nothing to do with any butcher.'

Sandro sat back at the memory of Johanna Nielsson's pallor, her otherworldliness, the sort of gossamer transparency of her, and he felt something ebb, at last, after so many years. An early proponent of veganism was what it amounted to. 'I see,' he said.

A cliché, all gone to dust. 'I was told you were away the first two weeks of August?'

'On business,' said Gorgone, very prompt. Unruffled. 'Aspen, Palm Springs, Miami.'

Damn, thought Sandro. Damn, damn, damn. He suddenly wanted it to be this pampered airhead. 'When did you get back?'

'Last Sunday,' said Gorgone, and then he leaned forward over his desk and lowered his voice. 'She's really dead? You're sure it's her?'

Sandro hesitated. 'There was a tattoo,' he said, raising his wrist and tapping on the tendons inside it. 'We're waiting on tests but, yes, it's her.'

And to his surprise, as he watched, the man's face crumpled at last, and he brought his hands up to cover it. After a moment's hesitation, Sandro rose from his seat and came round the desk to rest a hand on the man's shoulder. Gorgone raised his head to look at him and his face seemed washed clean, somehow, the pomposity gone.

'I never thought she'd die,' he said. 'We all thought we'd live forever.'

Chapter Seven

BY THE TIME GIULI GOT HOME it was dark, and Enzo had cooked polpettone: she knew before she got up the stairs to the door of their apartment. The intense savoury fragrance of meat cooking with herbs. Wine and fennel, sizzling pork fat, she could even smell nutmeg and pepper.

It was madness. Giuli had never in her life had any interest in food. Getting older was bizarre.

She paused, her key in the lock, trying to work it out from bits and pieces of medical information gleaned over the years. Could it be her thyroid? Again the flutter of anxiety, followed by an excess of impatience with herself. She wasn't going to google her symptoms – she was well aware that that way lay full-blown hypochondria and panic attacks. She couldn't ask Luisa: although Luisa's breast cancer was now five years in the past and they were entering safer territory, Luisa had enough on her plate.

Besides, she knew what Luisa would say. *Stop it, Giuli, you're just hungry.*

She turned the key and there was Enzo waiting, beaming at her with his apron on. He was looking even dafter than usual with a smudge of flour on one cheek and a wooden spoon in his hand.

'Darling,' she said fondly and he folded her in his arms. She looked over his shoulder into their home – lamps on in the living room, pictures on the walls – still every night a surprise to her that she had one.

They had bought this apartment – a little modern box with a tiny balcony in whose compact, orderly dullness Giuli absolutely delighted – when they married, the year before. In a small development on the southern edge of the city, overlooking a corner of an olive grove across a stretch of busy road, it had been the first place, at forty-three, that Giulietta Sarto had been able to call her own. Giuli had grown up in a succession of the squats and *monolocali* her mother – junkie, hooker, painter of little pictures, arranger of flowers in jam jars, teller of sad little stories – had dragged her to, then, when her mother had died, mostly the streets. And worse than the streets, but that was another story, an old story that had only begun to come to an end when Sandro had arrested her and had been swept away when Luisa had dragged her under their wing.

A funny old family history. Enzo never seemed to make remark on that; he never made her feel like she was any different, that their stories – his growing up in absolute safety as the child of simple country people, helping his father with their travelling *porchetta* van, working in his father's hardware store – might in any way be incompatible. He had faith. He had – without a religious bone in his body – absolute faith in Giuli and in his love for her. As for Giuli, who resolutely did not believe in love, if you asked her, or faith either, for that matter, she had been converted to both by the simple fact of his steadfastness.

He released her, beaming, and Giuli went into the tiny bedroom to change. It had been a long day.

Neither Sandro nor Luisa had called back.

Hanging up her coat, Giuli mused on that. It wasn't like them.

Sandro was on a job, he was in the station with Pietro on some old case – but Luisa? Luisa had given up work the year before. Of course a woman like Luisa was never going to be idle. She did house-to-house collecting for the women's centre, for example; she was on a rota to empty the used-clothes depository; and there were at least two very elderly and bad-tempered ladies she took to the supermarket twice a week. But somehow Giuli didn't think it had been any of those errands that had made Luisa breathless and hurried.

She'd call later.

In the office, she'd left it till after lunch and then she'd called the number back again, her unease mounting as she found herself inhabiting that child a little too much. If they'd had a landline in any of the places she'd lived with her own mother she'd have been calling the police once a week at least, but as it was she'd had to sit tight and let the crises pass, one after another. Her mother refusing to wake up, that had happened more than once. One or other of her mother's boyfriends battering on the door, ditto.

She'd heard no background noise when the child had called, no TV, no raised voices. A preschool child? Or just truanting?

The anxiety had had an odd effect on her: her appetite gone, her stomach queasy with worry. At lunchtime Giuli had lain her head down on the desk and slept.

'*Tesora?*'

'Coming,' she called back, tugging off the jeans that had been driving her crazy all day, nothing about them comfortable. They ate.

'So how was your day?' he asked. He was happier now she'd stopped working at the women's centre. She remembered about the blood tests tomorrow: she hadn't cancelled. Too late to phone tonight.

Giuli hesitated. Her instinct generally was to protect Enzo from the detail of her day. She always thought he'd find it either boring or upsetting, although in the event he usually seemed happier to know. 'It was weird. A little girl phoned, asking for help, then hung up.'

'She wanted Sandro?'

Her mouth full, Giuli shook her head. Chewed carefully: this appetite business. 'That was what I thought straight off – I mean, he would be the guy to call, right?' Sandro who had rescued her. 'But then I thought maybe she was looking up private detectives and chose him at random. It could have been a game, or it could have been just punching in any old number.' Her appetite gone again, as suddenly as it had come, she set down the knife and fork.

'So you called back?' Enzo was eating stolidly, but his eyes didn't leave her.

'More or less straight away,' said Giuli. 'It was a landline, a Florence number. But there was no answer.' She was sitting quite still now and his hand went out to touch hers. She gave him a quick look. 'I phoned again after lunch.'

'And?' said Enzo.

'The grandmother answered,' she said, her shoulders dropping. The woman had sounded nervous, apologetic. 'Gigi just learned to read and she's full of it,' she'd said, anxious. 'My daughter's out at work, and I'm not so quick on my feet these days. I'm so sorry to have bothered you. Did she actually say anything?'

'I told her the child asked for help,' Giuli said to Enzo. 'And then she went silent for a bit. Eventually – she sounded ashamed, I was ashamed of myself for asking – she told me her daughter's husband had left them six months before, they were struggling for money, she'd had to stop work, the state nursery nearby had closed down. She thought maybe the child, Gigi, wanted us to find the husband –' Giuli broke off, shaking her head wearily.

Enzo still had her hand. He patted it.

'I asked her,' said Giuli, 'if that was what Gigi's mother wanted, and the old lady said it was the last thing they wanted, even if she had the money.'

Enzo released her hand, smiling now. 'Sounds like you managed to help a bit, then.'

'I told her to call me if there was anything I could do. She said she would.' Giuli felt curiously happy at the thought. Maybe Enzo was right.

He got up and began to clear the plates. It came to her muffled, over his shoulder as he bent at the dishwasher, but still she was alerted by a note of wariness in his voice. 'Is it true,' he said, 'that Sandro's got something to do with this business at La Vipera?'

*

Luisa lay under the covers, unable to get warm although they'd been in bed hours, and Sandro was flat on his back and snoring beside her.

They'd tried everything with the snoring, nose-clips and no wine with dinner and no pasta after six and her nudging him on his side. Nothing worked. Luisa had learned long since to sleep through it. Sometimes she thought she wouldn't be able to sleep *without* that sound, and it certainly wasn't what was keeping her awake tonight.

He had come in late and dog-tired: she'd had a dish of beans and sausage covered on the stove for him but he'd waved it away, already walking past her into the bedroom, dropping down on the bed to pull off his boots and sitting there a moment as though he had forgotten what to do next. He wouldn't have noticed the long scratch on her leg even if she hadn't carefully hidden it beneath her best silk pyjamas. He didn't notice the pyjamas, either.

Now she stirred under the sheets, feeling the silk against her legs, an unfamiliar sensual luxury. She had bought them years ago. Five years, to cover herself after the operation, and Sandro always noticed when she wore them, although he rarely said anything.

What would have happened if Sandro had surrendered to the fascination of Johanna Nielsson forty years ago? Luisa and he would have gone their separate ways. She'd have married someone else? Probably. She'd have got pregnant with a different child, a baby that might have survived, unlike their own. She might have had many children. The thought stirred an ancient, indelible anguish. It didn't, though – and this came as a surprise to Luisa – make her want to go back and try a different path. To start again. The thought of all those years, all yet to be got through. And she and Sandro were grown together now, like the ivy circling those spindly trees she'd walked through this afternoon with a stranger.

For certain, Sandro would not have ended up with Johanna Nielsson.

It had taken Bartolini five minutes' uphill walking to ask again how Luisa had known Johanna Nielsson. She told herself she would have been surprised if he hadn't asked, and there'd been something about his manner – pleasant, educated, unassuming – that had by then made her relax. Persuaded her to consider this an almost-natural situation, the man being polite to a visitor to their little backwater. It seemed safest to assume the best in that moment.

They had just paused on the quiet road, where there was a rusting gate and beyond it an overgrown path. 'Well –' and Luisa had hesitated, deciding on an approximation of the truth. To hell with it, shameful or not. The woman was dead. 'Actually, my husband knew her better than I did.' Was it her imagination or was that a nod of recognition? 'It was a long time ago. But I was jealous of her.' Bartolini had cleared his throat, then, and stepped forward to open the gate for her.

'You're not married?' she asked, an innocent question that sounded the opposite when it popped out of her mouth.

He stopped, his hand on the gate, and regarded her for long enough to prompt a blush. He shook his head gravely. 'No,' he said. 'I never married.'

It was then it occurred to her that she didn't know this man and she was alone with him, out of earshot of the road or any building but La Vipera. Then that she faltered, because perhaps that was how the worst was allowed to happen: when you hoped for the best, assumed people were decent.

At any rate, the worst that had happened that afternoon was she had lost her footing and fallen against some old fencing.

'Well, if it's any consolation,' Bartolini had said, head down, 'I don't think your husband was the only one to have strong feelings about Johanna Nielsson. I gather she was – very charismatic.'

'That's one word for it,' said Luisa, before she could stop herself. 'You didn't know her yourself?' She stopped then to give him a quick glance, which confirmed her first assumption that he was more or less her own age. Late sixties.

With a sigh, Bartolini shook his head. 'I didn't know her,' he said. 'The two years they were here – the Vipera cult – I'd been packed off to Milan by the family. I was up there trying to make my fortune.' He grinned cheerfully. 'Or not, as it turned out.' He took his hand from the gate and turned to look down the hill. 'Maria Clara has always been my informant,' he said with a smile. 'We might look like an odd couple –' and catching Luisa's expression '– not that kind of couple. Friends. We were kids together, and my mother never liked me playing with her.' He shrugged. 'So of course that was what I wanted to do. She was always a tomboy.'

They were on the path now, and it was not quite wide enough for two to walk abreast, but nonetheless that was how they progressed. His arm brushed hers but he seemed unaware of their proximity. He had smiled, cheerful. Warm.

In bed now, Luisa raised her hands to her face, softly, at the memory. Would Sandro have accused her of flirting with Bartolini? She had not been. It had felt like walking a tightrope: the dangerous intimacy of confiding in him, of trying to get information from him, and placing herself in his hands to do it. Perhaps that was how the other kind of intimacy started. Sandro had gone to La Vipera, after all, in search of information too.

Once he'd removed his boots, Luisa had made Sandro drink a tisane, lime flower tea, if only to postpone the moment at which he would fall like a log into bed and to allow him a little window in which to unpack the day, to share it with her.

He'd drunk the brew in silence, without even his usual grimace, and only as he'd handed the cup back to her had said, abruptly, 'She'd been back in Italy since the spring, it seems. No more than a couple of hours from here.'

And then, without another word to mitigate or explain, he was under the covers, eyes closed. And the one fact he had retained from the day's journeying had been that for the last months of her life Johanna Nielsson had been within his reach.

Charismatic. Well, you could say that again.

Was it a cult?' she'd asked, breathless, catching up with Bartolini as he paused above her at a fork in the path, looking away from her. 'And look – I haven't – I need to get home. Is it much further?'

She looked around. There were so many trees, all very tall and spindly, clogged with ivy here and there, as far as the eye could see. It was quiet but not silent – there were tiny sounds, dripping, a rustle, her own breath as she panted – and the light between the trees was blurred to a haze with fine foliage and insect activity. Up above them was the shape of a low shack or shepherd's hut. Something flickered under the trees and was gone. Bartolini turned back to her.

'Were you here when she – found the body?' she blurted. 'Mrs Martinelli?'

He looked at her, a long judicious moment, then shook his head. 'I was – away. With my sister, as a matter of fact.'

She found herself wrong-footed and said nothing. He was watching her.

'It's not far,' he said. He didn't seem out of breath in the slightest and Luisa felt a twinge of shame, at her slowness, at the solidity of her small frame. She could walk for hours in the city but here – here was different. She didn't seem able to catch her breath. 'I'm sorry, I wasn't thinking. We could have gone on along the road a little further but from here –' He reached down to her, holding out his hand, and after a moment's hesitation she took it. He pulled her gently up to stand beside him and she saw that the fork in the path was where another track joined it, coming up from just around the hillside.

'As for it being a cult,' he shrugged, 'you tell me. You met her. Did you meet any of the others?'

She thought of the little group beside the Loggia dei Lanzi: the small blonde girl, the dark Italian, the man. The man had been Gorgone. Each face turned up to Nielsson, the laying on of her hand in dismissal or blessing. 'Not exactly, although I saw her with a group of them once.' She considered. 'Yes. There was something – sort of religious about it. If that's what's meant by a cult. But the local people – Mrs Martinelli for example – they would know better. What does she say?'

'Oh, Maria Clara, she's ... she's a little more broadminded than the rest, or more complicated at least. She's hardly a conventional person herself.' He was smiling again. 'It's why we get on. Of course there are plenty of others who thought at the time that they were Satanists or the place was a brothel or a drug den.'

'The police were called at one point, weren't they?' she ventured timidly. 'An anonymous call?'

He shrugged again. 'Like I say,' he said, 'I was in Milan most of the time. I just heard bits and pieces from my mother, although she always pretended she was too grand for gossip.' Luisa found herself smiling at that and then with a shock she realised something. 'But your mother –' she said. 'Your name's Bartolini?'

'My mother is the Princess Salieri,' he said. 'I was the product of her first marriage. My late father was not quite so noble.'

'Your sister –' Luisa broke off, confusedly. 'I helped with a wedding, a few years after –'

'Half-sister, to be accurate,' he said drily, 'but yes, Benedetta.'

Luisa had a vague memory of the old princess telling her Benedetta had gone to Switzerland. Years ago now, though. She realised it had been a long time since she'd had any contact with the old woman – she couldn't even claim acquaintance, although it wasn't a family you forgot.

She felt him contemplate her, tapping his teeth with a fingernail, and straightened. 'Do you know,' something dawning in his eyes, 'I think I remember you. In the big *salotto*, we men were kept away, weren't we? But Benedetta wanted me for something. I forget what. But you –'

Luisa moved away a little, feeling warmth at her neck. She didn't know if he was flirting or if he really remembered her. She only remembered Benedetta asking for a glass of champagne and a man bringing it.

'So you're all related,' she said. 'It's funny, I remembered the house – the entrance to the villa – differently.'

He must, she supposed, have been at the wedding, although she didn't remember seeing him. In the bridal dressing room, though, there had been only women fussing. And the father at the window. A strange cool atmosphere that she had put down to their nobility.

'We passed the back gate,' he said. 'The main entrance is a mile further on. The estate is very large – it more or less wraps around La Vipera.' And as if to illustrate the point he drew her closer, 'Look,' and set her in front of him. 'You get the best view from here.'

At first Luisa couldn't see what he saw – of course, he was taller than her. She took a step uphill, unsteady already with the climb and the odd light, and above them that something flickered again, white between the trees, and she recoiled, reached for his arm and missed. She went down. As she went down she saw it, below them, the roof falling in and the pale scrawled flank of the house, half-covered in ivy. She saw something drawn there, and then she was sliding.

And then Bartolini was grabbing for her, hauling her back from the brink, and that was when she felt the sudden sharp pain as it tore at her calf.

Sitting back abruptly on the uneven hillside, she had felt a dizziness that refused for a moment to be dispelled, as Bartolini, a stranger, knelt in front of her examining the wound. Looking down, she saw rusty barbed wire caught on her tights, the long ladder in the nylon and black blood underneath. Queasy, she looked quickly away, raising her gaze: over his shoulder, the side elevation of La Vipera was no longer visible, but it sat in her memory like a projection on a screen.

The gaping hole in the roof and the ivy, creeping black across the stucco, half-concealing the lineaments of a long-ago graffito that covered the whole side of the house. Had it been there all that time back? She'd never come here. The depiction of a gigantic spiral, spidery lines curling around on themselves like a snail, or something odder that from here she couldn't properly see, a distorted figure beneath the ivy, half-crumbled to dust.

'I want to go home now,' she had said then, stubborn as a child herself, looking up into Bartolini's face with its expression of mild concern. 'Please,' she said. 'I want to go home.'

In bed, she turned at the memory.

Beside her, Sandro's snoring had stopped, a hiatus that, as it prolonged, disturbed her more than the snoring. She waited – *Was he? Would he?* – and in a sudden uncharacteristic agony of fright she prodded him in the ribs. Don't. *Don't.*

A sharp, hoarse intake of breath and he was there again – if not quite in the land of the living, in the twilight land of restless sleep. Luisa lay back on the pillows and made herself be quiet, but her heart would not stop its fluttering.

Chapter Eight

SANDRO LEANED DOWN TO KISS Luisa goodbye, absently. It wasn't until he got to the street that he wondered if she had been a bit pale. He opened the door and the noise and bustle of the Via Ghibellina hurried him out and on.

Pietro had been surprised by the request to meet in the Via del Leone rather than at the station, but agreeable. 'Be nice to catch up with little Giuli,' he'd said, sounding upbeat. 'I can see being back in the station might be a bit – painful.'

Pietro knew him better than he liked to admit. The high-ceilinged dusty corridors of the police station with their long windows, the old faces, the memories. Of cases past, thievery and abuse and squalor; of his own misery. Had he been unhappy all that time? Not all of it. There'd been a turning point, when his career as a police officer had gone abruptly to dust.

He and Luisa didn't speak of it, never had. The week that had changed their lives, a week in which Luisa had given birth to their daughter, their only child, and – unable even to hold hands in the awfulness of their pain – they had watched her die, two days later, of a syndrome for which there was still no cure. The difference now was that the syndrome could be detected in utero, and the baby could ... well. There was still no cure.

There had been a moment in that hospital bedroom, as he sat helpless in the armchair beside Luisa, when she had started out of bed with the tiny creature in her arms and run – run, hobbling with all the loose-jointed disorientation of having given birth – to the window and held the baby up to it to see the sky. 'She'll have seen it once, at least,' she'd said, her face white in the pale light and, turning to Sandro, her eyes huge and black with it, the darkness too great for tears.

Work had not been a comfort, but it had been a distraction. He had fought on, grimly. Until he'd made a stupid mistake and he was out, on his backside, and his career was over.

Perhaps his going back to the station had stirred all that up for Luisa, too. Sandro stopped with the thought, got out his phone and sent her a text. *Is everything okay, sweetheart? Meet for lunch?* He walked on.

The day was beautiful. One of those September mornings cool and clear as crystal but the sun still warm on the golden house-fronts. Sandro took his time walking the long diagonal through the city, and by the time the pretty dome of the Cestello appeared at the end of the Vigna Nuova, bathed in yellow morning light, it had all settled somewhat.

When Sandro got to the Via del Leone Giuli was not there, but that suited him fine. Another moment or two of contemplation: suspects.

The primary motives for murder, in his experience, were emotion – hatred, anger, jealousy – or money.

Not Gorgone, then. Even if he hadn't been on the other side of the world when Nielsson died, and clearly hadn't known Lotti from Adam, he was wealthy already. And any passion or imagination he might once have had seemed to have long ago burned down to nothing. Sandro didn't think him capable of murder, but that didn't mean he liked him. He'd told Pietro as much on the phone already. *Not him, in my opinion. But he knows something.*

Nielsson's wrists had been bound. That told Sandro she had not been killed in haste, nor thoughtlessly. Lotti – well. That might have been a secondary murder, to hide evidence: he came upon the scene and found the murderer there and was killed. Possible – although coincidence played too much of a part in it for Sandro's liking.

The entryphone sounded. It was Pietro: Sandro buzzed him in and could hear him immediately cheery on the stairs, calling up. He believed Pietro was enjoying this reunion, and the thought heartened him. His old friend had two piping hot coffees in one hand and a briefcase in the other, and an overcoat concealing his uniform. He took off the coat and then the pale-blue uniform jacket immediately, the maroon trim at the pocket and on the sleeve giving Sandro an odd flip of the heart. Handing his uniform in all those years ago.

'So,' Pietro said, setting down the little paper cups and swinging the briefcase flat on to the desk. A quick glance around. 'You don't think he went down there and killed her. But does he know anything?'

'He's too dumb to know anything,' said Sandro, giving in to his dislike, reaching for the coffee, 'about anything.'

What had she seen in him? Just the body? He hadn't been quite the same man back then, had he, Sandro thought: idle, a main-chancer, wandering through the rooms of La Vipera in search of entertainment and no more.

That was too glib, though. He sighed. 'I'm not sure he's told me everything,' he said. 'I think he's scared of being involved and is just saying the bare minimum. But he did give me Kaufmann, at least. To get me off his back, no doubt. I'm seeing her this morning at eleven.'

She'd been polite on the phone, *yes, no, tomorrow morning*. She'd been expecting his call, she said, a deep voice, with a trace of an accent. She'd hung up before he could ask any more.

Pietro sat down next to Sandro, pushed one coffee towards him and, between the cups, Sandro laid the big dog-eared pad he preferred to any computer.

'What did she say, "Means, motive, opportunity – and intuition"?' he said. 'So ...'

'So, there's Martinelli, who found the body,' said Pietro, taking a pen and beginning to write.

'There's whoever's left of the La Vipera community,' Sandro said. 'So that's Gorgone, Kaufmann, Grenzi – wherever she is – and Helen Mason. Who else is left in the village from back then?'

'According to the *questura*,' said Pietro, 'almost no one. There's one farmer, but he's in a wheelchair, no dependants.' Pietro hesitated. 'There's the Salieri clan, obviously. The princess and her son and daughter – the princess was here all summer, as was Martinelli, but the rest of them ...' He sighed and laid the pen down. 'August people move around, don't they?'

'Okay,' said Sandro, knocking back his coffee and squinting at the list. 'That's a start, anyway. I'll see what I can get out of Martine Kaufmann.'

'I still want to get up to Sant'Anna, too,' said Sandro, the paper between his hands – the crime scene always told you something. But even as he said it he wasn't sure if he did. He was frightened of La Vipera – he was daring himself to return – and he didn't protest when Pietro held up his hand.

'All in good time,' he said.

From downstairs came the sound of a key in the door, then slow steps on the stairs.

'So,' said Pietro. 'Do you remember her from before? This Kaufmann?'

'Yes,' said Sandro. 'I mean, vaguely. Not much about her ...' Standing in the doorway watching. Bedrooms with mattresses on the floor and drawings on the walls, doodles everywhere. 'Just the blonde hair, the German accent, Baratti interviewed her while I was – talking to Nielsson.' He looked down at his list of names and birthdates: Kaufmann was his age, a little younger. There was Chantal Buisson, the oldest, the one who'd died: he ran a pencil through her name.

'Nielsson was in charge, then?'

Sandro thought about that. 'There was a lot of stuff about it being a communal house, a co-operative living experiement. But she owned the place and she – well, she had a sort of natural authority.' He could feel himself begin to flush.

What would Pietro say if he knew that Sandro still thought of Nielsson, on and off, at odd moments in all the intervening years? He might have him up as a suspect. He shifted in the chair, uneasy.

'I bet old Baratti liked that,' said Pietro, not appearing to notice.

'He hated it,' said Sandro reflexively. Baratti had said she needed a good seeing to, in the car on the way back to the station that first time.

Pietro glanced at him. 'Just as well he's wheelchair-bound these days, then,' he said. 'So who else have we got still alive?'

'Grenzi,' said Sandro. 'I think she must be the one Gorgone thought was running a ski school up north. And Helen Mason, in Nova Scotia.'

'Panayotis managed to leave a message for her at that convent or whatever it is, bless him,' said Pietro, 'asking if she might be prepared to talk to the Italian police. That boy's the best of them, actually. He works away at things. I'll get him on to Grenzi next.'

'Mmm,' said Sandro absently. On the desk his mobile buzzed and impatiently he turned it face down.

The steps had paused on the landing and they both turned their heads: the door opened and there was Giuli. Exasperated, Sandro examined her. She was late but that wasn't it. *She* was looking distinctly under the weather too. Dragging herself up the stairs like she was a hundred. He checked himself. 'Giuli?' he said.

'Sorry,' she said, setting her bag down on her desk in the corner. Giuli was no longer his assistant but an investigator in her own right, and thus had her own workspace. 'I'm not sleeping at the moment then the alarm didn't go off. Don't mind me.' She began to take off her coat and, in the second or two before Sandro turned back to Pietro, he thought, *she's ill.* Everything about her, the drooping shoulders, the odd – what? – shapelessness of her. But Pietro was leaning forward.

'One thing I forgot to mention that could be important,' he

said. 'That wasn't Lotti's usual dog walk, by no means. It would seem he positively avoided the path going up behind La Vipera.'

'And who told you that?'

Pietro sat back. 'Well, I told you I went up to the Salieri place.'

'One son, one daughter, both away,' said Sandro. 'Yes, I remember. You didn't go into detail, though.'

'Well, the old lady's gaga,' said Pietro. 'I mean, she was sitting up in a chair, and she gave me one of those looks, as though I was a footman who'd been caught stealing from the pantry – but I'd say her short-term memory's gone completely. She remembered La Vipera all right, but she seemed to think they were all still there. She told me to talk to her son, but then she seemed to be under the impression he was in hospital.'

Sandro didn't understand. 'She told you about Lotti's dog walk?'

A faintly sheepish look came over Pietro's face. 'Not her.' He cleared his throat. 'It was the housekeeper – Gianna Marte, she's called, from up north in the lakes or somewhere. Actually quite … chatty – so chatty I sort of tuned out.'

'Like a man in uniform, did she?'

It was Pietro's turn to flush. 'She was useful, as a matter of fact. I needed an interpreter, what with the old lady prone to digressing.'

'The woman – Marte – was there while you were talking to the princess?'

'Not exactly,' said Pietro. 'This was after the old lady got the hump and sent me out with a flea in my ear.'

'Right,' said Sandro drily. 'Let me guess. She offered you a coffee in the kitchen.'

'Not against the law, is it?' said Pietro defensively. 'Like I said, I wasn't really listening. The old lady quite freaked me out and I was just decompressing. I wasn't taking notes – yes, yes, I know – but it came back to me this morning. She was talking about how superstitious the locals were, that they didn't walk up behind La Vipera. No one did, Lotti included. He always walked the dog over the other side.'

'Which is perhaps why Nielsson was killed there,' said Sandro thoughtfully.

'Well,' said Pietro, 'it does lend credence to the theory that the killer was surprised by Lotti while returning to the body, for whatever reason. Might have expected not to be interrupted.' He scratched his chin. 'But that's back to the coincidence theory.'

'You know what interests me more?' said Sandro. He didn't trust coincidences. 'Why he *did* walk his dog there. There must have been a reason. There's always a reason.'

Behind Sandro, Giuli sighed heavily and the chair creaked as she sat. He leaned back. 'You okay?' he said to her warily. 'You called yesterday – what was that about?'

'Something and nothing,' said Giuli, waving him away. 'I'm fine. Don't fuss.' He turned back to Pietro.

'What about the original anonymous tip-off?' Pietro said. 'That interests me. You traced the call to the bar back then?'

Sandro nodded. Only three houses in the village had had phones in 1976, he remembered. They'd gone into the bar to ask but of course no one knew anything, no one remembered anything. You had to pay after you used the phone booth – behind the bar they had a little meter that showed how many *scatti* you'd used. It was inconceivable that the barman wouldn't remember a call being made, but the blue-jawed type hadn't.

'No one remembered anything, no one saw anything,' he said to Pietro, who nodded, his smile ironic. 'The barman would have been – sixty?' said Sandro. 'He'd be long dead.' He mused, thinking back to that little café, the long bar stretching into the gloom, the dusty bottles. He wondered if it was still the same and felt a pang of nostalgia. 'But he wasn't the only one working the bar. You know who I'd like to talk to?' Pietro leaned forward eagerly at the tone of Sandro's voice, and Sandro had to smile – it was nice, after all. 'The woman of few words. Maria Clara Martinelli. She found the bodies. And she used to work in the bar as a teenager. Way back when.'

'Right,' said Pietro, sitting back, satisfied. 'That's where we'll go this afternoon then.'

A silence, of satisfaction this time. Surreptitiously Sandro turned his phone over: the buzz had been a message from Luisa. *I'm fine. At the homeless shelter at lunch, sorry.* He put the phone in his pocket.

'Pietro?' They'd both momentarily forgotten Giuli's presence. There was something diffident, timid, in her voice that Sandro didn't associate with her.

Pietro turned to her in surprise.

'Sorry,' she said, 'I mean, Commissario. Can I ask a favour?'

He shook his head impatiently. 'What is it, Giuli?' he said, as she hesitated. 'Anything.'

'It's just – if I gave you a telephone number,' she said, 'could you trace it for me?'

*

Is everything okay, sweetheart?

So Sandro *had* seen something. She'd put on trousers to hide the dressing she'd applied to the scratch. White blouse: maybe that had made her look sallow. If not the trousers or the blouse, he would only have had to look at her face properly.

It had felt as though he was never going to leave.

She could have lied about the scratch. Or she could have just told him the truth. *I hated that woman and I wanted to know what had happened. I wanted to see for myself.* Vindictive – for more than forty years! – and a rubbernecker into the bargain. Sandro would have been shocked; he would have been disappointed.

And then Giuli had phoned, walking to work, sounding tired, and Luisa had remembered, too late, that there'd been a missed call from her yesterday. 'Angel,' she said, 'I'm sorry, I was – yesterday was a busy day.' Giuli sounded tired. She had some story about a child calling the office and she'd been worried she was in danger, the child, and Giuli had called back and spoken to the grandmother.

'So all's well, right?'

'But what if –?'

'I think, look,' and Luisa tried to make it lighthearted, 'maybe it's my age, but I think if it was just the mother, yes, you might worry that perhaps the mother was under stress, the child was at risk. But the child has a grandmother, too. That makes it safer, don't you see?'

There'd been a silence. 'Yes,' Giuli had spoken slowly, uncertain still, but Luisa could hear some of it had gone in.

'You want to meet up later?' Luisa said, but perhaps Giuli heard the equivocation in her voice because she just murmured something non-committal and was gone.

Luisa wasn't going to the homeless centre: she was going to the emergency room at the big central hospital of Santa Maria Nuova. When she'd looked at the gash under the light there had been an aureole of red around it, and it had felt hot to the touch. It added to her general discomfort: deceiving Sandro was on the same continuum. There was something bad in her system.

And some secrets were noxious; they festered. Johanna Nielsson had been noxious. Luisa could have brought it out into the open all that time ago, with Sandro, but she had not. She could have given him an ultimatum, *her or me*. But she knew what he'd have said, *I don't know what you're talking about, nothing has happened*. He'd have lied and walked away – because that was what men did.

The fact was, Luisa was proud and she hadn't wanted to look jealous back then, and still now.

The big forecourt to the old hospital, as wide and sunlit and grand as a piazza and arcaded on three sides, was busy with ambulances. An elderly woman was being unloaded, lying flat on her back with an oxygen mask over her face. Much older than me, thought Luisa, hobbling past in a fierce hurry suddenly. The emergency room was busy too, and a hubbub rose, of mostly foreign voices, the wail of a child. She should have got here earlier. She gave her details, took a ticket with a number on it and found a seat beside three Roma women, one holding a motionless baby. Their feet were brown and bare on the hospital linoleum.

Nielsson had been barefoot when Luisa saw her kissing Sandro all those years ago in a side street near the Uffizi, barefoot in the city, not even a sandal between her and the stone.

Back then, Luisa had stepped under the arcades of the gallery to hide and felt her heart pounding. She had felt sick, had hardly had time to think about what she'd seen, when the woman walked past her, tinkling somehow, scented with patchouli or one of those incense-smelling oriental perfumes that gave you a headache. Luisa hadn't known straight away who she was – and then she had. Because he'd described her, only in a few words but in a wondering sort of way, lingering on her: long hair parted in the middle, hippy clothes. Barefoot in that kitchen. Johanna Nielsson.

Head down, Luisa had seen the bare feet, long and brown, not pearly toed, like the Roma girl beside her now, but long, strange prehensile toes that you might imagine curling around a branch, dusty-soled monkey feet, and the source of the tinkling, an anklet of little bells in Indian silver.

A name was called and Luisa looked up to see a green-smocked doctor standing there in weary blankness and then all hell broke loose. On the wall a red light began to flash and a trolley came around the corner with paramedics at each corner, one of them holding down a machine she recognised as a defibrillator. They barged through the heavy polythene doors and disappeared, everyone staring after them.

As she watched the doors flap shut, suddenly Luisa felt odd. Unsteady in her seat. Too hot, her heart beating too fast. She had only been in this hospital once since the operation to remove her breast, a year after when she'd panicked over a rash along the scar line, and she felt those feelings surge back: extreme anxiety, a sense of having been removed from her own body as its heart clattered on. She felt lightheaded.

In a hurry, Luisa got to her feet because she could not bear the idea, suddenly, of slumping to the ground among all these people. A hand to the wall, she went through the polythene curtain where the crash cart had disappeared to find it on its way back towards her at speed. One of the nurses sat astride the patient, pumping at its chest. Luisa pressed herself flat against the wall to allow them to pass, feeling sweat bead on her forehead. The patient was a woman: a slender liver-spotted hand hung down at the side of the gurney, heavy with rings. She registered that much and then the cart was gone again between the doors.

Luisa stood there a long moment, struggling to get her breathing back to normal, and suddenly, fervently she wished not to die there. Anywhere, in the gutter, rather than here, out under the sky, rather than here. Then someone approached down the long corridor, between its long windows, a tall person, a lanky stride. A living healthy person. She looked up and in that split second she knew that she was hallucinating, because it was Luca Bartolini, frowning. He stared at her. 'What on earth –?'

Had she thought in that hallucinatory moment that he had been following her or that he had somehow – where her own husband had not – worked out that she was in trouble? He seemed genuinely surprised to see her. 'I'm with – I came –' He gestured towards the entrance to the emergency room. 'I've got to get in there. It's – Benedetta's had one of her –'

'That was Benedetta?' said Luisa, not hearing the question. 'I thought she was in – wasn't it Switzerland?' The paramedic kneeling astride her trying to get her back to life. Benedetta Salieri was Luisa's age.

'She's been back home for twenty years,' said Bartolini, glancing sideways at the door. 'In Florence, that is. I've got to get in there – my mother's fussing. Are you all right, is it –?'

'Just the leg,' she said, 'the cut,' in desperation. 'Just go. Go on.' The woman was dying. His half-sister. He went.

Fussing.

The door flapped. Bartolini was back.

'Is she all right?' said Luisa.

He sighed, still pale. 'They seem to think she will be,' he said. 'It's her nerves. She really wasn't well for a long time. She's had a place of her own for ten years now, and for a while it looked as though she – she was getting better.'

'We haven't seen her in the shop,' said Luisa, almost to herself. 'Not in years.' She wondered if Frollini, the old gossip, knew about all this.

'She doesn't really get out much,' said Bartolini. 'But we did think – she seemed to be making friends, she, well ...' He sighed. 'She can't do this many more times. Her heart won't stand it.'

'Do what?'

Bartolini rubbed at his forehead, as if considering whether to answer. His other hand was on her elbow, steering her a little so her back was to the door and the waiting room behind it. 'She –' he hesitated '– took too much of her medication.' He spoke stiffly, then sighed. 'She's had a hard time. She – there was a – she lost a child. Then divorce –' He stopped, as if he'd said too much.

Luisa's hand was at her mouth, remembering. That wedding, and the husband, nervous, pacing up and down on the gravel with a cigarette in his hand as they came up the cypress-flanked drive to the great house. A sallow man, uncomfortable in his wedding clothes, but Luisa had thought nothing of it then. People were always nervous at weddings, weren't they?

Benedetta herself, a small upright figure, had been perfectly still and silent throughout the fitting. A seam had needed letting out a little: it was usually the other way around at weddings – the bride lost weight through nerves. She had said nothing all the time Luisa was there, not when Luisa asked her to breathe out or to raise an arm, not in response to her mother's highly strung tirades about the florist or uncivilised responses to the wedding invitations, nor to her father's murmurings from the window.

It had felt like a dream to Luisa, her first such occasion, first time in a grand house, walking through the echoing stone-floored hall then up a broad staircase to the damask-hung state rooms. She'd been in awe. Downstairs in the subterranean kitchens they'd been preparing the wedding breakfast and there was a smell of meat cooking. It had been drizzling outside, a mist hanging in the trees. October: an odd un-festive month for a wedding.

'She lost a child?' she asked now. 'How long after – I mean, when?' And flushed, knowing instantly that she had overstepped the mark

Bartolini regarded her. 'Not so long,' he said, stiff again. 'Look,' he said, 'it's rather ... private. You understand, I'm sure.' Apologetic.

'I'm sorry,' said Luisa, staring down at her shoes. 'Of course.'

Had Benedetta been pregnant when she married, then? Another memory came to Luisa, of Benedetta's father's hand coming to rest tentatively on his daughter's shoulder as she passed out through the door to the dressing room, and of Benedetta flinching minutely at the touch. Luisa could see it all now, in that small movement. Something had been wrong from the start, with the marriage, with Benedetta.

Bartolini sighed. 'It's all right,' he said. 'It's just that for years her state of mind has been ... a rollercoaster. She moved to Switzerland with her husband, but the marriage broke down very quickly. She returned to Florence eventually, some twenty years ago. She came home initially and then wanted to live independently – she seemed to find stability, friends. But recently it's been impossible. Last week –' he hesitated '– for most of the last two weeks she's been in a specialist clinic, under sedation. I went with her. She came out three days ago. My mother –' his handsome mouth turned down, disparaging '– my mother's not really up to dealing with it any more.' And abruptly he released her arm, his face resigned.

'Did you get on with your stepfather?' Luisa heard her own voice as if from a long way away and saw his eyebrows lift a little in surprise at the non sequitur, but she could see in his eyes that he had not liked Salieri. She could see contempt: she didn't need to hear what he said, which was just as well as his voice seemed to come from underwater.

And as his mouth opened and closed, abruptly it all reeled in her head, a carousel of new information: the face of the spotty boy who'd driven her up to Benedetta's wedding turning to her as they passed La Vipera; Benedetta flinching to see Salieri look down at the place as she was being fitted for her dress. It occurred to her that Sandro needed to know these things. When this was done. She felt suddenly faint; her ears rang. The last thing she saw before she hit the floor was Bartolini's face peering down, curious, ironical, almost amused, into hers.

Chapter Nine

'I DON'T UNDERSTAND.'

Giuli stood over Luisa in the bright hospital corridor. She was being stubborn: with these two, you had to be sometimes. Particularly with Luisa, who wished never to admit to weakness of any kind.

'You fainted and you just happened to be in the emergency room at the time?' She frowned.

There'd been a man with Luisa when Giuli arrived. She'd been seated with him standing beside her, tall, probably Luisa's age, but good-looking for all that. Assured. The kind of guy Giuli was deeply suspicious of. Luisa, she thought, did not have enough experience of men. She only knew Sandro and that old goat Frollini, her employer, and she had been immune to his charms for years – she knew too much about him.

The tall man had leaned down to say something into Luisa's ear as Giuli hurried towards them down the corridor, then he'd disappeared through the swing door to the waiting room before Giuli was even within earshot.

The call had come not long after Sandro and Pietro had left.

Giuli had been just sitting there in the office, wired, waiting. When he'd heard her story, Pietro had frowned a moment, examined her face, then said he'd get straight on to it. He would trace the number, get a name, get an address. 'It's a five-minute job,' he'd said, giving her a smile of reassurance at last. So someone thought she wasn't a nutjob: she relaxed a fraction.

Of course, once they'd disappeared Giuli couldn't get on with anything else, although there was plenty. There was the agency's licence renewal to deal with, for starters. Before all this she and Sandro had been talking about making it a partnership, her and him.

And so when her mobile had begun to buzz it had made her jump. And Luisa's voice at the other end of the line, not Pietro's, her voice almost unrecognisable, wavering, weak. 'I'm at Santa Maria Nuova, in the emergency room. I had a funny turn.' A man's voice echoing in some lofty space behind her, probably this corridor, probably the man who'd leaned down to whisper something before buggering off.

'Who was that?' It had been Giuli's first question on arriving, ramming the *motorino* into a parking space and jumping off, running into the hospital with her helmet still on.

Was it normal to get angry when someone you love gets hurt or ill? Giuli wasn't angry. She was frightened. She'd got used to it, hadn't she, so stupid, got used to the luxury of having someone between her and the world, the buffer, the grown-up, the wise ones. Not always wise, parents – not that Luisa was her mother, nor Sandro her father. They were more than that. They'd *chosen* her.

So why now was she being rude and graceless? She could feel tears ready to fall, and pulled herself together.

'Who was he? That man?'

'He's just – he was there when I fainted. He helped. He was here bringing his sister in –' And Luisa had broken off, tormented-looking suddenly, and Giuli had relented. Folded her arms around Luisa, felt how much less of her there was these days.

Giuli tried for kind, but it had come out stubborn. 'And what were *you* doing here?'

'Don't fuss,' said Luisa, confirming it, her hands agitated in her lap. She was very pale still.

'Don't *fuss*?'

'They say there's nothing wrong, I just – they won't discharge you without someone to take you home.'

Round in circles. It wasn't until Luisa got to her feet and winced, putting a hand up, that Giuli got to the bottom of it. 'It's your leg?'

'They gave me antibiotics,' Luisa said weakly, sitting back down again. She pulled up her trouser-leg a little and Giuli saw a large dressing. An area of reddish skin extended beyond the bandage, tinged yellow with iodine, and the leg – Luisa's slim calf, elegant from a lifetime in heels – seemed a little swollen to her. 'I scraped it on some barbed wire.'

'Right,' said Giuli briskly. 'You need something to eat and something warm to drink. No arguments. And I want to know what you've been up to.'

*

It took a coffee, a sandwich and finally a small brandy in the nearest bar to get the whole story out of her.

'So you basically went up there to make sure the woman was really dead?' Giuli couldn't help laughing. Luisa looked sheepish and Giuli felt an odd pang, warm and sad and longing all at once, at the thought. That after all this time Luisa felt that for him, her man Sandro. And the thought of them so young, all those years ago.

'There was something about her,' said Luisa slowly, taking a tiny sip of the brandy. The colour had returned to her cheeks. 'She was a witch.' Giuli's eyebrows went up, because Luisa had not a mystical bone in her body. 'I'm not joking,' said Luisa. 'She had power over people.'

'Over Sandro, you mean?'

The pink deepened in Luisa's cheeks. 'Over him – a bit. Yes.'

'Because she was beautiful? You mean it was a –' Giuli hesitated, uneasy '– a sex sort of thing?'

Luisa's flush had ebbed. 'I don't *know*. She was ... modern. Free love, all that, that was what they were all about and if you didn't like the idea ...' She fidgeted. 'I didn't like the idea.'

Giuli would have been sceptical about the idea of free love even if she hadn't worked the streets for close to a decade. 'It was the time of the Monster. *He* obviously didn't think it would work out. He didn't like foreign hippies one bit, did he? Or anyone having sex outside marriage.'

Luisa was still frowning. 'Well, old ways don't disappear overnight.' A pause. 'Are you comparing me to a serial killer because I disapprove of free love? I don't trust it, that's all. And I didn't trust *her*.'

'Plus you were mad as hell and jealous,' said Giuli. Luisa just shrugged a little and sipped the brandy again. 'I can't believe you wrote her a letter,' Giuli went on, 'demanded to meet her.'

Luisa sighed. 'There were no mobile phones in those days,' she said. 'I don't think they even had electricity at La Vipera, let alone a landline.'

Giuli had seen photographs in the newspaper, over Pietro's shoulder on the tablet he'd set up on the desk in Via del Leone. A big old farmhouse, the roof half-fallen in, the tall trees right up close. 'You went up there on the bus,' she marvelled. 'Had you seen the house before?' Luisa shook her head stiffly. 'So you went right up to where – did you see the place where they found the bodies?'

Luisa's expression was veiled. 'Yes,' she said. 'It was stupid.'

Giuli examined her. 'You went up there with this, this neighbour guy, who you'd never met before. I'd say that was ... reckless. Not like you.'

'I know,' she said quietly. 'I thought if I went I'd understand something. About the place, La Vipera. Get it out of my system. Back then I used to dream about it, you know. Wondering what it was like – Sandro had told me bits and pieces. The dirty kitchen, the communal bedrooms. Indian things hanging up, the woods around it and wildflowers. He was fascinated by it. I could tell.'

'Yeah,' said Giuli drily. 'Funny. All my life I've wanted the opposite. I've wanted normal stuff, a boring life.'

'Well, it was ugly,' said Luisa. 'It was derelict and ugly and ... sinister. Give me a boring life any day.'

Giuli felt Luisa's eyes rest on her and suddenly she wanted to cry. Jesus Christ, what was the matter with her? Either she was stuffing her face or bursting into tears. She cleared her throat. 'So, back then. You wrote to her, you asked to meet. And then – you warned her off?' Luisa's face was hard to read but she nodded. 'Sandro never knew?'

'He never knew. He thought,' Luisa gave a faint smile, 'he thought he'd done it all by himself. Walked away from temptation.'

'He said you were at the homeless shelter today,' said Giuli suddenly.

Luisa's mouth twisted, wry. 'He's going to see one of them,' she said. 'He thought I wasn't listening, but I was. What if –?'

'This Martine Kaufmann?' said Giuli. 'I was listening too. She's in the Oltrarno, San Niccolo. You want me to check her out for you?'

Luisa looked embarrassed. 'I've already googled her.'

'Look,' said Giuli, sighing. 'You're going to have to tell him eventually. That you've been up there. Apart from anything else, you could help him, you know? With the investigation, I mean – you've got chummy with the neighbours already.'

'Or it might mess things up for him,' said Luisa quietly. 'He's got to do this. A chance to work with Pietro again? To be rehabilitated by the force? And –' She hesitated.

'And it might help him exorcise some old demons along the way?' supplied Giuli. 'And what about when he sees your leg?' She stopped, seeing Luisa pale again, seeing she'd undone all the good the brandy and the ham sandwich had done.

'If Pietro thinks I'm involved he'll get worried it's all too personal,' she said. 'He might kick Sandro off the case again and that would be a disaster. You know what Sandro's like.'

Giuli relented. 'All right,' she said. 'All right, in your own time.'

There was a silence. The bar had emptied out: the lunch hour was over.

'What surprises me,' said Giuli, leaning forward across the tiny table, an attempt maybe to lighten the atmosphere, to rouse Luisa again, to rile her even, 'is that you managed it. That she *did* walk away from Sandro.' Leaning down to smile into Luisa's face. 'I mean, little Luisa against the high priestess, right?'

No spark, though, from Luisa, only something else, a stillness coming over her, but Giuli pushed on. 'I mean,' she said, 'what did you say to get her to leave him alone?'

Luisa pulled her coat together, a hand at the neck.

'I told her I'd kill her,' she said.

*

Sandro walked along the cool dark length of the Via dei Bardi, away from the river. He liked this street, it was always silent.

The female cadaver *was* that of Johanna Nielsson.

Pietro had got a call as they walked away from the Via del Leone with confirmation that the chances – based on the DNA sample sent over from the Danish lab – that the body found in that hut in the woods was *not* Nielsson were infinitesimal.

He thought of her in that chair, her arms pinioned, plastic embedded in what was left of her flesh, sitting there in a long print dress, her hair loose. Stabbed in the lower abdomen, multiple times. All of those details felt to him absolutely significant. The man, the butcher – Lotti – had been killed carelessly, heedlessly: either he was incidental, or an afterthought, or simply despised.

The murderer had known Johanna Nielsson well, had known her a long, long time.

Lotti killed with that single casual blow: the murderer could have waited behind the door but instead stood in front of him. Didn't care about being recognised or actively wanted to be. Wanted to be the last thing Lotti saw. After his dead dog and Johanna Nielsson.

As he walked, Sandro wondered a few things. Where the message was that had summoned Lotti up into those hills, because it had not been his usual route and Sandro did not believe it was coincidence that had led him there to be killed. Was it on a mobile? Apparently he had not had one.

He had reached the halfway point on the Via dei Bardi, where the Costa Scarpuccia branched off and headed uphill, where a long wall barely contained the earth and foliage of an old overgrown garden, and stopped to think some more. Some late wild irises overhung the wall above his head and the entrance, unusually, to the tiny church of Santa Lucia dei Magnoli opposite the turning was open. He stepped without thinking into the great doorway, standing diffidently to one side and looking into the lofty, serene space. Dimly, he could make out a bowed figure in the front pew.

Sandro stood there, just a moment more; he waited, hoping for some kind of antidote to the images in his head of the ugly heap of death in that hut, hoping for the sense of a great good to set against the brutality. But the church was dark, and he must have made a sound because the kneeling figure stood up abruptly and, in a hurry, Sandro stepped back.

He was late, he realised, or almost: Martine Kaufmann's studio was a bare three minutes away, but he had only two.

Feeling it would be undignified, not to mention uncomfortable, to run, he proceeded at a trot. Aware suddenly of being watched, he half-turned as he stumbled on to see the woman emerge from the great church doors. Not the black-clad humble sort of person he'd imagined at all but the figure of a woman, from this distance perhaps a little younger than himself, stout, pulling a helmet over short, light hair, climbing on to a *motorino*.

Hurrying on, Sandro found himself at the studio, stacked canvases inside confirming it. He tried the door but it was locked. He pressed the buzzer.

He was peering inside again, hand cupped round his eyes, when he felt a tap on the shoulder. Turning, he saw that it was the woman who'd been in the church, pulling off a scooter helmet, the hair springing up. She held out a hand. 'Martine Kaufmann,' she said.

Short and stocky, with silvery pale spiky hair and light-coloured eyes, a face softened by exposure to the elements, a small gold crucifix glinting at her neck. She pushed open the door and they went inside.

Everything was very neat. Beside the door sat a couple of bulging plastic bags of the sort charities give out for old clothes, carefully labelled with their destination, a children's charity of some sort. So her presence at Santa Lucia dei Magnoli was down to mundane good works. He gestured at the bags. 'Having a clearout?'

She smiled, her eyes crinkling. 'My students donate – these foreign children, they buy so much stuff while they're here and then they just leave it behind.' True enough, thought Sandro. 'Help yourself,' she said, smiling.

'I think my denim-wearing days are over,' said Sandro.

Kaufmann barked a laugh. 'This way,' she said, gesturing towards the back of the space.

The stacked canvases ranged against the walls were a combination of abstracts and garish nudes, a few shelves with some pottery with price tags. She saw him looking. 'Student work,' she said, smiling, as they reached a desk with a chair to either side of it. 'We sell that too, for the charity, the pieces they don't want to take with them. Please, sit.'

She was organised all right, thought Sandro, looking round. He sat obediently. 'How's business?' he said.

Kaufmann pulled out a chair on the other side of the desk. 'I make a reasonable living,' she said with a frown, scrutinising him. He nodded. When people said that it always meant they were coining it.

And then abruptly she sighed. 'So,' she said. 'Is it her?' Her gaze was direct and memory did stir, at last. Her blue-grey eyes. 'Yes,' Sandro said simply. He had no idea if condolences were appropriate.

He was trying to work out what was familiar. She had been slender but she was well-built now, a little barrel of a body in a plain shift. Around her hung a scent at odds with her nun-like appearance, something floral, like jasmine. She rested her elbows on the table. 'Have we met before?' she said, mildly curious, her head tilted, and he caught a glimpse of that girl, years ago, watching him from a doorway.

Baratti had taken them back for one last visit, pretending he suspected the inhabitants of growing opium poppies as an excuse to return to the house and try it on with one or other of the girls. Sandro had stayed outside that time.

Now, he hesitated. 'I was one of the attending officers at La Vipera,' he said, 'when someone made an anonymous call. All that time ago.'

'Oh,' said Martine Kaufmann, pushing herself back in her chair to look at him again, her eyes darkening to slate. 'Oh, you. I remember. I remember you.' Her gaze on him was steady. 'Those visits you made to La Vipera didn't reflect too well on the police force, in my opinion. The senior policeman –' she was stiff with the memory of it '– he was not a pleasant man.'

'Commissario Baratti,' said Sandro, trying not to agree with her too openly. 'Things have changed since those days. I'm sorry if we –'

'You were very young,' she said, with a diffident gesture. 'It was a long time ago, as you say.'

'Well, I was still in training, yes,' said Sandro. 'We were probably the same age, weren't we? Aren't we?' She didn't reply. 'I've – I've come out of retirement to help with this case, as a matter of fact.'

'This case,' Martine Kaufmann said, passing a hand over her face. 'I – I can't believe it. Honestly, I can't – I – I –' He felt her struggle to regain her composure, and gave her time. 'I was so – oh, never mind,' she said with dignity, smoothing her shift, small square-nailed hands. 'You want to know about when I saw her?'

Sandro nodded. 'Among other things,' he said. The long room felt cold to him suddenly; you could smell the cold in these old *fondi*. They used to be the cellars, for wine.

Kaufmann gave him a quick, sharp look. 'Well, anyway, I was up in Liguria for a weekend back in April,' she said. 'Levanto, the other side of the Cinque Terre, the weekend after Easter, if you need to know. A painting trip, a visit to the churches.' She looked at him with a trace of defiance, as if she needed to defend her faith. *I'm not Baratti*, he wanted to say.

'Anyway.' She tugged at her shift again, uncomfortable. 'I booked myself into a campsite. I woke up the first morning, 29 April, and there was Johanna, climbing into her camper-van – she was just leaving. She laughed when I recognised her.'

'A camper-van,' said Sandro, his heart sinking. All that money and living like a hobo? 'So she wasn't living what you'd call a settled lifestyle? Had she fallen on hard times?'

Kaufmann shrugged. 'She didn't say so.' Her eyes were on him, mild but scrutinising. 'Settling down would never have been Johanna's thing, would it?' She smiled sadly. 'She was always a loner. We all are, really. It was one of the lessons that place taught us. Self-sufficiency.'

'All of you that were at La Vipera? Mr Gorgone said you kept in touch a little.'

She rolled her eyes good-humouredly. 'Oh, Marcantonio ... We've got very little in common these days. We run across each other – it's inevitable. And of course when I saw Johanna I mentioned it to him. But as a rule – it's like families, you know, they know each other too well. Outgrow each other.'

Sandro nodded. 'Mr Gorgone said something of the sort. Yes.'

'That time at La Vipera –' she was hesitant, apologetic '– it was formative. Living outside society, without comforts, no electricity, all that. I think it did set us apart, women working together, for each other. We had to do everything for ourselves.'

'Five women and one man,' said Sandro thoughtfully. 'And it wasn't like he was king of the hen-coop, either, was it?' Kaufmann drew herself back a little, wincing at the vulgarity of it, but Sandro remembered Baratti jeering at Gorgone, a hen-pecked cockerel. Gorgone just sitting there picking his bare toes, staring like there was nothing behind his eyes, insolent and stupid.

'Why did you have a man at all?' he asked, curious.

Kaufmann shrugged. 'We did try to be just women, for a while, but then Marcantonio came along ...' She frowned. 'Johanna liked him, was the truth of it. He had his uses.' She looked away a little and sighed. 'She liked to shock. She used to say, "They don't like the thought of men being sex objects, do they?"'

Sandro felt as though he was being tested. 'I don't like the idea of anyone being a sex object,' he said, too weary suddenly to think of anything funny to say. It wasn't funny. Two people were dead.

'Have you been in Florence all summer?' he asked, not quite casually, and she tilted her head to one side. Nodding.

'Pretty much, yes,' she said, 'since that trip to Liguria. Oh – except for last week. I was teaching a course in Le Marche. Ascoli Piceno, do you know it? It's very beautiful.'

'When did you get back?'

'Two – no, three days ago.'

Was this woman a suspect? If so, she was around when Nielsson was killed. Away when Lotti was killed. The thing went round in circles. If Martine Kaufmann had wanted to kill Nielsson she could have done it in Liguria. And why would she want to?

She was looking at him with a faintly perplexed air. 'I can give you the name and number of the course organiser if you like?'

He inclined his head graciously, disguising his disappointment. 'In due course, yes, please. You know there were two bodies?'

'I did know,' she said, head on one side, judicious. 'A butcher?'

So Gorgone had been in touch with her. 'Called Lotti.'

'I don't remember the name,' Martine Kaufmann said, apologetic.

'When was the last time you *did* go up there?' he asked lightly. 'To Sant'Anna?'

She shook her head. 'Back to La Vipera?' Her gaze was level. 'I don't know what I would go back for. I don't – haven't. I – what would I do there? Talk to the locals about their allotments? It's the past.' She shifted in her chair, uneasy. 'I can't believe Johanna did, either. She didn't say anything about it to me. She said she was touring in the north. She said she might go over to Venice, to the mountains.'

'And you believed her?'

'Why wouldn't I? Johanna wasn't a liar.'

Sandro found himself nodding. No. Not a liar.

'You don't think the man, Lotti, might have killed her?' said Kaufmann, a hand to her crucifix, anxious. 'I mean – a butcher.' She shifted, uneasy.

'Killed her, why?' he said, softly, quickly, and she coloured.

'I don't know,' she said, faltering for the first time. 'They didn't like us, those villagers. Some of them hated us, I think.' Her pale eyes rose to his again, asking him for something.

Asking him to understand. 'Because we were different? Or because they wanted us, desired us, because we were in control and that made them feel powerless?'

'Well –' Sandro hesitated, aware that he shouldn't be giving any more information than he had to '– Lotti as a suspect is one of the lines of inquiry we'll be pursuing.' It wasn't quite a lie: he might have done it. Sandro just didn't think he had.

Kaufmann seemed more composed again. 'She didn't care about people liking her, you see. I expect he's dead himself, now, but,' she said, 'she called the barman a eunuch. That *was* to his face. The barman at the café. When he'd kept her waiting.' She laughed bitterly. 'Johanna said something about his wife being frustrated too, something like that, about him not being able to get it up.'

'Did you know a girl who worked at the bar called Maria Clara Martinelli?'

She shrugged. 'I'm sorry,' she said. 'Oh – wasn't she the one who found the bodies?'

'She was. Well, never mind.' He sighed. 'Look, I can see you've worked hard to ... move on from that time, anyway.' He gestured at the bags of cast-offs. 'Your relationship with the community seems to have improved.'

Kaufmann seemed to subside. 'We were young. We were experimenting.' She rubbed her eyes. 'Italy wasn't ready for us.' The soft dark memory of Johanna Nielsson, of being alone with her, stood between them.

'I understand,' Sandro said gently. 'But you do see that we can't help but connect her death to those years at La Vipera. So if there's anything you remember, anything that happened that might contain the seed, if you like, of these murders, that might point to a killer, will you let us know?'

Opposite him, behind the desk, she nodded, pushed her fingers through her short hair, and the sleeves of her smock fell back. Sandro saw something on the inside of her wrist. A tattoo. She saw him looking and she held it out to him: a curled thing like a snail or a series of tiny concentric circles, the same tattoo as Johanna Nielsson had. 'I got it done to be like her,' she said, as he fumbled for his glasses for a better look, but she had pulled down the sleeves defensively and folded her arms on the desktop. 'We all wanted to be like her. We'd have done anything she asked.' Her voice rose a little, faltering. 'I can't believe she's dead. I thought she'd live forever.'

Which was what Marcantonio Gorgone had said. *We thought we'd live forever.*

He stood, at last, and held out his hand. 'You've been very helpful, Miss Kaufmann,' he said, although in fact all he'd learned was that she had an alibi for the time of Lotti's death. At the door he hesitated: there was something, after all. One piece of concrete information he could extract from this exchange. He turned back and saw her still standing behind her desk, watching.

'Perhaps,' he hesitated, diffident, 'perhaps you could you let me have the name of the campsite and your exact dates before I go? The campsite in Liguria.'

He called the campsite as he stood on the pavement outside. A young lad answered, mercifully bright and keen, eager to help. So eager he wasn't suspicious, didn't ask for ID. Yes, a Miss Nielsson had been there in April, checked out on the twenty-ninth. He gave Sandro the licence plate.

Before he forgot, Sandro typed it into a message and sent it over to Pietro. *Nielsson had been living in a camper-van. Licence plate DY17306, get a trace?*

As he put the phone away, he turned to see Martine Kaufmann emerge from the door to her studio, bent over. She was hauling the bags of old clothes out on to the pavement. He felt a weary nudge of conscience at the sight.

'Miss Kaufmann?' She straightened stiffly. He wasn't sure if the look she gave him contained reproof or if that was his imagination. He sighed. 'Maybe I could help you with those?'

She was rubbing her hands where the plastic ties on the bags had already cut into her palms. More gently, he said, 'Why don't I take them over to the collection centre for you? Is it far?'

She put her hands in her pockets, regarding him, stiffly upright, and he remembered her again, more slender all those years ago, but the determination intact. And then abruptly she inclined her head, gracious.

'Thank you,' she said. 'Thank you. They collect them at that little convent beyond the Carmine – do you know the one?' He did, and it was on the way back to the office. 'It's been – it feels like it's been a long morning. That's very kind.' And with another stiff nod, she retreated inside, leaving the bags on the pavement.

He regretted the gesture before he'd reached the end of the street, and by the time he got to the convent his hands were raw. In the side-room a swarthy man in a brown janitor's coat took the bags from him with a grunt, glancing at the tags. There were bins marked up for different items – shoes, overcoats, jeans – and overtaken by idle curiosity, Sandro lingered.

'Is Miss Kaufmann a regular contributor?' he said and the janitor looked at him, not understanding.

'Contributor? It's her charity. She organises everything, picks up bags every couple of weeks.' He undid the bags and upended them on to the counter. 'Some orphanage or something.'

What had he expected? He looked down at the heaped clothes. The bags contained just what Kaufmann had said, things only teenagers would wear. Skimpy sweaters, jeans, cheap shoes. Market-stall stuff.

His phone buzzed with a message from Pietro. *You done? I've got sandwiches. See you at the car in ten.*

Martine Kaufmann was doing some kind of penance. Charity work? What wrong had she done, and when?

Sandro turned and retraced his steps.

Chapter Ten

MERCIFULLY LUISA WAS BACK HOME, had taken more of the medication they'd given her at the hospital with a pot of camomile tea and feeling closer to normal than she had in days, when Sandro called. Sitting at the round table in the dim kitchen with her hands at the little teapot, listening to the children in the street outside.

How old would she have been now? Their Beatrice, their baby. Approaching thirty-three, and perhaps with children of her own. A ball was bouncing rhythmically out there, and the children's voices were like music. Then on the table the mobile buzzed.

He launched right into it, his morning and Martine Kaufmann. 'Runs a sculpture studio in San Niccolo,' he said. 'But it's all about good works, her life. What is it they're all trying to clean out of their lives? Gorgone and his wellness centres. She runs some children's charity. I just hauled a ton of old clothes over there.'

There was a silence, and she heard him wondering why she had not yet said anything. She took a deep breath and decided to leave it, to say nothing – yet.

'I'm worried about Giuli,' she said. 'I – we just had a coffee together in town.'

A last resort. 'What?' She could hear panic in his voice and wished she'd just come clean. 'What do you think's wrong? Should I go up there, back to the office?'

'I think she'd know you were keeping tabs on her – don't do that,' said Luisa hurriedly. The last thing she wanted was those two conferring. 'She's – she just seems so tired all the time. And weepy, and pale.' All true.

'Yes,' he said. 'She thinks it's the menopause.'

For some reason the thought made Luisa want to burst into tears but all she said was, 'Oh.'

He heard it in her voice, though. 'It's you I'm worried about,' he said. 'You were white as a sheet this morning.'

'Nothing gets past you, does it?' she said, and it came to her as easy as anything, the white lie. Something about a scratch in the rose garden and she thought it was infected, she'd gone in to the emergency room and they'd given her antibiotics. There was silence: he accepted it.

'Where are you?' she asked, hearing the hiss of steam.

'Piazza Tasso, waiting for Pietro.' He cleared his throat. 'We're going up to Sant'Anna now,' he said and she could hear it in his voice. He didn't want to go: the idea frightened him. But he was brave. She wanted to tell him, *it's okay, I've been there, it's just a hillside*, but he mustn't know she'd been there first.

Something occurred to her: a way.

'You'll never guess who was being admitted,' she said, 'when I was in the emergency room for my leg.'

'Who?' His voice was sharp with anxiety and she hurried on.

'Benedetta Salieri,' she said. 'I spoke to – her half-brother, is it? A man called Bartolini. Lives in the Salieri house with the old mother – and Benedetta too, I guess. Her marriage fell apart, he told me. She's – Benedetta's – unstable is what they call it. Mentally unstable. And the old lady's –'

'Losing her memory,' said Sandro. 'I heard that. What was Benedetta in for? Did you talk to her?'

'No, I –' Luisa hesitated, not wanting to admit it had been Bartolini she'd recognised, not Benedetta. 'She was in a bit of a state. I think it might have been an overdose, I'm not quite … Anyway, the main thing is she's going to be all right.'

Then mercifully, just as she felt herself entangled in her own stupid deception, there was a clatter behind him, traffic noise as if a door had opened, and Sandro said, 'Look, Pietro's here. Call you later, okay?'

Luisa had to get up and pace a little after he'd gone. This was so unusual, keeping something from Sandro, it made her heart beat too fast. To distract herself she went to the medicine cabinet to put away the dressings they'd given her in the emergency room and to make sure they had iodine and sticking plasters. There it all was, neatly stacked, carefully maintained. Luisa went through it regularly to throw away medicines past their date. She lifted out a tube of ointment for mouth ulcers. She'd been afflicted with them at one stage of her chemo: she remembered that vividly now, those days in dark rooms in pain, and her mouth dried at the memory. Although she had an urge to throw the tube out, she checked the date carefully and put it back in.

Although the name had meant nothing to her – it wasn't as though she'd been introduced forty years ago – she *had* googled Martine Kaufmann that morning. An indistinct mugshot, half-hidden behind a large sculpture in a bright studio. She wondered if the Princess Salieri had known any of them had still been hanging around all this time later. By the sound of it, she would have been past caring.

She drew up her trousers: the skin around the dressing was no redder, at least. It was not hot to the touch. She wanted to peel back the gauze and look but the dressing was freshly applied so she let the trouser-leg down again. She went to the window and looked down: the boys with the ball were leaning against the opposite wall looking at something on their phones.

She thought she would call Frollini, her old boss, with his silver hair and his cufflinks and his flirtatious manner. He would know what was going on with the Salieri family. He would know Bartolini, surely? Would he wonder why she was asking? He would. But Luisa just needed to keep her head. The thought popped into it that this was Johanna Nielsson from beyond the grave, still causing trouble. Stirring things up. What had they done down there to cause this so many years later?

Frollini answered straight away. 'Enrico?' she said, suddenly nervous. But he sounded absurdly delighted to hear from her. *A drink? But of course.* He insisted that they meet at Paskowksi in Piazza Repubblica at – when? – Luisa could hear him calculating, just as she had heard Sandro. The two men she knew like the back of her hand. Six. Which she knew would allow him to get home to his wife for dinner without an eyebrow raised. Not that there was anything for her to raise her eyebrows over and never had been, for all Frollini was still pretending he had a special bond with his ex-vendeuse.

Luisa sighed and reached into the street to pull her shutters closed.

*

Giuli stood on the Via del Parioncino and looked up at the long windows on the first floor of number three. The telephone on which the child had called her was registered here, in the name of Ticino. It was a good address, which was both reassuring and annoying. Reassuring because, statistically at least, the children of the wealthy were less likely to be ill-treated than those of the poor. They were less likely to be left at home alone, less likely to be malnourished, to truant from school, less likely to be frightened and anxious. This was down to money.

Would Giuli have had a better upbringing if her mother had been middle class and comfortably off? Sure she would, but then again, it couldn't really have been worse. On the pavement, in the blue shadows of late afternoon, Giuli looked up at the shuttered windows.

Pietro's voice, calling from Sandro's car, Sandro cursing in the background about the potholes in time with the old car's rattle, had conveyed respect for the address also. 'Look, Giuli,' he'd begun anxiously, 'you won't barge in mob-handed, will you? I mean, be discreet. These people,' he meant the wealthy inhabitants of the Tornabuoni district, 'they don't take kindly –'

'I won't say how I got the address,' she said, knowing where he was heading with this. 'I won't say anything at all if I can get some kind of reassurance from the neighbours or whatever.'

'Good luck with that,' said Pietro. 'It's not San Frediano, you know, or even down where you are, you and Enzo in your newbuild. I bet you've already got nosy neighbours down there, haven't you?'

He was right. A plump short woman with shiny black hair and three noisy little boys who'd moved in downstairs in the spring had already started hanging out on her front doorstep, calling stuff to Giuli as she passed. Nothing mean, just, *God, this weather* in the summer when the temperature had risen steeply and neither of them had the money to leave for the seaside. And *who'd have kids* when hauling her smallest out of the street by the scruff of his neck. The preparatories for establishing a neighbourly relationship: next she'd be asking if Giuli had kids, even though she knew full well there were none. Giuli had just agreed obediently. She thought the woman was called Gemma, and she hadn't seen a husband.

'No,' Pietro had said, raising his voice over Sandro murmuring something in the background, engine noise indicating that they were going up a steep bumpy road. 'You don't get neighbours as such in those areas. Either they don't even live there at all – they're in Gstaad or Sardinia and just drop in for a bit of shopping – or they're foreign, or they're above hanging out of the windows.'

No one was hanging out the window on the Via del Parioncino, which was in any case a tiny street, three doors long, that united the Via del Parione with the Via del Purgatorio. The street of purgatory: even Giuli with her rudimentary knowledge of Christianity knew that hell looked inviting next to purgatory. Number three was on the corner.

None of the shutters was even open in any of the buildings on the narrow street. Nervously, Giuli approached, found the buzzer for Ticino and rang. Listened. Nothing.

She felt only relief. This was an elderly lady babysitting her granddaughter. Would they be sitting inside in the dark on a fine cool afternoon? No. They'd be out in the park, the Cascine or over the river to the Strozzi gardens or the Boboli. The old lady pushing the child in a stroller or holding her hand. Or the daughter would have come for her – it was coming up to five o'clock, after all. There was something in that thought, though, that set up a ticking of anxiety in Giuli. What?

She stepped back, looked up. Still nothing. Took the three steps that would return her to the Via del Parione, where there were shops at least. A designer leather-goods shop, an antique shop, closed like they always were, with a number to ring in the window. A furrier's, closed still after the summer. She stepped into the leather-goods place. There was an array of shiny handbags on two shelving units, and a huge leather horse, and a very tall, very skinny girl with a long nose on her phone behind the counter. She looked up from the phone only when Giuli was standing right in front of her, not bothering to smile. Probably she was enough of a salesgirl to know Giuli wasn't in the market for a thousand-euro bag; maybe she hadn't even needed to look higher than Giuli's shoes for that insight. Giuli cut to the chase.

'I'm looking for Signora Ticino,' she said. 'An old lady in the Via del Parioncino, number three, maybe you know her?'

The girl shrugged, impassive. 'Dunno who you mean,' she said, her eyes flicking down to the phone screen then back up again.

'About, I suppose, sixty-five, seventy?' said Giuli. Still nothing: the girl looked back up at her without interest. In Giuli's pocket her own phone buzzed: a text, but she very deliberately did not look at it. 'You might have seen her out and about with a little girl, her granddaughter, or her daughter?' Because every Italian noticed children, didn't they? The girl wasn't foreign: she even had a Florentine accent. The crinkle of a tiny frown between her eyes, at the waste of her time.

'No,' she repeated. 'I don't know any old lady, and I'm not interested in kids. Little sods leaving sticky fingers on my window.'

'So you have seen the granddaughter?'

The girl's expression hardened. 'I told you,' she said, gesturing at the window. Giuli turned to follow her gaze. 'I come in here for eleven, I leave at seven, I see customers if they come in and that's it.' The window display did indeed block most of the view of the street, but Giuli couldn't understand how anyone could sit here all day, not go and hang out on the doorstep like normal people. Looking back at the girl, though, she got it. She didn't need real life – she had her phone. These days that was what was normal.

'Okay,' said Giuli, defeated. As she stepped out, though, the girl said something, and she turned.

'Round the corner,' she said. 'In the next street. I went there once.'

'What?' said Giuli.

'The shoe guy,' said the girl, impatient already. 'What d'you call it – cobbler, guy who mends shoes. He'll know her, won't he? Old ladies love those places.' Her lip curling. 'I mean, why buy a nice new pair of fashionable shoes when you can spend half an hour gassing with an old guy in a hole in the wall about make do and mend and young people these days.'

'The next street?' said Giuli, eager, because the long-nosed girl was right.

'Via del Purgatorio,' said the salesgirl, and with a flick of her hand dismissed Giuli.

Hurrying across between the tall stone facades, Giuli felt the chill of the approaching evening, although overhead the sky was still blue. Turning the corner, she slowed: up ahead was the battered sign of a boot. The Via del Purgatorio was a dead end, and the cobbler's was tucked in to the base of the narrowest house she had ever seen. Approaching, she saw that it was open at least – these tiny places could either be open round the clock with the owner sleeping behind the counter, or almost never because the cobbler was an elderly man with a heart condition and no one to cover for him.

An old guy, maybe in his late sixties but wiry, healthy. In front of him his customer, another old guy, a disreputable black shoe clasped between gnarled fingers, holding forth. On young people these days, as it happened. Young people and their drug taking, on this occasion, a complaint about the things they left littering the pavement. Giuli hovered. The cobbler, glasses on his nose, peered at her a second over his customer's shoulder, but said nothing. Giuli stepped back: in her pocket the phone buzzed again and she came out on to the street and stepped aside from the doorway.

It was from Enzo. *Don't forget, sweetheart,* it read. *Six p.m., Labo X, Via Verdi.*

What?

'But I cancelled it,' she murmured to herself, leaning back against the stucco wall with the phone in her hands. But she hadn't, had she? She had been about to, sitting in the office, but then the phone had rung. Giuli banged her head gently against the wall, two, three times.

Shit, she thought. *Shit, shit.*

She googled the place: Labo X. A website, lots of pictures of smiling faces, a price list. She gulped. She recognised the building, long, modern. A phone number: she dialled.

'Of course, madam, would you like to reschedule?' A bright female voice.

'Well, I – no, I –' and suddenly, violently, abruptly Giuli *did* feel ill. *Maybe when I'm feeling better* hovered on her lips, prompting a queasy, miserable laugh. 'I'll call back ...'

'Just to let you know,' said the female voice, confidentially, 'we have a policy, and a same-day cancellation does incur a charge, which will be drawn on the card used to make the booking.'

Giuli felt sick, remembering the price list. 'A charge?'

'Well, if a cancellation comes this late,' the voice lowered, apologetic, 'we charge the full fee.'

Giuli leaned back against the wall again, and the heat came over her, rising from her breastbone, and sudden, extreme nausea. 'I – ' and she gave in. 'In that case, if I hurry, maybe I –' She swallowed, squeezed her eyes shut at the thought of doctors and needles. Of what might be wrong. 'I should be able to make it.'

The female voice agreed comfortably that that would certainly be the best solution.

Ah, shit, Giuli thought, hanging up. It was five forty and she had the *motorino*. It would take her ten minutes or less to get there. She stepped back into the doorway of the cobbler's but they were still gassing and the look the cobbler gave her this time was wary, as if she was looking unhinged. She felt unhinged. She turned away, reaching for the keys to the *motorino*.

Cut and run.

Chapter Eleven

THE FEELING OF DREAD CAME, unexpected, as they took the narrow turning off the *strada statale* towards Sant'Anna.

It had seemed to take them forever to get going. Pietro had been summoned to a meeting with the super, there'd been paperwork to file and Sandro suspected both were connected with his secondment to the case. Perhaps they were having second thoughts about using him as a consultant: he half-wished they were.

The scene of the crime. He knew what you had to do was talk – talk to people and watch them as they talked back. But these people had closed their doors, they wouldn't talk. And at the thought of Sant'Anna he got a shifting, shadowy feeling, like the dark river at night, the river that whispered as it flowed black beyond the parapets, sliding under the bridges. The feeling that came when he thought of the place where it had happened: the woodland path; the tumbledown hut; La Vipera itself. That house.

Sandro had collected his ancient brown Fiat from where he kept it under the trees of the Via Romana, the roof plastered with birdshit and dead leaves, and went to meet Pietro in the Piazza Tasso. The incredulous laugh at the passenger window: it had been a while since he had been in Sandro's car.

'Business good, then?' said Pietro, but he knew that even if business had been booming Sandro wouldn't have traded in this car. He would drive it till it dropped.

He might have upgraded it if Luisa ever drove, but she'd gone off it after the baby, so almost thirty years ago. Luisa had slowly come back to life in small ways, out of the house, back to work, but something about driving still panicked her. He never mentioned it.

'What if some big job comes in,' said Pietro, climbing in, brushing down the passenger seat with a comical grimace, 'someone you need to impress?' Sandro just gave him a look. They'd set off, out up towards Poggio Imperiale, under the green shade of the long avenue of trees where the groomed gardens of the wealthy sat behind high walls, and as he drove Sandro pondered. Luisa had sounded odd on the phone. Not herself.

'Luisa told me she was in the emergency room at Santa Maria Nuova this morning and Benedetta Salieri was brought in,' he said abruptly to Pietro, eyes on the road. They were sailing round the hillside high above the red-roofed city now, in the striated shade of the huge leaning umbrella pines. 'Took an overdose, reading between the lines.'

'The daughter?' Pietro was interested. 'I hadn't heard.' Hospitals were supposed to report drug overdoses.

'Well, early days, isn't it,' said Sandro. 'It could have been prescription drugs. And we all know they sometimes give the patient the benefit of the doubt, don't we?'

'What was Luisa doing in the emergency room?' asked Pietro, and then, not waiting for an answer, 'Who did she talk to? Who brought Benedetta in?'

'The brother, apparently,' said Sandro. 'Or half-brother.'

'Right,' said Pietro thoughtfully.

'And you said Bartolini was away when – well, for both murders?'

Pietro nodded. 'The lads spoke to the Greek friend – Bartolini was quite free with the number – that he'd stayed with in Paros. Apparently he didn't leave the island for his whole stay. I also got the name of the –' he cleared his throat '– rest home where he spent the ten days with his sister. Actually, I called the place this morning, it's up in the lakes, and they confirmed that they were both there when Lotti was killed. Left four days ago.'

Sandro shifted at the wheel, obscurely disappointed. He'd have liked to make that call himself. It felt uneasy, coming in to this late, after uniformed officers had already been in there. Greece wasn't far away, he observed in stubborn silence. The lakes even closer. He didn't know what he had in for Luca Bartolini, except a certain warmth in Luisa's voice when she'd mentioned him. A certain hurry, too, as if to distract him. One of the advantages, or maybe disadvantages, of four decades together: it was like being the same person, sometimes.

They were on the *superstrada* now, leaving the city behind. The car rattled and jolted. The old road was in a terrible state, patched and potholed. The woodland to either side was still in full leaf, the colour only turning slightly here and there, and the trees overhung the carriageway, turning it dark.

'He showed me pictures on his phone,' Pietro went on, 'Bartolini did. I didn't get as far as asking for corroboration or dates, but ...' He shrugged as if to say, you know what it's like. These big houses. And then he surprised Sandro by saying, 'But maybe we should.'

As if on cue, as they rounded a curve in the road a row of black cypresses came into view, leading up to a villa surmounting a hill – two hills, in fact. Grand houses were ten a penny in this part of the region, their owners always moaning about the upkeep and the taxes. Worth a fortune, though, and the Salieri place was close to town.

'We didn't speak to any of them back then,' Sandro said, uneasy. 'Why would we? We did go up there, just a formality, to see if they had any complaints about the house. There was an old caretaker, told us the family had gone to the sea for the summer.'

He'd forgotten the visit completely, but now it came back to him: a violently windy day, one of those August tempests whipping up the Arno and sending tiles off roofs and showers of leaves down the drive to the Salieri place. Rather late in the season still to be at the seaside. The big ornamental gates had been locked, and although they had rung and rung the doorbell set into one of the stone pedestals, it had taken the old man forever to appear, with his truffle-dog. Truffles were like gold: maybe that's how the Salieri managed the upkeep.

'Benedetta, though –' Sandro hesitated. 'Did you say she was in the city in the summer?'

'I'm not sure,' said Pietro thoughtfully. 'And I wonder what the prompt was for this suicide attempt. I mean, it could have something to do with all this?'

'I wonder,' said Sandro. 'It's possible that just reading about a murder on her doorstep could do it. If she was fragile. Luisa said she'd been fragile for years.' He didn't much like the idea of talking to Benedetta Salieri: mental illness was very hard to interrogate. He glanced sideways at Pietro, who was chewing his lip.

'Well, when we were up there, there was no evidence of Benedetta,' Pietro said at last. 'Marte said something about her living in town, not at home.'

'She sounds very co-operative,' said Sandro and Pietro frowned this time, not in a joking mood, obviously.

'She didn't really talk about her employers, for obvious reasons, not under their roof. We certainly should talk to the brother again,' he said stiffly. 'I can see you'd like to get up to the grand house. You have to understand, at that stage I didn't know if Manzoni would agree to getting you involved.'

'Never mind,' said Sandro mildly, although it did intrigue him, the big house he'd never been allowed up to last time. 'He's probably still at the hospital.'

Beside him Pietro said nothing.

'I'd like to talk to the maid, though, or housekeeper, whatever she is,' Sandro persevered. Pietro grunted. And he said nothing more until they reached the exit for Sant'Anna.

Sandro wondered if he'd taken offence. It was only to be expected, he told himself, resuming a relationship after such a gap. A little awkwardness. He wondered again what the boss had wanted Pietro in for. The journey was no more than half an hour, and Sandro had been about to get up the nerve to ask when the turning came, out of the blue, along with that bad feeling, and he had forgotten the question.

They'd driven past signs to Sant'Anna since, he and Luisa, on their way down to the sea or driving off to other woods on a sudden urge of Luisa's to pick mushrooms or forage for chestnuts. He always noticed the sign; once or twice he thought Luisa did too but neither of them ever said anything.

Sandro swung the wheel and almost immediately the first houses of the hamlet that was Sant'Anna came into sight, a bell-tower beyond them. It had been so long and it was all so familiar. The faded lettering of an advertisement for some long-gone amaro painted on the flank of a house. La Vipera's graffiti, or whatever it had been scrawled across its wall, came into his mind, a monstrous advertisement for their careless way of life.

'There,' said Pietro, breaking in on his thoughts as he pointed to a small stone house on the edge of the village, its window boxes bright with geraniums. 'Marte lives there. I checked with her before we left, and she said to meet her at home, not up at the Salieri place.'

Sandro pulled in. 'So you'd already –?'

Pietro permitted himself a tight smile. 'I know you,' he said.

*

You could tell Gianna Marte wasn't from these parts. She wore her greying blonde hair in a coiled bun at the back of her head and was very bright eyed, very eager, very wholesome, with a singsong edge to her accent. She brought with her a whiff of gingerbread.

They sat at a table covered with an embroidered cloth while she made them her special herbal tea. 'Madam enjoys it,' she said, laying out pot, cups, saucers. The tea was yellow and tasted of absolutely nothing to Sandro, who wished for a small strong coffee but didn't say so. She came, she explained before they had even asked, from a village on the Swiss border. She kept dimpling shyly at Pietro.

'And how did you get the job down here?' he asked politely. 'Didn't Benedetta – Miss – the princess's daughter move there at one time?'

She smiled again, not answering. Very discreet. 'Cookie?' she said, pushing a plate of flower-shaped biscuits towards him.

'So,' Sandro said. 'You knew Mr Lotti.' Her eyes went round as saucers and she dimpled at Pietro again, as if asking permission, but there was a flush to her now. She shifted in her seat and fussed with the cup and saucer in front of her.

'Yes,' said Gianna Marte, her mouth set in a line. 'He was friendly. He suggested once or twice that we might visit the cinema together and I – well, he was considerably older than me, you understand, and I wasn't quite sure what he –'

'I understand,' said Sandro. 'But you were on good terms? You hadn't actually turned him down?'

Her flush deepened. 'Not in so many words, no,' she said. 'Yes, we were on good terms. I think he had hopes, you know.' She nodded at a garish teapot on a shelf above the stove. 'He bought me gifts.'

Sandro glanced up at it. 'Very nice,' he said, standing for a closer look out of politeness. It was hideous and vaguely familiar.

Marte sniffed, extracting a balled tissue from her apron pocket. 'He brought me that back from the city barely two weeks ago.'

'From Florence?' She nodded. Sandro lifted it and looked on the base, where the potter's mark had been pressed into the clay.

'You had an opportunity to observe his habits?' Pietro prompted from the kitchen table and she smiled, more happily now. Sandro set the pot back down and returned to the table.

'I did,' she said, her head bobbing up and down, obedient. 'As I told you, Commissario, Mr Lotti didn't usually walk his dog up at that end of the village. Not many people went up there, they – it's cold. Damp. The sun doesn't reach that far up the valley, not even in summer.'

'Not many people?' Sandro was gentle, diffident.

'Only that Martinelli, she lives up there. She and Lotti were not friends, so perhaps that's why he didn't –' She broke off, the flush returning. 'She was rather unpleasant, as a matter of fact. When she saw me speaking to him, she gave me such a horrible look. Only a couple of weeks ago, not long before –' She sniffed, clutching a napkin to her mouth. 'He told me she didn't like him. He said she was an old prude. They'd had an argument over something or other, long ago. He wouldn't tell me what, he only seemed to find it rather amusing.'

'Ah,' said Pietro. 'You didn't mention that last time.'

'People in this village are the least friendly I have ever met,' Marte burst out. 'Mr Lotti was the only one who would talk to me. Must I just stay inside my house silent when I'm not at work, keep my mouth shut and mind my own business? And now he's dead.'

Pietro patted her gingerly on the shoulder. 'Please don't upset yourself, Miss Marte. I can quite see there's not much in the way of conversation at your place of work.'

'No, indeed,' she said, subsiding. 'Mr Bartolini is very – he is a gentleman, good-mannered but hardly says a word when he's here.'

'He was away all the summer?' She nodded. He pressed her further, 'And more recently?'

'He came back in the third week of August and, almost immediately, off he went again. Taking his sister away on – well, they called it a retreat. He said it would be good for both of them. She has these – she has nerves.'

'Benedetta Salieri doesn't live at the villa?'

Marte folded her arms complacently across her front. 'She has her own place in town, some fancy place, she's supposed to live there. Only, when she has one of her turns –' She stopped, discreet again.

'What are they like? These episodes?' asked Pietro quickly.

'Hysterics,' said Gianna Marte, putting a hand up to smooth her bun. 'Honestly, I think they indulge her. They call it depression but ... she pretends to harm herself. Rants and raves. And then off she goes to a luxury hotel –' She checked herself, smiled more stiffly. 'Anyway. You haven't touched your tea!' Reproving. Sandro suppressed a prick of irritation. 'Eat up!'

Pietro obediently picked up a biscuit and nibbled. 'And when she has one of her turns?' he said.

'Off goes poor Mr Bartolini to look after her. I suppose that's family, and his mother's hardly able to look after herself.'

'Could we go up there to see her, do you think?' said Sandro. 'The Princess Salieri?'

'You could,' Marte said doubtfully. 'She's usually asleep by now, though. When I left her, she'd already taken her pill, and Mr Bartolini said he would be back late.'

Sandro looked down at the tea. 'Did Benedetta Salieri know Mr Lotti?' he asked.

'Oh, no,' said Marte firmly. 'If she was here she never went into the village. Agora-something. Hysterics.'

'Agoraphobia?' said Sandro. 'Was she here this summer?'

'She stayed in town.' She shrugged. 'So there's no one for me to talk to,' she went on. 'The princess, God bless her,' and she crossed herself, several times, 'Madam, I mean, she has almost stopped talking. It used to be going over the old days, when her husband was alive, the dresses she used to wear, the balls they used to attend – I quite enjoyed that – and now she says nothing. Not a thing.' She sniffed again and put down her crumpled napkin.

'So,' said Sandro gently, 'the last time you spoke to Mr Lotti would have been when Mrs Martinelli saw you together?'

Her lip quivered. 'I suppose it was,' she said.

'And what did he say?'

'He said he –' A tiny wrinkle appeared above her nose. 'He said he wanted to invite me to dinner. He intended to cook truffles for me.' Again the blush. 'He was sometimes a little ... perhaps a little crude. He asked me if I knew they were an aphrodisiac. He was very pleased because he –' she hesitated '– he knew where to find them.'

'Did he say,' Sandro kept his voice light, pondering that

hesitation, 'did he say who'd told him? About the truffles? A friend?' Watching her, he saw the pink of her cheeks deepen, just faintly.

'I think he overheard it,' she said airily. 'Perhaps in the bar?' She smiled, as if pleased with her deduction. 'He did drink in the bar. Brandy. In fact, that was where we were when he asked me. About the truffles.'

Sandro heard it, the sound he was tuned to: dishonesty. He held her gaze and the pink deepened further. She looked down into her lap a second then up again. 'Well,' and again she compressed her lips, 'it might have been – I might have heard it myself. And passed it on to him.'

'And where did you hear it?'

'I can't remember,' she said.

Sandro tilted his head, inquiring. 'You can't remember?' he said.

She shook her head tightly. 'I honestly can't! Isn't that funny? Perhaps in the supermarket. In the next village?'

A silence that grew. Her smile fixed. Sandro and Pietro exchanged glances. 'You've been so helpful, Miss Marte,' said Pietro, pushing his chair back.

Gianna Marte got to her feet in a hurry, clattering the cups together. 'Yes, well ...'

They offered her their thanks and left before she dropped all the cups on the floor.

They walked back to the car, and Sandro became aware of Pietro falling into silence. 'So Miss Marte heard about the truffles somewhere but she's not saying where,' said Sandro to fill it. 'All that *can't remember* nonsense. Someone told her in confidence?

She's afraid of giving away someone's truffle secrets? I know it's a cutthroat business but still. And if there were truffles around here these woods would be a lot more popular.'

'Maybe she really can't remember,' said Pietro.

Sandro glanced sideways. 'Those dimples, is it? I didn't know you were susceptible, Pietro. I wonder if Bartolini is. After all, she didn't have a bad word to say about him, did she?' No answer. 'I was wondering, perhaps we could just go and peer in at Lotti's place? You know, just to get the feel of it?'

'Sure,' said Pietro, but he wasn't meeting Sandro's eyes.

'So what else did we learn?' Sandro persevered. Pietro had never been such hard work. 'That Martinelli and Lotti had a row and Benedetta really is a nutjob – but unless Marte is covering for her, she wasn't out here but in town when Nielsson was killed.' There was no response so he mused on. 'Town's not the other side of the world, of course, and Johanna Nielsson had to get out here somehow. Did she drive herself in the camper and if so where is it?'

Pietro just jammed his hands in his pockets.

'Look,' Sandro said, stopping. 'Is everything all right?'

Pietro stiffened. 'Yes,' he said guardedly.

'What did the boss want to talk to you about this morning?'

Pietro sighed. They were at the car, and Sandro got the key out, waiting.

'She'd been digging around,' Pietro said. 'She came across something in the original case files.'

'Something?'

'A sarky comment Baratti made about you in the files.'

'That old bastard,' said Sandro, feeling his jaw clench.

'Listen, Sandro,' he said. 'It's a bit rich, you joshing me about the housekeeper – and there was nothing – she's not a bad-looking woman, yes, I may have flirted a bit ...'

Sandro stared at him. 'It was a joke,' he said eventually. 'What do you mean, a bit rich?'

'You never said,' said Pietro, dogged, still flushing. 'You never mentioned that there was something between you and her. Nielsson. You should have said.'

'There wasn't anything between us,' said Sandro quietly.

'Nothing?' said Pietro flatly. 'Sandro,' and there was a warning note in his voice, 'how long have we known each other?'

Sandro felt choked, suddenly, words sticking in his throat. 'Nothing happened,' he said.

'No – intimacy?' And Pietro was looking at him full on now, the flush gone from his face, and the interior of the car seemed very cramped. They were at a deadlock. Fucking Baratti, thought Sandro again. Dirty-minded Baratti. He felt sick.

'All right,' he said. 'Get in and I'll tell you. I should have told you before, but I'll tell you now.'

Chapter Twelve

AFTER SIX YEARS working at the publicly funded women's centre in the dingy Piazza Tasso, the reception area of the Labo X was a revelation to Giuli. No rough sleepers, no buggies, no druggies. Designer chairs and glossy magazines and a huge TV, and frosted windows onto the Via Verdi behind which the silhouettes of passersby were visible.

Giuli, who was ten minutes early after all that, found herself a corner as out of sight as she could manage. She felt out of place here, as though she might be ejected at any moment, although the receptionist had confirmed she had an appointment. Even the receptionist had a manicure: if she'd known, Giuli would have washed her hair.

She sat down with a form to fill in and a pot to pee in. She peed first. The washrooms were sparkling, the size of a bedroom, and the towels folded by the sink felt warm.

Date of birth, medical conditions. *Have you ever been treated for the following: cancer; diabetes; a sexually transmitted disease?*

And suddenly Giuli didn't feel like joking any more. She wanted to run away.

With a life like hers she'd been lucky, or perhaps her death wish hadn't been what she thought it was. Young enough to know all about HIV in time, even if she'd told herself she didn't care often enough back then. She'd injected drugs only for a very brief period; she'd used condoms. All the same, it was a long time since she'd been tested. She focused on the page and answered truthfully. As truthfully as she could.

They called her three minutes early. The room was blindingly white, with modern art on the walls, and the nurse – Cinzia Messi, phlebotomist, it said on her lapel – wore lipstick and gold earrings with her white lab coat. She looked down at the form Giuli had filled out, then up again, and smiled. They would be about the same age, although only one of them had taken proper care of herself for forty-five years. The smile seemed real, though, and Giuli knew the difference.

'I see your husband has sent you along,' said the nurse. Cinzia. Phelobotomist, not nurse. 'Yes,' said Giuli wearily. She took the pee pot out of her pocket and slid it embarrassedly on to the desk between them where a kidney-shaped cardboard dish sat containing a syringe, vials, plastic bags. 'I've been feeling ... under the weather. He bullied me into it.'

'Under the weather?'

Giuli listed the symptoms. 'Mostly tiredness,' she said. 'Mostly like I could just go to sleep and not wake up. I feel hungry then I feel sick. Nasty taste in my mouth.'

'Obviously, we need your agreement,' said Cinzia gently, 'for these tests, blood and urine. We'll look for anaemia, white blood cell count, cholesterol, glucose, fertility levels –' She broke off. 'You know we're doing this all the wrong way round? You should have visited your physician first. Doctor – what is it? – Hartmann.'

Giuli, who couldn't have said what sex her doctor even was, looked down at her hands, guilty.

'I'm guessing you're not really a regular at the doctor's?'

Giuli shook her head. 'Not really,' she mumbled. 'I've – I never really looked after myself, if you know what I mean. I haven't always been ... careful.' She hoped desperately that the woman, Cinzia, would not frown at her, or edge away, or, worse, ask her what exactly she meant.

She did none of those things: she took Giuli's nearest hand in both of hers. 'But you're being careful now,' she said. 'And your husband –'

'He's so good,' said Giuli desperately. 'He's such a sweetheart. I can't bear for –' and she broke off. She couldn't bear to think of him on his own. Until she met Enzo, life had been something she could take or leave. Even with Sandro and Luisa in her life, she had just been waiting, she could see now, for it all to end. But Enzo had changed the game. Enzo with his daft fringe and his shyness and his kindness and the way he looked at her.

'The best thing,' said Cinzia carefully, still holding Giuli's hand between hers, 'the very best thing is to know what your situation is, don't you think, and proceed from there? I think,' still gentle, 'under the circumstances, we can include an HIV test and a hepatitis C test. I can look into getting help to pay for them if that's out of your budget – and there are other test centres, too, you know? Free ones.'

'No,' said Giuli quickly, looking down at her hand, still in Cinzia's, and holding back something that felt dangerously like tears. 'I worked at the women's centre in Piazza Tasso. I know all about what's out there.' Guilt added into the mix – after all, what had Giuli ever done to deserve private testing? 'We can afford it,' she said.

And then the woman let her hand go. Reached up to touch her gold earrings, as if for luck, then pulled the little cardboard tray of equipment towards her.

*

Giuli walked back out into the reception area in a daze, one hand pressed absently still to the inside of her elbow where the blood had been drawn. One vial after another, dark red. Not as bad as she thought – in some ways. It was done. But the worst bit was waiting for the results, wasn't it? The worst bit was always waiting.

'You need to visit your doctor too,' Cinzia had said as she stood to say goodbye. 'I mean, that goes without saying, right? You need a full check-up, just to be on the safe side. We'll send the results on to him, but if there's anything to worry about, if there's anything urgent, we'll call you. All right?' Looking into her face. 'Promise me you'll make the appointment?'

Giuli had promised. She walked through the airy white space, focused on the frosted glass doors that would let her back out into the real world. The smells and the noise and the people, the grey pavements, the blue-grey hills in the distance, clouds white and fluffy above them. She was almost there when she heard her name.

She wouldn't have recognised him. It was thirty years – he shouldn't have recognised *her*. She was a different person. She didn't know his voice, low and hoarse: on instinct, she kept walking, she didn't turn to look at him.

And then she was on the pavement, dizzy in the bright day, a horn blaring as she stepped blindly off the kerb. Someone held her: someone pulled her back and she turned and saw him.

He'd always been a big man, but something had shrunk him. He'd always been big enough to floor her mother with the back of his hand, big enough to hold Giuli down. He wasn't wearing greasy jeans any more, though; his hair wasn't lank to his shoulders. He wore an expensive waxed leather jacket, shiny shoes. She calculated he would be about sixty-five years old.

'Giulietta?' His voice pleaded with her.

He wasn't well. Why else would he be there? She looked down at his hand on her arm.

Don't you know I'm a different person?

Roberto Ragno. His hair slicked down, dyed, she'd have said, but expensively done. Roberto Ragno who had been her mother's pimp during her early childhood, when they'd lived in the bedsit on the Via Pisana where Giuli had slept on a mattress on the floor. He used to walk through the door and kick the mattress, whether she was lying on it or not. By the time her mother overdosed in the bedsit one summer day while Giuli was at school, Ragno was long gone.

She shook his hand off, feeling her face frozen, all of her frozen. His clothes were expensive but he looked old and sick. His face was yellow. The whites of his eyes were yellow.

'You must have come into some money, Roberto,' she said, contemptuous, gesturing at his shiny shoes. 'Look at you.' And she felt it seethe and rise up her gullet, the hatred like bile. The memory of hatred. It occurred to her that bile was what was wrong with *him*: the liver malfunctioning, that's what made you yellow, and she could feel her rage acting on her like that, toxic in her body. She stood her ground.

'What's wrong with you?' she said.

'I'm dying,' he said, and she heard self-pity. 'I need to – I need to –'

'You need to what? To say sorry?' His lip trembled at the scorn in her voice and she saw she'd hit home. 'What, found God, is it, or Buddha or whoever?' He still had the big gold signet ring on his pinky finger, the one that had left a dent in Giuli's forehead one time. 'If you've got to get to everyone you've ever shat on, Roberto, you'll be a while doing that.' He stepped back. 'Where did the money come from?' His mouth moved. 'Don't bother,' she said. 'I know.'

It came from other women's shitty lives. After he left her mother he'd gone back to running the girls who stood by the country roads to the south of the city. Giuli's mother had told her as much in one of her long, rambling, recriminating rants. Foreign girls, mostly, from all over, from Africa to Russia, anyone hopeless enough. Women standing shivering in some disgusting lay-by, servicing van drivers behind the trees among used condoms and needles. Her mother dissing the girls because only the desperate would do that, because even she had to feel superior to someone. Let no one tell you misery made you strong or noble. It made you into a scavenger and a thief. Something sparked among the memories, something stirred. Those girls on the road beyond Certosa, winding on up into the hills.

But Ragno was speaking. 'Let me – let me help you,' he said, beseeching. 'You need money?' He looked at her more closely with his yellow eyes, looking her up and down, uncertain. The last time he'd have seen Giuli the only calories she got came from cheap wine. She'd been dressed out of charity dumpsters and sleeping against a fence in Osmannoro under the airport flight path. He looked like he was trying to work out what had happened to her, how come she was wearing a suit and a wedding ring and looked like she ate real food, off plates. With the thought, Giuli felt saliva come into her mouth, and she didn't know if it meant sickness or hunger but she wanted to get out of there before she threw up on him.

'I don't need money,' she said and was about to say, *and I don't believe in forgiveness*, but something stopped her – an urge to do her bit for this case that seemed to burden Sandro a little too much.

'You worked the girls down near Sant'Anna, didn't you?' She made her voice quiet, not conciliatory exactly but not angry any more. He mumbled something she couldn't hear, taking a step back from her. His yellow hands were shaking: she thought of Cinzia Messi taking hers. 'Didn't you?'

When he didn't answer, only staring with that mixture of craftiness and stupidity that came back to her down the years, keeping her patience, Giuli said, 'You wanted to help me, right?' He nodded. 'Before – mum,' keeping her voice level, 'before – you worked the girls down there. In the seventies?' Ragno stared still. 'You remember that place? That house where the foreigners had the commune?'

'I had nothing to do with them,' he said quickly, too quickly, with a sudden step that brought him up against the wall.

'La Vipera, it was called,' she said, examining him coolly. His mouth opened and closed but he said nothing. The yellow of his skin had turned greyish.

'What's the matter with you?' she said. 'I mean, what are you dying of?'

'Liver cancer,' he said through cracked lips and Giuli nodded without comment. 'They can't – I asked about a transplant but they said it's spread anyway,' his voice holding a sob, ready to break.

She told herself, *have no pity.* 'Well,' she said, and from her upper pocket she took one of her cards, holding it between thumb and forefinger until he looked at it. 'If you change your mind about helping me.' And she held it out, printed side up. *Giulietta Sarto, Private Investigator.*

For a long second they both looked at it, and then reluctantly, as reluctantly as though the card might harbour poison, the yellow fingers came out and he took it from her.

*

The Piazza Repubblica was noisy and chaotic as the day faded to grey. Luisa thought she had glimpsed Giuli on her *motorino*, zipping and swaying between cars, on the way over and had raised a hand, but if it *had* been Giuli her mind had been elsewhere.

Luisa picked her way across carefully: she hadn't worn heels in a while. She shouldn't have worn them this evening, really, nor should she have taken any care at all with her make-up, but she knew how Enrico Frollini's face would fall if she turned up in trousers and boots and a bobble hat. Enrico was of the generation that believed women should be beautiful: he had built a career on the belief, and Luisa had worked in one of his large, luxurious shops for more or less her whole life, so on went the heels.

The sky overhead was clear and pale and luminous, and a nice cool was descending. Luisa skirted the carousel that had been in this square since she'd been a child herself. Increasingly it surprised her, with all the entertainments available to kids, that they still pleaded with their parents for a ticket, two euros to clamber on to a painted horse and be whirled in the dusk, among the sparkle and mirrors. *Soon*, Luisa found herself thinking as she came into the golden light that fell through Paskowski's window, *they'll start dying, all my generation. Things will be forgotten.*

'Luisa!' Frollini was hurrying forward in his camel coat, the one with the fur collar, both hands outstretched to seize her by the elbows. '*Carissima!*' She allowed him to envelop her in a lingering embrace. He would never have called her darling when she had been his employee. Stepping back, she saw his shrewd eyes taking her in.

Some business with the bar's owner to remind her that he knew everyone who was anyone, and Enrico had them escorted to seats in the cosiest corner of the dining room, standing behind Luisa to take her coat with scented ceremony. The terrace had gone modern, with uncomfortable hard white sofas, but inside it was the same old Paskowski's: walnut panelling and Murano chandeliers that shed a pearly soft light and deeply upholstered banquettes.

'What a treat –' he began, taking off the camel coat and hanging it carefully on a polished brass hook.

But Luisa cut him short. 'I want to pick your brains, Enrico.' Pulling off her gloves. He looked crestfallen, but you had to be firm with Enrico Frollini. Gossip was like a swamp: it could swallow you right up if you didn't choose your route through it carefully. 'It's about the Salieri family.'

He sighed. 'Can't we at least order first?' Controlling her impatience, Luisa sat back and ordered a Negroni. Frollini twinkled. 'So,' he said, passing a hand over his thick silvery hair. 'What about Margherita Salieri? You know she has ... whatever they call it nowadays. Alzheimer?' His old tortoise eyes widened and for a moment she saw genuine anxiety. 'Sometimes I think we're all going to get it, Luisa.'

'Not you, Enrico,' she said, breaking a promise to herself and patting him on the hand. He brightened. 'When did you actually last see her?'

He sighed. 'Two or three years ago. She remembered me eventually but at first' – outraged – 'she thought I was her father!' Luisa suppressed a smile. 'She can't have looked in a mirror in a while,' he said, 'if she thinks she could be my daughter.'

'Maybe she doesn't recognise herself in the mirror,' said Luisa, at which Frollini simply looked depressed. 'Anyway,' she went on, 'I don't want to know about her, not really. It's the others.'

'Well,' said Enrico, sipping his malt whisky, grimacing. He drank it because he thought it sophisticated, she knew, but he had as sweet a tooth as she did. 'The prince died, oh, years ago now,' he said warily. 'Old Alberto. He was – it was never – he wasn't quite –'

'Come along, Enrico,' said Luisa, choosing her next stepping stone through the gossip swamp. 'Not as other men?' It dawned on her that she'd always half-known that. 'Theirs was a marriage of convenience, dynastic.' When he looked wary, she spelt it out. 'Alberto was gay.'

'Oh,' said Enrico, slightly miffed. 'You knew.' She thought of Alberto Salieri at the window of that old house, looking down. He would have been looking at La Vipera.

'Well, I suppose I must have guessed,' she said. 'I'm certainly not surprised. Was it top secret?' Frollini shrugged helplessly. 'He must have had lovers,' she probed. 'Not all of them can have been discreet.'

'Margherita didn't much mind,' said Enrico. 'She had the house, the beautiful daughter, the money.' He shrugged. 'And she quite liked him, you know. Marriage,' he shot her a glance, 'it has to be a flexible thing.'

'I'm sure yours has had to be, Enrico,' she said. 'I'm quite happy with mine as it is.'

He sighed, not visibly put out. But was it true? Was she happy? Luisa had forgiven Sandro things, he had forgiven her. They had learned when to bend. But there were limits: didn't there have to be? She had never slept with Enrico Frollini, although there had been a time when he'd wanted her to. She had never slept with anyone but Sandro.

'What about the children?' she said. To her surprise she had almost finished her drink. She felt a warmth, a softening, as she sat back against the velvet upholstery. Beyond the large windows the piazza twinkled in the twilight.

'Benedetta?' He was looking shifty now, undoing a button on his impeccably cut tweed jacket. Scottish tweed, Italian cut, he always specified. Avoiding her eye.

'We could start with her,' Luisa said. 'I was in the emergency room this morning and she was brought in on a stretcher. An overdose, apparently.' She spoke carefully, eyeing him, but she saw no shock or even surprise. 'It sounded like she was going to be all right,' and belatedly he murmured something like relief. 'I don't know what kind of drugs, I mean, whether it was sleeping pills or ...'

Enrico sighed. 'Probably tranquillisers,' he said. 'I know she's done it before. She's always been – sensitive. Delicate, if you like. Her mother despaired of her.'

'Always?'

He shrugged. 'Perhaps not as a teenager.' He hesitated, never enjoying a conversation where his age might come into it. 'Of course I hardly knew her then but – no. I remember her as a normal sort of adolescent. Parties, dressing up, boyfriends. All that.'

'So, it was marriage and settling down that did it?'

Frollini shrugged, evasive. 'Possibly. It doesn't suit everyone. Switzerland certainly doesn't suit everyone. I wasn't surprised when she came back.'

'All this time, though,' said Luisa, 'I thought she was still up there. You didn't say. Did they keep her under lock and key? And I hear she lost –' She broke off, not wanting Frollini to remember that Luisa too had lost a child, and the understanding looks that would entail. But she need not have worried: as usual Enrico showed no sign of having been listening properly.

'The whole business was a source of pain to her mother,' he said sententiously. 'Not all things may be talked about, you know.' Luisa opened her mouth to laugh at this, from him, but he was leaning forward across the little table, almost tipping the glasses, so close she could smell his Cuir de Russie. And he seized her hands. 'But what were you doing in the emergency room, *cara*?'

'That reminds me,' she said, gently withdrawing her hands from his to fish in her bag. 'I need to take a pill.' Seeing his eyes darkening with alarm at the sight of the antibiotics, Luisa extended her leg to show him the bandage, which she had reapplied more discreetly. 'I cut myself on some barbed wire.' He recoiled, grimacing, and she tucked her leg back under the table, satisfied with the effect. She signalled for a glass of water.

'What about the son,' she said, sitting back, casual. 'Benedetta's stepbrother?'

'Bartolini?' Frollini appeared indifferent. 'I don't know the man. He runs the estate for her now. He spent a little while in the fashion business at the beginning but it didn't suit him. A dilettante like his father.' He sniffed and Luisa detected a tinge of jealousy: the younger man, turning up his nose at the rag trade.

'Well, it does take talent,' she said warmly. 'Fashion, I mean.'

'I suppose it does.' Frollini was mollified. 'And he's protective of his sister. Half-sister.' A pause: they both sipped their drinks. 'It can't be easy, not being the heir,' Frollini conceded.

Luisa sat up straighter. 'No?'

'Well, he wasn't the prince's son, was he? I imagine the money goes to Benedetta.' He shrugged. 'Perhaps Mamma has made provision for him. His own father certainly left them on their uppers until Salieri came along.'

Luisa took a sip of her drink, thoughtful. 'He doesn't seem to hold it against her,' she said. 'Benedetta, I mean. He was really distressed when I saw him in the hospital.'

Frollini nodded, complacent. 'Well, half-blood's better than no blood relation I suppose. Neither of them has anyone to pass it on to. I'm sure I don't know whose hands that property will end up in. Imagine that.'

There was a silence during which Luisa knew he was contemplating his own two plump sons and five grandchildren with satisfaction. She moved on before he got on to looking sorrowfully at her.

'I expect you've heard about what happened down there,' she said carefully. 'The murders? Was there any connection between them? The Salieri and the – hippies?'

Enrico didn't reply: instead he sat back and then the waiter was there beside them, bending in his long white apron with her water and gone again in a quiet flurry.

'I have heard about it,' he said. 'I don't think the son was around when those people lived at Sant'Anna.' He looked pale, suddenly and uncharacteristically.

Breaking her rule again, she took his hand, impulsively. 'It's awful, isn't it?' she said with feeling, a chill right around her heart as she remembered the damp air, the smell of the leaves, the deep cleft in the valley. 'It's horrible. Those bodies. I knew her, you see. I knew her.'

'You knew her?' Frollini was aghast. 'But how could you have?'

'Oh, very briefly,' she said, 'very briefly. She wasn't someone you forgot, though.'

Enrico Frollini settled back on the banquette, but he looked shaken. 'She mustn't hear about it,' he said, 'the Princess Salieri. It would upset her to hear about it.'

'But she must have already heard about the murders?' Luisa wondered if he'd lost his marbles. How could it be kept from her? And why? Because her long-dead husband had been sleeping with one of them? The only man Sandro had mentioned was Gorgone, Nielsson's lover.

Could it be him? Enrico must know something. But she hesitated. He'd taken his hand out of hers. Usually it was the other way about. His face changed, as though something was dawning on him for the first time. 'I heard Sandro's involved with it,' he muttered, avoiding her eye. 'Perhaps he could just ... keep them out of it?'

Of course, Enrico Frollini would know about Sandro's involvement. He knew everything. Or perhaps it was common knowledge; Florence was so much a village. Sandro was probably talking to the old woman right now. Not for the first time, Luisa wished she'd never embarked on this ridiculous deception. She wanted to talk to Sandro; her hand crept to her mobile in her pocket.

'Yes, he's been called in,' she said, but Enrico had sat back, ashen, and was waving a hand, weakly impatient, at her.

'Never mind,' he said. 'Forget I said anything.'

Holding on to the mobile still, she allowed him to pay the bill. She waited, saying nothing more, eyeing him as he patted down his pockets, retrieved his glasses, put away his wallet, fumbled for his coat, and his colour returned.

He was almost back to normal as they said goodbye under

the lights, pulling on his silk-lined gloves, buttoning the lovely vicuna coat and then kissing her on both cheeks. Not lingeringly, though, and there was no embrace.

'Always a pleasure, Luisa,' he said. But as, walking away from him past the bright café terraces and towards the painted carousel, she turned quickly back to see him still standing there, Luisa had the distinct impression Enrico Frollini had never been so glad to see the back of her.

She got out the phone and dialled.

Chapter Thirteen

T HEY CLIMBED OUT of the car without a word, as if both in agreement that the car had become stuffy, but they weren't going anywhere. His hands in his pockets, not looking at Sandro but at the trees on the other side of the road, Pietro finally spoke.

'Well,' he said uneasily, 'I can see why – you've kept quiet about it.'

Sandro was still taking gulps of the fresh damp air. They were standing outside Lotti's house, a squat stone dwelling side-on to the road. The village sat a little way above them, grey in the twilight. The sun had almost completely gone from the narrow valley: just the tips of the trees on the eastern ridge were golden in the dying rays. He felt curiously lightheaded. It was done. Pietro knew and despised him.

'It's all right,' said Sandro, stiffly. 'It's –' but Pietro's arm was around him, so sudden and forceful he almost lost his balance.

'You've got nothing – nothing – to be ashamed of,' said Pietro fiercely into his ear, before releasing him.

There was a sharp honk and they turned to see one of the blue buses that served the region round the bend below them. They paused, standing back against the car to let it pass in a hiss of oily exhaust.

'So,' said Sandro as it disappeared. 'We could add me to that list of suspects, couldn't we?' Jamming his hands in his pockets.

'I'd have Luisa in the frame before you,' said Pietro, half-smiling, but the words turned Sandro's heart over.

'She never – knew anything,' he said.

'If you say so,' said Pietro, shaking his head and smiling, just in time. 'Maybe we should put Gianna Marte on the list, too, what do you think?'

They turned towards Lotti's house.

The windows were all shuttered but one, either in error or because it simply didn't matter now the man was dead. In the small patch of garden there was a stake with a chain: he kept the dog outside. The dog that was now dead. He had liked the dog more than any human, and he'd left it outside. Not a sentimental man. Sandro turned to see Pietro watching him, and he moved along the side of the house towards the unshuttered window. Reluctantly he peered inside.

A sitting room. In the dim light its surfaces shone blue and empty. A coffee table. A kitchen corner with counter. A telephone. A cold, dead, place: hadn't Pietro said that? A place where a man sat alone, in silence And all around them the village was silent, and grey. Soon it would be dark. Sandro made a decision, and strode back to the car.

'We're going to La Vipera,' he said, before he could change his mind. 'And in the car. If we walk from here they'll see us.

They'll be wondering already by the time we get back down.'

Sant'Anna seemed deserted, though, as they bumped between houses along the potholed road, not a pedestrian, not a dog and all the windows shuttered.

'See?' said Pietro, peering through the passenger window. 'Ranks well and truly closed. Like getting blood from a stone getting more than a yes or no. Half the houses are derelict now, anyway. Kids moved to somewhere else, Germany or Canada or wherever, if they want more out of life than to sell wine to tourists.'

The bus was moving off from its stop in the small triangular piazza but there was no sign of any passenger having alighted. The benches under the piazza's dusty plane trees were unoccupied; the bar on the far side had no outside space for sitting, even if it hadn't become suddenly cool – the pavement was mean and narrow. But a light was on inside; the steamy windows were yellow. They drove on, slowly, not wishing to draw attention to themselves, and almost immediately they were out of Sant'Anna again.

The road that wound uphill out of the village was unlit, and a wind had got up, swaying the trees overhead. To either side of them the woodland was dense and full of movement, between dark and deeper dark and probably boar. Then there was a big old gateway half-overgrown, a bend, a smallholding set back under trees, a ramshackle house with a small lit window.

'Maria Clara Martinelli's home,' said Pietro. 'We can call on her on the way back, right?' Sounding like he was trying to keep his spirits up.

'Sure,' said Sandro tightly.

He'd never told anyone about that late afternoon with Johanna Nielsson, the sun streaming through a window upstairs in the old house and voices from downstairs as she knelt in front of him. The sound from downstairs of Baratti browbeating the Italian girl. And the panic in Sandro's breast at all of it, banging like a bird in a chimney. Keeping it quiet all that time, and then when he brought it out like that, sitting in his stuffy car by a country road, it looked such a small thing, insignificant in this day and age. These days eight-year-old boys know what porn is.

And yet. He had known it was wrong: whatever Pietro said, he had known it then and he knew it now. He couldn't judge other men.

Around a corner and there was the place itself. La Vipera. Oblique to the road, facing up the valley just as he remembered it, blind and obstinate with its back to the world. The flank set in against the hillside was half-covered with ivy now, the windows – that window, which one had it been? Afternoon sunlight seemed an impossibility; perhaps he'd imagined it – without glass, their frames rotting, some gone completely.

He was out of the car and walking fast towards it without waiting for Pietro. From the front door the tatters of police tape fluttered in the strange wind that had picked up just at sunset, a wind apocalyptic under the reddening sky that blew Sandro's hair up in tufts and flapped at his trouser-legs. Behind him, Pietro called something he didn't hear.

Sandro felt cold as he came into the deeper shadow at the door and caught a horrible whiff of decay and urine beneath the clean smell of leaves. The door, rotten at the hinges, gave easily under his hand, and he was inside.

This. *This* is where it came from. As if the house was a well of darkness. Sandro knew it immediately as none of Pietro's men could have known it. This place began a chain of events that ended with a man's head in a dead woman's lap in a mean little hut.

His eyes were still unable to process the dim space he entered, yet Sandro's brain still held its layout. A broad tiled hall, a wide staircase, kitchen to one side, salon to the other, bedrooms upstairs. Bedrooms, each with mattresses on the ground, things hanging like cobwebs, decorative things from far-off countries, cloth birds, dreamcatchers. He felt something and turned around and saw it was Pietro.

'Did you do forensics in here?' said Sandro, and Pietro hesitated.

'Not really,' he said and they both looked around at the same moment. 'We checked it over. You might have expected it to have been used, kids or someone kipping down a night, but there wasn't anything. No beer cans, no dirty magazines. And no obvious sign of any violence in here, no break-in.' He cleared his throat. 'No blood.'

'You wouldn't have had to use violence to break in, though,' said Sandro, half to himself, the rotten wood from the front door still dusty on his fingertips. 'And as for blood – did you do light source detection?'

Blood showed up black under powerful UV, some other bodily fluids – semen, for example – glowed, phosphorescent. Just asking the question made Sandro uneasy – he wasn't a police officer any longer so who was he to tell them their job, and he was so far behind the latest technologies – but Pietro was shaking his head.

'Lotti was definitely killed where we found him,' he said. 'And we –' he hesitated '– we're pretty sure she was too. There was some animal interference and insect life with – the body – that would imply it hadn't been inside all that time.'

'I think it happened in here,' said Sandro, without knowing that was what he was going to say but quite sure as the words came out that they were true. 'It began here. I don't know when, of course.' He turned his head. 'Maybe forty years ago.'

Pietro opened his mouth then closed it again. 'All right,' he said cautiously. 'But there was an awful lot of her blood at the scene.' He coloured and Sandro knew he was embarrassed, thinking his partner was losing it. That this was all just a big mistake. 'But if you –'

Sandro held up a hand to him. 'Look,' he said, more brusquely than he meant, 'do you mind if I go upstairs on my own a moment?'

If Pietro said something – anything – about crystal balls or sixth sense, Sandro was out of there. He was uneasy enough about it himself, this sensation that had come unasked, had no idea if it was guilt or superstition. But Pietro just looked at him then pulled the bag he'd brought around his body, a flat nylon satchel, and extracted a torch. Sandro looked at it. 'It happens to be UV,' Pietro said, sheepish. 'But also, it's dark up there.'

As Sandro pocketed the torch, Pietro took a hurried step back, away from him, to the threshold, as if he needed the air. Sandro began to climb. On the wooden stairs as he drew up to the level of the first floor he heard something, an odd whistling, almost groaning, and paused, waiting, listening. He turned and saw that Pietro had stepped outside and the doorway stood open and empty.

The wind. The light was strange in here, dark yet not quite dark; the odours were unusual. Sandro kept climbing. The last time he had walked up these stairs, Johanna Nielsson had been ahead of him, her narrow hips swaying in something long and tattered. He couldn't have said he found her beautiful, even, but she had mesmerised him. Her large light eyes, her narrowness, her cracked pale lips.

And he was on the landing, feeling the wooden ball at the top of the banister under his hand. She'd turned here, a finger to her lips. Lucia Grenzi in the kitchen with Baratti, shouting at him in Italian, *porco maiale*: she was in the Dolomites running a ski school now, Gorgone had said. Was it even possible that the women that had been here had dissolved back into normal lives? Martine Kaufmann turning away and walking into another room as Nielsson held her hand out to him.

He shouldn't have taken it.

The wind rattled something and he could feel the breeze on his face. No glass left in these windows, loose in their frames. He wouldn't go into that room yet.

He stepped into the doorway opposite him. A large room with a single window in the back wall, a black square that emanated chill: a great piece of plaster hung down from the ceiling between the rafters and the room was empty, not a stick of furniture. Sandro stood a moment and let his eyes adjust to what little light there was, filtering up from the hall behind him, then closed them to set it as it was, as it had been. Back then there had been a chair, a small table and three big mattresses on the floor.

People came and went, didn't they? There had been visitors.

He heard a small sound from outside and opened his eyes. The crunch of footsteps on gravel: he stiffened, then relaxed. Pietro walking around the house. Sandro backed out of the room and turned to his right. The room that faced up the valley: like the first, it was quite empty. The wind must be eddying in the valley because in here it rattled the old shutters, one of them hanging askew from the frame. Sandro stepped over to the window and pushed the shutters back to see that the sky above the ridge at the head of the valley had turned a deep electric blue; the wind roared in the trees. Pietro must have heard the shutters because he appeared around the side of the house from the back. His face was very pale in the gloom.

'All right?' he called up, his voice sounding thin.

'Give me another minute or two,' said Sandro, his own voice carried away unearthly on the wind, but Pietro seemed to hear and nodded. Sandro stepped back into the room. This one he had more trouble remembering – it shifted around him somehow. He left the shutters open for the light they admitted. Something odd about the irregular shape of the room, and then he understood that there would have been a fireplace in one corner, above the kitchen, but it had been removed or sealed up. He stepped over to the place and tried to remember if it had been like that before, and failed.

For a moment he felt a kind of despair, tinged with fear: they were too old to go back. Old women, old men. All too old. And the fear grew. *Please*, he thought, *please, let me give up. Give it up.*

But he turned as if her hand was still in his and he was following. He stepped across the landing and into the room she'd let him into. Two large windows, one of them shutterless so the air and what was left of the light came in. He'd stood here, looking around at the floor, a sea of quilts and clothing, mattresses, but he had stopped counting now; everything had slowed since he came into this room.

Then she had put her hand on him.

She'd tugged at his trouser button, his newly issued pale-blue and maroon uniform trousers, one hand down there and another at his neck, pulling his face towards hers, and her body touching his, the nipples touching him through the fabric of her shirt. She had been wearing – and he could remember it now as though it was still there between his body and hers – a thin blouse of pale blue, something like muslin, almost transparent it was so light, undone to her breastbone, and he had stared and sweated against her and stood there as Baratti's voice, lower now downstairs, insinuating to whatever girl he was grilling, filled his ears. Jeering, taunting him: *call yourself a man?*

His erection had sprung up, unbidden, treacherous, because when you were a boy that was what happened, and her hand had gone down to it and he'd heard himself make a sound – not a groan, a sound more high-pitched and desperate, or at least that was how he had heard it, over the roar of blood in his ears. She had knelt down in front of him and he had felt the hair go up on his head as she put him in her mouth.

Pleasedontpleasedontpleasedont.

And he'd stumbled back. Too soon for her, too late for him, spilling himself on her hand, making an incoherent sound, a sob, and she laughed at him. She had laughed.

Never a boy to put it about, never, Sandro had been a shy

young man. He had loved his mother and father and had begun to love Luisa, to love her way of holding his hand diffidently, of picking it up at regular intervals and lacing her small fingers between his. That had been the extent of their intimacy. He had no way of understanding what Johanna Nielsson had done to him.

She had said something to him as she pressed against him that had sounded like her explanation but it wouldn't come back to him now: it sat like a cobweb in the corner of his brain, a sticky filament waiting to settle on his skin if he took one step too far.

Johanna Nielsson's skin as she had stood, wiping her hand, and pressed herself hard against him, murmuring something. The smells of grass and incense and warm unwashed skin, of dead leaves and the soft silt of sluggish rivers.

And then she'd come to find him in the city, to taunt him; she'd stood on tiptoe in her bare feet in the Uffizi's courtyard and kissed him, and he hadn't been able to stop her. He'd wiped his mouth, again and again, but too late. Love her? He hated her.

He managed to get out of the room, his boots loud and clumsy on the stairs, and registered Pietro's face in the hall, less pale now, his head turning as Sandro pushed past him to get outside before – before –

Before he vomited, a sour spatter of minestrone across the stone step and the gravel beyond it.

'Sandro?' Pietro was talking to him, Sandro could feel a hand on his shoulder as he bent, hands planted on his knees, and vomited between them again, but for a second he was blind, and his old friend's voice seemed distant over the sea-roar in his ears.

At last it felt safe to stand up. He wiped his mouth with the back of his sleeve and didn't look down at what he'd done.

'I didn't want – in there – I didn't want to contaminate the ...' He couldn't quite finish the sentence. Pietro patted him helplessly on the shoulder, peering uneasily into his face.

He'd told Pietro. But hadn't. He'd made it sound like – it had been something men do, not *boasting* of it, he couldn't have done that, but dismissing it. A joke, an oddity, a titbit for the locker room. A blow job. He couldn't say, *I couldn't stop her.* He couldn't say, *it made me cry.*

He swallowed, bitterness in his throat, and took the three, four unsteady steps away from Pietro over to his car. There was a bottle of water in the glovebox and he drank it thirstily, standing in the open car door. He'd cried, that night, in the lavatory at his parents' house, and he had wondered if his mother had heard him because she had stood a long time behind his bedroom door that night, without coming in.

It had been his last visit to La Vipera – until today.

*

When he saw her name on the phone's screen, he thought, *why did I never tell her? I never told anyone. Luisa.*

'Darling,' he said, composing himself. They'd just pulled up outside Martinelli's house 'We're going to be late tonight, is that all right?'

She had something to tell him: a couple of things.

'Hold on,' he said, because she was talking and he was still half in a daze. 'Say that again? You think what?'

She'd been talking to Frollini. The thought, which once might have nettled him, passed over him like water.

'I think the old prince, Salieri, might have been having an affair with the man – Gorgone.'

Sandro made himself digest this information but it said nothing to him in connection with this case. The old prince was long dead. Was it plausible? Yes. Gorgone – Gorgone was enough of a narcissist to take all homage offered him. And enough of an operator to know a golden goose when he saw one.

'And Frollini doesn't want me to go upsetting the princess.'

He can whistle, Sandro thought but didn't say.

Luisa sounded tired. 'Well, I did wonder if Benedetta might have had some kind of traumatic revelation back then. Witnessed something between her father and Gorgone. That could explain … all sorts of things. And did you know –' she hesitated '– she inherits the estate? Did you know that? Not her half-brother?'

'Well, I suppose,' Sandro mumbled, 'I suppose so, I haven't thought about it. And she's no children, has she? Who gets it if –?' He stopped.

A small noise, a sigh, a clearing of the throat. 'She might leave it to her half-brother, although he's older than her so …' A sigh again. 'Or the husband, wherever he is. Anyway. Maybe it's just Enrico gossiping. You know he's obsessed with money.'

Sandro said nothing, thinking only dully that she was probably right. None of this amounted to a motive for luring Johanna Nielsson back here and murdering her and an old butcher, or not yet.

'I'll leave something out for you,' Luisa ventured into the silence. 'A bit of soup?'

'Oh, don't worry,' he said quickly, and regretted it immediately. 'I mean, I don't know when I'll be in – only if it's no trouble.'

'It's no trouble, sweetheart,' she said.

How could he tell her, after all this time? He couldn't. Wasn't coming back here enough?

Pietro was standing with his back to him, looking up at the windows and the half-collapsed roof. The chimney halfway along the end of the house facing up the valley, there where the fireplaces must be. The kitchen below it which would have had a chimney corner for grilling and above it a fireplace in the coldest bedroom. Sandro stepped away from the car and back towards the house. He felt lighter, suddenly, or at least emptier.

'There's something,' he said, pausing beside Pietro, nodding towards the house. 'Just one more thing.'

Chapter Fourteen

B Y THE TIME THEY got to Martinelli's it was quite dark, and they had had to brush down the plaster dust from their clothes before they climbed the unlit path up the hillside to her front door. A yellow light shone under the scrawny trees and from behind one shuttered window.

It was seven thirty. They'd been at La Vipera an hour and a half.

'Do you think Marte was telling the truth about the princess being out?' said Sandro.

Pietro shrugged. 'It's far too late to call on her now, anyway,' he said cheerfully.

'But we *will* talk to her. Right?' said Sandro. He didn't want anyone, not even Pietro and certainly not Frollini, suggesting that they might bow to the desire of the nobility to be kept out of any dirty business on the borders of their land.

'Sure,' said Piero. He'd cheered up, which soothed Sandro. He didn't like Pietro itchy. 'And we'll get forensics up here first thing. I mean,' he pondered, 'that thing. In the fireplace. It's almost certainly just ... nothing – dead bird, whatever – and too late to call them out now, but to be on the safe side.'

A blocked up chimney breast concealing nothing more than a little pile of ancient cinders.

Sandro nodded. It seemed like a strange dream now they were on their way back to civilisation, and it gave Sandro a shiver. Something had sent him back inside the building, something he didn't quite understand, except that in that upstairs room there had been a fireplace forty years ago, he remembered it distinctly, an upstairs fireplace, and now there was none. So back in they'd gone.

Using a crowbar Sandro kept in the boot of the car, with a shared sense of transgression – Pietro stopping, rubbing his head, expressing anxiety at regular intervals – they had managed to open a hole in the plaster about the size of a football. Big enough to shine the torch through, the UV torch that showed black where blood had been, black fading to grey as it aged. They'd both leaned abruptly forwards, because blood there had been, a stain on the brick of a hearth. The beam of the torch moving, picking up a filament of dusty cobweb.

'Dead bird,' Pietro had said, after a long moment in which he looked intently, then handed the torch to Sandro. Because that was what became clear, the dessicated splay of a wing half-glued to the brick by putrescence, on the edge of the dark splash. Dust and bird bones and shards of pottery – tiles or a chimney pot.

A dead bird.

They climbed now. The ground under the trees was littered with junk: an old chest freezer, the rusting shell of a car. Martinelli was single – a widow – and Sandro told himself she had no one to help her with the place. Or tell her what to do. With trepidation, the image in his head of the stern broad face with its blunt fringe, Sandro stood back and let Pietro ring the bell.

'Who talked to her last time?'

'Me and Panayotis,' said Pietro. 'She came into the station. And answered everything we asked her but, somehow, we came out of it none the wiser. She found the bodies, recognised the bodies, was here the whole summer and saw nothing.'

They waited, and finally the door opened. Maria Clara Martinelli seemed quite unsurprised to see them. She accepted the explanation for Sandro's presence as a plain-clothes colleague and stepped back to admit them without objection. When they followed her inside, Sandro could see why it had taken her so long to answer the door: it looked as though she was in line for a hip operation. She walked with a roll, like an old sailor in her wide jeans and sweater.

The house was like a Swiss chalet inside – grubby red-and-white gingham and hearts cut into wooden cupboards – and on every surface a cat. Two sat contented over folded paws on a large elderly sofa that had been laid with newspapers. Martinelli shooed them off fondly and began to remove the papers. One was the front page of a recent copy of *La Nazione*, covered with a large photograph of La Vipera.

'Sit,' she said and rolled off behind a breakfast bar in search of something. Sandro sat, watching Pietro gingerly follow suit, mouthing, *sorry*. Sandro just shrugged: what had he to be sorry about? To his abrupt surprise Sandro felt at home here. He found himself liking the woman with her square red face and her gruff manner. He liked her crowded, untidy warm house; he even liked her cats, although he could feel a sneeze coming on.

She came back with a bottle of walnut amaro and three tiny glasses. Sandro saw Pietro grimace, but they all accepted a dose of the treacly black stuff. She seemed to know that this was all rather unorthodox – two policemen out of uniform, still lightly speckled with plaster dust – and to be supremely unbothered by the fact. Keen, indeed, to compound the unofficial nature of the visit by offering them alcoholic drinks.

He had always found *nocino*, the liqueur, very unpalatable, like cough syrup, and perhaps that was just as well as he had to drive home. He raised the glass. '*Salute!*' and took a sip, feeling suddenly, ridiculously cheerful. Pietro murmured something before replacing his glass on the coffee table between them.

There was an element of hysteria – Sandro was aware of that. But if anything was an antidote to La Vipera, damp, cold, smelling of ancient weed and incense and shadowy with ghosts, this place was it.

'Have you been alone long, Signora Martinelli?' he asked, the treacle-bitterness of the amaro on his tongue. It wasn't, actually, as bad as he remembered it. 'I know you are a widow. This place is a lot to manage, isn't it?'

'Oh, twenty years,' she said, eyeing him almost with amusement. 'But we help each other out here. And work –' she paused, and he thought she knew everything about him as she looked, this stout old woman in her man's clothes, knew how many afternoons he had spent twiddling his thumbs since work, actual work, had kicked him out '– work's good for the soul.' She smiled a broad smile, the tiny glass still untouched between her rough old fingers.

'It is,' said Sandro. There was a silence. Pietro looked at him as if he was beginning to regret this whole business.

Sandro sighed, the need to ask the questions weighing on him suddenly. 'You were born here,' he said.

She nodded. 'And I was here when they arrived, Miss Nielsson and her merry band.'

'How –?' Sandro paused, delicate suddenly.

'How old was I?' Her smile was still broad, a woman entirely lacking in vanity or dissimulation, but there was something, the merest shadow of something. Who didn't feel it when considering their younger selves? Weariness. Something like that.

'Twenty-two,' said Maria Clara Martinelli, 'if you mean when they arrived. Twenty-four by the time they left.' She was one year younger than him.

'I remember you,' said Sandro and her eyes, which he noticed only then were blue, turned darker. 'From the bar.' She nodded slightly, and he knew she remembered him, too, if not before, then now.

'Well,' she said, 'I suppose that's your job.'

When they'd gone in there on their way to the first call-out forty years ago, Baratti had thrown his weight around and got nowhere, asking who'd used the phone. 'Safe to say there was no love lost,' he said, remembering what Martine Kaufmann had said about Nielsson calling the barman a eunuch, 'between the bar staff and La Vipera?'

She shrugged, eyeing him. He raised the little glass to his lips but to his surprise he found it was empty. He set it down carefully on the low table and a cat appeared by his hand, rubbing against his wrist. He patted it, forgetting that cats didn't like that, and it writhed out from under his hand and was gone.

Maria Clara Martinelli seemed entirely relaxed. 'I'm the only one left alive,' she said. 'A new guy runs the bar now.' She smiled. 'If you're looking for suspects.'

'It must have been a shock,' Sandro said, 'finding the bodies.' She looked down at her hands, her glass still full, then up again, and he could see only frankness in her gaze. 'I've seen dead things many times,' she said. 'The woods are full of dead things. Obviously a human being is different –' She hesitated. 'But – can I be honest with you?'

'Of course,' put in Pietro, eager, and they both looked at him.

'Johanna Nielsson never struck me as much of a human being. Between us. That is a shocking thing to say. That some humans are better than others? Maybe. I didn't like her. I thought she was immoral. Another thing we don't say.'

'Immoral,' murmured Pietro, turning the word over. He was beginning to enjoy this too, Sandro could tell. Maria Clara Martinelli took up the bottle and leaned over their glasses. Pietro had finished his too. An inquiring look: Pietro hastily covered his glass with his hand but Sandro nodded.

'So when you found her dead you were –?'

'Well, we could say, I wasn't surprised to find her murdered, even after all this time.'

'Because she was immoral?'

'Because she aroused strong feelings in people. Because she didn't care.' Was it his imagination or did her eyes slide over Sandro as she said it? He took a sip and grimaced.

'And what about Giancarlo Lotti?' he said, sliding in the

question. 'That was a shock for you. You must have known him your whole life.' Mildly.

She shrugged. 'We bought our meat in the next village,' she said.

'Had you had a disagreement with him?' Again she shrugged. 'Miss Marte says you had.'

She rolled her eyes. 'That one,' she said. 'So you've talked to her. She's sly. Didn't you think she was sly?'

'She said you and he had had a row recently,' said Sandro quietly, catching Pietro's eye.

Martinelli knocked back her drink at last, wiping her mouth with the back of a hand and setting the glass down. 'Lotti was a bastard who beat his wife. Come on, should I pretend I liked him?'

'His wife died ten years ago,' said Pietro, and she turned that look on him.

'Who forgets?' she said.

'Did he kill her?' said Pietro. 'I mean, between us?'

She shook her head. 'She died of cancer.'

'She have any relations?' said Pietro.

Martinelli shook her head again. 'She wasn't from here.'

Which would be why no one had said anything. Sandro felt his spirits dampen abruptly at the understanding and he set his glass back down half-empty.

'Someone *did* say something at the time,' Martinelli said, looking at him as if she could read his mind, those frank blue eyes. She *was* reading his mind. 'I mean, you may as well know because someone will tell you. *I* told him to lay off her.'

'Ah,' said Sandro.

'And the circumstances?' said Pietro quickly. Sandro could see a flush at his neck, and he would be embarrassed that none of this had come out in the police station.

'It was a year or so before she died. She came into the bar for a drink at nine o' clock one morning – and I don't mean a coffee – and she had bruises round her neck as if he'd tried to strangle her. So I took off my apron and marched down the street to his shop and shouted at him. I was only annoyed there weren't any customers in there because Lotti wasn't popular, not even before the big supermarket in the valley got a fresh meat counter. People have their ways of showing they don't like a person.'

Sandro caught a sideways glance from Pietro and he knew what it meant. This was going round in circles. There was still nothing to connect Lotti and Nielsson beyond their having lived in Sant'Anna at the same time.

'So you were running this place and still working at the bar?' Sandro asked. She nodded. 'You were working there forty years ago, when I last came into this village, weren't you?' She nodded again and he leaned forwards, elbows on his knees.

'I hear Nielsson insulted your boss, called him a *cornuto* or something.'

'A eunuch,' said Maria Clara, looking him in the eye. 'Similar but not the same,' and she sighed. 'She had a thing about that. Men and their dicks. Poor old Massimiliano.'

The memory of Nielsson's hand on him sat there and it came to him she'd been like a veterinarian examining an animal, nothing personal in it.

'So,' he said, aware of Pietro's impatience, 'you were working in the bar when we were called in. And back then there was a phone booth in the bar, am I right?'

'There was.'

'Did it get much use?'

'Oh, yes,' said Martinelli promptly. 'There were only a handful of telephones in the village.'

'And back then, if I remember rightly,' of course he remembered – it felt like yesterday, 'there was a counter at the till that said the caller had used however many *scatti*, units, and he would pay at the till.'

'He or she, yes.'

'But it was a man,' said Sandro carefully. 'A man called us anonymously from the bar on that day in September, late summer, a day just like this, an afternoon, to say that La Vipera was being used as a brothel with under-aged girls.' She gave the slightest shrug. 'We found no evidence that that was true,' he said. 'Do you think it was true?'

She made a gruff sound in her throat. 'I don't think they took money for it,' she said, watching him.

'Is that why nobody seemed to notice who was using the *cabina telefonica* that afternoon? Because you all wanted someone to go and see what was going on up there? You wanted the foreigners called out?' She said nothing. 'Do you know who made the phone call?' It was time to stop all this.

Martinelli leaned back on the lumpy divan. Out of nowhere, the soft grey streak of a cat leapt and was on her knee. She lowered a hand to it gently.

'Of course I know,' she said at last, her broad fingers finding the cat's throat and tickling. 'I remember thinking, what's he doing in there? Because they *had* a phone, you see, they were among the few, for the business I suppose, and back then business was good. People ate meat back then, people had money and meat was good for you, back then.' There was a silence in which the cat's purr was startlingly loud, a rumble, a train in a tunnel.

'They had a phone, and so why would they be using the public phone box, unless for anonymity?' Sandro was patience itself: why jump to the conclusion before her? It was clear who she was talking about. 'But of course, no one's anonymous in the village bar, are they?'

There was the faint trace of a smile on Martinelli's lips, but her eyes were sad. 'They're dead now, so what does it matter?' she said. Weary.

'Lotti,' said Sandro, eager at last. 'That's who, isn't it? Giancarlo Lotti made that call.'

She smiled again, and then she shook her head.

*

'We're eating with mum and dad,' said Enzo almost before she'd crossed the threshold. 'I hope you don't mind?'

'Who's cooking?' she said, dumping her backpack on the hall floor. 'Me or your mum?'

He'd called Giuli as she stood on the pavement outside the clinic and she'd picked up with relief at the excuse to turn her back on Ragno. Helmet swinging, she'd walked towards the *motorino*, calculating that she'd still have time to catch the cobbler on the Via del Parioncino before he pulled down his shutter.

'I'm just leaving the clinic,' she'd said, knowing he was checking up on her. 'I've got one or two things to deal with and then I'll –' But it didn't seem to be just checking up on her.

'I'm home already,' he said. 'Why don't you come back now?' And hearing the anxiety in his voice she had just said yes.

They'd have said, wouldn't they, if she looked as ill as Ragno? She had peered at herself reluctantly in the bike's wing mirror and thought she looked all right.

'Mum's cooking,' said Enzo now. 'She said – she said they hadn't seen us in ages and –'

'I'll just get changed,' said Giuli. She didn't want to interrogate him: he was prone to feeling guilty at the drop of a hat, and it was true, she hadn't felt up to going over there the last time Rosetta had asked them. That evening she'd come in from work and just fallen asleep on the sofa.

Enzo's parents – Rosetta and Fausto – had moved to be closer, from their rambling old house in the hills halfway to Umbria to a little flat out towards Settignano, twenty minutes away. They'd given most of the proceeds from their old home to Enzo to go towards this place, their modern box with its balcony that Giuli loved so much.

Enzo was quiet on the journey, driving even more carefully than usual. They'd bought a cake from the pastry shop on Viale Europa and Giuli balanced it on her knee. Once or twice he opened his mouth to say something, but didn't.

The little flat had all the possessions that had filled their old farmhouse crammed into it: samplers and china ducks and display plates and even the curtains that Rosetta had embroidered herself. They sat at the kitchen table, hemmed in by it all, as

Rosetta heaped enough food for an army in front of them.

Pappardelle with ragu, fennel sausages with potatoes, a huge dish of beans, Rosetta fussing to and fro and piling up the plates. Giuli loved Rosetta, who had never, ever seemed anything but delighted with her daughter-in-law, although Giuli knew she had been told about her past. Who'd want her only child married to a woman like Giuli? Ex-addict, ex-hooker and past childbearing, the perfect bloody package. Enzo said when he'd told her she'd just flapped her hands a bit and said she knew he'd only choose the right woman. So when they went for dinner, Giuli always made a point of eating everything Rosetta put on her plate, and she was obediently forking her way through the beans when she noticed that she was the only one. Enzo was pushing potatoes round his plate, Rosetta had had no more than a tablespoon of pasta on hers and most of it was still there and old Fausto in his knitted waistcoat, at the head of the table, was sitting like a statue with his cutlery in his hands, his face stricken.

Giuli laid her fork down and gave Enzo a sharp look. He gave her a pleading one back: he doesn't know either, she thought. He knows something's wrong but he doesn't know what.

Then out of nowhere, Fausto slapped his hands on the table. 'I'm sorry, Rosetta,' he said. 'We must tell them.'

Behind him, Rosetta paused halfway to the sink, frozen, a dish in her hands. A tear sprang, rolling down one of her old cheeks, and she was helpless to dab it away.

Oh shit, thought Giuli, *oh shit oh shit*, and her hand crept out to Enzo's. He didn't seem to notice: he was looking at his mother. 'Mamma?' he said.

Fausto stood up and took the dish from her. 'Your mother –' He set the dish down and gently, tenderly, put his arms around her. 'Your mother has a tumour.'

Inside his arms, Rosetta rubbed the tear away with a shrug of her shoulder and looked up at her husband, patient. They were both so small, suddenly, these wiry old people, both so stoical – but so fragile. Giuli tightened her grip on Enzo's hand, knowing, *feeling* what he felt in the sickening clench of her own gut. He turned to look at Giuli and for a second he hardly seemed to recognise her. 'A tumour?' he said and she could hear the effort he made to keep his voice calm.

'It's one of those –' Fausto made a sound of helplessness, almost exasperation. 'The pancreas. I'm not even quite sure where that is. I did think – I asked and asked. I thought there would be an operation, treatment, you know. But they can't. Apparently there are some cancers that still –' And then with a sound it all seemed to leave him, to deflate him. 'They say they can't operate.'

From that moment the evening turned. It was as though the little warm kitchen to which the old pair had transplanted themselves for Giuli and Enzo's sakes was a bunker, and it was the end of the world. Fausto led Rosetta gently back to the table.

There were details, more details: a minor operation to relieve or forestall the symptoms – itching, jaundice, sickness; there were some medicines that could help too. Fausto emphasised the positives and did not say that these things were all temporary. He didn't need to.

At one point Rosetta simply, quietly got back up out of her seat and went on with the clearing and washing up, and

Giuli helped her. When it was done she clasped Giuli, a quick second – they'd never been people for big demonstrations of anything – and Giuli felt the softness of her old cheek against hers and the hand patting her as if she was the one needing consoling.

'You're worn out,' said Giuli, and as she said it her own tiredness – temporarily kept at bay by the fear of all this, the awful fear of seeing Enzo suffer, a monstrous outrage she wanted to batter at with her hands – settled back on her shoulders like a great weight, and all it brought with it. She'd forgotten her afternoon in the clinic, but now it returned with a vengeance, the intrusion of another world into this warm one, a world none of them wanted to live in, that cold white world of medicine and doctors and machines. If she, Giuli, was ill too. Enzo – who would there be for Enzo?

'Giuli's right,' said Enzo, getting up, and he was there between them, resting his heavy head on her shoulder a second like a child, except that now she was so much smaller than him. And straightening, looking her in the eye, 'Mamma. Get to bed. Are you sleeping?'

Rosetta shrugged, her eyes bright with unshed tears. 'I'll get her to sleep,' said Fausto gruffly, taking her hand. 'Look, these young ones,' he said, gesturing towards Giuli, who felt heavy and bloodless as marble suddenly, swaying beside them. 'We've tired them out – they don't make them like us these days, do they?'

At the door, Fausto said quickly, quietly, 'It might be a year.' Rosetta was in the kitchen, in her easy chair, hands folded in her lap, doing nothing.

'No more –?' said Enzo, and Giuli wanted to cringe away

into a corner, to throw herself from a window rather than hear the tremor in his voice, but she couldn't. The time for self-pity was long gone. 'No more than that?' he said, recovering himself.

'It might be less,' said Fausto. 'She knows. It will probably be less.'

At home, under the covers, she held him, tight, for a long time until at last he slept.

*

'You asleep?' His whisper was in her ear. Luisa smelled something on his breath and stirred.

Well, if she had been, his clattering around in the kitchen would have woken her. Stumbling against a chair before he turned the light on, the cupboard opening, the tap running.

But Luisa hadn't slept: she never could without him, although she wouldn't have told him so. The air outside was thickening, another storm brewing, they said, maybe tomorrow, maybe the day after. She opened an eye and saw the time on the bedside clock: midnight. Sandro moved away to the edge of the bed and she heard his boots come off, pushed into the corner. The clunk of his belt hitting the floor. A sigh, but not miserable, more weary. He slid in beside her and laid a warm hand on her side. His hands had always been warm except for that brief time, after the baby.

'How was it?' she said.

'We made progress,' he said, sounding tired. His cheek against the back of her neck, his breath sweet and medicinal. 'We did. We met the maid, old Princess Salieri's housekeeper, carer, Gianna Marte.' The ghost of a laugh. 'She's got a thing for

Pietro, poor sod. She said they were so unfriendly, no one would talk to her in the village, although she seems to be besotted with her employer, the son, whassisname.' A pause. 'Bartolini.' He rolled away. Sighed. We –' she heard a hesitation, no more than a check in his throat '– we went up to the house. To La Vipera,' he hurried on past that, 'and then we spoke to Martinelli.'

She thought about him going where she'd been, of that hillside where she'd walked with Bartolini and not told him. Still hadn't told him.

'But what about you, getting something out of that old rogue, for once, old Frollini?' His voice turning into a mumble.

'I've been thinking about it,' she said. Silence. 'I think it's got something to do with Salieri.' She had lain awake a long time turning that over before he got back, listening to the *motorini* whining past, the puff and hiss of the buses, bottles clattering into the dumpsters. 'Sounds like you're not going to get anything out of her anyway. The old lady.'

A thought occurred to Luisa, with trepidation. Not Sandro, but her? She could offer to go up and talk to her. But if she did, she would have to tell Sandro she'd been up there already and all that went with that. She held a sigh, let it out slowly and turned onto her back. She lay looking up at the ceiling in the dark. His hand had slid with the movement but stayed on her, flat now on her belly. 'I always knew,' she said, before she could stop herself. 'I always knew something had happened with her, with you and that woman. I knew you couldn't get her out of your head, all these years.' She ran out of breath, gulped, kept going. 'So I went up to Sant'Anna,' she said. 'I went because I wanted to make sure she was dead.'

She waited, in the silence. The long, unnatural silence in which she couldn't even hear him breathe extended and then, with a volcanic sound of upheaval, he was shifting, up and over on his side away from her. He snored.

Chapter Fifteen

'I'M NOT SURE,' SAID SANDRO INTO the phone, his hand cupped over it. 'She's just being funny with me.' It wasn't his imagination. Luisa had seemed on the point of saying something since they got up, but every time he looked at her, she looked somewhere else.

Pietro had called first thing and Luisa, who had just brought him a coffee in the bedroom, two sugars, standing there with it in her hands as he sat on the end of the bed in his underwear trying to get his sock on, had made an exasperated noise when he dropped the sock, ignored the coffee and grabbed for the phone.

He'd called after her. 'Darling?' He had the firmest impression she had something to say – although usually when Luisa wanted to say something she just said it, and forcefully. So he'd had to begin the conversation telling Pietro that, although, yes indeed, he was very fond of him, the *darling* had been directed at Luisa's retreating back.

He stood up, creaking, one sock on, and went to retrieve the coffee from where she'd left it.

'Women,' said Pietro at the other end of the line. 'Still, though. Still. That Martinelli, she came up trumps, didn't she? Manzoni is going to be pleased with you, my lad. We've got our link between Lotti and La Vipera.'

Maria Clara Martinelli had put them out of their misery almost immediately, as if she'd suddenly had enough of the game, the light gone out of her eyes.

'His father,' she'd said, 'Lotti senior. It was Giancarlo's dad I noticed going into the booth that afternoon, and I remembered thinking it was odd because they had a phone of their own. Maybe he didn't want his wife overhearing – she was a tartar, old Mrs Lotti – or maybe he was smart enough to know they could trace calls. He wasn't stupid, old Lotti.' And without asking, she'd poured them both another sticky black inch of *nocino*.

Pietro had shaken her hand on the doorstep, then Sandro, then Pietro had grabbed it again.

Passing back through the square, the bar had still been open and, seeing the lights, they'd pulled up. It had been empty, a twenty-something behind the counter, playing a game on his mobile, who could barely be bothered to look up when they came in. The look he gave them was vacant, then he seemed to recognise Pietro and nodded, setting his phone down reluctantly to make the coffee. In the corner the old phone booth was full of stacked toilet paper.

The kid set down the cups and picked his phone up again, incurious.

'Saw nothing, knows nothing,' said Pietro under his breath. 'Not even freaked by it. It's like two bodies found half a mile from here means nothing.' They drained the cups, gave a nod that wasn't acknowledged and were back on the pavement in under five minutes. 'I blame those little screens,' said Pietro, looking up into the black sky – not a star. The cloud was thick and low. 'People don't listen any more. They don't watch. See no evil, hear no evil, speak no evil.'

And in the car back, rattling down into the city, they were still so mellow with the liqueur and the breakthrough that they'd sat in silence, he and Pietro, each separately going over what it meant. There was a brief heavy rain shower as they came into the city, the old wipers straining, but Pietro roused himself to comment on how much cleaner it made the windscreen, which was true.

Almost as an afterthought, as if the grimy windscreen had reminded him, Pietro said, 'And the fireplace. Do we really want to call them out because we found a dead bird?'

A dead bird. Could that be all it was? It felt like something more, something sinister. But Sandro had just agreed. 'Sure. We'll see how we feel in the morning.' And the wipers had flogged back and forth in the silence that ensued, opening their fan-shape of clear glass in the murk.

He had no desire to go back to La Vipera at all, not by night, not by day, not with a full forensics team behind him, and he had had a premonition, there and then, that if he did go back, he'd be alone.

He'd dropped Pietro off and driven on, in to the dark avenue of trees under the slope up to San Miniato, where there was free parking, and walked back down in the dripping dark, towards the light.

Lotti and Nielsson.

They had their list of suspects, but what good was it? Means, motive, opportunity and Sandro's intuition – all of them lacking something. Princess Salieri, gaga. Benedetta Salieri, in hospital, even if you could imagine her strong enough to wield a knife. Prince Salieri, who was dead. Gorgone, who'd been in America in August.

The other women: Kaufmann and Grenzi and Mason. One busy with her painting and her church works, one somewhere in the mountains, the last in her seventies and in a commune on the other side of the world.

Maria Clara Martinelli, sitting in her house under the trees, freely admitting she hadn't gone anywhere all summer and disliked both victims. But to tie a woman up and stab her in the belly? What made someone do that? What terrible place did that hatred crawl from?

The deaths were different. He held to that fact, tenacious. Connected, but different.

Bartolini, the brother: on retreat with his sister. Away in Greece. Find out why.

He heard Pietro clear his throat on the other end of the line, waiting, and Sandro sighed. 'Old Lotti, the father, could have just hated foreigners,' he said. 'And hated free love. Plenty of people do, after all, and not just old farts in the country set in their ways.'

Free love. The idea made him pace towards the window, the phone held to his ear.

'But –' said Pietro.

'But I don't think it was just that, either,' said Sandro. 'I think –' He hesitated. 'I think we need to talk to Lotti's cousin. Didn't you say she was in San Frediano?'

He took down the address; they arranged to meet there. Then – who knew. Then back up to Sant'Anna, up to the big house. The princess and her children: the thought gave him a buzz he hadn't felt in a long time.

There was business to clear up, though, first. 'I was thinking,' he said.

'Yes?' said Pietro. Sandro looked down into the coffee dregs and as he looked up there was Luisa in the doorway, something in her dark eyes, and then she had turned back in to the kitchen. He heard the click of the gas as she put on another pot. Mind-reader.

He'd thought of it, in fact, as he went to sleep, Luisa saying something or other he hadn't listened to; in the grey dark of their bedroom he had thought of the inside of Lotti's house. The gleam of the fading light on its surfaces, the neatness of a butcher's parlour. And the telephone on the wall.

'The landline,' he said. 'Remember Martinelli saying she noticed Lotti senior making the call all those years ago because they had a landline?'

'Yes?' Pietro knew enough to let him go on.

'Lotti didn't have a mobile, right?'

'Right.'

'I mean, I know those lads know their job but – did you, did they check the landline? Incoming, outgoing calls, say, the last few months?'

A pause that lengthened, then Pietro cleared his throat. 'Ah. Yes. Well – I'm not sure about that. Let me check.'

The silence threatened to grow again: was this how it was going to be? Awkward silences? Not if Sandro could help it. He leapt in. 'Any joy yet on the licence plate?'

'Oh, that.' Pietro brightened audibly. 'Nielsson's camper-van. Yes, as a matter of fact. Road traffic information comes in in dribs and drabs, you know. Cameras captured it at a tollbooth coming on to the ringroad in Milan and off again forty minutes later. Late June. Heading east. It was issued with a fixed penalty notice in Bergamo, which was paid locally, immediately, in cash. That's all we've got so far, although numberplate recognition takes a while, especially with old vehicles. But probably between now and then she'd either been stationary or touring back roads. My money's on that.'

'Any images of the actual van?'

'One fuzzy picture. It's an old camper, turquoise trim, nothing special.'

Sandro grunted, and there was a silence.

It was still there between them: he regretted having told Pietro about Nielsson. He couldn't work out if Pietro had understood or not. How could he, when Sandro hadn't understood himself, not then, not even now. As if her hand had marked him, in a place no one else could see. He sighed and got his coat.

'Luisa?' She was in the bathroom, door closed. 'I'm off.'

She caught up with him at the door. 'Can't we sit down and have a proper talk?' she said, but he was so buzzed he just looked at her, almost blank, and she let him go. It wasn't until he was out in the street that the thought recurred. She *was* acting funny. She wasn't herself.

And as he set off, something Pietro had said last night about putting Luisa in the frame for Nielsson's murder before he'd put Sandro there came back into his head. He'd almost given Pietro their alibi – at the seaside in early August – before realising it was a joke. But had Luisa known? All those years ago, had she *known*? Sandro stopped, turned, looked up at the window. But he didn't go back and ask.

*

The cousin was an angular, hard-faced woman in a pinny who ran a hole-in-the-wall tobacconist's on Borgo San Frediano that Sandro had walked past a thousand times and never entered. Sandro hadn't smoked in twenty years, and he didn't buy every *tabachi*'s other money-spinner, lottery tickets; nor, he thought as he entered the tiny space behind Pietro, was he in the market for the china shepherdess figurines alternating with statues of the virgin that seemed to occupy every shelf.

'She says it'll have to be at work,' Pietro had said on the phone, calling him back. 'She can't take any time off.'

Flavia Lotti – the spinster daughter of Giancarlo's uncle on his father's side – stood grim-faced behind her racks of chewing gum and lottery tickets in her flowered pinny, against a backcloth of cigarette brands. The effect was enough to give anyone a migraine, even without the glare she was giving them. It occurred to Sandro that she hadn't closed the place for mourning, as would have been traditional even twenty years ago.

There was nowhere for them to sit. 'So, Miss Lotti,' said Sandro, having opened by commiserating with her for her loss, which courtesy she listened to stony-faced, 'when did you last see your cousin? Giancarlo?'

She shrugged. 'Ten years?' she said. 'No, eleven. At my father's funeral.'

Sandro was startled. They lived barely ten miles apart. 'You weren't a close family?' She made a face of distaste and said nothing. 'But you asked him to your father's funeral?'

She shrugged. 'I didn't ask him, he simply turned up.'

Sandro tried another tack. 'We're trying to establish a connection between him and the woman whose body was found with his.' And he saw something, just for a second, an unmistakable gleam. 'Do you know anything about her? Her name was Johanna Nielsson. Forty years ago, when you would have been –' he hesitated, guessing '– a teenager, perhaps, did you visit the family then? In Sant'Anna?'

And finally, there behind her barricade of packets and boxes, something shifted: Flavia Lotti took a step forwards so that she stood in the space where customers would pay. 'I never saw them,' she said. 'I had stopped going by then.' Her voice had a new quality, something throatier.

'But you used to?'

'Yes,' she said. 'He and I – when I was a child, five, six. Our parents thought it would be good for us. Giancarlo was eight years older than me.' She stopped, a silence that grew. It seemed in that moment hazardous to say anything. Pietro and Sandro exchanged glances and waited.

'I never married,' she said. Still they said nothing. And she burst out, not loud but fierce, under her breath, 'He was a filthy man. A filthy boy and a filthy man.' And then she ran out of breath. They waited a beat, then another, then she went on. 'I heard my parents discussing him: they had had words with his father. It wasn't me – I –' She gasped a moment, then seemed to reset herself; her face that had been bright with spots of colour

'What, though?' said Giuli. 'What's actually worrying you?'

A silence. 'I – I just got the idea that Luca Bartolini might him he saw me out there at Sant'Anna. Saw this madwoman ndering around.' A pause. 'Bartolini even said he remembered e from all that time ago at his sister's wedding. What if he ows I'm married to Sandro? The old princess knows I am.'

'I don't understand,' said Giuli. 'And isn't the old lady gaga?'

'He might – I might have messed up the investigation mehow. I don't know.'

'You just need to talk to Sandro.' Giuli tried to speak ently, but the truth was Luisa's fears and panic seemed to her nreasonable.

'Before he goes back up to Sant'Anna,' said Luisa, stubborn.

'Okay,' said Giuli. 'Leave it to me.'

But she had no clue. How did she know how Sandro was oing to react? Luisa had lied to him. That was a big deal. Luisa ever lied. Never panicked.

There was too much to think about. There was Enzo this morning, awake at five and staring at the ceiling. Pale as a ghost t the kitchen table.

'We'll get through it, my love. We'll get her through it.'

'She's going to die,' Enzo said, as if she hadn't understood, nd she put a hand gingerly on his shoulder.

'I know, darling,' she said.

And then he'd got up all in a hurry, leaving his plate and cup ntouched, grabbing his coat. 'Got to get to work.' Her hand alling back to her side, useless.

Giuli didn't have to ask herself if he'd kissed her goodbye: he dn't. Flying down the stairs, away from her. She'd gathered

on each cheek turned pale. 'It was that he had been seen visiting that house, for sex with those foreign women, and his father drew the line at that.'

Behind them the door pinged and they turned to see a fat woman pushing her way in. There wasn't room for all of them and for a moment they all stood there, unsure of what to do, until Pietro took the initiative and, with some jovial remark, edged sideways and out of the door. Sandro followed him.

On the pavement Pietro was bouncing on the balls of his feet. It was cold. He looked uncomfortable out of uniform. 'No wonder they had him in for the Monster killings,' he said. 'Thoroughly nasty piece of work by the sound of it.'

'So he molested her,' said Sandro.

Pietro sighed. 'She might have killed him herself,' he said.

Sandro nodded. 'You could hardly blame her,' he said. 'But Nielsson? She didn't even know what the woman looked like.' He chewed the inside of his cheek, wishing for another coffee. 'It's got to be someone who knew them both. If he was a regular visitor to La Vipera for sex, and Nielsson sanctioned it –' He paused, thinking. 'Would a woman kill someone, so long after, for rape?'

Pietro shrugged. 'You fancy asking one of the women in your life? My guess is – maybe. Depends.'

He was right. 'We've got a number for Mason, the woman in Canada?' said Sandro. 'And what about this mysterious Grenzi who runs the ski school in the Dolomites?'

'Ah,' said Pietro. 'Well. About her –'

But then the door swung outward viciously, almost knocking him into the road, and the fat woman emerged, giving them both a funny look.

'You were going to tell me something,' said Sandro, 'about the girl in the mountains. Grenzi.' Although of course she wasn't a girl any more, was she?

His phone buzzed in his pocket and he saw there was a missed call from Luisa.

'There was a message about Grenzi from the station,' said Pietro. 'I'll call them back from the car.'

'Why don't you do it now?' said Sandro.

*

Comes home to roost, thought Giuli, putting her phone away in the bright panelled splendour of Rivoire in the Piazza Signoria. *Doesn't it? All comes home to roost.*

Time had been when she had been the one to run to Luisa with her troubles. She'd depended on them too much. Over the years she'd been the one to take, taking love, taking their roof over her head, taking the job Sandro gave her, taking money, taking comfort and consolation. When she finally found the tears to cry for her own stupid, idle, hopeless mother, for the women she'd met in prison for murder herself, for the baby she was never going to have, Luisa's shoulder had been the one Giuli had cried on. Never mind that Luisa had lost a baby of her own, and even when they'd found out Luisa had breast cancer (Giuli, who had not even a vestige of belief, almost crossed herself whenever she thought of that day, six years past and no recurrence, God willing), Luisa had been the one to comfort Giuli, not the other way around.

And when Giuli had found Enzo, she'd started leaning on him, too. However much she'd told herself, don't depend, take

nothing for granted, it's not safe, she'd lean[...] stranger still, he hadn't seemed to mind.

But now it was her turn.

'Ey!' The square, grumpy old barman of Rivo[...] only a mother could love, shoved the little cup to[...] had a heart of gold, Giuli knew, and when she [...] together and smiled he scowled even harder, lik[...] old American gangster actors. But the tips of his e[...]

Giuli had just got her ticket at the cash desk a[...] across the counter when her phone went.

'I've been trying to get Sandro.' Luisa had sounde[...] unsettled. Even an edge of panic, and Luisa never p[...] you know where he is?'

'Aren't they going back to Sant'Anna?' she said. [...] this city, no signal worth a damn.' Rivoire, a big ope[...] place with a wide piazza in front of it, was one of th[...] exceptions. Was that why she'd come? In case a ca[...] from – someone? She'd even had her phone on lou[...]

The clinic had said they'd call if there was anythi[...] She hadn't been thinking about the clinic, but per[...] down. Perhaps.

Deep down, she didn't want to know.

'What is it, Luisa?' she'd said sharply. Because if [...] firm Luisa would prevaricate, she'd draw back fro[...] 'Luisa?'

It tumbled out in a miserable rush. Luisa had trie[...] but he wouldn't listen. She wanted to stop him – sh[...] go up there with him, to Sant'Anna, but now he'd b[...] and how could they have a proper conversation – [...]

h means,' said Giuli, pushing the thought away, 'that
n't get you on the phone. And besides, do you think
ave a conversation with you while he's in the car with
What did the text say?'

couldn't tell Luisa about Enzo's mum. Not now.

id he probably wouldn't be back tonight – he was with
oing to some spa in Trentino. *Spa? All right for some.*'

'And some other stuff.'

er stuff?'

stuff. Nonsense about missing me.' The sulk turning
reluctant.

ht,' said Giuli. 'So it means you have time to calm down,
ver whatever it is you're panicking about, to talk to *me*.
ed to eat, yes? Lunch. Maybe we can sort this mess out
n us.'

lence for dignity to be restored. Giuli knew Luisa. When
oke, she sounded mollified, even grateful. 'All right,' she
All right, Giuli. What would I do without you, eh?'

call you,' said Giuli.

ings don't go away just because you don't want to think
them. She could have said that to Luisa, but she hadn't,
reflected as she turned down the Via Porta Rossa towards
a del Parioncino. The old bootmender should have put
n out by now. She could bring him a coffee from the bar
ter him up. Her phone sat in her pocket.

*Sarto, this is Cinzia, Cinzia Messi, from Labo X. We have
preliminary results.*

ey'd call back, in time. She knew enough about medical
nation to know they couldn't go behind her back and

her things slowly, setting their small space to rights. At least
he'd stopped worrying about *her*. But that was only temporary,
wasn't it? Unless –

Now, standing in Rivoire's doorway, at the thought of all the
precautions she must take, all the calls and lies and evasions
and pitfalls waiting for her, Giuli felt a kind of clamouring, a
dizziness. She felt the muscles in her face tighten and for a
wild, irrational moment she wondered if the coffee had been
poisoned, if someone was poisoning her.

She needed air – it was just that it was stuffy, the smell of
coffee and sugar making her stomach roil. Once outside she
paused, breathed and slowly things reasserted themselves. She
had really thought she might faint: when had she ever fainted?
All she'd put her body through and was the bloody menopause
going to do for it? Something was still buzzing.

It was her phone again. 'Sandro,' she said faintly.

'Bloody hell, this town,' he complained crossly. 'Missed call
from Luisa, and I can't get her back.'

'Look,' she said, 'she wants to talk to you. It's really – she's
got very upset about all this. I know you're busy but please.'

'She's not ill, is she?' Now it was his turn to panic. Someone
was talking in the background, and her heart sank as she heard
the acoustic of the enclosed space and an engine. They were
already in the car.

'Sandro, she's not ill. She wants to talk to you before you go
back up to Sant'Anna. It's important. Surely you can manage
that?' Her phone was doing something else now, a separate
buzzing – she held it away from her face and saw there was an
incoming call from a number she didn't recognise. She rejected

it. 'Sandro? Are you still there?' She could feel the sweat beading on her forehead.

'Well, what, then?' he said, sounding distracted, and when she hesitated, thinking she should just spit it out, he went on. 'Anyway,' he said, impatient now, 'we aren't going to Sant'Anna after all – something's come up. All right?' Giuli felt herself subside with relief. Temporary, she was sure. But relief. 'Giuli?'

'You're back tonight, though?'

She heard him hesitate. 'Maybe,' he said cautiously. 'It's – we're going up north. So we can't be sure – but I'll get hold of Luisa. I'll keep her posted.'

'Up north? Where?'

'Trentino.'

'Trentino? You're going to the *mountains*?'

'A place called Serenita, if you can believe that. A – spa.' Drily.

'No way you're going to be back tonight,' she said, exasperated.

'We're taking Pietro's Alfa,' he blustered, then sighed. 'Maybe not.' There was a pause, then he said, as stubborn as Luisa had been, 'You're sure she's okay?'

He knew something. He knew Luisa wasn't telling him something.

'Just talk to her,' said Giuli. And she hung up.

With difficulty, Giuli threaded her way across the flow of crowds on the Por Santa Maria, down the side of the Borsa Merci and into the respite of the secret space behind it, quiet and empty and cool in the shade. Overhead the cloud had thickened: they said storms were coming. Maybe tonight.

Maybe it was a good thing Sandro was going to be safely out of the way today. Giuli could at least tell Luisa he wasn't going to

Sant'Anna. At the thought of the p[...]

Sandro and Pietro, talking in t[...] there: talking about men making u[...] tight-mouthed villagers and secre[...] About the old farmhouse, and no on[...] Sant'Anna, Sant'Anna. She'd seen[...] eyes, the terrible old pimp, leaning [...] thought he'd seen everything, but [...] asked him about that place.

So it was good Sandro was going [...] but there then came a tingle of somet[...] two of them separated. Luisa alone in t[...] with God knew what going round in [...] up the motorway with Pietro, two lads[...] have felt safer at the thought of Sandr[...] of a Fiat.

She sighed and got out her phone [...] because you didn't want to know thing[...]

There was the missed call from the u[...] was a message waiting. Hesitating, Giuli [...] of the answerphone and listened, a wo[...] the end. Deleted the message and the[...] the number from the call list.

She dialled Luisa's number: Luisa p[...]

'He's sent me a text,' she said before G[...] She sounded angry. 'Didn't even bothe[...] going to be away a night.'

The dread settled. Why couldn't they[...] just Luisa. Sandro wasn't talking either.

contact Enzo. He'd know from his card statement that she'd been for the appointment, which was all he cared about.

She could only postpone it, though. Eventually they'd catch up with her.

If you could call me back at your earliest convenience? These results can't really wait.

Delete, delete, delete. Giuli kept walking. One foot in front of the other had got her this far, and all she could do was keep going.

Chapter Sixteen

BARTOLINI AND MARTINELLI there at the bar. Just a couple of locals, having a morning drink. The memory of that kept returning to Luisa, the particular atmosphere in the place, the vibration between those two. Childhood friends, he'd said, hadn't he? Despite the old princess's snobbery. She needed to talk to Sandro – but that would mean telling him she'd lied.

Sandro thought the answer to the murders lay in the house, in those who had been there, that was why he was haring round the country tracking them down. Luisa thought it was still there in the village, in the autumn air, in the forest.

She *would* confess. She just couldn't do it if he wasn't there, dammit. She got her things together, closed the shutters: she had an idea.

She might be in the centre of Florence but Sant'Anna was there, in the corner of her eye, just out of sight. The curving road through trees turning rusty, leading up, up to nowhere and the three points: the Salieri house on the ridge; Martinelli's smallholding scattered under mangy trees; La Vipera. She knew,

Luisa *knew*, she would go back there. She saw herself plodding up the potholed road in the dusk.

No dinner to prepare, no man to wait for: she was free.

If she had dwelt on the idea of living in solitude, it was not her but Sandro she imagined. How he would survive without her, if he would marry again: it was one of the patterns of thought the cancer had set scurrying, round and round. You could only discipline yourself: no more than once a week may that prospect be considered. She had never – and this was possibly the single advantage of a cancer diagnosis and one that she had not considered up to this point – thought about how *she* would survive without him. Luisa descended the stairs with the thought, suddenly uncertain of her balance: she had to put out a hand to the wall either side a second.

And then she was down and out into the noisy street, fragrant with the smell of bread from the corner bakery and some pale late blossom overhanging the rails of the little public garden between her and Santa Croce.

Sandro was a little overweight. He complained now and again of aches and pains. He had been to the doctor perhaps three times in his life. Sandro would be fine. Was it just mortality? You went from twenty to thirty in a fever of hard work, trying to get somewhere. Thirty to forty hoping, waiting for children that didn't come. Then before you know it fifty's there; sixty arrives even quicker but you're still moving, still up and out every morning. Something else sits there on the horizon, though. Waiting.

She'd read and re-read the message he'd sent her. *I'm sorry, darling. We've got to head up to Trentino to talk to some people. Might have to stay over.*

on each cheek turned pale. 'It was that he had been seen visiting that house, for sex with those foreign women, and his father drew the line at that.'

Behind them the door pinged and they turned to see a fat woman pushing her way in. There wasn't room for all of them and for a moment they all stood there, unsure of what to do, until Pietro took the initiative and, with some jovial remark, edged sideways and out of the door. Sandro followed him.

On the pavement Pietro was bouncing on the balls of his feet. It was cold. He looked uncomfortable out of uniform. 'No wonder they had him in for the Monster killings,' he said. 'Thoroughly nasty piece of work by the sound of it.'

'So he molested her,' said Sandro.

Pietro sighed. 'She might have killed him herself,' he said.

Sandro nodded. 'You could hardly blame her,' he said. 'But Nielsson? She didn't even know what the woman looked like.' He chewed the inside of his cheek, wishing for another coffee. 'It's got to be someone who knew them both. If he was a regular visitor to La Vipera for sex, and Nielsson sanctioned it –' He paused, thinking. 'Would a woman kill someone, so long after, for rape?'

Pietro shrugged. 'You fancy asking one of the women in your life? My guess is – maybe. Depends.'

He was right. 'We've got a number for Mason, the woman in Canada?' said Sandro. 'And what about this mysterious Grenzi who runs the ski school in the Dolomites?'

'Ah,' said Pietro. 'Well. About her –'

But then the door swung outward viciously, almost knocking him into the road, and the fat woman emerged, giving them both a funny look.

'You were going to tell me something,' said Sandro, 'about the girl in the mountains. Grenzi.' Although of course she wasn't a girl any more, was she?

His phone buzzed in his pocket and he saw there was a missed call from Luisa.

'There was a message about Grenzi from the station,' said Pietro. 'I'll call them back from the car.'

'Why don't you do it now?' said Sandro.

*

Comes home to roost, thought Giuli, putting her phone away in the bright panelled splendour of Rivoire in the Piazza Signoria. *Doesn't it? All comes home to roost.*

Time had been when she had been the one to run to Luisa with her troubles. She'd depended on them too much. Over the years she'd been the one to take, taking love, taking their roof over her head, taking the job Sandro gave her, taking money, taking comfort and consolation. When she finally found the tears to cry for her own stupid, idle, hopeless mother, for the women she'd met in prison for murder herself, for the baby she was never going to have, Luisa's shoulder had been the one Giuli had cried on. Never mind that Luisa had lost a baby of her own, and even when they'd found out Luisa had breast cancer (Giuli, who had not even a vestige of belief, almost crossed herself whenever she thought of that day, six years past and no recurrence, God willing), Luisa had been the one to comfort Giuli, not the other way around.

And when Giuli had found Enzo, she'd started leaning on him, too. However much she'd told herself, don't depend, take nothing for granted, it's not safe, she'd leaned on him and, stranger still, he hadn't seemed to mind.

But now it was her turn.

'Ey!' The square, grumpy old barman of Rivoire, whose face only a mother could love, shoved the little cup towards her. He had a heart of gold, Giuli knew, and when she pulled herself together and smiled he scowled even harder, like one of those old American gangster actors. But the tips of his ears went pink.

Giuli had just got her ticket at the cash desk and handed it across the counter when her phone went.

'I've been trying to get Sandro.' Luisa had sounded breathless, unsettled. Even an edge of panic, and Luisa never panicked. 'Do you know where he is?'

'Aren't they going back to Sant'Anna?' she said. 'You know this city, no signal worth a damn.' Rivoire, a big open luxurious place with a wide piazza in front of it, was one of the very few exceptions. Was that why she'd come? In case a call came in from – someone? She'd even had her phone on loud.

The clinic had said they'd call if there was anything urgent. She hadn't been thinking about the clinic, but perhaps deep down. Perhaps.

Deep down, she didn't want to know.

'What is it, Luisa?' she'd said sharply. Because if she wasn't firm Luisa would prevaricate, she'd draw back from the brink. 'Luisa?'

It tumbled out in a miserable rush. Luisa had tried to tell him, but he wouldn't listen. She wanted to stop him – she wanted to go up there with him, to Sant'Anna, but now he'd be with Pietro and how could they have a proper conversation –

'What, though?' said Giuli. 'What's actually worrying you?'

A silence. 'I – I just got the idea that Luca Bartolini might tell him he saw me out there at Sant'Anna. Saw this madwoman wandering around.' A pause. 'Bartolini even said he remembered me from all that time ago at his sister's wedding. What if he knows I'm married to Sandro? The old princess knows I am.'

'I don't understand,' said Giuli. 'And isn't the old lady gaga?'

'He might – I might have messed up the investigation somehow. I don't know.'

'You just need to talk to Sandro.' Giuli tried to speak gently, but the truth was Luisa's fears and panic seemed to her unreasonable.

'Before he goes back up to Sant'Anna,' said Luisa, stubborn.

'Okay,' said Giuli. 'Leave it to me.'

But she had no clue. How did she know how Sandro was going to react? Luisa had lied to him. That was a big deal. Luisa never lied. Never panicked.

There was too much to think about. There was Enzo this morning, awake at five and staring at the ceiling. Pale as a ghost at the kitchen table.

'We'll get through it, my love. We'll get her through it.'

'She's going to die,' Enzo said, as if she hadn't understood, and she put a hand gingerly on his shoulder.

'I know, darling,' she said.

And then he'd got up all in a hurry, leaving his plate and cup untouched, grabbing his coat. 'Got to get to work.' Her hand falling back to her side, useless.

Giuli didn't have to ask herself if he'd kissed her goodbye: he hadn't. Flying down the stairs, away from her. She'd gathered her things slowly, setting their small space to rights. At least he'd stopped worrying about *her*. But that was only temporary, wasn't it? Unless –

Now, standing in Rivoire's doorway, at the thought of all the precautions she must take, all the calls and lies and evasions and pitfalls waiting for her, Giuli felt a kind of clamouring, a dizziness. She felt the muscles in her face tighten and for a wild, irrational moment she wondered if the coffee had been poisoned, if someone was poisoning her.

She needed air – it was just that it was stuffy, the smell of coffee and sugar making her stomach roil. Once outside she paused, breathed and slowly things reasserted themselves. She had really thought she might faint: when had she ever fainted? All she'd put her body through and was the bloody menopause going to do for it? Something was still buzzing.

It was her phone again. 'Sandro,' she said faintly.

'Bloody hell, this town,' he complained crossly. 'Missed call from Luisa, and I can't get her back.'

'Look,' she said, 'she wants to talk to you. It's really – she's got very upset about all this. I know you're busy but please.'

'She's not ill, is she?' Now it was his turn to panic. Someone was talking in the background, and her heart sank as she heard the acoustic of the enclosed space and an engine. They were already in the car.

'Sandro, she's not ill. She wants to talk to you before you go back up to Sant'Anna. It's important. Surely you can manage that?' Her phone was doing something else now, a separate buzzing – she held it away from her face and saw there was an incoming call from a number she didn't recognise. She rejected it. 'Sandro? Are you still there?' She could feel the sweat beading on her forehead.

'Well, what, then?' he said, sounding distracted, and when she hesitated, thinking she should just spit it out, he went on. 'Anyway,' he said, impatient now, 'we aren't going to Sant'Anna after all – something's come up. All right?' Giuli felt herself subside with relief. Temporary, she was sure. But relief. 'Giuli?'

'You're back tonight, though?'

She heard him hesitate. 'Maybe,' he said cautiously. 'It's – we're going up north. So we can't be sure – but I'll get hold of Luisa. I'll keep her posted.'

'Up north? Where?'

'Trentino.'

'Trentino? You're going to the *mountains*?'

'A place called Serenita, if you can believe that. A – spa.' Drily.

'No way you're going to be back tonight,' she said, exasperated.

'We're taking Pietro's Alfa,' he blustered, then sighed. 'Maybe not.' There was a pause, then he said, as stubborn as Luisa had been, 'You're sure she's okay?'

He knew something. He knew Luisa wasn't telling him something.

'Just talk to her,' said Giuli. And she hung up.

With difficulty, Giuli threaded her way across the flow of crowds on the Por Santa Maria, down the side of the Borsa Merci and into the respite of the secret space behind it, quiet and empty and cool in the shade. Overhead the cloud had thickened: they said storms were coming. Maybe tonight.

Maybe it was a good thing Sandro was going to be safely out of the way today. Giuli could at least tell Luisa he wasn't going to

Sant'Anna. At the thought of the place, she suddenly shivered.

Sandro and Pietro, talking in the office, forgetting she was there: talking about men making use of women for sex, about tight-mouthed villagers and secrets and grudges, old hatred. About the old farmhouse, and no one knew what went on inside. Sant'Anna, Sant'Anna. She'd seen it, too, in Ragno's yellow eyes, the terrible old pimp, leaning on death's door; you'd have thought he'd seen everything, but he looked away when she asked him about that place.

So it was good Sandro was going in the opposite direction, but there then came a tingle of something at the thought of the two of them separated. Luisa alone in the dark in their apartment with God knew what going round in her head, Sandro roaring up the motorway with Pietro, two lads in a big car. She would have felt safer at the thought of Sandro in his little old tortoise of a Fiat.

She sighed and got out her phone to call Luisa back. Just because you didn't want to know things, they didn't go away.

There was the missed call from the unknown number. There was a message waiting. Hesitating, Giuli punched in the number of the answerphone and listened, a woman's voice, listened to the end. Deleted the message and then, considering, deleted the number from the call list.

She dialled Luisa's number: Luisa picked up straight away.

'He's sent me a text,' she said before Giuli could say anything. She sounded angry. 'Didn't even bother to speak to me. He's going to be away a night.'

The dread settled. Why couldn't they make it up? It wasn't just Luisa. Sandro wasn't talking either. What was going on?

'Which means,' said Giuli, pushing the thought away, 'that he couldn't get you on the phone. And besides, do you think he can have a conversation with you while he's in the car with Pietro? What did the text say?'

She couldn't tell Luisa about Enzo's mum. Not now.

'It said he probably wouldn't be back tonight – he was with Pietro going to some spa in Trentino. *Spa?* All right for some.' Sulkily. 'And some other stuff.'

'Other stuff?'

'Oh, stuff. Nonsense about missing me.' The sulk turning softer, reluctant.

'Right,' said Giuli. 'So it means you have time to calm down, to go over whatever it is you're panicking about, to talk to *me*. You need to eat, yes? Lunch. Maybe we can sort this mess out between us.'

A silence for dignity to be restored. Giuli knew Luisa. When she spoke, she sounded mollified, even grateful. 'All right,' she said. 'All right, Giuli. What would I do without you, eh?'

'I'll call you,' said Giuli.

Things don't go away just because you don't want to think about them. She could have said that to Luisa, but she hadn't, Giuli reflected as she turned down the Via Porta Rossa towards the Via del Parioncino. The old bootmender should have put his sign out by now. She could bring him a coffee from the bar to butter him up. Her phone sat in her pocket.

Ms Sarto, this is Cinzia, Cinzia Messi, from Labo X. We have some preliminary results.

They'd call back, in time. She knew enough about medical information to know they couldn't go behind her back and contact Enzo. He'd know from his card statement that she'd been for the appointment, which was all he cared about.

She could only postpone it, though. Eventually they'd catch up with her.

If you could call me back at your earliest convenience? These results can't really wait.

Delete, delete, delete. Giuli kept walking. One foot in front of the other had got her this far, and all she could do was keep going.

Chapter Sixteen

BARTOLINI AND MARTINELLI there at the bar. Just a couple of locals, having a morning drink. The memory of that kept returning to Luisa, the particular atmosphere in the place, the vibration between those two. Childhood friends, he'd said, hadn't he? Despite the old princess's snobbery. She needed to talk to Sandro – but that would mean telling him she'd lied.

Sandro thought the answer to the murders lay in the house, in those who had been there, that was why he was haring round the country tracking them down. Luisa thought it was still there in the village, in the autumn air, in the forest.

She *would* confess. She just couldn't do it if he wasn't there, dammit. She got her things together, closed the shutters: she had an idea.

She might be in the centre of Florence but Sant'Anna was there, in the corner of her eye, just out of sight. The curving road through trees turning rusty, leading up, up to nowhere and the three points: the Salieri house on the ridge; Martinelli's smallholding scattered under mangy trees; La Vipera. She knew,

Luisa *knew*, she would go back there. She saw herself plodding up the potholed road in the dusk.

No dinner to prepare, no man to wait for: she was free.

If she had dwelt on the idea of living in solitude, it was not her but Sandro she imagined. How he would survive without her, if he would marry again: it was one of the patterns of thought the cancer had set scurrying, round and round. You could only discipline yourself: no more than once a week may that prospect be considered. She had never – and this was possibly the single advantage of a cancer diagnosis and one that she had not considered up to this point – thought about how *she* would survive without him. Luisa descended the stairs with the thought, suddenly uncertain of her balance: she had to put out a hand to the wall either side a second.

And then she was down and out into the noisy street, fragrant with the smell of bread from the corner bakery and some pale late blossom overhanging the rails of the little public garden between her and Santa Croce.

Sandro was a little overweight. He complained now and again of aches and pains. He had been to the doctor perhaps three times in his life. Sandro would be fine. Was it just mortality? You went from twenty to thirty in a fever of hard work, trying to get somewhere. Thirty to forty hoping, waiting for children that didn't come. Then before you know it fifty's there; sixty arrives even quicker but you're still moving, still up and out every morning. Something else sits there on the horizon, though. Waiting.

She'd read and re-read the message he'd sent her. *I'm sorry, darling. We've got to head up to Trentino to talk to some people. Might have to stay over.*

And sometimes it comes before you see it. Johanna Nielsson didn't see it coming. Johanna Nielsson never thought she would die.

She'd laughed when Luisa had said, forty years ago, stay away from him. Stay away or I swear I'll kill you. Laughed and laughed until the barman had turned round from his coffee machine and stared at her.

Luisa wasn't surprised someone had killed her. But who? And after all this time – what had tipped the balance?

'I've got the secret,' she'd said leaning towards Luisa, the smell of her in the air between them, a musty smell of damp old cellars that hadn't at all made Luisa think of life but rather of a tomb. 'The secret, you see. Of eternal life.' And she'd held out her wrist, turned upwards as if offering it to be dabbed with scent, but it was meant to show Luisa something. The tiny tattoo, snatched out of reach.

Eternal life? Well, she'd been wrong about that.

Pausing by the drifts of browning blossom in the gutter, Luisa adjusted her bag and let out a sigh, involuntary, that would have had him turning sharply to her and saying, *what? What's wrong?*

Luisa supposed – very reluctantly, she supposed – that if she found herself alone, for whatever reason, Giuli would bear the burden. Poor childless Giuli and Enzo, and he had parents of his own to fret over. She'd look forward to a coffee with Giuli all week; like today, a lunch now and again; they'd take her out into the country once a month. She'd go home to a quiet, dark house and eat soup and sit on the divan with the telly on, not really watching, just for the noise.

Where had this all come from? It came from a sudden uncertainty, from the past stirred up murky as mud in a pond, about what went on in Sandro's head – and then on its heels came a sudden, uncontrollable, foolish surge of love for him. Because she knew there had been moments – when a child died on his watch, and when their own child died while they sat hopeless in a hospital room – when he had not wanted to go on, and all that had stopped him had been the thought of her, alone. He didn't think of himself. Never thought of himself. Only her, or Giuli, or Enzo even.

Giuli. There was another worry, despite the pep talk, the firm hand she'd taken with Luisa on the phone, that something was up with the girl. Luisa sighed. Lunch was still a way off. She got out her phone and there it was, Sandro's text. *I'm sorry. I miss you. Let's talk later: I'll tell you when. I love you.*

She turned north, towards the hospital of Santa Maria Nuova, and put the phone away. He wouldn't expect an answer. But why did one keep silent when one should speak? She got out the phone, where Sandro's message still sat, and tapped in, *I love you too.* And sent it before she could change her mind.

The long rectangle of the hospital forecourt – three sides porticoed, one of them dusty with old frescoes – was busy. Four ambulances were parked up in the sunshine and Luisa had to skip hurriedly sideways to avoid a stretcher that emerged from one of them without warning. Not the place, she reflected, to visit if you had started the morning dwelling on mortality, but too late now. She asked at reception and was sent to the emergency admissions, where she waited in a long queue. It seemed to her that half the people waiting on the plastic chairs had been there the last time she came.

'Benedetta Salieri? She was being brought in when I was here yesterday, a – an accidental –' She stopped because an elderly man with his arm in a makeshift sling was staring at her with extreme curiosity. And she didn't know, after all, why Benedetta Salieri had been brought in.

The woman behind the admissions desk peered at her. 'And you are?'

'Luisa Cellini,' she said, hearing the intercom's crackle, seeing them through the glass turn to look at her from the far end. 'A friend.'

There was a lot of sighing and conferring behind a screened-off area but eventually Luisa was directed two floors up, to a ward designated Short Stay Acute. There was an intercom beside locked double doors and she gave her name again and Benedetta's. She checked herself – she didn't know Benedetta's married name. The shifty little Swiss Italian bridegroom pacing up and down with his nicotine-stained fingers all those years ago – he had, beyond those details, been quite forgettable and his actual name was long gone. Salieri would have to do. And abruptly she wanted very much to talk to Benedetta. Or just to see her, to hold her poor hand, the liver-spotted hand that had hung down beside the stretcher, to hold it and say, *life, eh? Life, Benedetta*. They'd both lost a child.

The doors had small windows of grubby reinforced glass. Peering through, she could see nurses moving, and out of the dim past Luisa remembered she had wanted to be a nurse once. It occurred to her that she might not have been too bad at it.

Bossy enough. And on cue a voice bellowed at her through the intercom.

A sentence emerged from static noise, barking, 'Visiting hours two till six. Relatives only.'

Luisa peered back through the dirty little window and saw the nurse conferring with someone, a short figure in a coat, hat pulled down – she couldn't tell if it was male or female – and they turned to look at the door. Luisa leaned back against the wall, quite certain they had been talking about her. And weighing it up. She didn't want to get into trouble, did she? She peeped back again in time to see the small person turning, beginning to walk down the curtained ward towards her.

A woman. Blue eyes, northern complexion. Luisa stepped back in a hurry with only these impressions and looked about her. There was a door a metre or so back down the corridor: a toilet. She hurried there and pushed it inwards, stepping inside with her breath held, quickly turning to keep the door a crack open. Feeling foolish, handbag dangling, her breath too quick – *who did she think she was, James Bond?* – but she wanted to see that woman. The woman who'd been talking to the nurses about her. She heard the swish of the weighted doors and widened the crack. She could see the woman's back, a gleam of fair hair, grey or blonde. She was turning, looking to see where Luisa had gone.

A woman of Luisa's age. No more than a glimpse of features, fair ageing skin, a second's doubt – did she know this woman? – and then she had turned again and was gone, out of the frame, so quickly that Luisa started back, thinking the door would be tugged open and she would be exposed.

It didn't happen. Luisa heard steps receding, waited a second, another, and then gingerly she opened the toilet door and stepped out into the empty corridor. She stood in the corridor a second with her head lifted to catch it, a flowery sweetness on the air.

And then she heard the footsteps, brisk, coming back. Two sets. Too brisk for Luisa to escape this time and she stood there, pressed against the wall and suddenly unable to move or to compose herself. The owners of the feet rounded the corner at the end of the corridor and she resigned herself to being interrogated, reprimanded, frozen there and waiting for her fate.

Two men, one young, one old, in white coats. Doctors talking to each other, the younger an eager student gazing up at his professor, and they walked straight past her, as if she didn't exist, and buzzed themselves into the ward. Of course: men didn't bother themselves with unimportant matters like confused-looking old ladies.

And before she could even think about what she was doing, Luisa found that she had moved up behind them, clutching her handbag, into their slipstream, through the door and – her heart pounding – halfway to the nurses' station on their white coat tails before they turned in to a cubicle and were gone, and she was alone. There seemed to be a lull in that moment: the ward was hushed, quiet. At the far end a nurse in green scrubs emerged from curtains pushing a drugs trolley and disappeared again.

She fully intended to explain herself. To say she knew Benedetta, had known her for forty years, had been in the emergency room when she was admitted. *We've both lost a child*, she wanted to say to someone.

But in that moment the nurses' station was deserted. She even waited: she could see a woman's head through the half-glass of a door behind the station, nodding slowly, but the woman didn't turn; voices murmured through the door. A trolley trundled at the bottom of the corridor. Luisa looked, peered over the desk for some clue, and then she registered a whiteboard on the facing wall, written up in a grid. The patients' names, bed numbers, attending doctors. No Salieri.

Had they given her the wrong ward number, after all that? Ten beds. She scanned the names again, *Marzocco, C, Feltro, D* – that was it. The initials. There was only one B – bed seven. Emboldened now, Luisa moved off.

Bed seven was in a good position, by the window. It had a view. Luisa stood and looked.

There was a broad strip of golden ornamented plaster frontage that was the top floor of the Medici palace; there were red roofs and chimneys, steam rising from their pots. There were balconies with bicycles and air-con units and clotheslines; there was a tiny loggia perched precariously above it all, and a woman on it watering a gardenia as big as herself in a pot. There was the world.

In the foreground, between Luisa and the view, Benedetta Salieri – Luisa had instantly forgotten her married name again – lay still under a white cotton cover, as motionless as a figure on a tomb. Luisa took a step forward and peered at her. It *was* Benedetta, and Luisa felt a prickle at her scalp, not of fear exactly but of sadness, grief almost, at the years that had passed for both of them. Luisa could remember her standing in that great high-ceilinged room among the statues, as still as if she'd been one herself, a small, plump-cheeked infanta. The walls had been hung with some kind of cloth as they were in the Pitti palace, a golden damask, the great long windows and Benedetta's father looking down at La Vipera.

Not classically elegant then, and her father's sighing sort of look at her from the window underlined that, the old man with his hooded eyes and fine straight nose: his faint disappointment. Her lovely rounded face had been a child's still, if Luisa thought about it – at the time, Luisa not much more than a child herself, Benedetta had seemed aloof and dignified to her, a princess from a painting, allowing them to move around her easing the dress. The dress had certainly needed room at the waist. She could have asked Bartolini, couldn't she? Or perhaps not, not in the waiting room to the casualty department. *Did your sister get married because she was pregnant? When, exactly, did she lose the baby?* Up on a hillside out walking with him perhaps – he had given the impression of such ease and carelessness that he would have answered even those questions.

He'd been away in Milan. Had nothing to do with La Vipera.

And then she felt a different kind of shiver and she didn't know if it was remembering the smell of the hillside in that moment, dead leaves and damp in the air, or his hand on her arm to stop her falling, or the sudden memory of the side of La Vipera below them half-covered with ivy and that strange swirl of a drawing on it.

There wasn't a hint of plumpness about Benedetta now, the stony face on the pillow, so light she barely made a dent. Her hair that had been so thick the pearl pins kept falling out of it was carefully cut but thin and brittle, and her cheeks were hollow.

Luisa stole closer and put out a hand to touch Benedetta's, lying brown and thin against the snowy cotton. It was cool – cold even – and it didn't react. She looked around the bed, at the machines there, but none of the illuminated numbers made sense to her. She folded her fingers around Benedetta's, squeezed, and still there was nothing; she turned the hand over, the soft wrinkled palm, manicured nails. She had been well cared for, a life, Luisa imagined, of indolence, rest retreats and nurses. She found herself stroking Benedetta's hand, looking down at it as if she might in fact be able to read a life in that palm. Then something stopped her.

She'd taken it for a vein, a scratch on the inside of her wrist, something to do with a medical procedure, perhaps, but it wasn't that: it was older. Two blue lines, turned fuzzy, the beginnings of a curve that called something to mind – and then there was the tiniest sound, less than a sigh, the merest softest exhalation, and with it a high distant alarm from somewhere behind her at the nurses' station. Running footsteps in soft-soled rubber clogs.

Luisa was on her own feet when they arrived. She'd dropped Benedetta's hand and had stepped back in panic against the window sill. They didn't pay her any attention initially, too busy lowering the bedhead, one skinny dark nurse taking her pulse, another, a redhead, tugging at a drip stand Luisa hadn't noticed, a plastic tube dangling from it, and then the redhead frowning, looking round and seeing Luisa.

'Is she going to be all right?' said Luisa, breathless, desperate, realising too late that it sounded like an admission of something.

'Madam?' starting almost polite, with a gruff edge. 'Who let you in here?' Angrier. Behind her the other nurse had her ear to

Benedetta's mouth, listening for breathing. *She breathed*, Luisa wanted to say, *I heard her breathe*.

'Who the hell are you?' said the redhead angrily and then, lifting the dangling tube, 'Have you done this?'

But all Luisa could hear was that breath, that soft, despairing exhalation that sounded like nothing so much as an end.

*

They didn't get their coffee till they were past Mantova, in the end.

Even in Pietro's big Alfa, with its heated seats and cream leather, it was a slog up the motorway to Trentino, three hours of wooded hillsides giving way to orchards, then the featureless plain, the miles and miles of *capannoni*, light industrial units, pig barns, and by Mantova they'd both had enough.

Sandro hadn't wanted to be here. He'd wanted to be tracking Luca Bartolini down. He might not have been around forty years ago, he might not have been around all summer – but there'd been something in Luisa's voice when she'd mentioned him. Too casual. That family. Was this a man's crime? Not Gorgone's, that was for sure, and Bartolini was the only other man on their list.

But then Pietro – returning Parini's call as they'd walked in the cool morning away from San Frediano and Lotti's grim cousin – had stopped, stock still, with the mobile to one ear and a hand to the other, at the foot of the Ponte alla Carraia. 'What?' he'd said, scowling into the mobile. 'She *what*?'

Sandro could only watch and wonder as he got Pietro's half of the conversation. 'When? Did she – was there any note? Any explanation?' Pietro grimaced at him.

'She's dead,' said Sandro, not waiting to be told, as Pietro hung up. 'Lucia Grenzi's dead.'

'It came through this morning,' said Pietro. 'They finally tracked her down. I can't understand why it took so long –' He let out a long breath. 'Except the lads started with the foreign ones. She hung herself. A little more than a month ago. Parini said he'd email me the report but –' he made an explosive sound of frustration '– this city! The signal's so bad. We'll need to call in at the station.'

He turned around and around in the narrow street, looking for somewhere open, then marched, Sandro in his wake, until they got to the bridge. Below them the river was all gold and green in the September light.

'A month ago,' Sandro repeated. 'More than a month or less?'

'Five weeks,' said Pietro. 'In a luxury hotel, one of those fat farm places, up in the mountains.'

A silence. Pietro looking at Sandro, beginning to shake his head. 'No,' he said.

Hung herself in a hotel. The girl, the small, dark Italian girl, feisty: talking back angrily to Baratti. Not too feisty to be Nielsson's slave, beetle-browed, dogged, like she was her bodyguard – and a better one than Gorgone, mooching around trying to look like Jim Morrison. Why had it taken the news of her death to bring that back to Sandro? The little terrier who'd made a life for herself with the ski school, who'd grown old. And suddenly, now?

'A couple of hours' drive,' said Sandro.

'Less in my car,' said Pietro. Silence. 'Come on, be sensible. You haven't even got air conditioning.'

They'd called in at the station on the way. Parini and Panayotis were there. There was a tray with empty coffee cups, sticky dregs. Panayotis handed Pietro the coroner's report on Grenzi's death. 'There's a couple of things –'

But Sandro interrupted him sharply. 'They're sure it's suicide?' Pietro was busy scanning the pages.

Panayotis answered, 'They're sure. She left a note. She was in a hotel, drank the contents of the mini-bar then hung herself. She locked the door, left the note, her handwriting. There was no suspicion at all of foul play.'

Pietro looked up. 'Up there in the Dolomites, they're a thorough bunch,' he said. 'Look, call ahead, will you?' Addressing Panayotis. 'Let them know we're coming and why. And text me names. Manager, whatever.'

'Hold up,' said Parini, bouncing on the balls of his feet like a kid, practically putting his hand up for permission to speak.

'Yes?' said Pietro wearily. Sandro could kiss him, sometimes: he'd always thought of him as a little brother but now he was the grown-up in the room.

'Right,' said Parini, pleased, 'first off, we got Lotti's phone records.'

Sandro's mind was blank for a second, and then he remembered. The little stone house, clean and cold as a butcher's shop, and Lotti's old-fashioned phone, his pride and joy. One of only three in the village, all that time ago.

'And?' said Pietro.

'Easy,' Parini said. 'Seven calls in the last three months, all incoming, six of them from call centres. Cold sales. And then five weeks ago there was one from a public phone booth in Trentino that lasted four minutes.'

'Trentino,' said Pietro and reached for his jacket – they were both halfway to the door but Parini was after them.

'No,' he said, 'no, there was something else.' Looking past him Sandro saw a name, ringed in red, on the whiteboard. 'Davide – officer Ceri – took a call late last night. About ten.' And Parini said the name as Sandro looked at it. 'From Helen Mason, the woman in Canada.'

'Nova Scotia,' said Pietro, impatient. 'What did she say? Where's Ceri now?'

'Gone out for more coffees,' said Parini. 'But she said she'd only speak to' – he glanced at Sandro – 'Mr Cellini. She said something about the community being very strict and she can use the phone only between three and four in the afternoon their time. Davide gave your mobile number but she got distressed, said she wasn't sure if she was allowed to call a mobile. Davide said he wasn't sure if she was dealing from a full deck. Then she hung up.' And Parini let out a breath.

'Shit,' said Sandro. 'Give me the number. Shit.' They were all looking at him.

Pietro was on his mobile, looking up a route. 'It says three hours.'

'Come on, chief,' said Parini. 'You can do it in two.'

The ring road was crowded, roadworks everywhere, the new Palazzo di Giustizia rising out of the chaos to the north like a monstrous machine that had forced its way up from some underground metropolis. Sandro spent the time composing a careful message to Luisa, abasing himself, and thinking they might as well have been in his grubby little Fiat if they were going to creep along at two miles an hour.

Staring out of the window at the monstrosity, Sandro dialled the number in Nova Scotia Parini had given him. It rang and rang: he hung up.

Pietro's mobile, sitting in its holder giving them directions, rang as they emerged from a tunnel around Bologna into low grey cloud. It was on speaker phone, and Parini's excitable voice said, 'Boss? Boss?' His gingery face appeared on the small screen, eager. *These kids*, thought Sandro, *and their technology*. Young officers never seemed to bother with landlines.

'I'm driving,' said Pietro. 'Talk to Officer Cellini, will you?'

'Sandro will do,' said Sandro drily. Around them the hills were shrouded in mist, a ghostly landscape. 'What is it, Parini?'

'Update on the vehicle trace,' said Parini, 'the camper? I just took a call from traffic.' Sandro detected suppressed excitement. 'Some more info came in from a ZTL camera, at San Marco.' A pause, then getting only impatience, the boy hurried on. 'The camper was caught there coming in to the city a little over a month ago, August 12th. Into Florence from the north, entering the ZTL illegally.' He paused, triumphant. 'She can't have been in the city for a hundred years,' he said, 'not to know she'd get a ticket, even in August.' Then flushed.

'Or she didn't give a damn,' said Sandro. 'You don't know Johanna Nielsson. Is there an image? Can you send it?'

Parini's head bobbed down, looking at a screen, then up again. 'Will do.'

'*Cazzo*,' said Pietro, risking a glance away from the road down at Parini's eager face. 'In August there's campers everywhere.

And most of those ZTL cameras only record entry not exit. I don't suppose ...?'

'As a matter of fact,' Parini turned pink again, 'there was another sighting. Once I knew we were talking Florence I requested another search in the immediate city environs for the days after that sighting.' A breath. 'A week later tollbooth cameras caught the licence plate, a rear image only, on the southern junction, where the Siena road meets the ring road, that big roundabout re-entering the city –'

'Yes, yes,' said Pietro, impatient, his eyes darting from the road to the mobile screen and back.

'Hold on,' said Sandro. 'What date are we talking now?'

'August 16th,' said Parini.

'The day after Ferragosto,' said Pietro. 'The city would have been dead.'

For a moment Sandro felt as though his brain had frozen. 'A month ago, though?' he said. 'Didn't the pathologist say – hold on.'

Silence. Pietro's hands white on the wheel. 'This time there was no driver image?' said Pietro.

'Where's the – where's the –?' Sandro had the iPad open on his knee. 'Where's the pathology report?' Stabbing at the screen in frustration. And then it appeared, in black and white. 'Death estimated approximately four weeks before the discovery of the body on September 13th.'

'So,' said Pietro, frowning, 'she would have to have been killed almost the moment she arrived in Sant'Anna?'

'Or –' They all reached the conclusion at the same time, but it was Panayotis who said it, his dark-browed face appearing in the screen over Parini's shoulder.

'Or she was already dead.'

'Panayotis?' said Sandro.

'Yes, boss?' said the kid, and Sandro barely even registered the word.

'Find that camper-van, will you?'

Chapter Seventeen

A T THE MANTOVA AUTOGRILL they fought their way to the bar. Even though it was past midday they ordered the breakfast special: cappuccino, orange juice, bun.

The place was packed, five deep at the bar, so while Pietro queued Sandro got himself a napkin and extracted a sugar-dusted bun for each of them from the glass-fronted cabinet on the bar. After five wearisome minutes they were reunited in a cramped corner of the big service station, by the window. Sandro got out the iPad, sheepish – he never thought he'd be one of those: a busy executive on his screen in public.

In the first picture, the camper coming into the city to the north, you could see her face, indistinct but recognisable. A white oval, the long grey hair. You could even see the rings on her hands, on the wheel. As he looked, Sandro was so silent Pietro had to nudge him.

'All right?'

'It's her,' was all Sandro could find to say. His mouth was dry: he took a gulp of orange juice, like medicine.

There was moving footage of the car's exit. The fuzzy pictures of the rear quarter of an elderly camper-van inching its way jerkily round the big roundabout to the south of the city, exiting to the Siena *superstrada*. But no matter how much they enhanced the images they could get nothing on the driver, not a profile, not an eyebrow, not a pinky finger on the wheel.

'Leaving the city to the south,' said Pietro.

'To Sant'Anna,' said Sandro.

Pietro shrugged. 'Where else?' He chewed his lip. 'Lotti would have still been alive,' he said. 'What if – I wonder –?'

'Where would you hide a camper,' said Sandro, musing on his own track, 'where it would be invisible? On a site you'd have to register.'

'Sandro?'

With an effort Sandro transferred his attention to Pietro. 'Yes?'

'What if it did go down to Sant'Anna and Lotti saw whoever was driving it? If Johanna Nielsson was already dead, the driver would have to be –'

'The killer,' supplied Sandro. 'I think ... I think you're on the right track. At least, I think Lotti died because he knew Nielsson's killer. Once you're sure – and the pathologist was very sure – that he didn't kill her and then kill himself.' There was a silence. 'I'd like to find that camper,' said Sandro. They both picked up their teaspoons in the same moment to scoop the last of the cappuccino.

'I'd like to know what Grenzi said to Lotti on the phone,' said Pietro. 'That call from the phone box in Trentino.'

'If it was her,' said Sandro, cautious.

Pietro shrugged. 'If it was her,' he said. They were both anxious, twitchy. Wanting to be in two places at once.

'As for the camper,' Pietro began, reading Sandro's mind, seeing Sant'Anna there, seeing the faceless killer at the wheel, 'I think Panayotis is really good. The other two are less ... steady. But if it can be found, he'll find it. We're going north, I think your instincts – our instincts – are right on this. '

Sandro sighed, extracting the coroner's report on Grenzi. 'So,' he said. 'They're sure it was suicide but they don't have a motive.'

Taking a bite, Pietro spoke around his bun indistinctly. 'She wasn't at the spa for medical reasons, but for a holiday. She was seventy-one years old. No illness, terminal or otherwise, no depression, or at least not diagnosed.' Pietro brushed at himself in exasperation where the icing sugar had found its way to the front of his sweater. 'The note didn't really say *why* she'd done it, just that she was sorry for the maid or whoever found her body but she didn't know how else to do it.'

'No traumatic break-up?'

'No partner at all, according to the man she had running the ski school.'

Sandro held out his hand for the report and looked down at the photograph of the note attached to the email. Beautiful handwriting, was his first thought. Neat and firm, which indicated she probably wrote it before she worked her way through the mini-bar. He had only had one bite of his bun and didn't really want another. He set it down on the counter. '"I can't go on with this," it says.'

'That's sort of standard suicide note, though,' said Pietro, peering down at it.

'Yes,' said Sandro slowly. 'And this note is just for the maid, isn't it? I don't know if people bother to explain themselves to the maid. I wonder if she said anything to anyone else.'

'She didn't seem to have anyone, did she?' said Pietro. He had finished his bun and was wiping his fingers fastidiously. He drained his coffee cup and turned to look out at the pale light of the plains through the Autogrill's window. A truck hurtled past on the motorway heading north and just beyond the petrol pumps a small family was having a picnic on a patch of mangy grass.

Pietro spoke. 'She told the man who managed her ski school – sounds like she was more or less retired from it – that she was going to this place to recharge her batteries. He told the coroner she seemed very cheerful when she left.'

'The ski school's only twenty miles from the spa,' said Sandro absently. 'We can go and ask the guy while we're at it, can't we?' He looked down at the email again, the small neat writing.

There were other photographs attached to the report. Sandro tapped on the first one and took off his glasses abruptly: he had seen suicide by hanging and he quite suddenly did not want to see a picture of this one. Grenzi's body *in situ*, hanging from the back of a wardrobe. The next was a set of post-mortem shots, the body on the high hard bed from various angles, the skin discoloured against white sheets. Carefully he set the pages down on the counter of the Autogrill.

He found himself thinking again of that room above the ring road, the three young officers gazing in wonder at him and Pietro. He'd missed that, having back-up.

As they walked back out to the car, Sandro's phone rang. It was Davide Ceri from the station. He stopped, and Pietro did too.

'Has he found the camper?' said Sandro. 'Panayotis?' Then almost immediately had to shake his head no, at Pietro. Ceri was calling about the Canadian, Helen Mason.

'I'll fill her up,' mouthed Pietro, clicking to open the big black car. Sandro watched it glide towards the petrol pumps and slowly he followed.

'So?' he said to Ceri.

It turned out he didn't have much to add, but Sandro listened anyway. You had to listen to everything, and the kid was eager.

'She sounded pretty shaky,' said Ceri. 'I mean, literally, her voice shook, like she had Parkinson's or one of those. She tried to explain to me about their community, where she is now. It's some kind of religious thing – they keep mobiles and all that out, no computers. It's all about meditation and mindfulness. Whatever that is. She said she hadn't used a telephone in sixteen years, can you believe that? They have the landline for emergencies only.'

Sandro was standing by Pietro at the pump now. 'She wouldn't tell you what she wanted to say?' Pietro shook out the pump, replaced it, locked the petrol cap. They climbed in, but Pietro didn't start the car. In the padded, sound-proofed leather interior Ceri's voice was audible, and Pietro was listening.

'She said she remembered you.'

Sandro cleared his throat. 'Really?' The word came out at a higher pitch than he'd intended.

'She said she remembered two policemen, an old one and a young nice-looking one. She said if you were the young one she wanted to speak to you.'

'She had registered the nature of the investigation?' said Sandro stiffly. 'That it concerned a murder?'

'Two murders,' said Ceri. 'Yes. She repeated that she would like to talk to the young policeman.' He sighed. 'I'm not sure about her – mental state, to be honest. She seemed to wander. She started telling me about what she had eaten for her breakfast. I told her, the young one – I said, you do know he isn't young any more?'

Sandro laughed, not very happily.

'Anyway,' said Ceri, clearing his throat, 'she said she'd try you tonight.'

Sandro thanked him – because back-up was back-up, after all – and hung up.

'That's all we need,' Pietro said, reaching for the ignition. 'Another old lady who's lost her marbles.'

Sandro sighed now, the phone in his hand. Back-up. Would he miss it when this was over? Would he be able to go back to the little office, being nursemaided by Luisa and Giuli? The car started, and they glided away from the pump, smooth as silk.

'Okay, boss,' said Pietro, pulling over and coming a halt, engine running. It was the second time he had been called boss today. Ahead of them, beyond the slip road, the traffic thundered, and Sandro felt a knot of apprehension in his stomach. Pietro scrutinised him. 'Next stop, a spa break – diet and mud-baths and mineral waters, all-inclusive?' He leaned over and tapped to open something on the iPad in Sandro's lap.

The pictures sprang up. La Serenita. A gallery of expensively shot photographs: a snowy mountainside, a ridge of pines, the sleek silhouette of a hotel, all glass and stone, an infinity pool. A woman in a white towel face down on a massage bed.

Sandro sighed. 'I guess,' he said, then reluctantly, 'You want me to drive this bit?'

Pietro shook his head, smiling wanly. 'I value my car too much for that,' he said, and Sandro was relieved. Too much walnut and leather, too many dials and alarms.

On the picnic tables between the petrol pumps and the Autogrill the little family were clearing their lunch away, the mother holding a wriggling small boy by the arm while she swiped at his face with a wet wipe. No more welcome than the old days, when your mother spat into her hanky.

'How's my god-daughter?' he said to Pietro as they moved off, wishing for a moment to be back in the real world, not the world of post-mortem pictures nor of luxury spas. His god-daughter was Pietro and Gloria's only child, Chiara, and he knew better than most she hadn't always been plain sailing.

'Ach, you know,' said Pietro, but he was smiling. The big car purred down the slip road. 'She's been with this guy for a few years now.' Grudgingly, 'He's okay, I suppose. Gloria worships the ground he walks on, so he's all right with me.' Rolling his eyes. 'How's Giuli?' shooting a casual glance at the traffic as they glided effortlessly in front of a big German articulated lorry.

'Giuli,' Sandro said. 'Now she's got Enzo –' he paused, frowning '– she's fine, I think.' He wasn't sure, suddenly. 'You saw her as recently as I did.'

'Well,' said Pietro cheerfully, 'she's never going to be, you know, any doctor's poster girl, is she? After the life she's had. But as a matter of fact I thought she looked pretty good.'

Up ahead the mountains had just come into view, white-capped and spectral on the horizon, rising out of the cherry orchards and vineyards.

'She's got something on her mind,' said Sandro, although it

had only just dawned on him. 'She's stressed.' He groped for his phone, reflexively, superstitiously. He wanted to talk to Luisa, to Giuli, to ask each about the other, to make sure everything was going to be okay: the women in his life.

Up ahead came the flare of several sets of red brake lights coming on. Pietro indicated to come out and there was a brief blast of a horn, the hostile white flash of headlights, as an even bigger, even faster car hurtled past, and with an impatient sound Pietro came back in. The car slowed.

Is everything going to be okay? He knew without looking that the last message he'd sent to Luisa said, *I'm sorry. I love you.*

Something else was nagging at him. The woman taking herself off to a spa to kill herself. Why there? And then as if it read his mind – and they did say, didn't they, that machines almost could these days – the iPad came alive in his hand (he must have grazed something with his hand) and there was the last thing he'd looked at, the home page of La Serenita. 'I wonder,' Sandro said, then stopped.

'What?'

It was only when Pietro turned to look at him that he realised he'd spoken. 'I think it's possible that something happened,' he said, 'at the hotel. Or fat farm or whatever.' He looked down at the picture. 'Wellness centre.'

They both looked at each other, then Pietro looked back at the road just in time and braked. An ambulance zipped past, lights flashing, on the hard shoulder.

'Gorgone?' said Pietro.

'Doesn't do any harm to give the guy a call,' said Sandro as they slowed to a stop in four lanes of traffic jam. 'Does it?'

Chapter Eighteen

IT WAS GETTING COLDER.

There was a wet wind from somewhere. It came up suddenly, strangely, a stiff breeze that made Giuli stop in the Via delle Terme, wondering if it was just her. But the Via delle Terme was one of those streets that always seemed deserted and she could see no one to corroborate the sensation. Giuli actually shivered, in her thin summer jacket – and then the breeze was gone. She walked on.

The Tornabuoni was, as always, bustling with shoppers. The summer's potted jasmine and plumbago still in place, the pedestrians in light clothing, strolling. Windless. Giuli crossed it in a hurry, intent on her destination. As she saw the sign – a crudely jig-sawed and painted boot – and the open door, she slowed. She could hear the high whine of the grinder as she approached and there was his back. The narrow shoulders, brown apron strings, thinning hair, glasses just visible perched on the top of his head as he leaned down, his back to her, trimming a leather sole in the finishing machine.

Perhaps he had a sixth sense for a customer or the sound of a heel that – as Giuli's did – could do with tipping because the cobbler stopped almost immediately she paused in his doorway and turned. Brought the glasses down on to his nose and straight away looked at Giuli's feet: a professional interest. She scuffled, embarrassed: they were boots off the market, twenty-nine euros, and when he raised his eyes to her face she knew he could tell.

Not quite as old as she had thought yesterday. Sixty rather than seventy. It occurred to her that the girl in the expensive handbag shop wouldn't know the difference: once someone was over forty they were ancient. It occurred to Giuli that – perhaps since she never thought she'd even *get* old – ageing had never bothered her until now. Until she started feeling her body going wrong. Your periods stopped, and then the rest started up – she halted the train of thought.

Because it wasn't ageing that was bothering her, was it? It was being dead. Being gone, and leaving Enzo. His poor ma, the look in her eyes from Enzo to her husband, even to Giuli, the worry over how they'd manage without her. Life going on without her. Stop it.

'Sorry to bother you,' Giuli said. He looked at her a second, then went on fiddling with the shoe he had in his hands. Tiny, tiny. A little court shoe, from the days when women had little bones, little feet.

She tried again. 'I wonder if I can ask you something?'

He grunted. 'Can't stop you, can I,' he said.

'The girl in the bag shop said you might know.' His bad temper was familiar: like Sandro's. You had to approach it with care or he might just push you back out the door and shut up shop.

Another grunt, this time rich with disdain. 'Well, *she* certainly doesn't know, whatever it is,' he said. 'Doesn't know French leather from Patagonian, doesn't know if it's raining unless her phone tells her.'

'No,' agreed Giuli.

He held the shoe out in front of him, sighed, then reached up to a shelf of polish tins and selected one. Navy blue. Then a rag, clean duster, brush, lined them up on his bench. 'What is it then?' The glasses were back on the top of his head, a dab of polish on the rag, applied to the shoe. Giuli watched, mesmerised. She experienced an odd second of longing to reach for the shoe and offer to help. Was she too old to learn a trade?

'The old lady in Via del Parioncino,' she said.

The polish had all been applied and he raised his head; the glasses fell back down on his nose. He reached for the brush. 'Ha,' he said. 'You'll have to be more specific. Old how? Your age, my age, ancient?'

'I'm not sure exactly,' she said. Trying to remember the voice, thin, cracked, girlish. 'She's a grandmother, I know that much. Has a granddaughter of, maybe –' she guessed '– three, no, four. Preschool age. And a daughter – obviously, the child's mother.' He was on to the duster now, polishing the shoe to a high gloss.

The child had to have been at least four. It occurred to her that it was odd, though, wasn't it? Why wasn't the child in nursery? The call had come in during the day. 'Number three?' she said. They both turned to look back at the Via del Parioncino: you could just see the door.

He raised the shoe up, checking it under the light, then looked past it to examine Giuli. He was shrewd behind his glasses. 'Number three's Signora Ticino,' he said, shaking his head a little, frowning. 'We don't see many children down here,' and he removed his glasses completely, wiping his forehead with the back of a hand, suddenly weary, older, his face creased. 'You lot don't have them, do you? You younger generation? One at the most.' He shook his head. 'We'd have thought it a tragedy, in our day. I mean, they're work, aren't they, little kids, but without them, what's the point?'

Giuli felt tears start to her eyes, of outrage; her mouth opened but nothing came out. It wasn't as if she hadn't heard it said before.

'You think I'm an old fool,' he said, eyeing her beadily. 'Or – what's the word? Prejudiced. Well, we're all prejudiced, aren't we? One way or the other. You, me, her in the handbag shop, anyone who pretends otherwise is lying. Young folks the most prejudiced of all if you ask me. But I'm sorry if I upset you.' He gave her a closer look. 'If it's any comfort, we never had any ourselves.'

He picked up the partner to the mended and polished shoe and began on that.

Giuli felt herself subside: curiously, she actually felt better. 'So,' she began again, 'do you know who I mean? Mrs Ticino, or whatever her name is?' He sighed, and hearing reluctance she hurried on. 'It's not exactly her I'm after, you see. It's not her I'm worried about.'

'Who *are* you worried about?' the cobbler said, working away at the shoe. He didn't look up at her this time, and it occurred to her that it might be best to tell him it all, even if it sounded unhinged, the wild-goose-chase of a barren woman. She might be anyone.

'You see,' Giuli began, 'I work in a detective agency.'

He heard her out. By the time she finished the tiny shoes were done: re-soled, re-tipped, polished and put in a brown paper bag side by side. He clipped a pink ticket to them, with a scrawl on it only decipherable probably to himself.

'So you're worried that the mother or the grandmother is mistreating the child,' he said. 'Is that right?'

'I – I don't know. There's just something – something not right about it. Why isn't the child at school? When children dial at random they usually just hang up or laugh, don't they? They don't beg for help.' She *did* sound unhinged.

'Give me that boot,' he said.

'What?' Giuli didn't know if she'd heard right.

'Your boot,' he repeated, nodding at her foot. 'The heel tip's come off. Won't take a minute.'

'They're not worth –'

He gave her a sharp look. 'Everything's worth mending,' he said. Obediently she handed him the boot, averting her eyes from the scuffs. 'Not bad workmanship,' he said. 'You know, they're probably made out beyond Prato. Not all rubbish you get on the market.'

'Please,' she said.

'I'm thinking,' he said. 'I can only think while I'm working.' It took him thirty seconds, less. He gave the boot back to her and sat on his high stool, arms crossed, regarding her.

'Those are her pumps,' he said. 'The lady at number three. She left them a month ago and hasn't been back for them. She's there, or was there – I saw her a few days ago. I called over to her but she didn't seem to hear me. She's ... a bit funny in the head, if you ask me.' He paused, and she could see his eyes were grave, anxious.

Giuli felt a chill come over her, a prickle at the back of her neck, the same feeling she'd had when the wind sprang up in the Via delle Terme. 'But the child,' she pleaded. 'The child. They shouldn't be leaving a child with her if she's doolally, should they? Do you think the little girl's safe?'

He looked at her long and hard and then began to shake his head. 'I don't know,' he said. 'I've never seen the old lady with anyone but her fancy man.'

'There's a man? She lives with a man?'

'He used to visit, take her out now and again. Tall guy. I've never seen a daughter or a granddaughter.'

Giuli found herself breathless at the scenarios that unspooled in her head. An elderly couple keeping a child captive. Had they kept her quiet while the grandmother called her back? Was she sedated so neighbours wouldn't hear? The small voice came back to her, whispering.

'What should I do?' she said. 'What should I do?'

The old cobbler looked at her a long moment, wiped his hands on his apron and picked up the paper bag containing the tiny pumps. He climbed off his stool and reached up for the long shutter that would close his shop.

'Come with me,' he said, and the shutter rattled down.

*

They believed Luisa in the end, or believed her enough not to call the police. Hushing her, bustling her out of the cubicle: by that time the place was full, a North African orderly, two nurses and an unshaven doctor on duty.

The redheaded nurse had marched her back to the nurses' station. 'What on earth did you think you were doing?'

'Benedetta – I've known her since we were girls,' Luisa said, only half a lie. 'I heard –' improvising '– her brother, half-brother, Luca, told me she might not last the day. I didn't want to leave it too late.'

The redhead frowned, her broad freckled face sceptical. 'Mr Bartolini hasn't been in today,' she said. 'She is – well, she was – quite out of danger. It really doesn't help when people don't respect visiting hours or procedures.'

'Why did the alarms go off?' said Luisa.

The woman looked at her. 'Her heart rate was dipping,' she said. 'Her rehydration drip –' She broke off, examining Luisa closely. 'You didn't touch anything, did you?'

'No,' Luisa was aghast. 'Nothing, I'd barely – well, I took hold of her hand. She seemed to want –' She didn't know what Benedetta had wanted, in truth. It was Luisa who simply hadn't wanted her to be alone, if it was the end. 'I didn't want her to feel alone,' she said.

The redhead narrowed her eyes, wary. 'Well, no harm done, I suppose,' she said grudgingly. 'And she's had her visitors. Her mother's carer has just left.'

'The Princess Salieri's carer?'

'Yes. She came out to look for you. She said she didn't recognise your name when you asked to be admitted before. I mean, we can't let just anyone in off the street.'

'Well, you let *her* in,' said Luisa.

The woman looked at her stonily. 'The patient knew her,' she said.

Sandro had said something about a housekeeper. The woman from the north, who hadn't been in the village long and therefore was prepared to gossip. 'I – I didn't see anyone,' said Luisa, because it seemed the safest thing to say. Then, as it occurred to her, 'Surely she would have noticed if the drip had come loose?'

Luisa tried to remember what Sandro had told her about the carer. Only that no one in the village would talk to her. That she had been a friend of Lotti's.

The redhead gave her a look. 'What are you suggesting, Mrs –?'

'Cellini,' said Luisa resignedly, seeing something dawn in the nurse's eyes.

'You're married to the detective, aren't you? He was in the newspaper a few years ago, and you with him.'

This city. It would have been the girl: it had been in the papers. A foreign girl held captive and Luisa had been with Sandro when they found her. It occurred to her that the maid, the carer, whoever, who'd been standing at the reception desk, who'd been interviewed by Sandro *Cellini* only a day ago, might have recognised the name.

'Don't you think you're letting your imagination run away with you?' said the nurse, with kind condescension.

'You were the ones who seemed to think someone had tampered with the line,' said Luisa. 'You even asked me if I'd done it. And I'm a friend of Benedetta's.'

'Well, we have cameras, you know,' said the nurse, giving her a sharp look, affronted.

'Oh, yes,' said Luisa, 'so you do.' She held the nurse's gaze: the previous year a woman dressed as a nurse had tried to steal a gypsy child from the emergency room and had only been apprehended when she began to run, on the hospital forecourt. It had been in the local paper. Security cameras had been installed all over the place.

'Well,' she said, holding herself upright, 'I suggest you look at your footage. And in the meantime I am going to wait patiently for visiting hours.'

The nurse flushed, very pink against her flaming hair, and said haughtily, 'One moment.' She hurried off through the door behind the nurses' station, from behind which Luisa heard muffled angry voices. The redhead emerged with her colour still high and said haughtily, 'You may sit with Benedetta for fifteen minutes. Do not touch her, or indeed anything, and do not interrogate her. Is that clear?'

'Have you looked at the footage?' said Luisa gently.

The woman pursed her lips. 'That's our business,' she said. 'Not yours, or your husband's for that matter.' And she made a gesture of elaborate welcome, sweeping a hand in the direction of Benedetta's bed, then stalked off behind the desk to busy herself pointlessly with some papers, not looking up when Luisa went.

Benedetta's skin against the pillow was still dry and papery, but there was a trace of colour to her at least. Luisa pulled the curtain round them a little and sat down on the chair that still stood beside the bed. She hadn't promised anything, had she?

She looked up, around the bed, searching for the camera, and saw none. All bluster, then.

Sandro, she thought. Sandro. She stepped to the window and dialled his number, her back to the glass, watching Benedetta.

As it began to ring, she suddenly thought, *what if he's driving*, and panic overtook her, a panic that seemed to have been lying in wait all day, since she'd got that message. *I'm sorry. I love you.* He'll answer and he'll crash – but before she could hang up the answerphone cut in. Hastily she whispered into it. 'I'm at the hospital, I came to see Benedetta. I worry about –' about what? About too many things. 'About her brother. Luca Bartolini. Not sure if he knows I'm married to you, if he's trying, I don't know, to hide something.'

On the pillow Benedetta's head moved just a little; a tiny sound, not even a moan, came from her. Luisa cupped her hand around the phone to mute her voice.

'The Salieri housekeeper, carer, whatever,' she whispered, 'the woman you met. Blonde? She was here at the hospital. Before me. I think she –' she spoke hurriedly, so it wouldn't sound so silly, so melodramatic '– I think she might have tampered with Benedetta. With her drip.'

She paused. Benedetta was still again; only the up and down movement of her thin chest gave a clue that she was alive. 'Give me a call back, will you? When you're there safely.'

It made no sense. Did the carer – what had Sandro said her name had been? Marte. Did she have a reason to hurt Benedetta? Luisa searched her brain and came up with none.

There were footsteps beyond the curtain. She hung up hastily, but the footsteps walked on past. She sat again, beside Benedetta, looking at the motionless profile.

Damn it: she hadn't promised the nurse anything in the end. Once again she reached for Benedetta's hand. The drip was there, in place, no alarms sounded. She raised the poor soft hand to her own cheek and kept it there. She expected nothing, only to sit there with her, so she wouldn't be alone. The minutes ticked by, the ward beyond the curtain was silent and Luisa was about to go when Benedetta's head turned on the pillow, and her eyes opened and looked straight into Luisa's.

'Benedetta, no – don't try – shh,' said Luisa in a whisper, not wanting her to use any of the energy that barely pulsed beneath her pale, papery skin. She was light and frail as dust on the pillow but her large blue eyes gazed, steady, into Luisa's.

'You remember me, don't you, Benedetta? It's Luisa.' There was the slightest movement of her head that Luisa took to mean she did. 'Did she take out your drip?' said Luisa in a whisper. 'The woman who was here? She's not your maid, is she? She doesn't work for your mother?'

The ghost of a smile appeared on Benedetta's lips. 'I must have done it by – by –' she seemed to have difficulty with the word, perhaps due to sedation '– by accident,' she finished.

Luisa looked into her eyes, trying to decipher the truth of it, and gave up. 'I was helping at your wedding,' she said, and as she spoke the words something came to her, a musty memory, an invitation with a gold tasselled cord, the name on it. 'All that time ago. At our age – those things seem to be clearer, don't they? Things that happened a long time ago.' She didn't know if she was talking to Benedetta or to herself.

The smile on Benedetta's face evaporated, a weak sun obscured by cloud. Luisa hurried on. 'It was always nice to see you, when your mother brought you into the shop.' Now, with hindsight, she could see that Benedetta's silence on those occasions hadn't just been recalcitrance. She must have been on medication for years.

Benedetta turned her head on the pillow, seeking the wall, then turned it back and looked at Luisa again. 'The child,' she said. 'The child. She's alone, you know. Will she be safe there?'

'The child?' Luisa whispered. 'What child, Benedetta?'

Something changed in Benedetta's eyes, turned them crystalline. 'They took her, they put her in the dark. You knew that, though, didn't you? They put her where it was cold and dark. You knew that.'

Luisa felt the hair on her head stand on end: the words meant something that in that moment she felt only she and Benedetta would understand. 'My child?' she said, although she knew in her rational mind that Benedetta wouldn't have known what happened, thirty years ago, to their child, hers and Sandro's – unless her mother – well, of course, yes. Her mother would have told her: other people's misfortunes were currency to those like the Princess Salieri.

But Benedetta could not have seen inside Luisa's head and known her thoughts as they buried their child, their daughter. In the cold and dark.

Benedetta smiled, a long, sad smile. The hand in hers wasn't soft any more, it was only bones, it clutched at her.

'She died,' said Luisa, as gently as she could. 'Benedetta. My baby died.'

'Oh no,' said Benedetta, 'our child will never die,' she said. 'Our child.'

And the head turned back on the pillow and was motionless. Her chest still rose and fell, no alarm sounded, but the beaked profile was the statue on a tomb.

There was a sound beyond the curtain, of voices, the nurses', and among them a new one. A man's voice – Luisa recognised it as Luca Bartolini's. And at the sound Benedetta began to struggle.

Chapter Nineteen

I T CAME INTO VIEW at the head of the valley as they wound up in the big black car. A scattering of large, pale, modern buildings, white as sugar cubes, set under a forbidding ridge against the sky. Climbing out of the car, Sandro could hear the thunder of a waterfall.

There was a message from Luisa but it had been delivered in a whisper and he couldn't make half of it out against the sound. Something about visiting Benedetta Salieri in the hospital. Something about Gianna Marte. What did she know about Gianna Marte? He gave up: they'd wait.

Pietro had called Gorgone from the car as Sandro drove. At the wheel, Sandro had found he needed to concentrate hard or the big car ran away with him. So easy to drive too fast when the car was so powerful and so silent, quite insulated from the world. It was difficult to drive and listen but he could tell, even with all the distractions, that Gorgone was hiding something. That he didn't like the questions. And that the news of Lucia Grenzi's death was a shock to him. Sandro had reached his hand for the phone, but Pietro shook his head.

'He knows La Serenita,' said Pietro after he hung up, 'but it's not one of his wellness centres. He said everyone knows it – it's the classiest and most expensive place in the Dolomites.'

They'd just come round Verona, past the ubiquitous commercial centres, furniture shops, eight lanes of traffic completely concealing the ancient city. And beyond it all, close now, the ghostly white peaks of the mountains, the great barrier to the north. Sandro was most definitely not a mountain person. The Brenner wound up into them, the wide square valley with rock climbing abruptly to either side.

'He was shocked to hear about Grenzi's death?' said Sandro. 'Genuinely?'

'I thought so,' said Pietro, frowning. 'He's – like you said before – a bit like he's on autopilot.'

The valley had begun to narrow around them. The afternoon wasn't much advanced but the mountains' long shadows had started to creep across the vineyards and barns. They were called suicide valleys, when you got to where the sun barely entered, Sandro knew that.

'I know what you mean,' he said, eyeing the rock face as though it might make another step towards them. 'Like his hard drive's been wiped,' he went on, 'burned out. They could easily have been doing drugs there at La Vipera – in fact, it would have been surprising if they weren't.' He fell silent, wondering. It seemed too easy to blame drugs.

It had been raining up here and the motorway gleamed: he shifted carefully into the slow lane.

'Or a lot of therapy,' said Pietro.

'Yes,' said Sandro absently. Something chimed with the

thought, some memory of standing on the landing outside Gorgone's offices. And that moment, at the end of his interview with the man, when a chink, an odd chink, had appeared in Gorgone's apparent imperviousness. 'Yes,' he said again. 'I thought he was just stupid. Maybe it was something else.'

'But he did seem very shocked to hear she'd died,' Pietro said thoughtfully. 'I believed that. *Committed suicide* – he kept repeating it. He sounded frightened. I asked if he'd had any word from her at all and he was adamant he hadn't.'

'Talking of drugs,' said Sandro. 'You did send the forensics people out to La Vipera to look at what we found? In the chimney breast?'

'Yeah,' said Pietro, leaning back in his big seat. 'They said they'd email preliminary results, could be this afternoon.'

And then the wet road had narrowed, a shining ribbon winding steeply uphill, and they'd stopped talking until La Serenita came into view.

They were standing in the car-parking area, screened from the hotel complex by a wide paved road lined with cypresses so neatly clipped they might have been cut-outs. They looked distinctly odd up here. The air was almost sparkling, cold and crystalline: tentatively Sandro inhaled, his old lungs used to carbon monoxide and the warm damp of the Arno, and coughed immediately.

Beyond the trees the bulk of the hotel buildings rose. Large windows, balconies, a sculptured parkland. A wide stream flowing across it and, somewhere he couldn't perceive, the waterfall. Now and again he'd read about these places in magazines, the fat farm, the wellness centre, and all he had ever wondered was

– other than, how can anyone afford a thousand euros a day – if they caught you wolfing down a plate of *spaghetti cacio e pepe* in the nearest mountain refuge, would they haul you back in under guard? With sorrowful looks, for re-education? He'd even remembered saying to Luisa, *they could tag them*. The inmates.

He surveyed the scene at higher level, and sure enough there they were, two cameras on poles at the entrance: no doubt more elsewhere.

It could have been the ridiculous purity of the air or the cold or the sound of the crashing water that never let up, but Sandro was feeling distinctly unusual: it was as if everything was in too sharp a focus here. As if the place was too clean, too full of nature. Grenzi had exiled herself up here for that very reason, perhaps. And Helen Mason in Nova Scotia, another cold, clean place of exile.

'Right then,' said Sandro, deciding to use this odd clear-headedness before it evaporated. 'We're meeting the director, right?'

Pietro had called ahead. 'Right,' he said. 'Two o'clock.' It was a minute after: the Alfa had done them proud. The old Fiat would have taken an hour and a half longer, if it had got here at all. They began to walk briskly towards a wide glass entrance, flanked by two large lumps of granite that might or might not have been sculptures.

'Any impressions?' asked Sandro quickly. 'Of her, I mean, the director of the place, when you spoke to her on the phone?'

Pietro looked at him sideways. 'German,' he said. They stepped up their pace.

She didn't look particularly German, a petite woman with a

lot of thick black hair, and her name was Maria Scarpa, a name from the Veneto. She gestured towards two chairs that looked faintly medicinal: the kind that were good for your back, all pale wood and oatmeal tweed.

Her voice did have the Tyrolean edge, it was true. They were different up here – but then weren't they different everywhere? Sitting down carefully, Sandro instructed himself to keep an open mind.

'Gentlemen,' she said and looked at her watch.

Sandro bridled, but he knew better than to take offence. 'Dottoressa.'

One wall of the large room had a display of certificates and qualifications – nothing vulgar, all very discreetly and tastefully presented. However, he had seen similar qualifications elsewhere. In the reception area of Luisa's hairdresser's, for example, where he'd whiled away many an hour examining them while waiting for her to finish inquiring after Fabio's family.

Why was he so against this kind of thing? Because aromatherapy wasn't science? Because it charged unhappy people, mostly female, a thousand euros a day for laxatives and broth and round-the-clock massage? That, maybe. But a woman had killed herself here and Dottoressa Scarpa was treating them like door-to-door salesmen. This most decidedly was not going to be easy.

'I know it's a little while back,' intervened Pietro quickly, getting the measure of Sandro's mood. 'And this is extraordinarily helpful of you, to offer us access –'

'I'm not offering you access,' Scarpa interrupted him smoothly.

'Of course not,' said Sandro, taking over. 'We understand absolutely that your –' the word *inmates* sprang to mind '– guests are here for privacy, their treatments are confidential, and we don't want to interfere with that.'

Pietro continued. 'But,' his voice was gentle, solicitous. He was good, Sandro reflected. 'We are pursuing a murder inquiry. Three people have died, if, as I think we must, we connect Signora Grenzi's death with our investigation.'

'Why must you?' said Scarpa swiftly.

'She lived with the dead woman in a commune, long ago, in the village where the murders occurred.' Scarpa said nothing, frowning, and Pietro spread his hands. 'You can see that we really have no choice.' He gestured back to where they'd come from. 'We've done our best to be discreet.' Implying that they could return in a squad car or two if she wanted.

There was a long pause, during which Maria Scarpa returned his look with steely poise. 'What do you want?' she said.

'We'd like to talk to anyone who was in contact with her while she was here for that last stay,' said Pietro quickly.

'Beginning with yourself, perhaps?' said Sandro.

Scarpa turned her head. 'I wasn't here,' she said. 'I was in Bermuda, on my annual break.' Her voice was quieter, regretful. If he'd known her for more than five minutes he'd have guessed it was sadness. But she went on, and he didn't pursue it.

'I spoke to everyone myself on my return,' she said. 'It was a tragedy. Lucia was much loved.'

'She was a regular guest?' he asked quickly. 'That must have been awful, for all of you.'

'I wasn't here,' said Scarpa again, looking older and more

tired – and nicer. 'I did wonder if I had been ...' She waved a hand, a gesture of helplessness more vague than her body language had been hitherto, more human.

'I'm sure –' Sandro began but Scarpa shook her head impatiently.

'I don't flatter myself I could have prevented Lucia from doing anything she wanted to do. She was a person of great determination. But,' and she looked uncertain, 'she would come here to restore herself. It was her safe place, her sanctuary. Perhaps my absence made it feel less so, less stable – I don't know.'

'She needed a safe place? She was – troubled?' Pietro spoke too quickly.

Scarpa put her hands flat on the table. Manicured, short straight-cut nails, unpainted. No rings, no jewellery of any kind. 'Commissario,' she said. 'I'm not a doctor. I'm not a psychiatrist. I run what is essentially a hotel. But allow me my professional scruples. I told the coroner what I knew about Lucia Grenzi. It is a matter of public record. She had fears, as we all do, episodes of anxiety. She came here to clear her mind, as many do. I told the coroner I had never seen any sign that she was suicidal.' She allowed a pause to lengthen. 'Never. I don't make guesses about my guests' mental health or the causes of their distress. I only try to create an atmosphere of calm and – sanctuary, if you like.'

'But there is no doubt it *was* suicide,' said Pietro gently.

Scarpa nodded, spots of colour in her cheeks. 'It would seem so. My staff tried very hard to revive her,' she said. 'She left a note beside the bed – I saw it, and it was her handwriting – apologising for the distress she knew it would cause them.' She took a piece of paper from a drawer to the side of her pale desk. 'These are the members of staff who spoke to Lucia Grenzi at any length.' She had it prepared, with details: she had always intended to co-operate. Sandro sighed inwardly at the foolishness of judging by first impressions, especially where northerners were concerned.

She stood. 'I have made sure that they are working today. There's a conference room you can use – number three, follow the signs.'

Sandro glanced at the paper: Scarpa had been thorough. Dorcas Ogunwi, Congolese, aged twenty, maid of two years' service; Vincenzo Nutri, restaurant waiter, forty-five, who had been with the spa since it opened; and Eleonora Castrozzi, born in Sardinia thirty-seven years ago. She had worked for La Serenita as a masseuse for six years.

'I'll have Dorcas sent up,' said Scarpa, with a thin smile. 'Eleonora is in a treatment. You may have to go to her – she's very busy today.'

And they were dismissed.

They proceeded to the conference room, up a limestone staircase and down carpeted corridors. The place was kept very warm. A middle-aged woman passed them going the other way in a towelling gown and turban, giving them a dirty look. Cold and hungry, no doubt, thought Sandro, nodding to her.

The maid, Dorcas Ogunwi, arrived promptly, peering round the door. A slight girl, looking younger than her twenty years in the pale-grey button-fronted uniform, a tiny cap on her cropped head, but sparky and cheerful as she introduced herself. All Sandro knew about the Congo was that there always seemed to be a civil war going on there, but he didn't say so. Obviously. She looked nervous when Sandro asked her instead, only because he could still hear her strong accent, how long she had been in the country.

'No, no,' he said, cursing himself. 'I am very happy you're here. Listen, I am not even a working police officer any more, and if anyone asked me, I would say we need more of you not fewer. Hard-working young people? Of course.' And he even believed it. Where were the young? There were so few of them.

Dorcas subsided. 'I have been in Italy seven years. I came when I was thirteen. I work here two years. You want to know about Lucia?'

Already Sandro liked Lucia Grenzi. He couldn't remember her more than in outline, small and dark and fierce, cropped hair. He had a stronger memory of Martine: he could remember Martine's voice in La Vipera now, hear it somewhere else in that house. But Lucia's name on this girl's lips, as though they'd been friends. She'd encouraged a maid from the Congo, made her feel at home up here in the cold white mountains.

'Yes,' he said.

'She was a very nice lady,' said Dorcas, putting a hand to her head to make sure the little white cap was in place. 'She always left money for me after her stay, even when she only came for a few days. She never became angry, never complain. Of course, I don't give cause – but there are plenty of guests who complain anyway. Who accuse of stealing even if they lose something themselves and when they find again –' She broke off. 'It wasn't the tip. She was kind lady. Ask about my family, give me money for them.' She paused, her bright eyes clouding. 'I – when I –' and she couldn't go on.

'You found her,' said Sandro gently. She nodded, sitting up very straight. He could see tears welling in her eyes and saw her hold herself very still so they wouldn't spill over.

'Hanging,' she said. 'You know. In Congo, we see dead people. Some guest wouldn't think about the maid at all, or if they think, would consider, a girl from Africa, she seen all this before, no need to protect her. She leave me a note, in the place where she always leave the tip. I had to give it to the police. It say, *I'm sorry Dorcas.* Say, *I can't go on but you must go on. For your family.*' She stared down at her hands. 'She left me money too.'

There was a heavy silence, the weight of a human life departed.

'Did she arrive here in particular distress?' asked Pietro. 'Was she worried? Did she talk to you about her – feelings at all, ever?'

The girl shook her head slowly, withdrawing a crumpled tissue from the sleeve of her uniform tunic and tugging at it between her fingers. 'She was okay the day she arrived. She seemed very happy to be here, very relax when she put down her bag. She give me a hug.' Dorcas looked down at the tissue, at her fingers that were shredding it. 'She was supposed to be here six days. She was here three days when I find her body.'

'You last saw her – alive, I mean – the previous morning?' said Pietro. Dorcas nodded. 'And how did she seem?'

'Normal,' said Dorcas, rubbing at the corner of her eye. 'Nothing strange about her. Getting better already, feeling better. Looking forward to her treatments. She enjoy them.'

'What treatments did she have? The same every day?'

'Yes,' said Dorcas. 'There are different plans for different guests. Lucia was not on the weight loss regime, but the wellness regime because she – she –' She hesitated, not knowing the appropriate words to use. 'She was not fat. Too skinny, in fact. She eat what she want – though everything here is very healthy.' She wrinkled her nose and darted them a rueful, comical glance. 'No French fries. Breakfast, swim, lunch, massage. Usually she go for a walk but that day it was raining.'

'So the waiter –' Sandro looked at the page again '– Mr Nutri, he would have seen her in the middle of the day?'

Dorcas nodded. 'Yes,' she said. 'She like Vincenzo, he was always her waiter.'

When they told her she could go she jumped up eagerly, like a child let out of school. At the door she turned back. 'I wish she tell me,' she said. 'I wish I see her one more time and she tell me why. I wish.' And she was gone.

Nutri was a square sort of man with a pink complexion and very little hair: he seemed shy, for all his substance, and anxious. 'I hear you were a favourite of Miss Grenzi,' said Sandro, to put him at his ease.

'She was a favourite of mine,' said Nutri proudly. 'I served her for seven years here, since she began coming, when the spa opened. A very nice lady. Very thoughtful. She could eat what she wanted but she always chose so as not to upset the guests who were on the weight loss diet. Always interested in me and my family.'

'I imagine it was a terrible shock,' said Sandro, 'to lose her.'

Nutri set his elbows on the table and briefly rubbed his big face with his hands. 'Terrible,' he said slowly. 'That's the right word. Shock – I don't know. I don't know. People come here because there's something missing. We don't talk about that –

I'm a waiter, it would be impolite. She was a sensitive person.' He spread his hands. 'So if something happened, if something went wrong – I just don't know.'

'How do you mean?' said Pietro.

'I mean, this is the place where they are safe.' Nutri gestured. 'Among friends. Lucia in particular. We were her friends, the director was her friend.' He hesitated. 'If their trouble, whatever the trouble is, the bad husband, the bad lover, the bank manager, the illness – if it follows them here –' He broke off.

'Do you think that's what happened?' said Sandro quickly.

'I don't know,' said Nutri.

'Did you say this to the coroner?' said Pietro. Nutri looked at him, his big shiny face.

'I didn't think of it,' he said simply. 'He just wanted to know if she had been distressed when I saw her, at lunch, the last time I saw her. And I said she had been maybe preoccupied, only. Not distressed. When he was asking me, I couldn't really say why.'

'Could you try to think?' said Sandro, as gently as he could. 'To think back to that day?'

Nutri rubbed his eyes again and was quiet for a moment, his hands to his face. Then he took them away. 'She had been swimming – her hair was still wet. She kept looking around whenever anyone came into the room. As if she was looking for someone?'

'She didn't say anything to you, though? Not that –' Sandro hesitated '– perhaps she'd seen someone she didn't want to see?' Nutri shook his head. 'And she didn't come in for dinner?'

'No,' he said, and there was anguish in his voice.

'You didn't see her again?'

Nutri began to shake his head, and then stopped. 'I think she went for a walk. As I was serving the second sitting I saw her come in through the front door and go upstairs. I didn't think much of it. It was such a beautiful evening.'

When Nutri was gone, Sandro stood from the long table and walked to the window. From where he stood at the wide triple-glazed hermetically sealed wall of glass, to his left he could see a flat-glazed roof that came out from that wing of the hotel, and beneath it the shifting pale blue-green of a swimming pool. The water extended further, beyond the roof into the open air where steam rose from its surface, and as he watched, the broad-backed figure of a female swam out, head in a rubber cap and employing a slow breaststroke, turning back in under the canopy as another swimmer emerged.

Sandro was aware of Pietro beside him, nodding down at the pool. 'What are you thinking?' he said. 'We go down to the massage rooms to find that busy masseuse?'

Sandro chewed the inside of his lip, still thinking about Scarpa and what Nutri had said. 'Sure,' he said absently. But when they turned from the window and it all shifted around in his head – the timing, the people, the thought of Lucia Grenzi at her lunch table – as they slotted into their places, Sandro stopped.

'No,' he said. 'You know what? A little detour.' He could see Pietro's face turn wary. 'Don't suppose you brought your trunks, did you?'

*

However hard you tried to disguise it with room fragrances and incense, you could always smell a pool. Chlorine and feet: the feet of the rich smelled just like everyone else's. Pietro and Sandro had been challenged at the door and admitted only after being supplied with disposable spongy flip-flops, Pietro's face a picture as he stripped off his socks and trainers. The pool was very long and narrow in a room of the same pale stone as the rest of the place, and at the far end a sort of rubber curtain allowed the swimmers to swim out into the open air without admitting too much cold. As they watched, the large woman they had seen from above breached the curtain, swimming doggedly back inside.

They stood against the back wall. Pietro hadn't asked why they were here, yet.

Sandro watched the woman. 'Lucia Grenzi came in with wet hair. Didn't wait to dry it,' said Sandro.

'Do women always dry their hair?'

'I'd say they do if they're not at home, if they're eating lunch in public. I'd say she was in a hurry. Distracted.' The pool had four lanes and, as they watched, held only the woman and a man, both in caps and goggles. There had been a discreet sign at the door insisting on both. A lifeguard paced.

The long space was flooded with light: it entered the room from three sides, bouncing and twinkling from its surfaces. But it had been raining, mused Sandro, when Lucia Grenzi had come swimming on the last morning of her life. Had she known when she entered the water that it would be the last? He thought not. But something had been set in motion by the time she climbed out.

'With goggles and those rubber caps on you wouldn't recognise your own mother, would you?' said Pietro, and bang on cue the female swimmer reached the aluminium steps and stripped off her cap. Damp tawny curls sprang out around a broad freckled face; the goggles were next.

The male swimmer had reached the end of the pool and, just as the woman had done, removed his cap. They nodded at each other circumspectly, climbed out and walked off in different directions.

'I think she saw someone. Someone she thought she knew. Or someone who reminded her of something.'

The lifeguard was approaching: they waited for him to reach them.

Chapter Twenty

GIULI STARTLED HERSELF by yawning and hastily lifted a hand to stifle it. It felt to her as though they had stood in the doorway of the building engaging in easy conversation with the concierge for an hour before they got into the narrow vaulted hall. Her back ached. Was this age, too?

The concierge was a small Neapolitan woman in an apron, with suspicious eyes and short dyed red hair. She seemed to be on easy terms with the cobbler: gradually Giuli grasped that she had her eye on him, although he was probably ten years her senior. Sometimes it astonished her, the human urge to find a mate. Or just to mate. If she hadn't found Enzo ...

Surreptitiously she checked her phone. Another missed call, but not from Enzo, from a number the phone didn't recognise and therefore that clinic woman. She stuffed the phone back in her pocket.

The cobbler, she recognised, was something of an operator. He took his time getting round to the point, until she began to wonder if he was interested in the Neapolitan. He didn't give that away, which would have been Giuli's recommendation: the concierge looked like a little terrier who wouldn't let go once she'd got her teeth into him.

The narrow stone stairway smelled of incense and polished stone. There was a door at the back of the hall that had been left open, allowing a glimpse of a rug and a dresser in a dim, sunless space that must be the concierge's apartment.

'It's the lady on the first floor,' the shoe-mender came out with it, finally. 'What's her name, Signora –'

'Ticino,' supplied Giuli, regretting her intervention immediately when the Neapolitan shot her a narrowed look. Giuli twiddled her wedding ring casually, hoping that would convince the concierge she wasn't a rival, but the woman just settled her arms across her broad bust, turning a little so she couldn't see Giuli at all.

'What about her?' she said, glancing up the stairway. Giuli and the cobbler followed her gaze. At the bend in the stairs an ugly cactus stood on a ledge.

'Well, this lady –' smoothly the cobbler corrected himself, indicating Giuli '– this person is worried about her. Seems to think there's something wrong.' He lowered his voice. 'Some family trouble. The wellbeing of a child is involved. She's got a grandchild? Granddaughter?'

The Neapolitan became immediately agitated. 'I can't discuss the tenants out here,' she said, seizing the cobbler by his elbow and shoving him ahead of her down the hall towards the open door. Giuli hung back, a foot on the step, but the woman was too sharp for her. 'And you,' she said over her shoulder.

It was a single room, crammed with the contents of a whole apartment, and a door to the back that must lead if not to a bathroom then at least a privy. The room smelled of drains and damp and was dark. The concierge hauled out a set of mahogany chairs around a matching table too large for the room and they sat, squeezed against the highly polished wood. Giuli was beginning to feel queasy: she felt a stab of longing for her clean, small, bright flat, and for Enzo. A tinkling tray of glasses appeared on the table, some unspecified sticky liquid in them.

'What was that about a child?' said the concierge, her eyes beady-bright in the dim room. She handed a glass to the cobbler and plonked one down in front of Giuli.

The cobbler sipped, appreciative. 'I told, I told this lady –'

'Giulietta Sarto,' said Giuli, unable to sit quietly any longer. The smell of sweet booze settled over the sulphurous stink of drains. 'I work for Sandro Cellini, who is a private investigator.' The Neapolitan's suspicious expression hardened but Giuli took a deep breath and carried on. 'The child phoned our offices asking for help, from this number. I spoke to the grandmother the next day, who explained the situation to me – but there was something odd about it. I can't explain.'

'I've never seen a child,' said the concierge slowly. 'Never.'

'That's what *I* said,' said the cobbler eagerly. His glass was empty: the concierge reached for the bottle, but absently.

'There's a man, her own age, brother or cousin. He took her when she went on her holiday, a few weeks ago, he brought her back, then –' she hesitated. 'He took her home with him a day or so ago.'

'But no daughter? No child?'

'There's a woman visits, but I always thought she was some kind of carer, checking up on her. No family resemblance, none.

A blonde. Never brought a child with her, and not the motherly type, I'd have said.'

'So you've never seen the child?' Giuli sensed something coming, something she was afraid of. It sharpened her senses, the air thickened, the room squeezed tight around her and she felt saliva rush into her mouth. 'You haven't seen one – but –'
She was half to her feet at the table, cold sweat on her forehead, her hand to her mouth.

'There,' said the concierge sharply, pointing to the door at the back of the room and Giuli stumbled, barking her shin painfully on something, blundering through the crowded space. She got through the door just in time and found herself on her knees in a tiny, shockingly cold space, face to face with the ancient scale round a porcelain toilet bowl.

She vomited, luxuriously. The door behind her was open – there wasn't room to close it with her on her knees – but Giuli was past caring. She could hear a tap running, could hear them muttering together at the table, scandalised. *At* her *age*, she heard. They probably thought she'd been drinking. *I'm sick,* she wanted to say. She heaved and retched until there was nothing left and she sat back, drained. Her face felt clammy; shakily, she stood up. A tiny basin sat against the wall, above it a small square of speckled mirror: she looked green. She splashed water on her face and rinsed out her mouth, and went back in.

'All right?' said the concierge warily. The cobbler just looked appalled.

'I'm sorry,' said Giuli. 'It must have been something I –'

'Something you ate,' the Neapolitan finished for her, sour. Giuli knew she thought she was a drunk or a junkie. 'Yes, well.'

She pushed a glass of squash across the table to Giuli, and beside it a cracker. 'Just have a nibble on that.' She and the shoe-mender exchanged glances.

Gingerly Giuli nibbled. The salt on the cracker might have been ambrosia. There was a silence.

'You were saying,' said the cobbler, leaning towards the concierge, his elbows on her polished mahogany, 'were you?'

The woman hesitated a moment then got up, crossed to a board of hooks beside the door where keys hung, ran her finger along, selected one.

'I've never seen a child come into this building,' she said. 'But up there, in that room with the old lady – with Signora Ticino – I've heard her.'

'You've heard her?'

'I've heard her crying.'

*

Luisa was halfway home when finally Sandro got hold of her. She was at the foot of the steps that led up to the loggia of the Ospedale degli Innocenti, where a stone bench presented itself. She climbed the steps and gingerly lowered herself to sit.

She was still reeling from the look Luca Bartolini had given her when he saw her at the bedside, Benedetta beside her struggling upright in adoration when she heard his voice, her beloved half-brother, her protector. Contempt? Was that it? Irritation. The kind of look an aristocratic employer gives a clumsy servant. She'd been right: he'd played her. She'd got up in a hurry, apologetic – although what had she to apologise for?

'Luisa?' Sandro's voice crackled.

'Darling,' she said.

Sandro sounded a long way away. How rarely, it occurred to her, were they separated, and the distance doubled, tripled, by the weight of what she wanted to say and couldn't. He was busy. He was out there in the world: he had no time for nonsense of that sort, for jealous imaginings.

She let him speak first.

This tangled mess.

He told her that a woman who'd lived at La Vipera had killed herself up at some hotel, months ago, early in the summer. Before all this. One of those women. Her name had been Lucia Grenzi.

Luisa remembered again standing in the loggia of the Lanzi watching the people from La Vipera approach, all that time ago. A very different loggia to this one: the Innocenti, where she stood now, had been a foundling hospital. Where the desperate left their unwanted babies, setting them in a wheel to turn and be drawn inside to the sisters who would feed them and clothe them and neither the nuns nor the infants would ever know what their mother had looked like.

She would take a child, even now, if it came to her in the night, she would take another woman's child from that wheel and hold it, a baby – Luisa tightened her grip on her handbag. Stop that.

The loggia of the Lanzi was where the bodyguards of the Medici would stand and wait and watch. Luisa forty years ago had stood there among the statues and the milling tourists with their big cameras slung around their necks, no mobiles back then so you had to look, and look hard. She had watched

Nielsson, listened to the voices; she had determined that one of the women was Italian, the stocky dark one with the Roman nose and the accent of the Po valley.

Another had been blonde.

Something shifted with that memory, a tiny tingle of recognition.

'I think she saw Nielsson up here,' he was saying now. 'She had a camper-van. Martine Kaufmann, the one with a studio in the Oltrarno, came across her in Liguria. She was in the camper.'

A thought occurred to her about that day: had Johanna Nielsson told them all who she was meeting under the Loggia dei Lanzi, and why? Gorgone, Grenzi, Kaufmann. The idle, loafing man, hands in his pockets. Nielsson upright – a blonde, a smaller dark woman. Had she laughed with them about Luisa, this silly little Italian girl with her uptight ideas, with her family and her cooking and her little job selling dresses to the bourgeoisie, at the thought that she might be there to threaten them?

The girlfriend of the policeman. Something crept at the back of her neck, the thought that she was tied to this horrible murder case as tight as Sandro was. She thought of the nurse turning to look at her down the corridor, with Benedetta's visitor beside her, as she said her name.

Sandro was talking. 'The lifeguard said someone else was swimming there that day, a woman who'd taken a swimming ticket to the spa. Not a local, a foreigner. Hair too long for her age, he said, grey hair and –' he hesitated '– Nielsson had long hair. Long white hair.'

The reason Sandro knew Nielsson's hair had been white and still long was because he'd seen photographs of her decomposing corpse. She was dead, and Luisa's spite looked pathetic.

'So Grenzi saw Nielsson – and then she killed herself?'

There was a hesitation. 'Trouble is, no one actually saw them talking. The lifeguard said they didn't speak. Grenzi rushed off to her lunch and the other, let's assume Nielsson, took forever drying her hair and didn't use the restaurant. But yes. But – maybe.'

'Have you spoken to the man? Gorgone? I thought you said he ran a chain of wellness centres, spas?'

'Pietro spoke to him,' said Sandro. 'It's not one of his places, although he did say he knew it. I think there was something he wasn't telling us.'

'About Nielsson?'

'Maybe,' said Sandro. 'He said the only one he kept in contact with was Martine Kaufmann. He couldn't remember Grenzi's name, even – that seemed convincing enough.'

She saw them again, in her mind's eye, even though she was in the wide empty piazza and not the throng of the Piazza Signoria. 'I spoke to Benedetta,' she said. 'In the hospital. I think she's involved, somehow.'

Sandro didn't seem to be listening. 'We've been trying to trace the camper Nielsson was travelling in.' His voice seemed to fade in and out, hesitant.

'Are there things you aren't telling me?' said Luisa.

'Where would you hide a camper-van?' he said, his voice suddenly clear. 'Not a caravan site, you have to check in, give documentation. If you wanted it to just – disappear?'

It came to her straight away. 'In one of those places, you know. Van parks. Where people keep their campers when they aren't using them. There's about five of them down on the ring road, near Firenze Sud.'

A silence. Then Sandro said reverently, 'You little genius. You little sainted genius.'

'Darling –' she began, not knowing how to start on the phone like this. To tell him she knew about his feelings for Johanna Nielsson. To say it was all right. To confess she had hidden things from him. 'Darling –' But she broke off.

'Tomorrow – tomorrow. I'll be back tomorrow.' He thought she was saying she missed him. His voice faded, faltered, uncertain.

Luisa cleared her throat. 'Did you get my message?' she said. 'About the maid from the Salieri villa at the hospital? Visiting Benedetta?'

'Yes,' he said distractedly. 'I couldn't work out what you were saying. The maid visited her employer's daughter – well, that's not too strange?'

'It's not that,' said Luisa. 'There was something about her – when she heard my name. I don't know if she recognised me or something. She came rushing out to look for me when I asked to be admitted to the ward and I –' She broke off. 'There was a scent – she smelled of –'

'Gingerbread,' said Sandro and she stopped in her tracks.

'Gingerbread?' She wasn't sure if he was winding her up.

Sandro was energised. 'Marte? Why would she know you? I'd never seen her before in my life. She was a funny woman, very Austrian-looking. I don't think she knew what she'd got into, associating with Lotti. Although –' He stopped.

'What?' said Luisa.

'She sort of admitted she'd told Lotti that he'd find truffles on that hillside, though God knows where she'd have got that information from.' He was thoughtful. 'She pretended she couldn't remember. You had the idea maybe she had messed about with the life support?'

'Something had certainly happened,' said Luisa. 'There were all sorts of alarms and the woman, Marte, was nowhere to be found. Benedetta said she'd done it herself, got tangled up in the wires ...'

Should she tell him? And then it spilled out anyway. 'Sandro – Benedetta was talking about a child,' she said. 'A baby, a lost baby alone in the dark.'

There was a silence, and she heard his unease. They didn't talk about lost children, never had.

She swerved, abruptly. 'In any case, she seems to be on the mend. They think she'll be well enough to be discharged. They're taking her back to Sant'Anna. Her, her half-brother is. So he must trust Marte to look after her.'

Before the curtain had been pulled back she had heard him saying that to the nurses: something about her being safer in the country.

Something else. But Sandro was off the phone, talking to Pietro.

'Look, I'd better go, the masseuse is free.'

'What? You're getting a massage?' In that instant she simply wanted to scream.

'No, I need to talk to her. She was the last person to talk to Grenzi.'

'Okay,' she said hastily. 'Sorry, but it seemed important. There's this thing –' she hesitated '– it's Benedetta.' Don't mention the baby again. Don't. 'She had this thing, this, like a sort of homemade tattoo on her wrist. And didn't you say, didn't you mention –' for a panicked second she couldn't remember if he *had* said '– she had, Nielsson had, a tattoo, on her wrist? Like a –' she might as well bluff it out, now, skate over how she knew '– like a spiral sort of thing, a curly snail shell thing?'

And he was listening. *No, wait,* she heard him say to Pietro. *Hold on.*

'Yes,' he said.

'And there's a drawing like that on the side of the house,' she said. 'La Vipera?'

'Yes,' said Sandro slowly and she could hear him wondering how she knew. 'Yes, it's all covered up with ivy, some kind of symbol. Like a – a rune or something. Concentric circles, or a spiral.'

'I think Benedetta has the same tattoo, or tried to make it herself. Funny thing is, it didn't look like a snail, the one she did, hers had a sort of –'

More noise behind him then, and Sandro said quickly, 'Can we talk again, darling? Can we? I need to see you, I miss you, can't we – I've got to go.' And he was gone.

'Hers had a sort of – a sort of face,' she murmured, to no one.

Opposite her in the pale autumn sunshine a crocodile of tiny children was being led diagonally across the big square, past the equestrian statue, to the great pillars of the church, the Santissima Annunziata. The most Holy Annunciation. Only occasionally did Luisa look at the great buildings of the city and wonder about their meaning: they were so much the fabric of her life, her childhood, her workday wanderings.

A church dedicated to the annunciation of the birth of Christ, an angel coming to the virgin to tell her she was pregnant. The children trailing across the square from where Luisa sat, under the loggia of a hospital for the care and protection of the newborn. The blue majolica medallions along the arches depicting the swaddled child. What did it mean, without a child? What did life mean?

The coil traced blue on the inside of Benedetta's wrist had a face. It was the curl of a child, a foetus. Luisa closed her eyes and saw the circles half-exposed on the flank of La Vipera and knew that was what they meant, too, their significance perhaps more disguised, but Benedetta was beyond hiding her meaning, Benedetta's pain was all on the surface, it needed to be subdued. Who knew about it? Who subdued it? Her half-brother? Her mother?

In the soft dark of her closed eyes she saw Benedetta, saw her wandering in that effort to ease something, to subdue it, from hospital to seaside resort to sanatorium. That was what they used to be called, now they were wellness centres. Her eyes sprang open on the bleached space of the wide piazza: the children were gone. No, though. No, she was getting confused. It was Grenzi at the wellness centre, it was Nielsson.

The loss of her child? But the loss contained a mystery, a darkness that Luisa couldn't quite make out; it was as coiled and convoluted as the symbol on the wall of the farmhouse. Was it possible that Benedetta had lost a child *before* her marriage – that the thickness around her middle, her catatonic blankness at the dress fitting had been as a result of a pregnancy not ongoing but recently miscarried? And what of her departure to Switzerland with that husband, that temporary person, that stop-gap – had he been the father? Could he shed more light on this than Bartolini had? Luisa struggled to think of his name after all these years. What name had been on the admissions board at the hospital Luisa had just left?

Hurriedly she got to her feet, unsteady, half in shadow, half in light, her eyes still adjusting, and a nun in pale grey was there beside her, steadying her, and for a panicked second she thought she'd forgotten the antibiotics and then she remembered, yes, she'd taken one this morning. She needed to get home and take another.

But when Luisa did get home, up the dim stairs, into the quiet, shadowy apartment, she didn't go straight to the kitchen for the packet of pills that stood beside the sink but to her bedroom. The bed was made; the room was neat in the striped light that fell through the shutters, where she and Sandro had slept side by side for forty years. Where had she kept it?

Her underwear drawer, silk things never worn, bras neatly folded. She'd never had a reconstruction since the mastectomy but wore nice bras anyway, carefully rolling a cashmere sock to replace the missing breast. At the bottom of the drawer were treasures, treasures Sandro had never seen.

Luisa hadn't been invited to so many society weddings that she would throw it away, a card turning soft with age, printed in silver with a silver tassel, and there it still was. Next to a small tin that had once contained violet-flavoured pastilles and had a picture of violets on the front but had for twenty-seven years –

twenty-seven! – held a curl of dark hair. She had asked the nurse to cut it from their baby's head when Sandro was gone, to work or somewhere, sent unwilling to buy a coffee in the hospital cafeteria, and she had placed it inside her bra, taken it home when the baby stayed, their daughter stayed, to be prepared for burial. Luisa had taken it home and she had placed it in that tin and had never looked at it again. Her fingers touched the tin lightly and moved on.

The invitation was in a small pile of similar relics, a party at the Palazzo Corsini, the presentation of a medal to Sandro for some forgotten accomplishment, a handful of newspaper cuttings.

The Prince and Princess Salieri invite you to celebrate ...

Of course Luisa hadn't been invited. Hovering, nervous, in the anteroom to the palace's chapel after the guests had all filed out in case she might be needed still to tweak Benedetta's dress, she had picked the card up from a plastered niche where it had been carelessly discarded by a young woman who doubtless attended a dozen such celebrations a year and found them dull.

The light was better in the kitchen. Setting the invitation down on the table, Luisa went to the sink, filled a glass, dutifully popped one of the pills from its blisterpack and swallowed it.

There would be a bus out there. Her heart quailed at the thought of them, the Salieri up on the hill, the nurse, the brother, the two women on their separate sickbeds. But that was where the answer lay. In the coiled tattoo, in the crumbling house, in the undergrowth of the hillside.

She picked the invitation up again, the silk tassel soft as thistledown against her hand. *The wedding of their daughter Benedetta Fiamma to Arturo Ticino.*

Could she track him down, ask him, the husband, Arturo Ticino? There was Facebook, there was Google. Ask him what had happened to Benedetta to turn her from a sturdy girl into a frail and trembling old woman? But perhaps he wouldn't care, or wouldn't remember, or perhaps part of the deal had been that he keep his mouth shut. Perhaps there were a hundred Arturo Ticinos.

The Salieri would tell her nothing. She knew that from the expression on Bartolini's face. They closed ranks.

In the pocket of her coat her mobile hummed, electric against her side, and she took it out. It was Giuli.

'Luisa? Luisa?' In the background, voices squabbling, a shrill female and a man's murmur, and Luisa felt a great despair overcome her at these distances between her and those she loved, these interruptions, these unwelcome spectators.

'Giuli?' Even to her, her voice sounded dead. It was the tiny tin with its violets; it was the past, rising like a mist from a valley.

A pause, only the voices in the background. 'Are you all right, Luisa?'

Luisa cleared her throat. 'I'm fine.'

'I need you,' said Giuli, and the mist swirled and was gone.

Chapter Twenty-One

THE MASSAGE SUITE was in the basement.

Before they descended, Sandro had called Panayotis with Luisa's suggestion about looking for the camper-van among the camper parks. 'One of those, you know, rundown ones, where no one pays much attention to comings and goings, would be my guess.'

Panayotis had agreed eagerly. That boy, he thought wryly, would go far. The rest of what Luisa had told him had had a strange ring to it. Gianna Marte in the hospital, hovering over Benedetta Salieri: he didn't like the sound of that. And Marte had been the one to tell Lotti about the truffles, she'd admitted that. It was all fishy. All of it. The idea of Chinese whispers occurred to him: the Sant'Anna whispers.

And then there was a baby. Benedetta Salieri rambling about her lost child.

The therapy suite was a long, dim, warm room, scented with something bracing, like eucalpytus. Sandro was surprised to see two curtained cubicles, a little like a small ward in a luxurious private hospital.

'Temporary,' said the masseuse with a touch of defensiveness as she saw them look around. 'Mind you, it's been temporary for nine months now. We have a whole massage studio, but the drains collapsed underneath it last Christmas.'

Eleonora Castrozzi was a tiny woman in a pale-grey tunic with white trim. She had very short black hair and corded muscles in her forearms and gave the impression of having nothing wasted about her, no spare anything, all compact and useful energy.

'This is where you treated Lucia Grenzi,' he said, 'the afternoon of May 21st this year?'

'The afternoon before she died,' said Castrozzi. 'I gave her a massage every day when she was here. It was the third massage of that stay.' And with an abrupt movement she rubbed her eyes, leaving her face softer, weary. She pulled back the curtain to reveal the massage bed and two chairs. She perched on the bed and gestured to the men to sit down.

Pietro asked the next question. 'How had she been? Since she'd arrived?'

'Normal, for her,' said Castrozzi. 'She was a woman with a lot of – struggle in her. She fought against something, I don't know what. She didn't talk very much, but the muscles tell you their story. I understood she would have episodes of stress. She once said to me that massage was her lifesaver.' Castrozzi stroked the pillow abstractly. 'She said it stopped her thinking.' She exhaled, a sigh, almost angry. 'Anyway, when she arrived she was tense, as always. The second day I could feel the difference. It wasn't simply the massage, but it was her ritual, of letting go.' She hesitated. 'But that last day. That last massage was not normal.'

They waited for her to go on. The atmosphere in the room was hushed, the lighting low, the scented air subtle, but for a second Sandro had the sense that it could suffocate, turn claustrophobic in the blink of an eye: he had the urge to run up the stairs and throw open the door.

'Maybe it was because – well, I don't know. When she came down the room was empty. There was another massage booked in halfway through, in the next cubicle, but when she arrived it was just me and Lucia. We knew each other well, there was no need for any preliminaries and she wasn't a talkative woman – but still. There was something constrained about her. Tense.'

'She gave no explanation?' said Pietro.

Castrozzi shook her head. 'She undressed very hurriedly, lay down. It was as though – I don't know. As though she wanted to run away.'

Sandro heard himself murmur in agreement: the feeling he had had himself the moment before. He wasn't sure about all this, about these *feelings*. They seemed very real, very concrete, but they weren't facts, were they? But there was a crossover: what Castrozzi had said about the muscles having a voice, those were feelings.

Castrozzi glanced at him and went on. 'She did seem to relax, eventually. After about – well, until the next client appeared.' Her expression was anguished. 'It's not ideal, massaging two side by side.' She put a hand up to the curtain behind her as if to show how insubstantial it was. 'But sometimes it is unavoidable. We keep the curtains closed, and as a rule clients prefer not to talk, it was just that this time –'

Sandro leaned forward on the hard white chair. 'You saw the other client?'

The masseuse shook her head. 'The curtains were closed. I only heard her,' she said. 'And that was when I felt Lucia grow tense. The junior masseuse, the one with the other client, was temporary, from Denmark. Perhaps she didn't really understand our rules, perhaps – we were very quiet – she didn't know we were there. Anyway, they weren't talking loudly, it was whispering, and I couldn't exactly stop and reprimand them without making things worse.'

Sandro and Pietro exchanged a glance. 'Were they talking Italian?' said Pietro.

Castrozzi looked puzzled. 'Yes, of course, the Danish masseuse spoke Italian and English as well as her first language.'

'So you understood what they were saying?'

Castrozzi's face clouded. 'I didn't eavesdrop, if that's what you mean.'

'That's not what we mean,' said Sandro patiently.

She gave him a hard look then waved her hand. 'The patient was murmuring. A kind of monologue, rambling. I tried not to listen because, to be honest, I felt she was not quite well. Some of our patients unravel a little here. But,' she took a breath and they let her go on, 'she was saying over and over that you could never escape your past. That people come back to you, like ghosts. That she had seen a ghost here, and the ghost had said things she didn't understand. And as I was massaging Lucia, instead of the muscles relaxing, they were becoming more tense, more and more tense.'

'Do you think,' Pietro was diffident, 'in your opinion, was

it the woman or what she was saying that was disturbing Lucia Grenzi?'

Castrozzi had pushed herself off the massage bed and was standing, rubbing her forearms in an anxious movement. 'I think it was both. I was on the point of stopping and suggesting I come to Lucia's room to resume the massage. And then the patient discovered the masseuse was Danish and her voice became louder. She almost started to rant – she was calling the woman names. She kept saying *vipera*, over and over again. It was as though she was a different person.'

'You told this to the coroner?'

The masseuse shrugged, uneasy. 'I just said she had been tenser than usual. I mean, discussing another client –' She took a pace away from them, then back. 'I can't do that.'

'Do you know who that other client was?' She stared at them. They stared back. Deadlock.

'Did she – was she perhaps a day visitor?' Pietro tried. 'One of those who come in just for a treatment or two?' The masseuse shrugged. 'It wasn't,' and Sandro could hear in Pietro's voice the same strain of keeping his temper, 'a woman we know was using the swimming pool on that day, a woman with long white hair?'

'I didn't see the patient,' said Castrozzi carefully, 'but it wasn't that woman.'

'How do you know?' said Sandro, intent at last.

'Because that woman had a foreign accent, northern – perhaps, in fact, even Danish – and the woman we heard in the next cubicle was certainly Italian, rather well-spoken too. And because I encountered the woman with long white hair in the lobby on my way down to Lucia. She was very rude: she pushed in front of me as I was coming in for my shift, practically knocked me over. She seemed fired up about something. Muttering to herself.'

'What time was this?' asked Pietro, 'Did you see where she came from? From the swimming pool?'

Castrozzi shook her head. 'She smelled of alcohol, though, so perhaps she'd been in the bar.'

'There's a bar?' said Sandro, unable to restrain his surprise.

'Even in hospitals they have bars, this isn't rehab,' said the masseuse stiffly. 'Look, I didn't see the client and I didn't recognise her voice, so I can't swear to anything, of course. I can only give my opinion. She wasn't one of my regulars, if I knew who –' She broke off. 'Of course we have a log of all bookings.' Stiffly. 'It's confidential.'

'This is a murder investigation,' Sandro reminded her softly, and her eyes widened.

A pause, then she spoke. 'This murder investigation – do you think the woman in the next cubicle who said she'd seen a ghost, was she the victim?'

Sandro shook his head. 'No,' he said. 'She's not. From what you've told us, that's one thing we can be sure of. As to who she *is* ...'

An idea began to form, a possibility. He stood up, quickly, before it dissipated, and hastily Pietro followed suit.

'You've been most kind, Miss Castrozzi,' said Pietro. 'I, we, appreciate –' and he held out his card. 'If there's anything else ...'

She nodded, looking down at the card, the frown still there.

Hurrying down the dim, warm corridor with its soft diffused light, Sandro said mildly, 'They all seem awfully keen on respecting the privacy of the clientele, from Dottoressa Scarpa down. D'you think we're going to need a warrant to look at that log of spa bookings? Or the hotel register?'

Pietro made a sceptical sound. 'Well, we can try,' he said cautiously. They climbed the stairs into the cool pale light of the lobby, where they stopped a moment.

'Would you ever come to a place like this?' said Sandro, looking around. No voices raised above a murmur, figures moving beyond layers of glass in white bathrobes, outside on the heated terrace.

'Well, Gloria's always saying ...' Pietro's voice petered out: he cleared his throat. 'Never,' he said. 'It makes me think of – you know when they describe heaven, when you're a kid, and you think, hold on, doesn't sound like much fun?'

Sandro nodded, smiling at Pietro's sheepish expression. 'Nor me –' he began, and then in his pocket the mobile throbbed. Around them nothing changed, no one looked around, but he knew he was supposed to go outside to talk in anything resembling a normal voice.

The clean, dry chill of the air on the forecourt struck him all over again. It was like Pietro said: heaven didn't feel that welcoming.

'Hello? Hello?' the voice gabbled. 'Is that Cellini?'

'Calm down,' said Sandro. It was Gorgone.

Gorgone sounded different: he sounded terrible. He sounded like the drugs had worn off or the therapist had died or the bank had gone bust.

'I don't know,' he said, 'I don't know if it means anything, if it matters.'

'It usually does,' said Sandro, 'when it sounds like this. What is it, Gorgone?'

Through the big glass doors of the entrance he could see Pietro standing there. He looked like a boy on his first day at school, lost. Obedient and lost. He saw him jump a little, then scrabble in his pocket, remove the mobile from it. He held it to his ear. Saw him turn and begin to walk further inside the hotel.

'She – I never thought – I didn't mean – I had forgotten, truly.'

'Start from the beginning,' said Sandro.

'His daughter,' said Gorgone desperately. 'The prince's daughter from – back then. Back there, Sant'Anna, La Vipera. I didn't even remember her name, the daughter. I met her on the stairs of my building – can you imagine that? Months ago, in the spring – I can't remember exactly when. She said she had been recommended the shrink by a hospital in Florence.' A ragged sort of gasp. Sandro wondered at the man. He'd seemed so bland and composed, so confident. Perhaps it only took a chink, a hole in the fabric he'd woven around himself – like Lucia Grenzi.

'You had an affair with her father,' said Sandro quietly. 'Isn't that it?'

'I – I –' Gorgone stammered, didn't answer. 'She seemed quite … She asked me if I could recommend a spa. It was all very civilised. I told her about La Serenita. I assumed, I thought – how was I to know the other woman would be there, how was I to know?' he gabbled. 'I just wanted to get rid of her and I said the first place that came into my head that wasn't one of ours. God knows I didn't want her at one of our wellness centres.'

'You didn't know Nielsson was in the area, either?'

A silence, as of horror. 'Johanna? How could I know? I kept away, I kept my distance, that was the agreement when we all went our separate ways, that was what we decided.' Sandro heard him swallow, the sound of a child caught out, the dry mouth of a liar. 'I didn't see her. I didn't see Johanna.'

'That's not quite the truth, is it?' said Sandro, sensing only that.

'I didn't.' Gorgone was insistent. 'She phoned, Johanna –' He broke off and when he spoke again his voice was broken, horrified. 'It wasn't long after but, I swear, I'd forgotten all about Salieri's daughter. Johanna said she was on her way through Italy. She asked if I knew where – people were, I couldn't even remember the names, I told her I thought the Italian girl, Grenzi, was in the Dolomites.' He broke off and Sandro heard him swallow again. 'She said she was "doing the rounds".'

'What did she mean by that?' Sandro interrupted him swiftly and Gorgone gave a frightened gasp.

'I don't know. I don't *know* – I'm not a mind-reader, am I?' A pause, but Sandro said nothing and Gorgone went on. 'Catching up with people, that's all. And I – I –' he was gabbling and Sandro could imagine him doing the same to Nielsson, a gabbling torrent of evasions and half-truths '– I told her I couldn't see her, I was too busy. She laughed and said she was coming anyway and so I went to America. My receptionist will tell you, she came and I was gone. I was thousands of miles away, I can prove it.'

'No doubt you can,' said Sandro drily. 'Why didn't you want to speak to her?'

'Those days,' he said, pleading, 'dragging all that up, I don't know, perhaps she was feeling the need to – have closure. We can't be held accountable for those days, can we?'

Closure, thought Sandro. What did that mean? 'I don't know,' he said, still dry. 'That depends on what you did.'

Gorgone didn't seem to have heard. Sandro had seen this phenomenon, years of therapy that served to convince the subject they need take no responsibility. He controlled his anger: he let Gorgone speak.

'And then she turned up. The daughter. His daughter. I couldn't remember her name.' As though wondering how much else there was he might not remember.

'Benedetta,' said Sandro. 'Her name is Benedetta.'

*

Giuli looked out of the window and saw Luisa at the door of the building, staring at the brass nameplate. 'Second floor,' Giuli called, and then Luisa looked up, in some kind of daze. Giuli retreated inside and pressed the button to admit her, again.

What had happened now? This Nielsson murder had done something to Luisa, to the quiet sensible pair she had come to think of as her parents. What had she been thinking of, calling Luisa? It was only that she had felt suddenly out of her depth. Still wobbly from vomiting in the concierge's icy privy, climbing the narrow scented stairway had brought on an access of vertigo – and walking into the small apartment everything had swirled around her. The faces scrutinising her, this woman no better than she should be insisting on being allowed to poke around a lady's apartment.

A noblewoman's apartment. Because it hadn't only been the faces of the concierge and the cobbler staring at Giuli, this upstart. Even in the tiny lobby she'd been greeted by a full-length painting of a woman in a long red dress, pearls in her hair, the kind of thing you saw in a museum – and as Giuli followed the concierge into the small sitting room, thirty other faces gazed down at her from the walls. Ancient heavy gilded frames, popes and cardinals and princes, lapdogs and olive groves and tapestries, velvet gowns and a treasury of jewels, all in oils, all crammed in to a sitting room barely bigger than the concierge's.

'I've just got to –' Turning from them with hands suddenly trembling. 'Can I open a window a minute?'

And it was there, standing in the clammy air – she no longer knew if the storm was brewing in the atmosphere or in her own head – that she dialled Luisa. She saw the Neapolitan with her pomegranate-coloured hair mutter to the cobbler. What could she say in front of these people? *Come. Help me.* When Luisa had answered, Giuli was flooded at first just with gratitude, that she answered, that she was *there*, but almost immediately she heard a weakness in Luisa's voice that seemed an echo of her own, and she checked herself.

Luisa said she was all right. That she was at home. Her voice steadying.

The Neapolitan had started a muttered argument with the cobbler. He had put a restraining hand on her forearm and her voice rose, shrill.

'Would you mind?' Giuli half-whispered. 'Could you just come?'

'Where are you? Who are those people?'

'They're just – they're helping.' She gave the address hurriedly. When she hung up they had fallen silent again and were looking at her suspiciously. The room loomed, its coffered ceilings too high for the narrow walls, and she stepped back into it, under all the painted eyes.

How could you imagine a child in here? There was nothing for a child to play with. It was dark, it was crowded. A child would be frightened.

There wasn't a sound.

The kitchen was a galley, you could barely turn around in it, and it smelled stale, unpleasant. An old lady's kitchen, dust thick on the counter, a row of glass jars with bleached and desiccated herbs. Giuli found herself thinking for some reason of Enzo's mother's kitchen, the warmth, the air fragrant with good things. One child between them and him grown but theirs was a family, right enough. She might be dying but there was life. Here there was no life.

'Seen enough?' said the concierge, but Giuli had knelt and was opening the fridge. If there was a child there would be orange juice, there would be chocolate puddings from the supermarket, there would be cheese strings. If she had provided a grandchild for Enzo's parents – and the thought barely checked her, she was past all that, wasn't she? – that was how their fridge would look.

But Signora Ticino's fridge, a small old model that wheezed and shuddered as she opened the door, held only a withered lemon and a tub of margarine – and still it smelled of rancid neglect. Giuli felt a warning growl from her stomach as the sourness rose to her nostrils and abruptly got to her feet, and that was when the buzzer sounded. Luisa had been quick.

Behind her the concierge was saying something about knives.

She hurried past the staring pair to the lobby and pressed the buzzer to admit the caller without checking who it was, and then of course she had to run, awkward in her hurry, blundering through the sitting room to lean out.

She heard Luisa's breathing on the stairs, laboured, and panic set up under everything else, for the things she put her through, and then Luisa was there in the doorway.

'It's her,' said Luisa. 'Ticino. She's Ticino.' She looked past Giuli and nodded perfunctorily at the Neapolitan and the cobbler, not asking why they were there.

'It's who?' said Giuli.

'Mrs Cellini,' said the cobbler from behind her, sounding uncomfortable. 'Salvatore,' said Luisa stiffly. Giuli turned to catch him bowing.

'You know each other?' growled the Neapolitan, affronted.

The cobbler bowed deeply. 'Mrs Cellini used to send customers to me,' he said. 'From Frollini?'

The concierge subsided fractionally. Of course, Luisa knew everyone, thought Giuli.

'She was living here all that time?' said Luisa, ignoring her. 'Benedetta was?'

The man shrugged.

'Benedetta?' said Giuli, unable to understand. 'Isn't that –?'

Luisa shot her a glance, a tiny nod. Benedetta was the woman admitted to the hospital after an overdose, whose brother Luisa had been talking to in casualty. Who lived out there in Sant'Anna. Things slipped, half-fell into place. 'I thought she was Salieri,' said Giuli.

'The man she married was called Ticino.'

The Neapolitan bustled two steps forward, eager, newly respectful. 'He calls her Benedetta, the brother, half-brother. And if I might say, madam, Mrs –?'

'Cellini,' said Luisa quietly. She was ashen. Giuli, newly purged of her own sickness, took an unsteady step forward and placed a hand on her arm. Luisa didn't seem to notice. 'Go on,' she said to the Neapolitan.

'She may have been living here but you wouldn't have known it, not really. She ventured as far as Salvatore's workshop once in a blue moon, but no further. She had some kind of condition, well – he tried to explain – nerves, you know. She'd be here and then she'd be gone again, to some –' she checked herself '– some rest home. Spa, you know.'

They were losing sight of it: Giuli felt the sickness rise inside her again. 'But what about –?' They turned to look at her. She opened her mouth but it wouldn't say the words. 'I need to –'

Where was the child?

Giuli turned. She wanted to call, *where are you*, because for all the coffered ceilings here, for all the china and mahogany and family portraits, the air was the same air she herself had breathed as a child, in the walk-up, oily with exhaust fumes, on the roaring Via Pisana where her mother had serviced punters, the same rancid emptiness – and how many times had she wished for someone to come up those stairs and call for her? On the dirty mattress on the floor, not even room for her to hide.

'Where are you?' she whispered, not even sure if she'd said it out loud.

'Giuli?' Luisa's voice seemed to come from far away.

She got as far as the signora's bedroom, a small room, almost fully occupied by a four-poster bed hung with dusty brocade, pink velvet counterpane, bedside table. She fell to her knees, crouching to look under the bed, not caring what they thought of her, but there was only dust on the soft-red tiled floor, furry in the distant gleam from the sitting room. Dust – and there, rolled away back against the wall, a tube of something. Flattening herself to the floor, Giuli reached for it and sat up against the bedside cabinet. She squinted at it in the light. Glue.

A tube of glue such as children use.

She looked up at them, standing in the doorway and staring at her. She pushed herself off the bedside cabinet, which had a key that was sticking into her back, and turned.

'You can't –' said the concierge, starting forwards, but Giuli paid no attention.

Inside the cabinet was a scrapbook. Faded cover. This was old. If this had been a child's scrapbook, it was from years and years ago. Giuli opened it and stared, and Luisa's voice, gentle, pleading with her, became part of the hum filling her ears.

Chapter Twenty-Two

THERE WAS A SMALL BAR at the end of the street, three steps down from street level, and with her instinct for these things – for places of safety, or at least relative safety – Luisa led Giuli there.

The scrapbook, wrapped in a clean tea-towel extracted from Benedetta's kitchen drawer – not only clean, but ironed: there must, Luisa had thought irrelevantly as she extracted it, be a small army of cleaners and laundries keeping Benedetta housed and hygienic – was in Luisa's tote bag.

There in Benedetta's strange, small, crowded bedroom, she had gone straight to Giuli's side. The scrapbook open on her lap, cuttings from the eighties: a royal baby from Britain on one side; on the other, *I lost my little angel* was the headline beside a baby's closed eyes, the face in tight swaddling. Luisa had swallowed. Giuli had turned a page, another. Involuntarily, Luisa had looked away.

Her glance had fallen into the bedside cabinet, its door still open. There was something else in there. A little worn notebook, leather, with BT stamped on it in gold. Benedetta Ticino.

'Look,' the concierge had said to Giuli, 'that's madam's private things.' Giuli and Luisa had looked back up at her and the woman had faltered.

'Could you get a glass of water, please?' Luisa had said with as much authority as she could muster. 'Can't you see she's not well?' And gently taking the book from Giuli, manoeuvring herself between her and the cabinet, she saw them turn away. Reaching behind her with a free hand, she slipped the little leather book into her pocket.

In the kitchen, Luisa addressed herself to Salvatore.

'I need to get this to the police,' she said, and the concierge started back with a small gasp as if burned. Salvatore's eyes merely narrowed, and he conceded a wary nod. Neither of them had more than glimpsed the contents of the scrapbook, but they had seen enough. 'I'll take it to Sandro,' she said. Salvatore and the woman had conferred, inaudibly: she knew what they'd be saying, though. Neither of them had any enthusiasm for going to the police.

'We'll say we were looking for the child,' Luisa said, coaxing. 'And we were, weren't we? How could you get into trouble for that? For caring about a child in distress?'

Salvatore and the Neapolitan exchanged glances and he said, 'All right. As long as you make sure they know it was about the child.'

The scrapbook lay between them on the kitchen table. It was closed, but that made no difference. They'd all seen it. The last five pages were crammed full, glue daubed here, there and everywhere. And all the cuttings referred to the bodies found in Sant'Anna.

Luisa grilled the two of them as to Benedetta's whereabouts the previous week. It seemed only wise. The cobbler had last seen her weeks earlier, when she had dropped her shoes off for mending.

'I told her,' he said, nodding towards Giuli.

'The half-brother came for her,' said the concierge. 'Third week of August.' She darted an uneasy glance at Salvatore, then at Giuli, then finally at Luisa. 'He took her to the place, a nursing home they call it, but it's for drunks, addicts. She was there two weeks, and they don't let them go, you know, once they're in. They have security.' Nodding, looking around at her audience. 'He brought her back, three, four days ago.'

'Just after the bodies were found,' murmured Giuli, and Salvatore shot her a startled glance, but the concierge didn't seem to hear.

'How did she seem?' said Luisa.

The woman shrugged. 'She seemed – steady.'

'But she wasn't always steady,' said Luisa, 'was she?'

'She was all right when I got here, a couple of years ago. They seemed to keep her on an even keel between them – he'd visit, her brother, and then the woman would – what with massage and churchgoing and that. Treatments. She hadn't had a turn in a while, but then this summer ...'

'About a month ago,' said Luisa. And they both nodded. 'And then again two days ago,' said Luisa. 'The night after she got back.' Bartolini, when she saw him in Sant'Anna, must have just got back too. Hadn't he said something about having been away with his sister?

Benedetta had come back here, sat here sticking in those cuttings, writing the dates – and swallowed a bottle of pills.

'I had to call them, of course, and the ambulance.'

'Them?'

'The brother. I've about had enough. She's not allowed sharp knives, you know.'

'She's a danger to herself? Or –?' Luisa broke off.

Benedetta couldn't have killed Lotti. She'd been in the rest home, under close watch, and her brother too. And the idea of Benedetta killing anyone gave Luisa pause. So frail, paper thin – but something inside her kept going, didn't it? It's the weak that kill: Sandro had said that to her long ago.

She couldn't have killed Lotti – but she could have killed Johanna Nielsson.

'The housekeeper, Gianna Marte?' said Luisa, almost to herself. 'Did she visit her at the hospital, do you know?'

'I don't know, do I? I don't know what she is or what her name is, for that matter – she just lets herself in. Do-gooding foreigner, religious nut, those moony eyes. She wasn't with him. She comes separately.'

'And what about friends? Her brother said –?'

The concierge shook her head. 'No friends I know of,' she said. 'Except you, of course.'

'Me,' murmured Luisa. She sat back.

At the bar she ordered Giuli a camomile tea. A tea-towel. She could imagine Sandro's eyes rolling to heaven at the thought, the contamination of evidence. Sandro, Sandro, Sandro. She got out her phone, which told her there was no signal down here.

Hands in her lap, Giuli hadn't moved. She was staring at something invisible. Carefully Luisa carried the glass beaker of yellow camomile to her. The smell reminded her of her own childhood. Surreptitiously she spooned some sugar into it and pushed it to Giuli, who gave a small, unhappy start and looked up into Luisa's face.

'The child ...'

'You know,' said Luisa, 'that there was no child – at least, no living, breathing four-year-old – to be rescued?'

Giuli looked at her a long moment, then nodded. 'I've heard of that kind of thing. I think I read in a magazine –'

'I don't really understand it,' said Luisa, 'but, oh, ten years ago, maybe less, Sandro told me about a – a woman they interviewed who did that. Who spoke in other people's voices. Perhaps, for example, a child's voice – and her grandmother's? Multiple personality disorder, something like that. It can be due to trauma. Or schizophrenia, I think –' She checked herself. 'God knows, I'm no expert, but it seems to me if Benedetta lost a child herself ...' And again she fell silent.

The first pages of the scrapbook had been photographs of film stars, women and dresses, cut from magazines. No more than four or five pages like that, the heads cut out carefully but with the hand of a child. And then there had been some boys, sweet-faced pop idols. A page or two of close-packed handwriting, mostly complaints about her mother, worship of her father, the usual. The usual. After that had come the baby pictures.

All sorts of babies, black, white, fat, curly haired, dark, pale. Cuttings of babies stolen and recovered, the headlines telling it all. *Reunited after twenty years, They stole my baby, Deranged baby-snatcher jailed.* And dead babies. Little angels, gone to heaven. Handwritten dates above them. Sometimes every day for a week, sometimes months between cuttings.

The last pages – four of them – had the fresh cuttings glued in. From several different newspapers, *La Nazione*, the *Corriere*, *Repubblica*.

Giuli was staring down at her phone, flat on the table. Luisa pushed the chamomile towards her gently. 'Drink it,' said Luisa, settling herself beside her. Giuli looked up again, and it was as if Luisa had hardly seen her for the past however long it was, as if she didn't quite recognise her Giuli, the daughter she'd never had. Her face was thin and pale; there were new lines to either side of her mouth; her lip trembled. Giuli wasn't a child: she was forty-five. Soon she would be old.

'There's something funny about all this,' Luisa said. 'I'd like to talk to this Gianna Marte. What about the friend Bartolini said she'd made? Or is it –' she paused, as the knots drew tighter '– the same person?'

Giuli didn't seem to be listening.

Remembering, Luisa felt in her pocket and extracted the little notebook. The leather was worn but of good quality. She opened it. Her first feeling was one of disappointment because it wasn't a notebook: it was an address book, the gilt-edged pages soft with age. She leafed through it: there weren't many names in it, and almost all the writing was browned with age. At least half the names were crossed out – some of them she recognised as old friends of the princess's long since dead. *What?* she murmured to herself, because there was something not quite right.

'There's something I haven't –' Luisa turned, not sure what she'd heard, Giuli's voice was so quiet, and saw Giuli looking at her. Her eyes looked huge and dark.

'Giuli?' She dropped the notebook and reached for her hand. 'What's wrong, darling, please?'

And then Giuli's phone buzzed, jiggling on the table between them, and as Luisa saw 'number withheld', no name on the screen, Giuli snatched it up and in the same movement rose to her feet, the colour draining from her face. 'Hello,' she stammered into it. 'Hello, I –' lifting her free hand to her ear to block the sound and grimacing, turning away from Luisa's concerned gaze. And then she stopped. Turned back.

'You,' Luisa heard her say. The colour was returning to her face. 'No – it's no – don't – I was expecting someone else, that's all.' She turned, paced away from Luisa, turned again. 'I can't – the signal's so bad –' and was walking away again, to the little bar's door and the two steps up into the street. Luisa snatched the tote from the table, and the little address book, and followed her.

Out in the Via del Parione Giuli was hanging up. 'I've arranged to meet him in the office,' she said.

As Luisa handed her her bag and coat, there was a rumble from overhead, and they both looked up to see cloud shifting, darkening in the strip of sky over the narrow street. 'Who?' said Luisa, managing to be patient now that Giuli's colour was back. 'And who were you expecting?'

'He's called Ragno,' said Giuli. 'He's a – I bumped into him a couple of days ago, he's – from the old days.' Her neck reddened. 'When I was a kid, when mum – he worked the Via Senese.'

'You mean –?' said Luisa and Giuli nodded. A pimp. Her mother's pimp.

'I asked him about La Vipera,' said Giuli, holding her gaze. Luisa took her hand, felt how cold it was, as she went on talking, oblivious. 'He said he had something to tell me. I'm going to meet him at the office.'

'Right,' said Luisa, releasing her, then agitatedly pulling on her coat and searching for her umbrella. 'I'm coming with you.'

At the corner, Giuli stopped. 'What had she done?' she said abruptly.

'Sorry?' said Luisa.

'What had the woman done, with multiple personality disorder, the one Sandro interviewed?'

Luisa opened her mouth, closed it, opened it again. 'She'd killed someone,' she said stiffly. Cleared her throat. 'As I remember it, she stabbed her mother twenty-six times.' And for a moment they stood there on the busy corner of the Via dei Serragli and the Borgo Santa Monaca as the lights changed and a bus thundered by, trailing cars in its wake.

Giuli put a hand on Luisa's arm. 'There's something I haven't told you,' she said.

A soft, ominous rain had begun to fall.

Chapter Twenty-Three

THE SKY HAD LOWERED VISIBLY, cloud drifting up the valley to settle. The light faded quickly in the mountains, those airy peaks taller than you thought when it came to sunset. One minute the grass sparkled, the stones were bathed in rosy light, the next it was all grey.

As he hung up on Gorgone, Sandro saw a missed call from Giuli and sighed.

'So it was Benedetta Salieri.' Pietro had his hands jammed in his pockets like a schoolboy, staring gloomily out into the twilight. 'Bloody hell,' he went on, 'the three of them here. You think that's a coincidence?'

'Nope,' said Sandro succinctly. He set a hand on Pietro's shoulder and turned away from the view. Inside the hotel was warm, and the lighting changed expensively, as if by magic. Beyond reception, the bar they hadn't noticed became visible, lights twinkling on tables, bottles glowing on glass shelves.

'No harm in sitting down in there a minute,' said Sandro wearily, 'is there?' They chose a table by the window. Outside the dusk was turning velvety. Although the insulated glass meant no sound reached them, some spotlights had come on, revealing some large shrubs agitated by what looked like a rising wind.

The place was deserted, although the chink and clatter of a dishwasher being unloaded came from beyond a door behind the bar.

'So not a coincidence?' Pietro was impatient, drumming his heels below the table like Ceri.

'Well,' Sandro spoke slowly, 'it doesn't sound as though Lucia Grenzi was expecting to see Benedetta or Nielsson. Or that Benedetta was expecting to see Nielsson. I think Gorgone, in his dimwitted way, sent Benedetta here just wanting to get her as far away as possible, out of his hair, not thinking Johanna Nielsson might come this way to find Lucia Grenzi. Had Nielsson heard about the ski school, perhaps from Kaufmann in Liguria, and called ahead to find out she'd come here? I imagine something like that. I think she came here to talk to Grenzi.' Sandro paused. 'We don't, of course, know if she did that.'

Pietro nodded. 'Gorgone – what did he say? That she had told him she was "doing the rounds"?'

'We don't know why, what prompted this little road trip. But it looks like that's what it was. She'd bumped into Kaufmann up north already; she'd contacted Gorgone but he ran away rather than see her. Next would be Grenzi.'

'And the call, the telephone call from a public phone here?'

Sandro nodded. 'I think that would have been Johanna Nielsson. I think Lotti was next on her list. She told him she was coming to see him, too.'

'He killed her!' Pietro burst out. 'He killed her after all.'

Sandro sighed. 'Do you know, I really wish he had. I really do.'

Pietro subsided. 'What then?'

'I think Nielsson never saw Lotti. I think she told Lotti she was coming, but she never arrived. Who knows what else she said to him. And when she didn't turn up, when she was killed, might Lotti perhaps wonder where she had got to and what might have happened to her – and who might have wanted her out of the way? Perhaps he told that person, or perhaps he spoke to someone else who told that person.'

Pietro sat back in the little velvet seat abruptly. 'It's like Chinese whispers,' he said gloomily. 'That place. Sant'Anna. Like a bloody relay race – you take this, I'll take that, you run this way, I'll run that way. You can't pin anything on any of them.'

Sandro stared at him. Relay race, he thought. One kills the first, another kills the second. Co-operative effort. Now *that* made sense.

And then his phone blipped again. He extracted it to see a message from Giuli: *We've found someone who knew them at La Vipera back then and Lotti too Roberto Ragno he's a pimp*

No bloody punctuation, as if she'd broken off halfway through. He waited a second to see if any more of the message appeared, then lost patience and swiftly began to jab at the keyboard. He'd had enough of all this, missed calls and no signal and half-finished messages. He'd had enough of being without Luisa. Not being able to talk to Luisa.

Not being able to see her face.

Skype call please. You and Luisa, in the office, six o'clock.

Pietro peered over his shoulder and raised his eyebrows. 'That gives us an hour and a bit,' he said.

It would annoy her to be talked to like that but ... There was movement in the room and Sandro looked up to see a barman appearing behind the bar, stopping in his tracks with a dishwasher basket in his arms. Sandro walked over and rested his arms on the rough stone of the bar, which was hewn, it appeared, from the mountain. 'Afternoon,' he said to the barman, who warily lowered the wire basket to the counter.

'Can I help you?' He began to unload the glasses, looking from Sandro to Pietro and back, warily.

'We're from the police,' Sandro said.

'The *dottoressa* mentioned you,' said the barman, reaching up to put highball glasses on a shelf above the bar. 'But I didn't – Miss Grenzi didn't drink. She never came in here.'

Pietro was ambling over, laidback. 'It's about two other guests,' said Sandro, keeping his voice easy, 'who were here at the same time. You were working that day? The day before she – died?' The barman nodded. 'And do you remember a woman with long white hair, a foreigner? Around midday?'

The barman drew himself up. 'Huh,' he said. 'I do remember her. She had a pass for the pool that didn't also allow her access to the bar. She was very ... insistent. She wanted a drink. I told her it was for guests only. '

'She got her way, though?' said Sandro and the man straightened.

'She did not,' he said stiffly. 'At least, she wouldn't have. Except that there was a guest, in the reception, who heard her voice, who recognised her. I – the situation got rather difficult.'

'It's all right,' said Pietro mildly, comforting. 'This lady, she was like that, I understand. She liked to stir things up. Can you tell us what happened, exactly? Did you hear their conversation?'

'Stir things up,' said the barman, 'you can say that again.' He finished putting away the glasses, frowning. 'The guest, a frail-looking lady, recognised her, but the white-haired woman –'

'Johanna Nielsson,' Pietro slipped in.

The barman shrugged. 'If you say so. She had no idea who the guest was to begin with. One of those people who expects to be remembered but never bothers to remember other people.'

'The guest introduced herself?' said Sandro.

He nodded. 'And then she – this Nielsson – was all over her, slapping her on the back. "Buy me a drink, Benedetta," she said. Of course, I was ready to intervene, but it was tricky, you know. This Benedetta, she obviously was … not up for it. Just stood there like she'd been turned to stone. Whereas the other, Nielsson, was all over the top. Trying to put her arms around her. But she bought Nielsson her drink and what was I supposed to do? And the drink – Nielsson had a double scotch, and that's simply rude, in my book, to order the largest drink you can think of when someone else is paying – the drink just made her worse.'

'Did you hear their conversation?'

The barman looked uneasy. 'They were the only ones in here. I couldn't help but –'

'What did you hear?'

'Nielsson said something about being on her way down to find her and what a coincidence this was. She was here looking for a mutual friend – she didn't give the name – she was catching up with everyone. She'd been in Canada, she said. She wasn't well, she'd understood a few things and she wanted to lay things to rest. Something like that.'

'Lay things to rest,' murmured Pietro, disbelieving.

The barman shot him a glance. 'The guest –'

'Benedetta Salieri,' said Sandro.

'If you say so,' he said again. 'She looked like she was having none of it. She just stood there, stiff. And then this Nielsson grabbed her, practically strong-armed her away from the bar. They moved to where you sat, by the window, so I didn't hear much after that. Until she left.'

'How long were they talking?'

'No more than ten minutes – though Nielsson had finished her drink in two. She started signalling for another but I pretended I couldn't see her then I went into the kitchen. She made me angry. Something about her. Everything about her.'

'Yes,' said Sandro. He felt on the edge of beginning to shiver himself, the sense of her here was so vivid.

'When I came back out of the kitchen she was on her feet, then they both were. Nielsson was waving her arms about. The other, Signora – what was it? – Salieri, was just standing very still. She was much smaller than Nielsson, but she stood there, sort of holding herself still while the other one ranted. Saying something about being a victim herself too. About it all having been someone else's idea. I started going over there, you know, to break it up – Salieri was a guest, and she was obviously under attack somehow – but then Nielsson just stormed off.'

'You heard nothing more?' said Pietro.

The barman looked from one of them to the other. 'Salieri just stood there as if she didn't understand, then she said, "You're a liar."'

It was very quiet, suddenly, among the flickering lights. So quiet you could hear the howl of the wind beyond the glass, an unearthly sound, as though it had come down from the mountains like a ghost.

'She said it quite clearly but Nielsson didn't turn around,' said the barman. 'She just stalked off, out into the reception area. Nearly knocked someone over as she was going out.'

'That would be Miss Castrozzi,' said Pietro, but the barman didn't seem to hear.

'And then she said it again,' he said, 'even though there was no one to hear her. Salieri did. Standing quite upright, like – a bit like a kid trying to be brave. "You're a liar." With her fists clenched like she wanted to kill the woman.' Pietro and Sandro exchanged a quick glance. 'And then she phoned someone else, a friend, it sounded like, who calmed her down.' The barman sighed. 'And then some other people came into the bar and she came over to me to make sure the cost of the drink was on her slate, white as a sheet. I told her there was no charge.'

'And she left?'

He nodded. 'She walked up and down in the foyer like she didn't know where she was for a bit, and then I think she went down to the massage suite.'

There were people there now, in the reception area, a woman in a fur coat, and expensive suitcases being wheeled in on a tall trolley. Sandro felt an itch to be gone from this place – but he couldn't Skype-call Luisa from the car. It all roiled in his head. Benedetta Salieri like a child, clenching her fists. *I'll kill you.*

'Can I ask you something?' he said, turning back to the barman. He saw a hint of greying five o'clock shadow, the ghosts of bags under the man's eyes, and felt sorry for him. Working in a place like this, feeling time creeping up on him – or maybe that was just Sandro.

The man nodded. 'Sure,' he said, careful.

Sandro had never seen Benedetta Salieri, not then, not now. 'You say she looked like – ' He rephrased it. 'Which of them would have come off worse,' he said, 'if she'd gone at Nielsson with those fists?'

The man folded his arms, in white shirtsleeves, across his belly and sighed. 'She was small,' he said, 'fragile-looking. But she was angry. She was wound up so tight – under those circumstances people can fight, can't they?'

A silence. Sandro felt Pietro looking at him for guidance.

'It's not just Miss Grenzi, is it?' The barman's voice was diffident. 'It's not just about the suicide. It's her. She's dead, isn't she?'

Sandro opened his mouth then closed it again. 'Who's dead?' he said.

'Salieri,' said the barman. 'Her.'

And as Sandro saw Pietro begin to shake his head, the shiver came at last. Not so much fear as recognition of a danger that had not passed, that was coming closer. Benedetta Salieri.

The barman was just standing there when they left, the little lights still flickering on the tables in the empty room.

In the reception area, behind the wealthy woman with her stacked suitcases, momentarily, neither Pietro nor Sandro could remember what they'd done with their things and they stood there turning, looking at the various exits from the foyer. All those doors.

'Conference room,' said Sandro abruptly and set off almost at random towards a door. His instincts felt all shot to pieces by the low-lit stone and glass blandness of the place, but the direction he took was right, it turned out. The door said 'Conference rooms 1–5' and opened on to a corridor he recognised. They let themselves into the room and sat, opening the little screen between them. There were a couple of emails from Parini.

Sandro opened the first: it was a report on the plastic ties used for Nielsson's wrists. Not agricultural, at least not specifically. They were ties for rubbish bags. In the mail was a close-up photograph of the blue plastic, embedded in what was left of Johanna Nielsson's wrists.

Behind him, Pietro sighed. 'Well,' he said, 'that's disappointing. Garbage-bag ties. Though they're usually yellow, the ones I buy.'

Sandro leaned in because he'd seen those blue plastic ties, and recently – then Pietro leaned past him and scrolled up.

The second email had an attachment.

Pietro peered in at it, blocking Sandro's view. 'Oh,' he said. 'Oh. Oh. Wow.' He sat back up. 'Not a dead bird, then. Or not only.'

'What?' Sandro felt his scalp prickle. *At last*, he thought. *At last*. He pushed up his glasses and focused. The attachment was the forensic report on the small pile of twigs and cinders from the walled-up fireplace. La Vipera's little secret.

The walls of the small room pressed in on him. The feeling came back to him now, the creeping sense he'd had on the threshold of the old farmhouse, that it was there, the origin of the violence. He'd thought it meant Nielsson had been killed there, despite Pietro's scepticism, despite the blood in the little hut. But it had been something else.

Dead bird, yes. The wing was unmistakable – and recent. The rest was much older: forty years old.

'Foetal remains,' said Pietro. They were both staring at the screen. 'Human,' said Sandro. 'A human foetus.' He felt his chest clench like a fist, and he made himself breathe.

Most of the 'recovered material' had been charred beyond useful identification. One bone, though, one tiny bone, had escaped. So small it might have been the bone of a bird except, of course, that to a forensic scientist they were easily distinguishable. A tiny bone, metacarpal, it said. The bone from a foetus's tiny hand: the little finger. The length of the bone indicating a five-month gestation.

Sandro felt his mouth open and close, *what, what.* He felt Pietro's hand on his arm and stood up abruptly. 'I can't stay in here,' he said. 'I can't.' Blindly he walked out. Hastily gathering up their things – coats too thin for the mountains, briefcase, iPad – Pietro followed.

*

The campsite wasn't empty.

'You know why I want to find it,' Sandro had said as they drove away from the pale buildings of La Serenita, into the night. 'Grenzi went for a walk that night. I think she found out where Nielsson was staying and went to find her.'

Five or six campers huddled in the shadow of a looming rock face. A small wooden chalet to one side had a light on. A kid in a big outdoor coat was in there, hunched over a computer screen. At first Sandro thought it was a boy but then she looked up. Scrubbed face, bright eyes, curly hair. She made Sandro feel about a hundred. He hesitated, and Pietro stepped in to the breach, holding out his badge.

The girl sat back in the chair, almost amused at the two of them tripping over each other in the doorway, and Sandro saw that the screen had a wide shot of some distant mountains on it, the high plains of somewhere like the Andes.

She was called Niki, and it turned out she had been in sole charge of the campsite since 2012, which made her older than she looked. Her amusement at these two bumbling cops didn't falter, even when Pietro told her it was a murder investigation, but she did sit up and take the iPad from him. It had the picture of the camper on it.

'A Swedish woman,' he said, 'about seventy, long grey or white hair.'

'Yes, I remember her,' Niki said simply. 'But her name will be in the book.' Fixing them with a beady look. 'We do things properly. She booked for four days but she left on her second night. I wasn't surprised, after what had happened.'

'And what did happen?'

'I think she'd come to see someone and it hadn't worked out as she planned. You could hear them arguing halfway to Bolzano. I had to go and tell them to shut up.'

'Could you tell what the argument was about?'

Niki shrugged. 'The Italian was remonstrating with her, trying to persuade her not to do something. The other one said something about all of them taking responsibility. Then there was –' her face stiffened, uncomfortable '– some rubbish about them all being cursed, a curse, and that's when I banged on the door.' She sat back. 'She was gone by the morning.'

'You saw the Italian woman? Could you describe her?'

Niki shrugged again. 'Sure. Not young but fit-looking, you know, active, short hair.' Pietro and Sandro exchanged a glance: Grenzi. 'I saw her walking away again, five minutes later, from here. Walking up towards the hotel. She looked – smaller, sort of hunched up. She walked more slowly. That's all I can say.'

Sandro and Pietro looked at each other, a mutual silent decision not to tell her Lucia Grenzi had also been gone by the next morning.

They thanked the girl, and it was with a sense of huge relief that they climbed into the big car and pulled off. Pietro drove fast, swinging at the bends with a hint of recklessness: they both felt it. They were going back to Sant'Anna.

'What about the Skype conference,' said Pietro, 'with Luisa?'

Sandro shot him a glance. 'I'll do it in a service station, in a public toilet, anywhere but here. I want to get out,' he said. 'I want to get away from here.'

By the time they reached the motorway it was 5.35, and twenty miles to the nearest rest stop. Pietro put his foot down.

Chapter Twenty-Four

THERE WAS NO SIGN of Ragno on the pavement outside the office, so they went up.

'When did he say?' Luisa asked her.

'He should be here,' said Giuli, uncomfortable. Luisa didn't know what they were like, people like Ragno. Luisa knew the inside of a fancy dress shop and the inside of a happy marriage. Luisa didn't know what Giuli was scared of, or she wouldn't have said what she'd said.

'Call them,' she'd said on the corner of the Borgo Santa Monaca. 'For God's sake, girl, call the bloody lab. Whatever it is – what*ever* it is – we'll get you through it.'

If it's AIDS? If it's hep C? Giuli had mumbled that she would. Luisa had stared at her, like she already knew. 'It's just that – Enzo's mum's sick too. He won't be able to handle it.'

'Enzo can handle most things,' said Luisa. 'He knew what he was taking on.' Which shut Giuli up.

'Okay,' she said. 'When this is done. When Ragno's done.'

Luisa had shaken her head, despairing.

Up in the musty office it felt damp, close, and a gust spattered rain against the window. Giuli set her bag down on the table and looked at the phone to see if Ragno had sent a message. There was one from Sandro instead, and her head jerked up.

'Sandro wants to Skype-call us,' she said, mind boggled.

'What?' said Luisa, pale. 'What's that mean?'

'At six.' It was 5.15. Luisa just went on staring.

'You know,' said Giuli. 'He wants the screen up – you talk and he can see your face, you can see his.'

Luisa turned away. 'Right,' she said, and there was a choked sound to her voice. As Giuli watched she laid the tote bag on the desk, extracted the scrapbook. 'He needs to know about this,' she said. They eyed it. Her hand was still in the tote. As Giuli watched she took out something else: a small bashed-up leather notebook. Luisa opened it between them on the table, spreading the pages, soft as old silk. Addresses.

'Stop,' said Giuli, her finger on a page. M and a number. The writing was less faded than the rest they'd seen. 'What did you say the woman was called? The housekeeper?'

Luisa frowned, dredging her memory. 'Gianna?'

'Gianna what?'

Luisa straightened. 'Gianna Marte.'

'My guess?' said Giuli. 'That's her number. Do you think we should call her?'

Luisa looked at her, thoughtful. 'A member of the Salieri household? Give away their secrets on the strength of a phone call?'

'But –' Giuli felt frustration build.

'And besides, we know where to find her,' Luisa said.

Giuli stared back, feeling a trembling set up, a chill creeping into her from the damp room. Sant'Anna was where she was to be found. 'But –'

Luisa held up a hand, shaking her head. 'There's someone else I'm looking for,' she said. Leafing on, through the pages, as Giuli peered over her shoulder – N, O, P – she stopped at T. Arturo Ticino.

'The husband? You think *he's* going to talk?'

'I only want to know one thing from him,' said Luisa. 'And it's ancient history.' Under that steady gaze, Giuli wanted to step back, to run for the door, but Luisa, who always knew, put a hand on her arm, detaining her. 'I'm going to go downstairs and call him, in the street – so there'll be no one listening when you call the woman from the lab for your results.'

Shit, thought Giuli, and she felt the sweat break again, her body going wrong, and there was nothing she could do about it.

'Do it for Enzo,' said Luisa, and she turned away, pulling out her little fold-up mac from the tote, stashing the address book in her pocket. The door closed behind her.

Hands trembling, Giuli took out her mobile and dialled. She walked towards the front of the building, into the little lobby where clients sat, when there were clients, which was not often. At random, all their dilemmas, their obstacles, their difficulties swarmed into Giuli's head, other people's lives. Unfaithful wife. Dishonest business partner. Missing child.

An automated message came and she almost hung up, but it wasn't telling her the place was closed: it was offering her options. *If you know the extension …*

I'm the missing child, thought Giuli, *lost, AWOL, adrift*.

To speak to one of our operatives, continue to hold.

She continued to hold. Down in the street she could see Luisa, hunched over the mobile, shaking her head. She looked down the Via del Leone, listening to the tinny music in her ear, and she could see the trees in the Piazza Tasso stirring in the wind, and beyond it, in the large garden of the Villa Strozzi that stretched up the hill, the leaf canopy rippled silvery like water. Her gaze came down again and she saw him appear, Roberto Ragno, in a waxed jacket held close at the neck, walking towards Luisa. The two of them facing each other as though it was high noon.

'Good afternoon, Labo X. How may I help you?' The receptionist – soothing, kind, complacent even at the ragged sound of Giuli's voice, put her through.

'Miss Sarto, Giulietta, I'm so glad you called.' She did sound glad, thought Giuli, and how mad was that?

If I stare down, if I stare down into the street, if I escape from my body and put myself down there on the pavement in the rain, in the real world, none of this is happening.

What did she think? That she could stop time? Giuli knew that didn't happen. She had learned to look at herself in the mirror and accept what was there. You had to take the consequences. Step out of your own life, and that way madness lay. That way you were Benedetta Salieri in her bedroom on the floor, filling in scrapbooks and talking in a child's voice.

'I'm sorry,' she said. She had heard the word *peri-menopausal*. 'Could you say all that again?' She hadn't heard HIV or hepatitis or cirrhosis or stomach cancer or further tests. Perhaps that would come. Be brave. 'Please?' She didn't know if it was in her head but she thought she heard the woman chuckle. Really? *Really?* Was it a joke?

Down in the street Luisa had hung up. She didn't know Ragno from Adam so she had turned to push her way through the door and he had stopped, hanging back. He was going to change his mind. Giuli lifted her hand, knuckles clenched, ready to bang.

But her hand never got there. And then she was listening. Then she was really listening. She turned her back to the window, to the world outside. She went hot, then cold: her hand went to her mouth and then it went to her belly.

Luisa had come up the stairs and was in the doorway, saying something about Benedetta's baby, the missing child, and Giuli felt her own insides contract, and then the buzzer was sounding. And everything went black.

*

Luisa got there just in time to stop her head hitting the floor. The buzzer was still going. Giuli's head flopped, then jerked upright. 'Get the door,' she mumbled, heavy in Luisa's hands, 'or he'll leave.'

Gently Luisa laid Giuli down then ran to the intercom, pressed the buzzer, long and hard. Listened for the click of the door but there was nothing, and then ran, ungainly, dripping still in her raincoat, through the lobby to the front window and shoved it open. 'Hey!' she shouted. He was five metres away, going back the way he came. He turned and looked up at her: a man older than her, thinning hair plastered over a yellowed face. For a moment they just stared and Luisa had no idea what she needed to say to persuade him, but then his shoulders dropped and he began to walk back towards the door. Luisa opened the inner door, pressed the intercom again, went back to Giuli.

She was sitting up in the office chair, colour returning to her cheeks.

'What were you saying?' Giuli mumbled. 'About the baby?'

Luisa examined her face, little Giuli's face. Saw something. The softness in her cheek. She put up a finger and stroked. 'You're not sick,' she said, wondering, 'are you?'

'You were saying Benedetta had a baby,' said Giuli, pale as a ghost and searching her face, and Luisa wanted to hold her tight as the revelation, after all these years, came to her, *it's you*. All this time she had only been able to think of the three-day-old girl she and Sandro had had, the tiny red feet, the face wrapped tight before they gave her away to be buried. And Giuli had been there all along, waiting.

'Benedetta never slept with her husband,' Luisa said. 'He told me. There was no child of that marriage. If there was a child –' she hesitated '– *if* – it was before. It was why they married her off. He was paid to marry her. To cover up the fact that her dad took her down to La Vipera on one of his trawling expeditions and she got pregnant. Family scandal, in spades. And then the baby –' She paused. 'I don't know what happened to the baby.'

Ticino's sour old voice when eventually he answered. 'She's died, has she?' She'd told him, no. He hung up. She called again. He let it ring a long time but she didn't give up, and eventually she heard him bark into the phone. 'Who are you?' She had told him she was a friend, and Benedetta was in hospital. 'We were married five minutes,' he said angrily. 'I can barely remember the woman.'

She'd asked him had he heard about the murders in Sant'Anna, and then there'd been a long silence. In three sentences, four, he'd laid out Benedetta's marriage. Three years of sobbing, locked in her room: once he'd touched her, and no more than touched her, and she flew at him, biting and scratching, then never again. 'I tried,' he said roughly. 'Believe it or not, I felt sorry for her.' She could hear forty years of cigarettes in the rasp of his voice and remembered him pacing outside the Salieri villa. She wanted to ask him more but he hung up. When she tried again, it went to answerphone.

Up in the office, they'd heard footsteps on the stairs, but no one had appeared. Giuli finished tucking in her shirt where it had come loose when she fell. 'Where is he?' she said. They both looked at the door from the lobby and on cue it swung open.

Luisa took charge, standing up. 'Mr Ragno,' she said stiffly.

'Who are *you*?' he said, looking cornered, panicky, then to Giuli, nodding towards Luisa, 'Who's she?'

'I'm a colleague,' said Luisa, softening her tone, her hand on Giuli's shoulder. She could see he wouldn't talk to her if she stood in judgement over him. A pimp, though.

'You all right?' he said to Giuli, frowning, ignoring Luisa.

Giuli got up from the chair. 'I'm fine,' she said, gesturing. 'Please, Roberto. Sit down.'

And Giuli *looked* fine, suddenly. She looked as though ten years had fallen away. Her eyes, never anything but watchful since Luisa had known her, were wide, wondering, her face smoothed. Hesitantly Ragno sat. Luisa stole a glance at her watch. It was 5.54.

Ragno sat there, in his good clothes, hands knotted humbly in his lap. Standing at his shoulder, Luisa could see how skinny his legs were. 'Luisa,' said Giuli, closing the laptop that sat on the desk and pushing it towards her. 'I think you've got a conference call, haven't you?'

Luisa took the computer, helpless. 'But I –'

'It's pretty straightforward,' said Giuli firmly. 'Just click on the icon at the bottom of the screen. Why don't you take it next door? You need to – I think Sandro would benefit from a one-to-one to start with, don't you?' She spoke brightly, but fixed Luisa with a meaningful look. Ragno just sat there docilely. Giuli said, pale but smiling, 'Password's *Luisa1975*.'

Feeling herself flush, Luisa took the laptop and retreated into the lobby. As the door closed behind her a murmur set up beyond it. The man was dying, Giuli had told her. What could he know? His voice was hesitant, low: she couldn't hear what he was saying. But in any case her thoughts were too hurried, scattered: she had the sense of something looming, something huge. She looked at her watch again. It was 5.58. In a hurry, she sat on the small hard chair by the window in the lobby and opened the computer, balancing it on the sill. She typed in the password: her name and the year they met. Outside, the wind rattled the window in its frame.

The screen opened: she saw the icon immediately and tapped on it. Nothing happened for a while. The clock in the corner of the screen ticked down; six came and went and next door the murmuring continued. And then a sound came from the computer, an unearthly sound like a sonar echo, and a face appeared. The icon of Pietro's face in a tiny circle.

She clicked Answer. *If Pietro's there, I don't have to say* – but it was Sandro's face that filled the screen. His mouth moved jerkily, the image swam and pixellated.

'Hello? Hello?' The screen settled, and the jerky mouth smiled.

'Darling,' she said, flooded with relief, and it came out like a sob. She averted her eyes from her own image, framed in a corner of the screen. It was dark behind him. She went to put up a hand to the screen then stopped. He was still smiling, as if he hadn't seen her in days, weeks. His mouth was muffled but recognisable. 'Where are you?' she said and he turned to look around himself.

'In Pietro's car,' he said, 'in the car park of a service station near Verona.' She could see the car's interior now. His smile was still there but his eyes looked tired. Sad. 'Where's my Juliet?' He leaned closer to the screen, and his face loomed, pale, unshaven.

'Are you staying there the night?' she said. 'The weather's awful here. Who's driving?'

Small talk. 'Pietro's driving,' he said, 'but he's pretty tired. I think he'll be persuaded to let me have a go. We're going to try and make it back tonight. The forecast's,' he hesitated, 'the forecast's not too bad.' A silence: she didn't know what to say. How to begin. She searched his face and caught a glimpse of her own, strained and guilty. 'Pietro's gone inside to get himself something to eat,' Sandro said. 'We've had ... something of a breakthrough. He's celebrating.'

'A breakthrough?' Overhead, as she said the word, there was a rumble then the crack and roll of thunder.

He hesitated again, looking from side to side. 'A couple of things,' he said. 'Most importantly, they've tracked down the camper-van – it's in Galluzzo in a camper park, just like you said.' A quick beam of gratitude. 'That's where we're headed first, all being well. Traffic's pretty sticky, but –' he moved, pushing himself back a little, and the screen pixellated '– I don't want to talk about the case. I wanted to talk to you alone.'

'Yes,' she said, her hand still up close to the screen, and as she watched his fingers appeared to meet it, over-exposed. She had the strangest, most desolate feeling, as if they had entered a new universe where this was all their communication, as if she'd never see him in the flesh again. She pulled her hand back a little.

From not far off she heard thunder, felt it roll around the bowl that held the city, coming closer.

'I've got something to tell you –'

'I need to –'

They both spoke at the same time and then both laughed, miserably. 'You first,' said Sandro roughly.

'I went up to Sant'Anna two, three days ago,' she said. 'I saw Maria Clara Martinelli and Luca Bartolini, thick as thieves in the bar.' She saw his face change and before he could speak she said, 'I knew her, you see. I knew Johanna Nielsson too.' Then she told him all of it, going back forty years. She didn't dare watch his face as she said it. She saw her own, foreshortened and fuzzy in the tiny frame, her white parting as she bowed her head.

From next door she could hear the murmuring still going, monotonous, insistent; she didn't know if it was Giuli or Ragno.

And finished, 'So I told her I'd kill her if she went on tormenting you.' Sat back, drained. A silence. 'So, you know. Want to investigate me for her murder?'

His face was still, watching her. There was something in it she averted her eyes from.

'Thick as thieves,' she said, because in that moment it appeared to her the crucial thing, the missing piece of the puzzle, 'in that village bar. It was like, right then, I thought, they know, they know just what's happened and between them they're covering it up. Between them, don't you see?'

But when he spoke he didn't seem to see, he didn't even seem to have heard. 'All these years,' and his voice was so low she could hardly hear it. 'What would we have done,' he said slowly, and he searched her face, 'if she'd come back into our lives? She was going around checking in with everyone she could track down who'd been there, at La Vipera, all those years ago. She wanted to expiate her sins, or find closure or peace, for –' and he hesitated '– for God knows what. She had five minutes in a campsite with Kaufmann, Gorgone ran away to America rather than meet her, Lucia Grenzi killed herself when they'd spoken. So who's left?'

'For the record,' said Luisa, 'I haven't seen her since then. Not for forty years.' And it came nearer, like a dark, cold mist, the thought that Johanna Nielsson might have tracked her down. 'But it wasn't just those who'd lived at La Vipera she was after, was it?' And she didn't want to tell him, suddenly. Her heart seemed to swell in her chest at the memory of Benedetta's thin liver-spotted hand, her sister in grief.

'No,' said Sandro. 'There was Lotti, Lotti who came to La Vipera for sex. She called him, too.' His face seemed to shift, his eyes evading her.

'But I thought you'd ruled out –?'

'We have,' said Sandro. 'Lotti didn't kill her and commit suicide,' and his face was watchful. 'I think he told someone he knew she was coming, and that signed his death warrant. Maybe the killer tried to make it look like Lotti was the murderer, killed himself out of remorse over the body of his victim. Two birds with one stone. And someone else told Nielsson she'd kill her. Someone she'd damaged beyond hope of a normal life.'

'But Benedetta was locked up when Lotti died,' she burst out, and he sat back. She tried to cover up, to save Benedetta. 'And who would he have told? He spoke to no one, you said. No one except for –' She broke off.

'Except for Gianna Marte,' said Sandro. 'Who told Lotti where the truffles were. Who had a soft spot for her boss. Maybe –'

Luisa interrupted him. 'Maybe she thought he was the heir,' she said wildly, because suddenly she had a powerful sense of this woman, this woman she'd glimpsed in the hospital corridor, this greedy, conniving woman. 'But he isn't, you know,' said Luisa. 'Benedetta is, she's her father's heir, and her mother's only her tenant, Bartolini too. She's a rich woman but it's brought her no happiness. I don't think *she* even knows.'

Her head ached, and suddenly the fuzzy image on the screen, Sandro but not Sandro, made her feel strange and sick, combining with the thought of Benedetta on a bed, Gianna Marte pacing the corridors.

Sandro's face moved closer. 'But still,' he said, 'why was she killed? What has Benedetta's inheritance to do with –?' and she saw that pixellation again as he shifted his face away a second. 'We still don't know for sure what they did, back at La Vipera, what Johanna Nielsson wanted forgiveness for.'

And then it swirled, it took shape. The coil on the wall, the tattoos on the wrists, the photographs in the book.

'We found something,' she said, and her face filled the small frame as she came closer to him. 'We found something, Giuli and I. In Benedetta's flat there was a scrapbook she'd had since she was a child. She had been pasting in photographs.' She hesitated. 'Babies. For years and years. And then the last week – cuttings from the newspaper. About the murders. I spoke to the ex-husband and he said there was no child, they had no child, no miscarriage. But I fitted her –' she paused, thinking of Sandro and what he might think of her citing female intuition, steady, cynical Luisa '– I fitted her for her wedding dress and I felt ...'

What had she felt? Under her fingers a softness at the waist of an otherwise slender child, and more: she had felt a chill in Benedetta's stillness, her silence on her wedding day. 'I think,' she said, 'I think the tattoo they have is of a foetus, and I think Benedetta had a child before her marriage. I don't know what happened to it.'

It was out. It was out, in a voice she hardly recognised as her own. Luisa felt a darkness open inside her, a cleft in the hillside, black and cold.

What was Sandro saying? Was he saying, 'I know. *I* know'?

If one needed a reason to kill Johanna Nielsson, even forty years on –

She tried desperately to cling to what she knew. 'The concierge in Benedetta's building said there was woman who came round, who said she was the housekeeper. A do-gooder type, churchy type, German or Germanic –' but she broke off at the sight of Sandro.

His face seemed to pale, to waver; he was silent and then, imperceptibly, he nodded. She couldn't read his expression. She didn't dare lift her fingers to the screen again, for fear his wouldn't come to meet them. And then he spoke. 'All these years,' he said, and his voice was so heavy with sadness.

'I know,' she said. The thunder rolled again, and the window lit blue-white, almost immediately afterwards. The image froze.

'I never –' His mouth was moving. And then he was gone.

Chapter Twenty-Five

'**A**H, SHIT,' said Sandro to himself, staring at the screen, a drumming in his ears. He'd heard a crack, the rumble of thunder, he knew what must have happened – the electrics had been blown – but all he could think was she was gone. He'd never see her again. And then the sound changed and he realised it was Pietro, knocking on the window, a cardboard tray of coffees in one hand and a greasy paper bag in the other. He leaned over and shoved the door open, and Pietro climbed in, handing him the bag.

Sandro took it, staring ahead. The windscreen was clear. The wind seemed to have dropped, ominously.

'All right?' said Pietro. 'Come on, eat up. You haven't had anything since this morning.'

Sandro looked into the bag and saw a limp *piadina*, the flatbread oozing melted cheese and a bit of curled ham. Reluctantly, he took a bite and a swig from a bottle of water Pietro passed him.

'Something's happened,' said Pietro. 'I may not be much of a detective but ...'

Sandro shook himself. Swallowed. 'I know what that – those foetal remains were,' he said slowly. 'Benedetta Salieri, Ticino, whatever, must have got herself pregnant while her dad was busy upstairs with Gorgone.' He thought of the mattresses laid about the upper floors: more mattresses than there were people. 'And they – I don't know what. A five-and-a-half-month foetus.'

'Jesus,' said Pietro.

The smell of the food in the car was abruptly sickening and Sandro screwed up the bag and let it drop. He felt dull, stupid. 'Luisa said that Benedetta had a homemade version of Nielsson's tattoo. Martine Kaufmann had the same one. Christ knows, it's fucked up. Horrible. Luisa says she thinks the tattoo is of a foetus. She said if you look closely –' and he paused, his throat tight, squeezing his eyes shut. That was what she'd said, all those years ago. Those were the words that had evaded him for four decades, that Nielsson had whispered in his ear.

You can be the one. He'd begun to shake his head, but she hadn't moved away, her hot breath on his neck. *Give me a child.*

'You don't think Lotti –?'

'Impregnated Benedetta?' Sandro felt cold. His mouth moved but his lips felt numb. 'I think it's a possibility. I mean, there may be DNA.'

Pietro growled in his throat. 'And then what?' But Sandro didn't want to think, then what. Benedetta had lost the child, that's what. Not under the care of a doctor, but in that dank farmhouse, and the child hadn't got any kind of burial.

Pietro grabbed the paper bag from where it sat between them, opening the car door and depositing it in a bin two paces from the car. Then he was back. '*Madonna santa,*' he said.

Sandro felt the weight of the laptop in his lap and mechanically began to stow it in the briefcase. He didn't even know if Luisa had forgiven him because he hadn't had the chance to tell her what he'd done. It only occurred to him as he zipped the briefcase closed that she had been asking *his* forgiveness, too. He hoped he would never have to tell her what they'd found in the fireplace of La Vipera.

'So,' said Pietro, and the engine roared into life, 'Galluzzo?' He brushed his GPS gizmo with a finger and it told him two hours, traffic moderate to heavy. Sandro sat back in the deep leather seat, stiff with dread.

Panayotis had been fizzing with it. 'Such a great tip, boss,' he'd said to Sandro. 'I mean, it was a pig of a job, calling round all those places with just a number plate, and the van park where we eventually located it – just like you said – was one of the old-school ones, no computerisation, no CCTV, just some old guy in a cabin, someone's granddad, no doubt. But he knew straight away. Knew the number, described the vehicle. Paid in cash, an envelope with the number plate on it stuck through the letterbox.'

Sandro had been cheered immediately by the scenario: Panayotis finding out what legwork meant and the advantages of low-tech operations – someone's granddad. Sandro's ears had properly pricked up at the sound of him: his brain was obviously still as sharp as any computer.

'So he didn't see who left it?'

'He said not.' Which left a certain amount of room for manoeuvre.

Pietro had been jubilant. 'You're kidding. They found the camper? It's going to be like Christmas.'

But now, as they eased on to the busy motorway, the outline of the mountains dark against the night sky behind them, the atmosphere in the car was more like the night before a funeral. The conversation with Luisa had sobered them both, and the thought of what they might find in that camper-van inspired more dread, in Sandro at least, than excitement.

South of Bologna the motorway grew busier, and the rain began to fall. At first a deceptively soft patter and then with a vengeance, by the time they hit the bottleneck as the road began to descend from the Apennines into the city, it was coming down like stair-rods. A nightmare drive under normal conditions – narrowing abruptly with constant roadworks, tight bends and trucks nose-to-tail, so close you could smell the diesel, you could hear the shriek of the brakes – in heavy rain it was a hellish rollercoaster.

Beside Sandro, Pietro was hunched over the wheel, his face pale in the dark and his knuckles white. Sandro could feel the tension right down his own arms to where his hands gripped the sides of the leather seat: he could feel the adrenaline battling his own tiredness, and God alone knew what Pietro must be feeling. He'd been driving for hours.

And then they were on the ring road, eight lanes, slow moving, brightly lit through the industrial outskirts of the city, and fractionally both men unbent. Pietro spoke.

'I hope the guy's still there,' he said, his voice rusty, still not moving his eyes from the busy road.

'Panayotis said he would wait for us.'

'We could have sent the lads,' said Pietro. 'I mean –'

'We're here now,' said Sandro. The thought had gone unspoken all through the long, dreadful drive: he knew Pietro had shared it, though. What were they thinking of? A pair of old lags insisting on getting the catch, serve them right if they ended up creamed under a truck.

Off through the tollgates, and they swung around the roundabout, turning back into town. Pietro lifted his hand to the horn, poised to startle some slow-moving oldster he'd cut up on the exit, but he never used it, his head jerking back, startled instead. 'That looked like –' Sandro sat up in the passenger seat but the car was behind them now and Pietro was shaking his head to focus. On to the scruffy congestion of the Via Senese and the tiredness began to catch up with them, and then there it was. Just as Sandro had pictured it, the very one, in fact, he'd had in his head. A piece of waste ground, no more than hardcore and rubble, on the edge of some scrubby trees, packed with six rows of camper-vans put up for the winter.

A Portakabin with a light still on.

'This is it, then,' said Pietro, and they climbed out. Stiff and weary and suddenly not ready, not ready at all. The door of the Portakabin opened and a wiry figure was silhouetted against the light.

*

By the time Giuli stood stiffly from the chair to thank Roberto Ragno, she understood that he had come to be forgiven, too. Don't we all want forgiveness, she thought, laying her hand on his shoulder. Maybe that was the church's secret. Giuli had never been in a church in her life.

'Thanks for coming,' she said, and her voice came out in a croak. 'You did the right thing.'

It had been hard for her to concentrate since coming round in the chair with Luisa's anxious eyes on her and that question she didn't dare answer on Luisa's lips. 'You're *not* sick, are you? You're not.' The hope in it, like the frightened leap in her own belly, that it was too early to acknowledge.

Five months. That was safe, wasn't it? A baby could be born alive at five months these days. With the right machines. Her brain jumped and fired in panic: she wasn't ready for this. She hadn't been prepared for this.

Second trimester, Cinzia from Labo X had said, judging from the date of her last period and the amount of – whatever it had been – in her urine.

'But I've never been regular, I'm not –'

'Go to your own doctor, Giulietta,' she'd said. 'Get a scan scheduled immediately. At your age, that's essential.'

'But you mean I'm not – not –'

'Liver function, heart, lungs, kidneys, everything we checked came back normal. You're not sick.'

So it should have been easy to answer Luisa's question. *I'm not sick, I'm pregnant.*

But then Ragno walks in. And once she said it out loud, she would be tempting fate.

Pregnant.

He sat down in the chair and almost immediately his hands in his lap were moving, restless. Looking around from side to side, as if he was waiting to be arrested. He was seventy, he'd lived a hard life: it was his time to go. Giuli set her elbows on the table, watching him. Would she be ready when it was her turn? Once upon a time she would have said she'd been born ready, but the trouble with getting clean and sober – her trouble, Ragno's trouble – was that the world came into focus. You could see the clouds moving across the sky, the new green on a tree, a couple sitting on a bench with their arms around each other. And then you didn't want to leave it.

Behind them there was a weird rushing sound, a clatter as something fell in the builder's yard, rain struck the window pane with a rattle like gunfire and Ragno jumped in his seat. Even thunder, you didn't want to leave.

'So,' Giuli said. 'You do remember La Vipera.'

He nodded. 'Before your time,' said Ragno, then looked at her again. 'Maybe not. Your mum had you already. You must'a been two, three. I remember you.'

Giuli stared at him. 'You're not going to tell me you're my dad, are you?' With horror.

To her vast relief, he laughed and shook his head. 'Not that your mum was the perfect mum, neither. But – well, what's the use? After all this time.'

But what? she wanted to say, but she overcame the sudden urge to reach across the desk and grab him and shake him till he told her. *Did she love me? Did she ever love me?* Giuli let it lie. 'Let's get back to La Vipera,' she said and he shifted, uneasy.

'She asked me if I had men,' he said. 'The woman there. Men with – I don't remember how she put it – men with petrol in the tank. They were all women. They decided they were going to have their own little commune, grow their own kids, live without men. Only needed them for one thing. So she asked me to get some men.'

Giuli stared at him. Between them on the table was Benedetta's scrapbook, full of pictures of babies. 'And you did?'

Ragno sighed, relaxed a fraction. 'It was daft,' he said. 'I thought it was a stupid game. I mean, they laid down these rules, got to be clean, got to be young, got to have it all in working order. Who knows that stuff even these days? Forty years ago, it was impossible, it was nuts, but who am I to argue? I managed to find a couple of guys to do it for money once or twice. But no one got pregnant and she told me not to come back. They had a local lad coming regular.' He sighed again, and he looked down into his lap, where his hands had unclenched, lay open, the yellowing skin of the palms vulnerable.

'The local lad would have been –'

The hands tightened in his lap. 'I don't want to talk to the police,' he said. She just went on looking at him. He stood up abruptly then sat down again. 'It was the guy they found dead,' he said dully.

She nodded. 'Lotti,' she said.

There was a crack of thunder and Giuli turned to look out of the window, waiting for the lightning. Two, three beats later a soundless flash illuminated the plastic tubing in the builder's yard, the orange showing black. In the silence that followed she could hear Luisa's voice, low and earnest, from next door. She turned back to Ragno.

'I saw him again,' said Ragno. 'I saw him here, in the city, maybe a month ago.'

Giuli laughed incredulously. 'After all this time? You recognised him?'

He clamped his mouth closed. 'I don't want to talk to the police,' he said, and she knew it was because she had sounded like she didn't believe him.

Rain rattled the window pane again. 'Come on,' she said. 'You're not going any –' and before she could finish the sentence there was a great bang right overhead and the lights flickered, died. For a second they were in darkness, only the gleam from outside on Ragno's face, and then the lights came back on.

'So you're sure it was him,' she said carefully.

Ragno almost smiled, wearily. 'We'd had a bit of – history in between,' he said. 'Lotti, he was a customer, wasn't he? Until he started smacking the girls around.' He shrugged, uneasy again, not comfortable with the role of knight in shining armour, thought Giuli. Which was to his credit. 'Last time I'd seen him was maybe ten years ago, when he gave a Nigerian girl concussion and I said that was it.'

'And when you saw him this time?'

'There's a bar open all August I go to – Rifrullo, you know it?' She shook her head. 'It was in there. He laughed at me when he saw I was sick. He started talking about the old days, said he'd been paying a visit to a friend from back then.'

Giuli felt a stillness come over her. 'Do you remember a young girl, from the big house in Sant'Anna?' she said. 'A girl called Benedetta? You might have seen her there with her father.'

Ragno tipped his head back. 'Christ,' he said. 'It's a long time ago.' His eyes narrowed. 'Maybe,' he said, curious. 'Slumming it, yeah. I remember a girl like that. Looking lost because her dad was having fun in the bushes with his boyfriend. You think that was the old friend?'

'I don't know,' said Giuli, in despair, listening out for Luisa to finish her Skype with Sandro, but she was still talking. 'Benedetta Ticino. She lives in the Via del Parioncino.'

He shook his head. 'Rifrullo's a bit of a hike from there,' he said, dubious. 'It's over in San Niccolo, just inside the city gate.'

San Niccolo. She tried to remember who'd been there recently, when and why. Someone. Sandro. He'd been there to see Martine Kaufmann.

'Can you remember the exact date?' she said softly.

He looked into her face and she saw how yellow the whites of his eyes were.

'Yes,' he said at last. 'Yes. The weekend after Ferragosto, it was – 17th, 18th, something like that?'

Giuli's head felt like it was stuffed with cotton wool. They thought the woman, Nielsson, had died the second week of August, didn't they? She couldn't remember.

She pulled a piece of paper towards her and began writing, to look like she knew what she was doing. 'That could be very useful to the police,' she said.

'Can't you tell 'em?' he pleaded.

She sighed. 'I can tell them, yes,' and as she said it she registered the silence. Luisa's connection with Sandro must have gone down.

'Can you remember anything else?' she said, and slowly he shook his head, his jowls, loose with the weight he must have lost, wobbling. He stood up, reaching for his coat. He seemed limp with tiredness, but at the door he stopped.

'It wasn't all her,' he said, and for a moment her heart leapt, but he was talking about someone else. Giuli got to her feet, took a step towards him. 'It wasn't all her. The other one dealt with the practical arrangements. I thought the Swede, Nielsson, she was just an airhead, if I'm honest: a frontwoman, if you like.' He paused, Giuli was in front of him now. 'I've seen women like her before,' he said. 'Born with it all, they mess about with this and that. They fuck ordinary folks over. I took her money, and I'm not proud of it, but if I hadn't it'd have been a cats' home or psychics or a homeopath. There's always someone who'll fleece 'em. But she wasn't the brains.' He was looking at Giuli in sorrow, now, as if he knew he wouldn't see her again.

'Who was then?' The silence beyond the door struck her in that moment and she pushed the door open. Ragno's hand was on her arm, detaining her.

'Listen,' he said, in the cajoling voice that told her some sentimental bullshit was coming. 'It wasn't your ma's fault. She *did* –'

But she was shaking him off, ancient history. All she could see was the laptop sitting there open on the little table, its screen dead. Otherwise the room was empty. Luisa had gone.

Chapter Twenty-Six

I F SHE'D STOPPED to tell Giuli what she was going to do, Giuli would have talked her out of it. Or worse still, insisted on coming with her.

The symptoms she had described earlier had been circling in Luisa's head ever since, refusing to make sense. All those years that Giuli was insisting, *I'm too old, no chance.* Saying she was menopausal, past all that. But what if she wasn't?

Either way, she wasn't in any condition to come where Luisa was going. Luisa's reasoning rang hollow in her head, knowing what Sandro would say, and in that moment she could only remember her last sight of his face, moon-pale and sad, on a computer screen, freezing then dissolving into pixels.

Blinking away the image, Luisa circled her own kitchen, trying to remember where Sandro kept them. The hook-board beside the front door was the first place she'd checked but it had been empty. She surveyed the dresser. Right. She pulled at one drawer and papers exploded out of it. The world was against her: she felt like wailing. *Pull yourself together.* She tackled the next drawer more judiciously. Promising. Old pebbles, broken pens, a paperweight. Gently, she eased it open more fully, felt in with her hand towards the back and something chinked: a chain, clever Sandro, a dozen sets of keys on a chain. She tugged and they were in her hand.

Luisa hadn't driven in thirty-odd years. She knew the exact date, in fact, because – that was the date. She'd driven herself to hospital, in labour. Sandro had been at work, it had been rush hour and she'd sat in traffic, bracing herself for the next contraction.

With trembling fingers Luisa sorted through the keys until she found the Fiat fob. Sandro would snatch them off her if he could see inside her head, but she folded them into her palm.

The car would be where he always left it. On the bridge, the rain whipping against her sideways, Luisa stopped, remembered her phone – had she even brought it? But there it was. A message from Giuli, *what the hell, what the hell*, and another from Sandro, businesslike. *Bloody weather, see you later, almost at the* tangenziale.

She didn't reply: didn't dare. She sent one to Giuli, saying, *Sorry. Leave this to me now. You need to get home to Enzo.*

Almost immediately the message pinged back. *Ragno says they were trying to make babies at La Vipera, some kind of all-women commune, getting all the women pregnant, no need for men. Lotti came to see an old friend in the Oltrarno, just after Ferragosto. He says Nielsson wasn't the brains of La Vipera, only the moneybags.*

Tell Sandro, she typed in. Trying to work it out and failing. Began to ask what did she mean – but before she could finish the message another followed on the first's heels.

I'm pregnant.

She stared. Stared and stared, trying to subdue the sensation, to moderate it, because it was dangerous – but it would not be moderated, like a song it rose inside her. A woman with an umbrella bumped against her with an impatient sound. *Go home, daughter*, she typed in, her fingers clumsy with joy. *I love you. We love you.*

As she sent it a little window popped up on the phone: Low Battery. She paused, considered. Replied to Sandro: *Who was it you went to see in the Oltrarno? Ragno the pimp says he knew Lotti from the old days and bumped into him in the Oltrarno the weekend after Ferragosto. Said he was visiting an old friend.* Her fingers hovered over the screen: she could tell him where she was going. But he'd only worry. She pressed Send.

With a stab of panic she turned it off then, stuffed it hastily away in her pocket and began to run.

The car was there. She'd almost been hoping it wouldn't be. She climbed in and immediately was surrounded by Sandro: old leather, the smell of his skin, his hair oil. Fumbling, she found the ignition. Twenty-seven years since – but the car started. If it had been a modern car, if he'd given in to Giuli's pressure, Pietro's, to get himself a decent machine with air-con and a radio, she'd have been lost. But she knew this car as well as she knew Sandro: it was old-school. Found the windscreen wipers, engaged gears, hauled on the wheel – and she was out in the slow-moving traffic of the Via Romana.

Dizzy under the assault of a dozen different lights – headlights, streetlights, the glare from a shop window, the tail-light of a *motorino* that undertook her with a buzzing whine – dazzling in the rain, Luisa gripped the wheel for grim death until she came under the Porta Romana, across the big roundabout and reached the relative calm of the Via Senese, when she managed to sit back in the driver's seat for the first time. Take a breath.

The traffic was heavy: rush hour. Just as well, take it slow.

Did she even know Benedetta would be there? Luca Bartolini had implied it back at the hospital, but she couldn't trust Bartolini, she knew that now.

But it wasn't just Benedetta that Luisa was going to see. She thought of the big old house on the hill, the dank overgrown drive, the cavernous rooms. She thought of Gianna Marte, whom she'd seen in the hospital, who knew her name; she thought of Luca Bartolini; she thought of the old woman, the Princess Salieri, who hadn't been seen in public for months, who was gaga by all accounts. Ahead, traffic slowed to a standstill, brake lights came on in the rain. If Sandro knew where she was going, he would start by telling her she couldn't possibly drive, it probably wasn't even legal after all this time, did she know where her driving licence was?

Then he would ask her if she thought it was safe, driving up into the dark hills in a storm, those country roads. He would say, *but why?*

What do you think you can find out on your own?

Going to visit someone you suspected of murder alone, in the dark. He would ask her what question she would put to Benedetta, supposing the Salieri would leave her alone with the woman, supposing she wasn't dosed up, supposing she was even still *alive*. Luisa shivered suddenly at the wheel and in the same moment a horn blared: the traffic ahead had moved. She engaged gear, barely escaped stalling, recovered momentum, put on speed. Quick. Quick.

She took the new tunnel bypass and came out at Galluzzo. A big black car cut her up on the roundabout and she braked abruptly as a profile turned briefly to examine her. Dazzled, she held a hand up, but he was gone and she was on the Siena road.

The turning to Sant'Anna took her by surprise, it came so quickly. She heard the tyres squeal a little in the wet as she took the curve and the wipers flogged back and forth. It occurred to Luisa that she didn't know if the car was roadworthy. It had been years since Sandro had spent any money on it.

In the dark, the country road Luisa had only seen from the bus since the day of Benedetta's wedding wound uphill, unrecognisably strange. A derelict barn loomed ominous on a sharp bend, old advertising fading on its flank, and she swerved around it. Her head ached with concentrating, in the rain, in the dark, looking out for the sign – and then there it was. She crept uphill, headlights feeble in the pitch dark, then the village appeared, small stone houses shuttered up, street lighting. The little square, trees dripping, the bar window fogged up. She crept on, because she knew the road now: this was the road she'd walked. Up ahead she saw a light a little way back, on a curve, under scrubby trees. She was going at barely fifteen miles an hour, frightened of missing the turn – and just frightened. Peering at the light, she saw it must be Martinelli's house, which must mean – yes, it was. Luisa braked.

The pillars that marked the rear entrance to the Villa Salieri stood there to her left, gleaming greenish-white in her headlights. Peering out of the side window, Luisa gauged the road that led up between them. It was overgrown, potholed, unlit – but she didn't want to use the main entrance. She didn't want them to see her coming, to hear her coming – and she didn't want to pass La Vipera. She turned the car between the pillars and began her bumpy ascent.

It was precarious and agonisingly slow: the wind buffeted the trees to either side, twigs and leaves and at one point a whole branch clattered on to the windscreen, but Luisa kept the little car creeping on steadily. The road turned steeper and the villa rose above her – at least she assumed that was what it was. A great dark wall, black against the blacker sky, no lights on – and then there was a crunch as, distracted, Luisa tilted the little car into a pothole. The wheels spun, useless, for a long, awful moment, the engine's revving deafening in her ears before, panicked by the sound, she cut it. Luisa climbed out into the dark and the rain whipped against her face. Far off she heard thunder rolling leisurely around the great basin of the city and a sheet of lightning backlit the road ahead, showing her the way up. She pocketed the keys and began to walk.

*

Pietro was looking back towards the roundabout as he climbed out of the car into the driving rain, his face still uncertain, but when Sandro asked what was bothering him, he just said, 'Never mind. I saw a car like yours, that's all.'

And then the camper park's caretaker was ambling towards him, keys chinking.

The camper was right at the back, under some overhanging plant that had stained its canopy with red splotches, shining dark as blood under the sulphur-yellow lighting.

The caretaker was a wiry little man of indeterminate age with a chin dusted with stubble. He asked for their identification and Sandro stood back as Pietro proffered his. 'Does it happen often?' Pietro asked him. 'Money in an envelope?' Then, as the man eyed him suspiciously, Pietro hurriedly said, 'We aren't the Finanza, mate. I don't care two hoots about what you declare to the taxman.'

The man shrugged. 'Often enough that I didn't think much about it,' he said. 'But I declare every payment.'

'And you didn't see the person who left it?' The caretaker shook his head stiffly, and Sandro watched him more closely. It never did to push them, not at this stage. 'Have you looked inside?'

'Of course not!' The man was indignant. 'I don't poke my nose in,' he said and took a step back, holding out the keys.

'You're all right with us looking?' said Sandro carefully.

'If the owner's dead, like you said on the phone,' said the man, wiping his hands on a grubby quilted waistcoat before sticking them in his pockets, 'then be my guest.' He regarded them a moment, then said, 'I'll be in the cabin.'

There on the threshold, they hesitated: it was too narrow to admit both of them at once, and they both stepped back politely. Pietro put a hand on Sandro's shoulder. 'You first,' he said, and Sandro knew he was consoling him for having had no official ID to show the caretaker. He stepped up and fitted the key in the lock.

Of course, it was dark: no more than a dim gleam from the outside lighting through the thin red curtain hanging across the camper's bigger window.

'Wait,' said Sandro, because he could hear Pietro fumbling for the torch he carried with him, but he wanted this moment, this first moment, without the cacophony of signals light would bring. He smelled it. He smelled *her*.

Musk and dead leaves and something else, a mineral scent that brought up the hairs on the back of his neck, the smell of slow rivers, of the woods in high summer, when decay is accelerated. The scent of a body found long ago but not far from here, a child dumped in a river that had diverted the course of his life with Luisa. And then the soft sound beside him of Pietro's sigh, a click and the thin gleam of an overhead strip light flickered on.

The eyes stared back at them. A whole wall facing them, plastered with images, some peeling and faded, some relatively new. A magpie patchwork of religion: Buddhas, Kalis, Madonnas with and without children, saints bleeding, saints tortured or beatific, saints with upturned eyes and outspread arms. The effect was grotesque, something between a teenager's bedroom and a Neapolitan catacomb.

Pietro cleared his throat. 'I guess she found God,' he said. 'Or something.'

'Something,' said Sandro.

He looked away. There was the usual galley kitchen and Sandro stepped into it: a tiny oven, two gas rings and a gas bottle. The smell was different in here and he knelt, took a pen from his breast pocket and flicked open the door of a small fridge. A dish of something sat under a fur of lurid mould, purple and green, but otherwise it was clean and empty. He closed the door again and saw something else. Something he couldn't identify immediately beyond its physical properties, a scrap of thin plastic, something printed on it, a scrap that had snagged on the vinyl of the floor tile – and yet it was familiar. Gingerly he took it by a corner and looked, but his sense of Pietro behind him, breathing heavily, eager, put him off. Carefully he stowed it, with the pen, in his breast pocket and straightened.

He found himself looking into a scoured stainless steel sink at something that cleared all other thoughts instantly. He beckoned Pietro to his side and they looked down together. A large butcher's knife almost filled the sink, on the diagonal from corner to corner. A long streak of black along the blade. They turned back into the bedroom in unison and in one stride Pietro was there. He pulled back the greying quilt.

The blood had faded to rust-brown, but the image was clear. Clearer, in fact, than it had been hitherto, when he'd seen it on the post-mortem photographs of Johanna Nielsson's bound wrists. He put a hand up, at the memory, to his chest, a reflex he couldn't quite explain, protective, superstitious. The curled spiral of what was not, after all, a snail but, as Luisa had said, the embryonic form of a child, drawn in smeared blood on Johanna Nielsson's sheet. It had a face, crudely drawn, and as he stared, Sandro heard himself swallow, a painful sound: he felt his heart in his throat.

Pietro had laid the quilt back, its underside marked with the faintest mirror trace of the bloodstains, and was taking a picture with his phone as Sandro stared. Benedetta's lost child.

And then Sandro's phone rang. His blood drumming in his ears, he hardly recognised the sound at first. He felt as though he was underwater, or in some terrible burial chamber, and all sound, all life was far off – and then with an effort he brought himself round. Answered, and as he did so saw that there were messages waiting from Luisa.

The voice sounded old, old as the hills. It laughed creakily.

'It *is* you,' she said, a ghost voice coming down the years, and although he didn't remember her at all, beyond the indistinct memory of a pale blonde who spoke Italian with a grating transatlantic accent, drifting almost transparent through the rooms of La Vipera, the voice was there still, rusty accented Italian.

Helen Mason. Helen Mason talking to him from Canada.

He had to leave the camper to listen to her without distraction; he had to pace between the rows of vehicles put up for the winter, resting shuttered and silent. She began by laughing at him and ended by telling him something he felt, somehow, somewhere, had been sitting at the back of his thoughts all along.

When she hung up, finally, he found himself at the end of a row looking at the silhouette of the janitor's head in the window of his cabin, bent over a screen.

At first Sandro looked without seeing, and then he saw. Perched on a pole at the entrance to the place, half-hanging off its wire, the battered eye of an ancient camera.

*

Giovanna Scarsa, staff nurse in acute care, fixed her red hair and looked on as little Cara, twenty years her junior, made a pig's ear of making the bed up again, before stepping forward with a sigh to tug the sheet into place.

'I don't know who she thinks she is,' she said, half to herself because it would be incompatible with her dignity to share her thoughts with her junior, 'telling us how to do our job.' She glanced up at the CCTV in the corner. 'Just because she was a policeman's wife once upon a time. I happen to know she's just a shop assistant.'

'He was nice, though, wasn't he?' said Cara warily. The last thing she needed was Scarsa in a temper. 'The brother?'

Scarsa sighed and her expression softened, just a touch. 'Lovely man,' she said pensively. 'Class, you see.'

He'd thanked them courteously for their help, reserving a special twinkle for Cara, which she was fairly sure Scarsa hadn't noticed. She tucked her dark hair under the little cap with satisfaction. There *had* been something odd, though. She didn't know if the staff nurse had noticed it too – but when they'd mentioned his mother's carer having come down to keep his sister company, a distinct shadow had passed over his face. 'Who?' he'd said. 'Gianna? Are you sure?'

Being classy, of course, he hadn't confided a thing in them, just turned a little stiffer in his gratitude.

The bed was done, and Giovanna Scarsa looked at it with satisfaction. The evening was quiet still but it was the calm before the storm. An elderly lady was on her way up from the emergency room having suffered her third heart attack. This bed would be hers, and probably her last resting place. But they wouldn't clear her for dispatch for another half an hour and in the meantime ...

'Cara,' she said, hesitating. The girl might be junior but two eyes were, she grudgingly admitted, better than one. 'I don't see how it would do any harm to look at that CCTV footage, though? Just to be on the safe side.'

It was a matter of minutes to get it up on the screen behind the nurses' station.

They saw her, moving jerkily. Something about watching someone who thinks they are unobserved, thought Cara. The stocky little figure crept. Her body language changed in front of the nurses' station: she stood straighter, with confidence. Scarsa had gone quite still, watching, her red hair a cloud around her face, and Cara darted a quick glance. The policeman's wife might be just a shop assistant but she had something. The staff nurse peered closer and clicked on the camera nearest to Ticino's bed.

Benedetta Ticino wasn't visible, the curtains were closed around the bed, but the small figure stood outside them, poised, hovering.

Looking one way, then another. Checking for who was watching, then her head tipped back as she scanned the corners of the long corridor, looking, looking. Looking for the camera.

And then she found it and looked straight into it.

Wide northern face, blonde hair. It sat up from her face, tufted silver in the light, and she looked back at them.

Chapter Twenty-Seven

ONCE SHE TOLD ENZO, Giuli knew, that would be it. Off active service, once and for all.

Sod it. She climbed on the *motorino*, pulling on her helmet. Why did everything suddenly feel so precarious? When she'd thought she was sick she'd felt like lead, weighed to the ground. And now she felt like thistledown, like the slightest breeze would knock her over.

Fastening the helmet's strap, she had to acknowledge that this was more than a breeze. The wind buffeted her so that she had to brace her legs either side of the little machine to stay upright, and the street gleamed slick with rain. Her phone blipped.

Don't come after me.

Luisa.

Well, she thought. We'll see about that. She hesitated, then texted Sandro.

I think Luisa's gone to Sant'Anna.

It was only after she'd pressed Send that it occurred to her that she might be wrong. Because how would she even get up there? Too late for a bus, and Luisa spending thirty, forty euros at least on a taxi? Inconceivable. But the alternative was – Giuli stood, straddling the bike, at a loss. Surely not. The thought of Luisa driving brought something like a laugh to her lips. Slowly Giuli leaned down and stuck the key in the moped's ignition: *now* Luisa decides to take up driving again, she thought, in wonder. She'd stopped when she lost her own baby, and now – She stopped the thought right there, with a shiver.

Riding the *motorino* gingerly, as if on a tightrope, she set off, hissing through the streets and over the Ponte alla Carraia. The lights strung out along the river like diamonds, the low curve of the Ponte Santa Trinita silhouetted dark against the bright jewel-shops of the Ponte Vecchio. The world looking dangerous and beautiful and new, and her head like a balloon about to float. She pulled up in the Via del Parioncino and pressed the bell marked Concierge. When the Neapolitan opened the door in her slippers, she looked down first and, following her gaze, Giuli saw that without realising it she had put her hand over her belly.

'I thought so,' said the woman. *Witch. Neapolitan witch*, thought Giuli in a panic. Then the woman smiled, a crooked little smile. 'I was the same,' she said, 'with my first. Throwing up left, right and centre.'

Giuli pulled off her helmet, and a gust soaked her. 'It's about the friend,' she said. 'The woman, Gianna Marte, the mother's carer.'

The Neapolitan stepped back, frowning, and admitted her into the hallway, but no further. She closed the door. 'I thought you were her coming back,' she said.

'What?' said Giuli.

'She just left,' said the woman, and when Giuli whipped round to look down the narrow, empty street she sighed. 'I mean, like, ten minutes ago. Fifteen.'

'Left for where?'

The concierge shrugged. 'Search me,' she said. 'My guess is back there. To the old lady. To the big house.'

'She was on foot?'

'Moped,' said the Neapolitan, gesturing towards Giuli's. Giuli frowned. Something about that struck the wrong note, somehow – but she supposed everyone rode a moped these days. Though not Luisa.

'What did she come for?' said Giuli.

The woman looked crafty. 'She said she wanted to collect some of Miss Benedetta's things.'

'But?'

'She went straight for the bedside cabinet,' said the concierge, folding her arms across her front. 'I told her –' hesitating '– I told her a friend of Miss Benedetta's had taken it already. The scrapbook. She wasn't pleased. I mean, I don't know any German but it sounded nasty.'

'German?' Giuli shivered abruptly, out of nowhere.

The concierge shrugged again, 'Sounded like it,' and extended a hand to Giuli's thin soaked jacket. 'You'll catch your death,' she said. 'You want to come in and sit down? I could call your – husband?'

'No, wait –' said Giuli. She did feel odd. Cold.

The woman sighed. 'Please yourself,' she said. 'Anyway, she asked about you and the older lady.'

'Luisa,' said Giuli, her voice sounding far off. There was a roaring in her ears and she didn't know if it was the wind or her own blood. Luisa out there. She groped for her phone to make sure the message had gone to Sandro.

The woman was still speaking. 'I guess it was her baby too –' and there was a hesitation in which the word hung in the air '– the scrapbook, I mean. Their ... project. The last time she came, three, four days ago, it was her brought the newspapers. A pile of 'em.'

'Her.' The single word came out like a gasp. The sharp little face peered up into hers, swimming. 'You saw it too, didn't you?' said Giuli and the face tilted. They'd all seen it and all pretended they hadn't. A smudge on the edge of the clipping pasted in, a smudge of a larger stain underneath that looked like blood.

The Neapolitan looked at her with curiosity. 'Look here,' she said, and Giuli was leaning on her small figure suddenly, more heavily than she would like. She felt a sweat break over her, felt her belly like a stone: she knew she was bleeding. Looking down, as if from a height, she saw that her phone was in her hand still and she raised it, her hand shaking. The woman's hands under her arms.

'Enzo,' she said. 'My husband's Enzo.' And the phone fell to the floor with a clatter as she fainted for the third time that day.

*

It took five minutes to reach the top of the road where it turned into a gravelled space, bounded by the trees where she entered it and what looked like a high black wall. Luisa could still discern no lights. Warily she entered the space and looked up: the sky was a deep inky blue, with clouds moving fast across it. There was no moon. She walked by the wall, holding a hand up to the rough plaster to feel her way, turned the corner and was in a courtyard. A rectangle of gloomy greenish light falling from a window high up illuminated a central well under an iron lid, shuttered windows and three steps up to a doorway. The space dripped with a strange echo. Luisa shivered: she was soaked to the skin but it was more than that.

She'd been here before. Servants' entrance. And as she remembered she swayed, dizzy a moment, feeling that the high walls of the courtyard were tipping around her. The thunder rolled again and as it ebbed she thought she heard something else, a thin high sound, not quite human, not earthly, coming from inside the building. In that moment she wanted only to turn around and leave – but she stood her ground. She walked: she came around the battened well and climbed the three stone steps. A cheap plastic bell-push sat beside a rusted iron handle, and after a moment's hesitation she pressed it.

A woman she assumed was a maid answered the door, in an embroidered red linen pinny, peering at her. A cavernous hallway sat behind her and there was a familiar scent of baking. 'Yes?' said the woman, her sharp voice at odds with the sweet, comforting smell and the apron, and Luisa took a step closer on the doorstep, listening. She could hear nothing.

She held out her hand. 'I'm Luisa Cellini,' she said.

'Cellini?' said the woman, turning her name over as if she wasn't sure if she knew it. 'What is it you want?'

Taking another step forward, Luisa saw her face, white-skinned, pale-grey eyes, braids folded across the top of her head. 'I'm a friend of Benedetta's,' she said, trying to sound casual.

'And of the princess, as a matter of fact, from long ago. At the hospital, Mr Bartolini said they were bringing her home. I know it's late but I was worried about her. Could I –?'

'Mr Bartolini has gone out,' the woman said more uncertainly. Her accent was singsong.

'I see,' said Luisa pleasantly. She gave it a moment, then said. 'I wonder if I could have a minute with her, Benedetta? I mean, just sit by her.'

'Was it you called her earlier?' The maid's voice rose, anxious.

'No,' said Luisa, wary, feeling herself go still, but the woman was fretting now, unburdening herself.

'Mr Bartolini had told me to take her phone away so she could rest but I had forgotten. I heard it ring –' She hesitated, and took a step backwards, and let Luisa in. Carefully, she closed the door behind them and glanced up the stairs. 'I didn't mean to listen.' She sighed. 'Whoever it was upset her.'

'I thought I heard someone cry out,' said Luisa, 'just now.'

But the woman shook her head a little. 'That was Madam,' she said. 'The princess. She has her moments – I've just given her the medication, she'll settle down, it takes twenty minutes or so.' Glancing up the stairs anxiously again. 'Perhaps you could go and see Miss Benedetta. You seem – your husband is the policeman, is that right?'

'Yes,' said Luisa, wondering how even this random person knew.

The maid was wiping her hands on her apron agitatedly. 'I'll take you up,' she said.

Obediently, Luisa followed her broad behind up the wide stone staircase. Portraits were hung all the way up, obscure in the dim lighting; Luisa supposed they must be economising on electricity, forcing herself to think of that, mundane thoughts to calm the pattering of her heart. 'Where did Mr Bartolini go?' she asked as they climbed. She didn't want to talk to him: she wanted access to Benedetta and he would stop her. She knew that suddenly. 'Back into the city?'

'Oh, no, down to the bar, no doubt,' said the maid, not bothering to turn around, 'or to her house, they're thick as thieves these days – ' But then she broke off to cast a quick glance over her shoulder, as if to remind herself who she was talking to, and clamped her mouth shut.

They stopped on the first floor, the piano nobile, and the long landing stretched out to either side of them, doors at regular intervals that would lead to the large rooms at the front of the house, just as Luisa had remembered it. The soaring painted ceiling, the intaglio tiles, the little gilded tables, the portraits and at either end a long shuttered window. There was a smell of church incense and floor wax and the house was very still and silent around them.

'Thick as thieves?' said Luisa stupidly.

The maid regarded her. 'Miss Benedetta's room is at the end,' she said. 'The little *salotto*. We – the ladies sleep on this floor, as the family doesn't use it for entertaining any more and the stairs are too much for the princess.'

'Thank you,' said Luisa. 'You're very kind.'

And as if the words sparked something in her, the maid said, 'I don't know what he sees in her, I'm sure. Dressed like a man and a good five years older than him.'

'Maria Clara Martinelli?' said Luisa. 'That's where Mr Bartolini is, with her?'

The woman nodded, fidgeting, then blurted, as if confessing, 'It was Mr Bartolini told me about the truffles, and I passed it on to Giancarlo. Will you tell him that? Your husband?'

'Yes,' said Luisa, without the faintest idea what the woman was on about.

Then the maid subsided. 'You want me to show you in?'

'That's fine,' said Luisa, but something was wrong.

The woman was halfway down the stairs, gliding in her haste on soft slippered feet, and then Luisa realised what that scent that hung around her was, the smell of foreign baking: gingerbread. 'Gianna?' she called, and the woman turned. '*You're* Gianna Marte?'

The maid was at the foot of the stairs and she turned, bobbed her answer, yes, and was gone, flicking the lower light off behind her. Luisa stared after her. Fair-skinned, blonde, sweet-scented, German-inflected – but this wasn't the woman she'd seen at the hospital. The deep gloom of the empty stairwell mocked her – and then from along the landing Luisa heard a groan.

Tiptoeing along the smooth old tile of the gallery, she remembered what Gianna Marte had said about medication – and the ladies. So both of them were here, the princess and Benedetta. She pushed open the first door and the great salon yawned, cold and dark, the only light the rectangle shed in from the landing. The dust-sheeted shapes of chaises and hard armchairs sat muffled in the dark, gilded side tables and armoires ranged along the walls and the three long windows. The room where Luisa had pinned Benedetta into her wedding dress, thirty metres of duchesse satin and bugle beads, and where the old prince had stood at the window and looked down.

Silently, she pulled the door closed and moved along. There were two more doors: Benedetta's was on the end. She knew that. But the princess's medication might yet have to take effect. She stopped. Gingerly, she turned the ebony handle of the painted door and took a step inside.

The room was dim, but not dark, and between the two long windows a four-poster sat, its heavy draperies concealing the pillows until Luisa took a step, then another, into the room. Behind her the door creaked shut. The Princess Salieri, whom she had not seen in five years, more, was propped up on her pillows with her arms laid straight in front of her, stiff as a doll. She was thinner – so much thinner. The flesh had fallen away from her face so it was all hollows and shadows, the eyes dark pools, and Luisa must have made a sound because she spoke, her voice as piercingly aristocratic as it had ever been.

'Who goes there?' And then a rusty laugh that turned into a despairing cough. Luisa took three, four steps and she was there, beside the bed. The princess's skeletal hand lifted and fell, patting, and gingerly Luisa sat.

'Luisa Venturelli,' said the princess, and on the pillow her head tilted, interrogative, and then she gave a sudden yawn. 'Excuse me,' she said, making as if to lift a hand to her mouth but giving up. 'You're married to the policeman but I can't remember his name.' The words came more slowly now, an edge of slurring.

'I've come to see Benedetta,' said Luisa, and the heavy lids that had been drooping lifted, like a doll's. The princess's eyes were dark and filmy, and she let out a sigh, and then the cough was back. Luisa saw a glass of water on the side table and offered it.

'That child,' said the princess, craning her neck to take a sip. 'That child.' And her hand fluttered, waving the glass away. 'You see what she's done now?'

'What has she done?'

The princess looked at her, judicious, and then her eyes turned vague, crafty.

'They told me,' she said, 'but I can't remember.' The hand came up, slow, slow, and just when Luisa thought it would fall back, the forefinger, no more than bone, reached her temple, tapping claw-like before dropping to her side. 'They think I'm gaga,' she said, and her face twisted in what Luisa did not immediately recognise as a smile.

'What happened to Benedetta?' said Luisa in a whisper. 'What happened to her baby?'

The old head moved restlessly on the pillow. 'What he did was none of my business,' she said. 'He took her down there with him – well, she was his daughter, after all, how was I to prevent them?' Her lip curled. Luisa knew she was talking about her husband and Benedetta. 'And she came back pregnant. I told her it was out of the question to have the child. A child whose father is unknown? Not only unknown but –' She struggled on the pillow and gave up, sitting back again. 'She was always headstrong. Well, she got more than she bargained for. Men from the street. The village butcher. I did wonder even if Alberto – but women weren't to his taste. If I'd given him a son ...' and her face turned away, the beaked profile against the white pillow.

Luisa stared and stared, her eyes feeling hard and round as boiled sweets with the staring. But the old lady was talking again, dreamy, slow. 'It was simply a medical matter. I told her. The doctor came to the house. I told her it was for the best. And then of course a marriage had to be arranged, in a hurry. Switzerland – to get her out of the way, before people talked, before *she* talked.'

This was disinhibition. Luisa had heard of it. The elderly said what they liked without fear. The only thing to fear in the Princess Salieri's case might be hell, but she probably didn't believe in it. Luisa had to suppress a powerful urge to press the pillow over the woman's face.

'The silly girl ran away. While we were paying the doctor, Alberto and I. I could hardly be blamed for challenging his price, could I? Thieves, they're all thieves ...' She seemed to drift a moment, back to some ancient quarrel with a long-dead tradesman, and then sighed. 'Silly girl, ran straight back down there.' On the bed the claw trembled, a finger raised. 'She could have bled to death, the doctor said afterwards. Although, all things considered ...' The shoulders rose minutely in a shrug, the mouth downturned in distaste. 'All things considered, she hasn't amounted to anything.'

Luisa started up as though the bed underneath her had begun to burn and took a step, two steps backwards.

The face all planes and hollows turned on the pillow to look after her. 'I remember,' said the princess, quavering triumph in her voice, 'I remember, d'you see. Not gaga. I remember what she's done now.' Patting the bedside table. 'Benedetta told me, the little bitch told me. Left it all to charity, some do-gooder. But while I live ...' The smile trembled, ghastly. 'While I live ...' and then the eyes closed, the lids quivered a moment and were still. On the pillow the head was motionless as marble. Either she had died or the medication had taken effect: Luisa found she didn't much care which. She backed out of the room, carelessly hasty. On the landing, the house felt like a great tomb around her.

Do-gooder. The Neapolitan had called Benedetta's friend a do-gooder, charity worker, churchgoer. The woman pretending association with the family, the woman Luisa had thought was Gianna Marte – until she'd seen Gianna Marte. The woman she had seen through a crack in the hospital bathroom door was not the woman who had opened the door to her.

M for Marte wasn't M for Marte, after all. M for Martine.

Benedetta's door, she saw as she got closer, wasn't quite closed and warily she peered through the crack. A narrow bed against the wall, a humped shape in it. She pushed the door open. Where the princess's room was grand this one was bare and cold and narrow, as though it had been carved out of a larger one. 'Benedetta?' she whispered, but the figure didn't move. There was no sound. With an awful feeling in her belly she came closer and put a gentle hand on the shape, but even before she leaned down to look for Benedetta's face she knew. Too soft, too shapeless: she tugged back the blanket and there were pillows in the bed.

With an exclamation, she was out of the door and on the landing, flying, flying. 'Miss Marte, Miss Marte,' she called, her breathless voice echoing strangely in the lofty space, 'Miss Marte,' and the woman came out of the kitchen door wiping her hands on her apron, wary, frightened, looking very small in the lofty hallway as Luisa flew down the wide staircase and stopped, abruptly, in front of Gianna Marte.

'What – what on earth is it? Is it madam? Is she –?' The dark soft air of the great building hung around them like a cloak, muffling secrets.

'No, no. It's not. Not her. It's Benedetta. Miss Benedetta. She's gone.'

'Gone?' Gianna Marte made as if to push past her but Luisa stopped her with a stiff shake of her head.

'You said someone called her. You said you didn't mean to listen, but you did. Who called her? What did you hear?'

'I – I –' The woman's face was slack with panic.

'Come *on*,' said Luisa, seizing her.

'Miss Benedetta was saying something about a baby,' said Marte, uneasy, struggling to get free. 'Look, let me –' Luisa released her. 'Something about a baby that needed her.' She stood sullen. 'You had to keep her away from babies. Miss Benedetta was – she always wanted to hold them. One time –'

'Could you tell if it was a man or a woman on the phone?' said Luisa, interrupting her. There had been a time when Sandro had had to lead *her* away from the mere sight of a pushchair in the street – the worst were those papooses, the soft head, the tiny legs ... 'Think,' she said.

'How should I –?' Then Marte stopped, pale brows drawn together under the stupid plaited hairstyle. 'Woman,' she said, her face clearing. 'She said, "I know you're my friend, my only friend," and she said amic*a* not amic*o*. The woman seemed to be persuading her of something.' She tilted her head. 'Mr Bartolini was very glad when it seemed she had a friend, years ago. We never met her.'

But Luisa was gone. Out of the door and into the dark and gone.

Chapter Twenty-Eight

T HEY PEERED IN through the glass, but the long studio space was dark. San Niccolo was buzzing. The bar over the road had spilled out into the street despite the weather.

'Shit,' said Sandro, 'shit, shit, shit.' There was no sign of Martine Kaufmann.

The wiry little caretaker of the camper park had started out by saying he thought the camera didn't work, hadn't worked for years, but they'd just stood there, impassive. 'We understand about privacy and all that – but this is a murder investigation,' said Pietro. They kept having to say that.

The man had stared at them stonily, and then abruptly gave in. 'Help yourselves,' he said, shoving the ancient computer screen towards them in his Portakabin. He located the August footage quite effortlessly, without explanation, his seamed old fingers surprisingly agile on the keyboard. No doubt a lot of surfing went on while he sat there with his electric heater.

And there they were. There *she* was.

Had Sandro known, even before the footage came up? The down-lit camper park half-empty in August, the camper bouncing slowly across the potholed waste ground to the furthest, darkest corner under the overgrown fence, and then the figures emerging, walking along the edge, one holding the other's hand as though to keep her under control.

Nielsson's camper-van, but neither of the women was Nielsson. Nielsson was dead.

Sandro had just come off the phone to Helen Mason, down the crackling line from Canada. She had meandered, querulous. 'Should I begin at the beginning?' And then had proceeded to jump forwards and backwards, tying herself in knots, making excuses, until she came to it, at last. It was her fault. It had begun with her, Johanna Nielsson's search for forgiveness: she'd gone out to Canada and found Helen Mason.

The voice rambled on, self-justifying. In the background chanting rose and fell.

'We were young, we didn't know what we were doing. It isn't as if we – it was only sex. And it isn't as if we aborted the child ourselves, is it? Leave it to the upper classes to do that.' Bitterness hiding under self-righteousness, a mess of excuses and spite – it didn't sound to Sandro as though Helen Mason had found peace. He didn't trust himself to say anything. 'I suppose,' grudgingly, 'the Salieri girl wasn't really into the sex.'

Rape, thought Sandro. *That's what we call it. Rape.*

'And after all,' she meandered on, 'we were punished, weren't we? In the end there were no children. Not one of us had a child.'

He didn't know how long he had to let her go on like this in the hope of finding anything concrete. It was quite possible her allotted telephone time would expire before he did. He had been about to give up hope when he heard it: Helen Mason drawing a wheezing, portentous breath. 'In the end, though, when Johanna came to ask me was she to blame, I told her she need not feel guilty. Should the fly feel guilty for catching the fish? She was just the bait.'

'Bait?' He was quick.

'None of it was her idea. She just smiled and went along with it. She was ... amoral, at worst. The other one was behind it all. She was the consigliere, the purser, the strategist. Her. Her.' An edge of panic to the voice now, of fear.

'Who?' said Sandro, holding his breath.

And she had answered, 'Martine,' with a hint of impatience, 'Martine Kaufmann.'

He had hung up and told Pietro. 'Benedetta Salieri got pregnant by Lotti or by Gorgone or by one of the men who dropped in. They had a plan to found a commune, just women, the men only for impregnation purposes. The one who got pregnant, though, was Benedetta Salieri, only along for the ride as cover for her dad and barely of legal age.' He took a breath. 'So the anonymous call back then wasn't so far off the mark.'

'And the child?' Pietro had been ashen in the car park's sodium lighting. 'Those remains we found in the chimney breast?'

Sandro nodded. 'She lost the child. Helen Mason got all vague on how. But it happened in La Vipera.'

And Pietro whistled shakily. 'Well, that's a motive,' he said. 'Even forty years later, that's a motive.'

And they went inside. Into the caretaker's Portakabin where the fuzzy film played out the camper's arrival in the park, and two figures emerged. They moved in the shadows and then, just as they reached the bumpy ramp that would have led them out into the Via Senese and out of shot, the slighter figure, so slight she might have been a child, made as if to dart away, pulling out of the other's grip. Was that Benedetta Salieri? Frail, the barman at La Serenita had said, or fragile. Yes. Yes.

And the woman cajoling her along was Martine Kaufmann.

'So what the hell –?' said Pietro straining to see. 'You mean both of them –?' But the caretaker had abruptly lost patience then, moving to switch the machine off, telling them it was the middle of the night and if they wanted to waste any more of his time he'd see them in the morning with a warrant.

They got to San Niccolo in seven minutes in the Alfa.

'Giuli said someone saw Lotti out here in San Niccolo, "visiting an old friend",' said Sandro.

'Let me guess,' said Pietro. 'Martine Kaufmann.'

'I don't understand, though,' said Pietro as they peered through the darkened window of the studio. 'Was Kaufmann trying to protect her?'

'Luca Bartolini told Luisa his sister had made friends,' said Sandro. 'What if that was one friend, and that friend was Martine Kaufmann? Kaufmann trying to make up for what they'd done to her, what La Vipera had done to her.'

It was a theory. Pietro was nodding, uncertain. 'So Kaufmann went along with Benedetta to visit Sant'Anna with Nielsson. So they could all – what? Find closure? Only something happened.'

'Something certainly happened,' said Sandro slowly. 'They came back alone, didn't they?'

And now Sandro cupped his hand around his eyes, looking in to the long studio space, looking for something he remembered, and saw the shelf of pottery – yes. Yes. Hand-painted mugs and vases and – teapots. Just like the one Lotti had given Gianna Marte, his love gift. His eyes ranged across the dark interior, the vaulted ceiling, the crowded walls, the desk – and down.

'Lotti had come here to the studio to find Kaufmann,' he said to Pietro as he looked, 'to tell her Nielsson was on her way, hadn't turned up yet. Maybe he was trying to cause trouble, or maybe he wanted money. She fobbed him off with a teapot for his lady friend. But from that day on, his days were numbered, weren't they?' Sandro said. 'She'd have warned Benedetta, maybe Benedetta told someone else about Nielsson doing the rounds. Benedetta was whisked off to the funny farm by her brother quick enough, wasn't she?'

Beside him, Pietro was shifting from one foot to the other, uneasy, beside the car illegally parked up on the pavement. In the dark street, a rowdy gang of young bucks outside the bar drinking beer were just beginning to notice the two old farts peering in at the window of Kaufmann's studio.

'Maybe it was Kaufmann the barman heard Benedetta phoning in a panic after she'd met Nielsson up at La Serenita,' said Pietro, slowly. 'And Kaufmann calmed her down.'

Sandro knelt, concealed by the car. Three plastic sacks sat near the door waiting to be taken to the charity's distribution centre. He looked down at his palms as if he expected to see the marks the blue ties had made in them, hauling her stuff across town. Slowly he felt in his pocket and extracted the scrap of plastic he'd found on the floor of the camper-van.

Benedetta hated Nielsson because of the rapes and because of the baby. Had she confessed to her brother that she'd done something terrible in that shack? And Martine was her friend, her protector.

How Kaufmann had made contact again with Benedetta Salieri, he didn't know, nor why, but it was clear she had, and some time ago. Covering her tracks, changing history, becoming the do-gooder, the redeemer: perhaps Benedetta had never known the part she'd played back then. *He* hadn't, after all, too dazzled by Johanna Nielsson's otherworldly beauty, by her strangeness: the bait.

Pietro was at his shoulder. Sandro pointed to the bags stacked inside the glass door and held out the scrap of polythene, which had black printing on it, as did the bags. 'It could be anything –' Pietro began but then he leaned closer. 'The blue ties,' he said. 'They're ...' and they both saw in their heads the post-mortem images of Nielsson's wrists, the blue plastic so tight it had cut into the stretched and desiccated flesh and tendons.

'So perhaps when Benedetta got back from La Serenita, they talked it over, decided they needed closure, or whatever? Healing. Kaufmann and Benedetta, for mutual support?' Pietro spoke slowly.

But only Benedetta needed support, thought Sandro. It must have been Kaufmann's idea. A trip back to where it all began. Clear everything up between them, once and for all. And they met Nielsson in her camper and the three of them went up there to the little shack, on some pretext, to the place where they'd carried out their rituals, perhaps, all those years ago.

'This *healing* outing back to La Vipera that went horribly wrong,' said Pietro slowly. 'But if –'

Sandro finished the sentence for him. 'If it was all about healing old wounds,' said Sandro, 'how come Kaufmann went prepared for a different sort of closure?'

'With bin bags,' said Pietro, 'and plastic ties?'

'I think Nielsson told Benedetta something about her friend Martine that Kaufmann didn't want her to know,' said Sandro.

'And where is Kaufmann now?' said Pietro, his voice going up a notch, alarmed. 'Has she done a runner or –?' And the phone rang, at that moment, in Sandro's pocket.

It was Enzo, and he was practically shouting. 'Don't you read your messages?' Beside himself: frightened, raging jerkily, half-weeping. This wasn't like Enzo. 'Don't you read your damn messages, Sandro?'

'What?' Sandro's heart was in his mouth now. 'What? Just tell me, for Christ's sake.'

'She's bleeding. I've got to get her to the hospital but she insists she has to go after Luisa – she keeps trying to leave.'

'Who's bleeding?'

Enzo was sobbing now, sobbing as if his heart would break. 'Giuli. She's pregnant – or was pregnant, I don't know. I didn't know anything until they called me. She's having a bleed. I'm in the ambulance with her now – they'll scan her as soon as they can.'

'All right,' said Sandro, 'all right,' his heart going like the clappers. 'I'm so sorry, Enzo. Shall I come –?'

'No,' said Enzo sharply. 'You have to go after Luisa. She went off while Giuli's back was turned and she, she thinks she can handle it but Giuli says she can't. If you'd read your bloody messages ...' His voice turned muffled and Sandro heard the sound of muttered voices in the background, of mechanical beeping, Giuli's voice straining to interrupt.

'But where –?'

'Read your bloody messages, Sandro,' said Enzo, wild with anguish now. 'She's gone to Sant'Anna.' And he hung up.

*

There was no more lightning, no thunder, only the rain coming down in sheets in the pitch dark. As Luisa stumbled downhill back to the car she could hear Marte calling after her but she paid no attention. She yanked open the car door and climbed inside on hands and knees, groping in the glove compartment. She didn't even try to get the car moving: she'd hardly been able to keep upright herself on the treacherous unmade surface, and she didn't want to waste time listening to the wheels spin in the mud.

Nothing but sweet wrappers and old envelopes. Luisa transferred her search to the side pocket, then the far one. And then as she shifted her weight back the car moved too and it rolled out from under the passenger seat: Sandro's ancient torch. She climbed out again and began her awkward, hasty descent between the trees, her shoes clogged with earth and sliding on the treacherous combination of rubble, mud and leaves.

The climb down seemed to take forever, her breath hoarse in her ears, her heart pounding in her chest and the rushing patter of the rain in the leaves all around her almost deafening. She could hear running water, too, gathering force, streams turning into torrents as they did in these hills. She thought of leaving the overgrown drive to cut across country to her destination but that ominous sound kept her on the straight path down. How far was it?

Because she knew where Benedetta would go now, even if her 'friend' hadn't lured her, talking of babies: to the same place, the old place. The place where Luisa had never been but where whatever had passed between Johanna Nielsson and Sandro still hung with the stale smell of drugs and cheap theories of love and life in the musty air, where Benedetta had fled her mother's private doctor to miscarry her child.

And then, with a last stumbling rush, Luisa reached the road and the water was gurgling down her side of it so she had to jump across a flooded metre. She was soaked, from her hair to her feet, but she hardly felt it: once you were that wet it no longer mattered. She hurried on up the dark road. It was as she came to Maria Clara Martinelli's house, no more than a chink of light uphill under scrubby foliage, that she heard a new sound, a gleeful roaring chatter, swung the torch around and glimpsed a moped parked under the trees, and then black water, running towards her.

Luisa felt it in the same moment as she saw it: almost a river rushing down beside Martinelli's house and across the road, gurgling and swirling over her feet – it was up to her knees, and as she tried hurriedly to back out of it, she realised too late that it was deep enough to have an undertow and she was down, on her backside, the water running over her. As she fell back on her elbows and for a second was under, she felt the strangest sensation, as though she was dissolving, as though she was becoming part of the river. As though, like Johanna Nielsson, she was dead and being drawn down into the earth, pulled into the leaf mould and dirt under the trees, and there was nothing she could do about it.

And then she sat up, scrambling, dripping – mumbling about God knew what. And the torch, which was somehow still in her hand, went out.

Shit. She heard herself say it. On hands and knees, she crawled forwards – the torch still in her hand, knuckles scraping on the tarmac – and was through the flood. Staggering to her feet, she registered that her tights were torn and one of her shoes was gone in the torrent. She abandoned the other in the middle of the road and, hobbling, began to run. She was soaked, dripping, feeling heavy as lead: in the back of her mind, a logical voice told her that she didn't even know where she was going, she didn't know what – or who – she'd find when she got there. But she kept on in a kind of awkward trot. She looked down, realising she still held the useless weight of the torch, and stuffed it into her pocket.

At the bend, the rain seemed to be easing, gusting now rather than falling straight down. Luisa's feet were cut and her chest burned but she kept moving, on, round the corner. She couldn't see it, but she knew it was there, a deeper dark in the black cleft of the hill that rose ahead of her, a blank dead end. She knew it was there with the curl of that monstrous drawing on its flank, half-buried in the hillside. She knew too that she was going slower, lurching in a zigzag despite herself; her skirt flapped soaking against her legs and she burned and shivered. Her cheeks felt hot but inside her it was cold. The temptation was there, after all these years, a lifetime of service, decades of fretting over Sandro, six years watching out for the cancer and

Giuli, the temptation simply to lie down in the rain and rest, but stubbornly her legs kept moving.

She didn't know what the sound was for a moment and then she understood that it was the cessation of one of the sounds: miraculously, the rain had stopped. The multifarious roar ebbed, reduced to the patter of her own heart, her own hoarse breath, the dripping in the trees and that far-off headlong rush of water downhill. Luisa slowed on the road, registering that there was just the slightest pearly edge to the dark, and she looked up to see a chink in the cloud. The moon was hidden still but a trace of its luminescence turned the edge of a cloud to silver and with that faint gleam of light she saw the roofline of La Vipera and stopped.

Think.

She moved to the edge of the road, where the trees gave shadow. The ground was more uneven here and her pace slowed even further, her bare feet numb and silent. She was on the same side of the road as La Vipera but she kept her head down, until she raised it and she was there. It rose above her. She put out her hands in the dark, as if to ward it off, and walked forwards like that, like a zombie in a film, across slimy grass and then something sharp, a broken bottle that tipped her sideways, arms flailing. She was there in the rubble and ivy at the back of the house, and the great wall rose above her. Half the remaining ivy had come away in the storm and Luisa raised her arms, as if to cover the curved concentric lines underneath. She flattened her body against the wall, trying to suppress a harsh sob rising inside her – for being lost in the cold and the wet, for the babies lost and cold and dead, hers and Benedetta's, and all the misguided idiocy that had led to this moment.

And then, as the moon came out from behind its cloud to show her her own outspread hand against the wall, she heard them. They were inside.

Chapter Twenty-Nine

'SLOW DOWN,' said Pietro in alarm, but Sandro barely heard him. They'd crawled the five miles out of town, traffic jams and burst water mains, and then quite suddenly the rain had stopped, a couple of miles down the *superstrada*. He didn't even have to think about putting his foot down – it did it all by itself, the big powerful car leaping under him.

Pietro had regretted letting him drive the minute he'd climbed behind the wheel, but he'd driven seven hours himself, more, and he was wiped out. 'Don't you understand?' Sandro had said, his hand out. 'I've got to. This is Luisa.' And Pietro, grey with exhaustion, had handed him the keys.

Luisa had gone to Sant'Anna. She hadn't said where, but he knew. Logically, it would be the Salieri house, once she knew about Benedetta and her baby – but this wasn't about logic any more.

They hit the village at sixty, tyres hissing through the little square, a moment when a pothole tilted the heavy car and then it righted itself. The streets were dripping and deserted, the window of the bar was dark, when Sandro's head turned, on instinct, remembering something someone had said about Maria Clara Martinelli and Bartolini in the bar, heads together. Thick as thieves. Bartolini who loved his sister. Martinelli who'd do anything for Bartolini. Who had said it? Luisa. And he'd been so busy realising that Luisa was confessing she'd told Nielsson she'd kill her that he'd hardly registered it.

'She even found the bodies,' said Sandro, half to himself.

'What?' said Pietro, and when Sandro waved him away, trying to think, trying furiously, his old friend let out an explosive sigh. 'Talk to me,' Pietro said. 'Sandro?'

'Yes?' said Sandro, turning to him with an effort.

'Where are we going?' said Pietro and Sandro flicked a glance across at him.

'Where do you think?' he asked. 'We're going back.'

And then he had to look back at the road because the big car was through the village and out the other side, tyres hissing, and the streetlights were abruptly gone and a wall of dark rolled up to meet them. The two pillars at the foot of the overgrown drive that led up to the Salieri place flashed past. Sandro felt the big engine surge effortlessly, asking to be told, faster. One more bend. A spot of light no brighter than a glow-worm under trees appeared in the dense black of the wooded hill. Martinelli's place. Sandro put his foot down.

Pietro sat up, stubborn, gripping the sides of the seat as the car swung.

'But I still don't understand,' he said. 'I don't understand why. What would Martine Kaufmann, supposing she – supposing – what would she have to gain from it? From any of it?'

Money.

The answer was in Sandro's head but he didn't know if he'd said it out loud because for a second time stopped, nothing changed and then he felt it. Flung forward with shocking violence and, as he moved, seeing from the corner of his eye Pietro's body jerking against the seatbelt and only then, as the car skidded violently under them, as he felt himself thrown towards the black glass of the windscreen, remembering to wonder if he'd fastened his own, before it hit him.

*

His awkward length pressed against hers on the hospital bed, Enzo stroked her cheek. Pale, pale, his pale beloved, paler than he'd ever seen her under the spiked aubergine halo of her hair that he loved, and when she opened her eyes so hopeless, brimming with tears, he lowered his cheek to hers on the hospital pillow.

'I love you,' he whispered, and he could smell her skin. That comforted him, that sustained him, the smell of his beloved. She closed her eyes and the tears leaked out, ran gleaming down her cheek. 'Whatever happens,' he said, with a pain inside him he couldn't describe, 'whatever happens, I love you.'

Outside the rain had stopped.

They waited.

*

Luisa heard it. They must have heard it inside too.

A crump below them that echoed in the blind valley, the tinkling of broken glass. Luisa turned, stumbling. She backed behind the house, trying to locate a memory of that combination of sounds. Car crash: the sound was of a collision. She'd hardly passed a car on the way. Who would be coming up here?

From inside she heard Benedetta's whimper. 'What – what is –? Martine, Martine ...'

She'd known, though, even before she heard the name. M for Martine. She'd isolated the face in her memory of the four of them standing in the Piazza Signoria, the small one, built like a gymnast, the northern cheekbones wide below pale eyes. The face she'd seen in the hospital corridor, the do-gooder with her charity work, the eyes looking, seeking, monitoring.

'Luca was so angry,' said Benedetta's voice, 'when I told him. I tried to say I wasn't myself when I did it, to say what you told me. I blacked out, the therapist said, you block things out – just like you told me. He –'

Another voice soothed, husky endearments. 'Darling,' it said, 'sweetheart, listen, listen. You know what we agreed. There's a way out: the best way out. You first, then me. It's too late for anything else. It'll be quick, the rope is quick, if we do it here –' A little pause, a gasp. 'You'll be with her. With your baby at last, where she left the world, you'll be here.'

As the meaning of the words dawned, Luisa felt something flame inside her and she came out from behind the house. Unable in that moment to control what she did, to be quiet or circumspect, she ran stumbling around the house to the front door, the stone step, the rotten wood ajar. As she reached it, the explosion came behind her, and she recoiled, her hand still on the door.

Through the trees Luisa saw it flash white and yellow below her, then she heard a new roar, of fire that leapt upwards, flickering: it was close, so close she could see the sparks rise in the air; it lit her. One bend below her, no more. And then smelling that other sweet scent, somewhere below the wet forest and burning fuel, mingled with acrid sweat: it was close. Luisa turned her head a bare centimetre and Martine Kaufmann's face appeared out of the darkness inside the house, and something hit her hard, above the ear.

Her face was on the floor, something slimy against it, dead leaves, dead animal. She scrabbled to get up, feeling her age in every joint and sinew, but Kaufmann was hauling on her shoulder, the fabric of her coat ripping in her fist as she was dragged into the house, and then she was on hands and knees and the door banged shut behind her. Luisa could hear Benedetta whimpering somewhere further inside. She swayed on all fours and looked up.

Moonlight came from somewhere, leaking behind a shutter, and she could make out the faint outline of a staircase and, standing on it, Benedetta. Above the stairwell in the dark something swung, indistinct, something Benedetta could reach out and take hold of if she wanted.

Doors opened off the hallway, dark apertures. The smell in here was musty, sweet-sharp, old leaves and damp, some long-dead animal, crawled in and unable to find its way out. How long would it be before they were discovered, as Lotti and Nielsson had been? When Benedetta reached out for the noose, what clue might Kaufmann come up with for Luisa's presence? An ancient feud, her hatred of Nielsson.

For a long moment no one said anything, long enough for Luisa to register a warmer flicker in the moon-glow, for the faint shouts from below to make themselves heard.

'There'll be police,' she said, her voice hoarse. 'There'll be fire engines.'

Martine Kaufmann stood over her, the wide cheekbones, the slanting pale eyes implacable in the gloom, the tattoo blue on the inside of her wrist. The image of an unborn child that none of them could ever forget. 'They'll be too late,' she said, then drew back her foot and kicked Luisa in the head.

The pain was shocking, and as Luisa felt her hands flutter out across the floor, her face down again, trying to hold on to consciousness, trying to brace herself for the next blow, she heard a sound from Benedetta, a choked gasp, and she reared back from it. She knew what she would see: the girl she'd dressed for her wedding who had for forty years been walking towards this moment, the moment when she could finish it.

'No,' she said, reaching out blindly, her vision full of stars, 'no, Benedetta. No.'

Chapter Thirty

S ANDRO DIDN'T KNOW the tall man bending over him, but he knew the woman at the man's shoulder. It was Maria Clara Martinelli. Sandro was on the tarmac, one side of his face wet with blood, and water was rushing over him: he tried to push himself up.

'No,' said Maria Clara Martinelli, 'don't!'

The man's face was gaunt, blank with fear. 'What are you doing here?' he said.

'I told you, Luca,' said Martinelli out of the side of her mouth, 'it's the policeman.'

They're going to let us die, thought Sandro, and he was scrambling upright, trying to get to his feet. Something gave under him, an ankle, but the man reached and grabbed him before he fell.

'Where's my – where's Pietro?' But as Sandro twisted to look for the car he heard an ominous sound, a sharp crackle, saw a quick, low, lethal flash, and then came the boom and he felt himself blown backwards, the man, Luca Bartolini, with him, and they were in the mud on the far side of the road. Sandro was scrambling up again.

'Pietro – my friend,' he said and something stung his cheek, he couldn't stop it, tears were pouring down his face. 'Please!'

'It's all right,' said Martinelli, behind him now, her voice rough and frightened, and Sandro turned to look for her. Her face, streaked with smoke, seemed in that moment to him like an animal's, when it lays its ears flat against its skull in fear. 'We got him out. He's in the house. We've called the ambulance.'

Sandro was on his feet, unsteady but upright, and they were closing in on him. 'Police,' he tried to say, but the word wouldn't come out right. 'Po– po–'

Putting both arms out, he flailed between them and began a hobbling run, swaying on the tarmac, zigzagging. He expected them to come after him, but he heard a phone ringing behind him, Bartolini saying something he couldn't hear, a loud voice of alarm, and he kept on going.

The tears wouldn't stop, although he knew Pietro was safe.

His fault: a life of failure and fuck-up. A car crash, beginning to end, and now he was going to lose Luisa. Hobbling on, he knew there were things badly wrong with his body but something prevented him from feeling them. There would be time for that. He rounded the bend, and there was La Vipera, and they were behind him now, they were coming after him. From down in the valley came the wail of sirens.

*

But Benedetta wasn't on the stairs any more. Kaufmann's arm was round Luisa's throat now and she could feel her peripheral vision begin to go, a white halo round what she could see, the empty staircase. The rope, swaying. She felt something hard underneath her, digging in, and, twisting, reached for it, but the weight of Kaufmann's body was too great: it pinned her to the ground, the pressure of her meaty forearm at Luisa's neck like iron.

She could hear sirens, now, too late, too late.

And then somehow, miraculously, there was a second in which Kaufmann's grip slackened, and in that second she heard Benedetta's voice, shrieking, smelled her chemical breath, and realised she was on Martine Kaufmann's back and hauling at her, pulling with her arms thin as a child's, her counterweight no more than a bird's. But in the brief respite, Luisa felt her hip shift on the slimy floor, and she managed to reach into her pocket and pulled it out from where it had been digging into her: Sandro's torch. She twisted, trying to see where Benedetta was before using it, but she couldn't, and then there was a grunt and Kaufmann was on top of her again.

'You killed her,' said Luisa, struggling, breathless under the weight. 'You killed Johanna Nielsson so she couldn't expose you to Benedetta. All that time persuading her you had been her friend, even to the point where she changed her will. Then you told Benedetta she'd killed Johanna and you were protecting her?' She heard Kaufmann's raw triumphant breath in her ear, all the confirmation she needed, but Kaufmann spoke the words.

'She should have died in the hospital,' she hissed. 'She would have done if you hadn't turned up, you busybody bitch. I'd have turfed those parasites out of their great palace and had the money and the world would have been free of one more nutjob.'

But in that moment of exultation Kaufmann's grip shifted, eased, and as Luisa felt her head fall back on the floor, she drew back her arm in one last hopeless effort, the torch in her hand, and brought it down as hard as she could where she thought Kaufmann's head must be.

There was a sickening crack as it connected, heavy as a cosh. For a second nothing happened, nothing. She was choking on that sweet flowery scent mixed with Kaufmann's sweat – and then Kaufmann went limp.

In the same moment, there was a splintering crash from behind her head and a swift movement of air past her, the grey rush and rustle as Benedetta flew by, and she heard Luca Bartolini's voice, she heard him murmuring, *darling, darling*.

She hardly had time to register her eyes filling, those tears for herself, alone, *where is my* – and then there was a commotion beside her on the floor, where Martine Kaufmann was beginning to struggle, and she realised there was someone else in the room, there was Maria Clara Martinelli. And he was there.

Kneeling by her head, he smelled of ash and water and petrol. His face was streaked with smoke and blood and too close to focus on, but she knew him, she would know him anywhere. She would know him at the end of the world.

'Sandro,' murmured Luisa. 'Sandro.' And setting a palm on each side of her cheek, he answered her. 'My love,' he said.

And then he turned and arrested Martine Kaufmann for the murder of Johanna Nielsson and conspiracy to murder Giancarlo Lotti.

*

The woman took so long to turn her head from the screen and look at Giuli that had it not been for the constant fierce pressure of Enzo's hand in hers she would have pushed herself off the high hospital bed and run for the door, run and run, run herself into oblivion, into the white light, rather than wait one second longer.

A heartbeat that didn't even sound like a heartbeat, too fast, too light, too muffled in flesh and bone. You could put no hope in a heartbeat.

The ultrasound technician's lips were moving, her eyes intent, her face lit by the screen Giuli and Enzo couldn't see. 'I just have – I just have to be sure,' she said, almost to herself. And then she turned, and smiled, and she turned the monitor, and she was there.

The bridge of a nose, the starfish of a hand, the ridge of a perfect spine spooned against Giuli's. There, cradled in her cocoon of flesh and blood built by Giuli's body, despite everything, there, safe and sound, the ghostly chambers of her tiny heart beating. The child that had been lost was found.

Afterword

LUCA BARTOLINI CONFESSED first, before they'd even left La Vipera. Holding tight to Benedetta, staring down at Kaufmann where she sat restrained by Martinelli and Sandro to either side of her, her face white, her eyes burning.

'I've always loved Benedetta,' he said, his voice weary, 'since she was a child – how could I not? So beautiful, so delicate, so loving. Of course, marrying my half-sister was out of the question. And mother –' For a moment words seemed to fail him. 'Every time,' and when he spoke again, his voice had been weary with failure in a way that Sandro recognised instantly, 'every time a crisis came I wasn't here to help her. In Milan, all those years ago, to come back only when – when her life had been ruined and she had stopped talking and was about to marry.' And then he twisted his head a little as if he was in pain. 'And this summer. When she came to me and confessed.'

'You helped her.' It was Maria Clara Martinelli's voice, rough and grating with an emotion Sandro couldn't immediately identify. 'You took her away, endlessly. Don't you understand? You couldn't always be there.'

'That place,' he said. 'That place. Those women: Nielsson and,' he gestured at Kaufmann between them, 'and her.' He leaned down towards her and spat, his aristocratic features twisting. '*You*. You took her child and burned it. You took an innocent like Benedetta and you twisted her. She branded herself at your insistence – your ideas of free love and some breeding paradise were never going to last, were they? She believed in love, and you gave her to men to rape. She believed in love – it would have saved her, but you took it away.'

It seemed to Sandro then that Luca Bartolini looked at him a second, then the look was gone. Love, he thought. And Nielsson's hand on him in the dim green room turned like smoke and was gone.

Luisa spoke softly then, out of the gloom. She took a step forward. Sandro saw her feet, bleeding, he saw her white beloved face and heard a sound in his throat.

'You didn't make that scrapbook on your own, did you, Benedetta?' On her half-brother's shoulder, Benedetta, her face hidden, let out a little moan. 'You had a friend to help you, didn't you? You had Miss Kaufmann.' Luisa held Bartolini's gaze. 'Did you know that? Did you know that friend she had made was someone she had known long ago, one of the women from La Vipera come back into her life?' Sandro saw Bartolini move forward, an incoherent sound on his lips, staring at Martine Kaufmann. 'I think Miss Kaufmann did more than help her stick pictures in an album,' said Luisa, white-lipped.

'I knew she –' Bartolini was almost whispering. 'She never said. She said a woman from the church. When she said she'd changed her will, that it was all to go to a children's charity ...'

His eyes swept the room. 'I didn't care what she did with the money if it helped her become herself again.'

'How did you find out Lotti knew?' said Sandro, and the man's eyes settled on him, questioning. 'You told Gianna Marte there were truffles up behind La Vipera, knowing she would tell him, knowing he would go up there. You made sure you and Benedetta were safely out of the way at the rehab centre when the deed was done.' Under his hands Kaufmann struggled.

'An anonymous note,' Bartolini said, faltering. 'It came in the post. It said, a friend of Benedetta's.'

'That was you, wasn't it?' Sandro gave Kaufmann's arm a tug, and she thrust her chin at him, aggressive. 'Lotti visited you and dropped hints – and you wanted him out of the way. It would just take a nudge, wouldn't it? Bartolini would do anything to save his sister from prison for a crime she didn't commit. So you sent the note and got yourself an alibi by way of a little teaching stint at the other end of the province.'

Sullen, Kaufmann said nothing.

'When Benedetta confessed,' said Sandro, his eyes on the head against Bartolini's shoulder, 'did she perhaps say she couldn't even remember doing it? Maybe she woke up covered in blood, a knife in her hands, in the hut?'

'She came to me,' Bartolini mumbled, not quite understanding. 'And I went to Maria Clara. We worked it out between us, the ruse with the truffles. I sent him there to die. I couldn't let him drag Benedetta into this again.' And then his eyes widened. 'You mean, she didn't kill Nielsson? Benedetta didn't kill her?'

'I'd bet my life on it,' said Sandro quietly. And in his arms Martine Kaufmann began to struggle and spit.

And then Maria Clara Martinelli took a step away from her and, standing her ground, confessed, stout and unashamed, to Giancarlo Lotti's murder, there in the old farmhouse while they waited for the sirens to reach them.

*

The chapel on the hill was tiny, the filmy-eyed priest old enough to understand that God's children did not always come in conventional shapes – they sometimes, indeed, had never before been in a church in their lives. But a child was a child, and a baptism, in Father Francesco's tired old soul, was no more or less than an expression of hope for that child.

His congregation sat obedient in the small cool space. Two middle-aged policemen – the older walking with a pronounced limp – and their wives, one dark, one with hair of faded red. In through the door behind them walked the happy parents, of whom the father, Enzo, the old priest had himself baptised forty-seven years ago – and Rosetta Luisa, their daughter, their first child, wrapped tight in a knitted blanket of a lacy fineness he had not seen in thirty years.

And behind Enzo came his father, moving slowly, leaning heavily on the wheelchair he pushed. And in the wheelchair sat Enzo's mother, Rosetta, no bigger than a bird, but her eyes brighter, her face more radiant than any bride's. There would be a funeral, too, in the days or weeks to come, but for the moment all were living, all were present: all bore witness.

Afterwards on the doorstep in the soft spring sunshine, the almond blossom spilling down the hill towards the marvellous red canopy of Florence's rooftops, the old priest stood back from them a little. He heard the quiet murmurings of their love for each other and he saw, standing humble above the great city where all of them had been born, that small unorthodox family in a kind of golden daze, and in that moment it seemed to him, after a lifetime of service to God in cold churches, an expression of everything that was holy.

*

It was late, so late – neither of them could sleep and, after long accommodation of nights like this between them, they both knew it. There was a baby now, and in both their heads that thought prompted a circling of emotions from anxiety to fear to joy and back again. Evenings fretting over school and doctors and friends and every fever, every tear, stretched ahead of them. And a broad open future where she danced and ran in sunshine.

Luisa pressed her cheek against Sandro's broad back that was turned to her in the bed and she heard his sigh, expressing all of that. Her hand crept to his side and his came to meet it.

'I know she hurt you,' she whispered. 'It's all right, I know.'

'I never –' said Sandro.

'I know,' said Luisa.